Christian Popular Culture
from *The Chronicles of Narnia*
to *Duck Dynasty*

Christian Popular Culture
from *The Chronicles of Narnia* to *Duck Dynasty*

ELEANOR HERSEY NICKEL

CASCADE *Books* · Eugene, Oregon

CHRISTIAN POPULAR CULTURE FROM *THE CHRONICLES OF NARNIA*
TO *DUCK DYNASTY*

Cascade Books
An Imprint of Wipf and Stock Publishers
199 W. 8th Ave., Suite 3
Eugene, OR 97401

www.wipfandstock.com

PAPERBACK ISBN: 978-1-7252-8120-2
HARDCOVER ISBN: 978-1-7252-8121-9
EBOOK ISBN: 978-1-7252-8122-6

Cataloguing-in-Publication data:

Names: Nickel, Eleanor Hersey, author.

Title: Christian popular culture from *The Chronicles of Narnia* to *Duck Dynasty* / Eleanor Hersey Nickel.

Description: Eugene, OR: Cascade Books, 2020 | Includes bibliographical references and index.

Identifiers: ISBN 978-1-7252-8120-2 (paperback) | ISBN 978-1-7252-8121-9 (hardcover) | ISBN 978-1-7252-8122-6 (ebook)

Subjects: LCSH: Popular culture—Religious aspects—Christianity. | Mass media—Religious aspects—Christianity. | Christian fiction, American—History and criticism.

Classification: BR115.C8 .N490 2020 (paperback) | BR115.C8 (ebook)

04/12/21

To my wonderful husband, Royce, for watching so many episodes of *Duck Dynasty* and even laughing along with many of them

CONTENTS

LIST OF ILLUSTRATIONS

ACKNOWLEDGMENTS

I am thankful to Fresno Pacific University, my academic home for nearly twenty years, for providing the sabbatical leave that allowed me to finish this book, and to my amazing dean Ron Herms for helping me find the right publisher. I have learned many things from the students in my C. S. Lewis classes over the years, and I owe a particular debt of gratitude to two alumni of that class, my intrepid copyediting team of Margaret Bowlin and Laurel Samuelson. I am grateful to Michael Thomson from Wipf and Stock for taking a chance on an unusual manuscript and to Rodney Clapp for his copyediting expertise and his provocative writings on the relationship between Christians and popular culture.

INTRODUCTION

Christian popular culture has tremendous influence on many American churchgoers. When we have a choice between studying the Bible and reading novels, downloading movies, or watching television, we become less familiar with Numbers than with Narnia. I have to open my Bible to find Gamaliel son of Pedahzur, but I know Ramandu and Rilian without looking at C. S. Lewis's fantasy series. I am not sure whether the Old Testament forbids eating duck, but I can talk for hours about the onscreen and offscreen dynamics of *Duck Dynasty*. However, the study of Christian culture remains a small corner of popular culture scholarship, since most academics have little contact with these authors, audiences, or subcultural contexts, and they often sidestep the biblical themes in mainstream favorites like J. R. R. Tolkien's *Lord of the Rings*, J. K. Rowling's *Harry Potter*, and Suzanne Collins's *The Hunger Games*. This book examines popular Christian narratives with rigorous scholarly methods and assumes that they are just as complex, fascinating, and worthy of investigation as the latest secular dystopian novel or *Netflix* series. While most scholars focus on the religious aspects of Christian texts, this study takes a new approach by analyzing their social responsibility in portraying the complex dynamics of race, class, and gender in a profoundly unequal America.

Thirty years ago, Clifford G. Christians wrote "Redemptive Media as the Evangelical's Cultural Task," a call to action for artists to set aside trite, unsophisticated media and take seriously our biblical role as stewards of creation, including the realm of human culture. Mature popular art should resist and provide alternatives to conventional media: "At that epiphanal moment when the taken-for-granted world is made problematic and the moral contours illuminated, the media could serve as signifiers of justice, peace, and harmony."[1] Christians goes on to ask, "Where are the evangelical attempts to broaden the moral landscape of a modern highly technological

1. Christians, "Redemptive Media," 344.

1

age?"[2] This book offers one answer. Close readings of six case studies uncover both harmful stereotypes and "signifiers of justice, peace, and harmony" and demonstrate the importance of Christians serving as leaders in social justice.

SCHOLARSHIP ON CHRISTIANS AND POPULAR CULTURE

Few scholars analyze evangelical novels and films, but many explore mainstream American culture's religious expressions, Christian themes, and Christian critics. In the category of broadly religious themes, Eric Michael Mazur and Kate McCarthy's *God in the Details* observes how Americans find spiritual meaning in practices from Southern barbeque to the Burning Man Festival, while Bruce David Forbes and Jeffrey H. Mahan's *Religion and Popular Culture in America* includes *Star Trek* fandom, the weight loss industry, and sports. David Chidester's *Authentic Fakes* investigates the religious work done by everything from Tupperware parties to firewalking to alien abduction, and Diane Winston's *Small Screen, Big Picture* considers lived religion in prime-time dramas from *Deadwood* to *The Sopranos*. Although they concentrate on nontraditional religious practices, the covers of *God in the Details* and *Authentic Fakes* include photos of a Virgin Mary shrine and Clowns for Christ, which seem to make them more accessible to readers by grounding them in a traditional faith.

The title of John Wiley Nelson's *Your God Is Alive and Well and Appearing in Popular Culture* summarizes the narrower focus on Christian or theological themes in secular culture, in which critics often bend over backwards to defend works that seem trivial or even heretical.[3] Catholic priest and sociologist Andrew M. Greeley's *God in Popular Culture* celebrates *The Cosby Show*'s family love, Bruce Springsteen's social protest, and Woody Allen's hope in the face of despair, while Craig Detweiler and Barry Taylor's *A Matrix of Meanings* considers the spiritual longings of postmodernity with compassion. Gordon Lynch's *Understanding Theology and Popular Culture* looks at violence in the music of Eminem, civil religion in the *Simpsons* episode "Homer the Heretic," and mystical experience in British club culture. In *Religion and Popular Culture*, Richard W. Santana and Gregory Erickson examine how texts like *Dogma* and *Buffy the Vampire Slayer* rescript the

2. Christians, "Redemptive Media," 347.

3. The catchy title is misleading, since Nelson's classic study discusses how popular texts and genres reflect dominant American belief systems that Christians must understand to present the uniqueness of the gospel.

sacred for Americans who revere the Bible but don't know it well. There is a huge body of work devoted to theological themes in Hollywood film, such as Robert K. Johnston's oft-cited *Reel Spirituality*. This type of analysis crosses religious boundaries in unexpected ways; for example, both the Catholic Greeley and the atheist Santana and Erickson sympathize with Madonna's unorthodox religious expression.

Christians also debate whether believers should avoid or embrace secular culture, although most agree that some familiarity is helpful in order to understand our neighbors. Kenneth A. Myers's *All God's Children and Blue Suede Shoes* sees the mass media as a major challenge to faith, but William D. Romanowski's *Pop Culture Wars* argues that we must overcome the desire for censorship and social control. Rodney Clapp's *Border Crossings* notes that we can learn much from *The X-Files*, jazz, and country music, and Romanowski's *Eyes Wide Open* urges readers to analyze mass culture critically rather than falling into the traps of condemnation, appropriation, or blind consumption. Dick Staub's *The Culturally Savvy Christian* returns to a more negative tone, decrying all popular culture and encouraging readers to develop a deeper relationship with God. Ted Turnau's *Popologetics* critiques previous approaches from "Ew-Yuck" to the "Cheerleaders of the Postmodern" and calls for a balanced response that sees both grace and idolatry in worldly media. Quentin J. Schultze's *Redeeming Television* and Walter T. Davis Jr. et al.'s *Watching What We Watch* recommend that television viewers expand their moral concerns beyond sex, violence, and profanity.

But what about the popular culture created by Christians to preach the gospel, illustrate biblical truths, and inspire other believers? Peter Horsfield's *From Jesus to the Internet* reminds us that people's views of Jesus are "based not only on the Bible but also on impressions gained through Christmas carols, cultural festivals, hymns, prayers, children's storybooks, Sunday School lessons, sermons, theological books, popular devotional guides, statues, paintings, and the movies."[4] Although Horsfield's account of church history is often unorthodox, he makes a convincing case for the media's role in shaping beliefs across eras and cultures. It matters whether we are listening to Jesus' parables or reading Paul's letters, worshiping in a house church or cathedral, traveling to Jerusalem on a pilgrimage or crusade, watching a public procession or execution, examining an illuminated manuscript or Lutheran pamphlet, reciting the Nicene Creed or hearing a sermon by John Calvin.

This project focuses primarily on Christian popular culture in the United States, with its rich history from the Cambridge Press publication

4. Horsfield, *From Jesus to the Internet*, 3.

of *The Bay Psalm Book* (1640), to the seduction novel *Charlotte Temple* (1791), to the first edition of the *Christian Almanac* (1821), to the first radio broadcast of the Moody Bible Institute (1925), to the finale of *Fixer Upper* (2018). Most historical surveys begin with the nineteenth century, such as Schultze's *American Evangelicals and the Mass Media*, which critiques the optimism about technology as an evangelistic tool that often leads to unsophisticated and ineffective texts. R. Laurence Moore's *Selling God* examines the cycle in which Protestants condemn a new medium, then accept family-friendly versions, and finally create their own versions. Colleen McDannell's *Material Christianity* looks at treasured places and objects such as Laurel Hill Cemetery, Lourdes water, and Mormon sacred clothing, while David Morgan's *Protestants & Pictures* demonstrates the complex uses of Millerite prophecy charts and Victorian lives of Christ.

Scholars analyze how more recent works reflect both evangelical and mass media trends. Randall Balmer's travelogue *Mine Eyes Have Seen the Glory* includes visits to filmmaker Donald Thompson—famous for his apocalyptic thriller *A Thief in the Night*—and the Christian Booksellers Association convention. Heather Hendershot's *Shaking the World for Jesus* examines how products like *VeggieTales*, Focus on the Family teen magazines, and Moody Institute of Science films negotiate with mainstream culture. *Understanding Evangelical Media*, edited by Schultze and Robert H. Woods Jr., shows how digital natives are moving beyond conventional radio and television formats. Journalist Daniel Radosh's creative nonfiction account *Rapture Ready!* narrates his trips to see *The Great Passion Play*, Bibleman, the Christian Comedy Association, and much more, asking why Christian culture looks so much like secular culture. Woods's three-volume *Evangelical Christians and Popular Culture* includes fifty-four essays covering every corner of the landscape from tattoos to candy.

Developments in Christian fiction, film, and television have inspired close readings, historical surveys, and humorous rants. Jan Blodgett's *Protestant Evangelical Literary Culture and Contemporary Society* looks at sixty inspirational novels, arguing that publishers and authors serve as gatekeepers of religious identity. Anita Gandolfo's *Faith and Fiction* argues that the wide gap between accessible evangelical publications and demanding literary fiction perpetuates the culture wars and prevents helpful dialogue between conservatives and liberals. Lynn S. Neal interviews women readers of inspirational fiction in *Romancing God*, and Valerie Weaver-Zercher seeks the appeal of Amish romances in *Thrill of the Chaste*.[5] Terry Lindvall's *Sanc-*

5. Reference works also help readers navigate the ever-expanding world of Christian fiction. Janice DeLong and Rachel Schwedt's *Contemporary Christian Authors* features living writers' responses to a questionnaire. John Mort addressed *Christian Fiction* to

tuary Cinema describes Protestant exhibition, distribution, and production of silent films, proving that "the relationship of the church to the moving picture in the first two decades of the twentieth century was engaging, vital, and robust."[6] *Celluloid Sermons*, his sequel written with Andrew Quicke, covers Christian filmmaking from the emergence of sound until videotapes ended the era of church distribution. Horsfield's *Religious Television* provides a rigorous scholarly investigation into the rise of televangelism, while Nadia Bolz-Weber's *Salvation on the Small Screen?* gives a hilarious account of a progressive Lutheran minister watching twenty-four consecutive hours of Trinity Broadcasting Network.

WHY RACE, CLASS, AND GENDER?

Social justice was a central concern when popular culture studies emerged in the 1970s, but Christian scholars' focus on religion divided them from the major issues of the discipline. With exceptions like the field of black gospel music, books about race or gender in Christian popular culture did not appear until the 2010s. There are several ways to explain this gap. Scholars often assume that Christian popular culture lacks the creativity and sophistication to speak to current social controversies. Myers dismisses it as "something of a parasite on earlier forms."[7] Romanowski complains that evangelical texts have "jejune lyrics, sweet-sounding music, didactic dialogue and Pollyannaish endings"[8] and calls them "sanitized and usually inferior imitations."[9] Staub attacks the "subculture that is defined by kitsch, that produces subpar music and books, and that is addicted to artistic mediocrity."[10] As Turnau points out, "The elitism of the 'We're-Above-All-That' response to popular culture often expresses itself in nothing short of all-out derision."[11] However, these assumptions have become harder to justify since the Mitford books became *New York Times* bestsellers and *Duck Dynasty* broke audience records for nonfiction cable series.

---

librarians and includes sections devoted to Catholic, Amish, Mennonite, Quaker, and Mormon authors. Nancy M. Tischler's *Encyclopedia of Contemporary Christian Fiction* juxtaposes evangelical favorites with literary fiction writers who have complex relationships to the church.

6. Lindvall, *Sanctuary Cinema*, 6.

7. Kenneth A. Myers, *All God's Children*, 23.

8. Romanowski, *Pop Culture Wars*, 327.

9. Romanowski, *Eyes Wide Open*, 29.

10. Staub, *Culturally Savvy Christian*, 33.

11. Turnau, *Popologetics*, 127.

Christians also view sociopolitical criticism as too entrenched in secular sensibilities. According to Myers, "Culture is not (as many scholars today believe) simply the battleground for a perpetual war of classes, races, and genders."[12] The lack of diversity in Christian popular culture may seem to support that perspective. Woods acknowledges: "Although North American evangelicals include many ethnic groups and races, audiences would hardly know it. Even more than their mainstream counterparts, evangelical media are owned and operated primarily by Caucasians."[13] Woods anticipates a near future which will include more African American, Hispanic, and Asian artists, but all three volumes of his study have white men on their covers: Billy Graham, Steven Curtis Chapman, and Rick Warren. Since I analyze the most popular texts in my communities, this study also focuses on white artists, which is merely a stepping stone to the important future project of examining Christian artists of color. Yet the perceived "whiteness" of the field does not explain the relative lack of scholarly interest in racial portrayals by white artists or the dynamics of class and gender that are clearly relevant to everything from Christian retailing to Christian romance.

Unfortunately, scholars may have sidestepped race, class, and gender because white evangelicals tend to define morality in a narrow way that excludes systemic injustice. In 1992, Schultze's *Redeeming Television* claimed: "If morality is only a matter of personal conduct, there is no reason to judge the values and practices of society. And, in fact, we rarely hear Christians complaining about televised racism."[14] Over twenty-five years later in 2018, Joshua F. Hoops observed that Christian periodicals continue to frame "moral issues" in terms that preserve current power relations: "Historically, this has meant that white Christian voters (e.g., the 'moral majority') inquire as to politicians' stances on abortion and gay marriage, whereas numerous other issues are overlooked as amoral, whether it be poverty, mass shootings, systemic racism, environmental protection."[15] Of course, Christians are not writing scholarly books on popular cultural depictions of abortion or gay marriage either, indicating that *all* political issues have been set aside as scholars argue about whether we should engage with worldly culture or whether Christian culture has artistic integrity.

In the past decade, two important studies reveal an emerging interest in gender and race. Kristy Maddux's *The Faithful Citizen: Popular Christian Media and Gendered Civic Identities* investigates the ideal forms of

---

12. Kenneth A. Myers, *All God's Children*, 27.

13. Woods, *Evangelical Christians and Popular Culture*, 1:xxv.

14. Schultze, *Redeeming Television*, 132.

15. Hoops, "Constitution of a 'Moral Issue,'" 27.

citizenship in *Amazing Grace*, *The Passion of the Christ*, *Left Behind*, *7th Heaven*, and *The Da Vinci Code*, including masculine interventions into public affairs, passive submission to injustice, feminized relational solutions to social problems, and civic nonparticipation. Omotayo O. Banjo and Kesha Morant Williams' *Contemporary Christian Culture: Messages, Missions, and Dilemmas* examines cultural and racial identity in Barack Obama's political discourse, gospel performance, newspapers, radio, contemporary Christian music, and churches: "While advocacy for multiculturalism is increasing, societal racial tensions persist and are evident even among fellow believers,"[16] including divisions over immigration, Black Lives Matter, and the election of Donald Trump. Banjo and Williams reinforced my belief that studying race, class, and gender in Christian culture is an idea whose time has come. Since most scholars analyze religious elements in mainstream texts, we need to provide a balance by analyzing mainstream elements in religious texts.

In *Christianity and the Mass Media in America: Toward a Democratic Accommodation*, Schultze argues that Christian media can be a valuable counter-narrative to secular assumptions: "From early American religious agitators to nineteenth-century abolitionists, and from the civil rights rhetoric of Martin Luther King Jr. to the pronouncements of a pope, religious rhetoric has a long history of using countercultural images and prophetic language to make the case publicly for truth and justice."[17] This is true for fictional narratives like *Uncle Tom's Cabin* as well as nonfiction forms like abolitionist newspapers. Rather than seeing an increasingly crossover Christian popular culture as a weak imitation of mainstream culture, we can view it as a sometimes-powerful countering of prevailing stereotypes and an always-legitimate voice in a pluralistic democracy.

My focus brings Christian texts into the center of the academic field while holding their artists accountable for the socially responsible portrayal of historically oppressed groups. Greatly beloved or controversial texts like *The Chronicles of Narnia* and *Left Behind* have attracted criticism from virtually every angle, but most Christian works have never been examined through the lenses of feminism, Marxism, psychoanalysis, queer theory, postcolonial studies, disability studies, or environmental studies. When I read papers based on this project at the annual conference of the Southwest Popular/American Culture Association, critical race theory was the common ground. The attendees were impressed by the clip from the Sherwood Baptist Church film *Courageous*, and sophisticated television scholars

16. Banjo and Williams, *Contemporary Christian Culture*, ix.
17. Schultze, *Christianity and the Mass Media*, 339.

laughed surprisingly hard at the clips from *Duck Dynasty*. Lynch points out that "the study of the everyday has an important *critical, liberatory*, or *ideological* function in raising our awareness of oppressive structures and concepts within our own cultural context."[18] Christian texts may have sentimental plots or bad acting, but we should be more concerned when they view Latinos as comic sidekicks, poor Southerners as white trash, and women as sex objects. Turnau reminds us, "God cares deeply about aesthetics, but I think he cares even more deeply about people."[19] He notes that scholars have listened sympathetically to the most rebellious artists: "That is simply an implication of Christian love, of treating culture-makers as human beings created in God's image and worthy of respect."[20] We should extend the same openness *and* rigor to those within the household of God. If Madonna gets to have her say, why not Francine Rivers?

We should also resist the temptation to generalize about Christian popular culture. Lynch's comments are highly relevant to Christian critics: "The broad debate about whether 'popular culture' as a whole has any merits or not has therefore tended to polarize critics and supporters of popular culture into positions where it becomes harder to think of the possibility of there being good *and* bad, better *and* worse forms."[21] As Turnau puts it, "by critiquing, we must not merely condemn; and by creatively engaging, we must not merely affirm."[22] Christian popular culture includes both impressive and appalling works; individual texts both challenge and reinforce stereotypes; and series and franchises evolve over time. The following three brief case studies will demonstrate this diversity, with high marks going to *Christy* for celebrating Appalachian culture and *This Present Darkness* for including strong heroines, while *The Shack* shows the pitfalls of white authors embracing multiculturalism.

"THE STRENGTHS OF A FINE HERITAGE": *CHRISTY*'S SENSITIVE PORTRAIT OF APPALACHIAN POVERTY

Catherine Marshall's *Christy* (1967) tells the story of a nineteen-year-old schoolteacher who travels to Cutter Gap, Tennessee in 1912, deepens her shallow faith, and finds romance. The beloved novel inspired the CBS television series with Kellie Martin (1994–1995), the television movies with

18. Lynch, *Understanding Theology and Popular Culture*, 18 (italics original).

19. Turnau, *Popologetics*, 129.

20. Turnau, *Popologetics*, 180.

21. Lynch, *Understanding Theology and Popular Culture*, 187 (italics original).

22. Turnau, *Popologetics*, 190.

Lauren Lee Smith (2000–2001), and the annual ChristyFest. Appalachia is one of the nation's poorest regions and often subjected to jokes about moonshine and incest. As we will see in chapter 3, Jan Karon romanticizes North Carolina's Blue Ridge Mountains but represents Tennessee as an impoverished nightmare that destroys unwary visitors. Marshall focuses on Christy Huddleston's labor to overcome her stereotypes and highlights the community's intelligence, hard work, and artistry, creating a Christian classic that has stood the test of time.

Christy is such a compelling character because she allows the mountain people to change her more than she changes them. The first sentence of the prologue, in which the author visits Cutter Gap with her mother and becomes inspired to write the novel, makes it clear that Christy's efforts will fail in a worldly sense: "On that November afternoon when I first saw Cutter Gap, the crumbling chimney of Alice Henderson's cabin stood stark against the sky, blackened by the flames that had consumed the house."[23] Cutter Gap is gone. While the opening sentence has the potential to erase the region's ongoing poverty and cover the novel with a haze of comforting nostalgia, the discussion of presidential politics quickly moves to the realm of social critique. "Appalachia's economic problem had never been solved" and Franklin Roosevelt absorbed the land into the Great Smoky Mountains National Park, replacing mountaineers with tourists.[24] The federal government may have removed this community and its problems, but Marshall devotes nearly 500 pages to remembering them.

Throughout the beginning of the novel, Christy's first-person adult narrator looks back on her youthful idealism. When she hears a missionary speak about a boy who walks to school barefoot through the snow, she looks down at her expensive shoes and decides to volunteer as a teacher. She is culturally ignorant and overconfident, "certain that I was about to take the world by storm,"[25] but comparing the cost of one's own shoes to the cost of someone else's education is a good start for a teenager in a helping profession. In her first weeks at Cutter Gap, she continually compares the mountaineers to literary and historical figures: Robin Hood, early American frontiersmen, and their own Scottish highland ancestors. Yet her confrontations with suffering bring her back to the present. When she first sees the O'Teale cabin, with trash and human feces in the yard and a disabled boy in an indoor pen, she goes back to the mission house and vomits. Alice Henderson challenges her to develop a mature faith that can handle the

---

23. Marshall, *Christy*, 1.
24. Marshall, *Christy*, 2.
25. Marshall, *Christy*, 17.

realities of poverty, mentioning her own crisis as a young missionary when she faced the rape and murder of a crippled girl: "Christy, evil is real—and powerful. It has to be fought, not explained away, not fled."[26] Christy learns to appreciate the practical compromises of the Quaker Alice, who carries a gun and earns the men's respect as a good shot, and Dr. Neil MacNeill, a Cutter Gap native who cannot change the people's contaminated drinking water or superstitions that kill infants, but continues to operate on gunshot wounds and research the causes of trachoma.

Christy becomes a model for the self-aware, humble attitude of service that is required for mutually transformative missionary work. While she continues to view the highlanders as romantic literary figures, she also starts to see them as potential readers, raising money for textbooks and teaching her best friend Fairlight Spencer to read. At the end-of-school exercises, Bessie Coburn recites "When, in disgrace with fortune and men's eyes"[27] and Lizette Holcombe wins a copy of *The Complete Shakespeare*.[28] By the end of the novel, Christy passes the ultimate test: "No one has greater love than this, to lay down one's life for one's friends" (John 15:13 NRSV). She stays in the Cove during a typhoid epidemic, changing the diarrhea-soaked diapers of her most obnoxious teenage student and scrubbing dishes for Bessie and her bedridden mother, only to succumb to the disease and narrowly escape death. Yet Marshall never loses sight of her heroine's flaws, and the novel ends with gratitude rather than triumph.

The mountaineers never appear as a monolithic Other because they change as we view them through Christy's zeal, David Grantland's condescension, and Alice's empathy. They may appear in the roles most comforting to the white middle class—the willing servant or grateful object of charity—but the variety of characters shows that impoverished people are not all alike. Some highlanders (mostly men in Marshall's feminist vision) stubbornly resist innovations that would do them good, allowing their bitterness over social injustice to excuse their violent, law-breaking, hard-drinking behavior and mistreatment of women and children. Others (especially women) are faithful, hospitable, and resourceful, with better understandings of social problems and their solutions than well-meaning outsiders. While some of the brief descriptions in the opening character list seem stereotypical, like "BIRD'S-EYE TAYLOR, feuder and blockader" or "LIZ ANN ROBERTSON, married at fourteen,"[29] the novel develops the

26. Marshall, *Christy*, 95.
27. Marshall, *Christy*, 356.
28. Marshall, *Christy*, 360.
29. Marshall, *Christy*, xi.

characters at enough length to show their complexity and to reveal growth and change.

Christy recognizes the people's practical and academic intelligence: her schoolchildren sing in parts, fifteen-year-old John Spencer asks for a harder math book because he has finished all the geometry problems, the parents demand that their children learn Latin, and Dr. MacNeill has a research laboratory in his cabin. Although the mountaineers speak in dialect, Alice draws Christy's attention to its seventeenth-century rhythms and vocabulary, imported from England and Scotland and kept intact in the isolated region. David dismisses the men as lazy until he attends a Working and takes much longer to clear his strip of land than the others, ending the day with bleeding hands. Christy marvels at the women who work day and night to maintain large families without modern technology. Alice shows her "the strengths of a fine heritage"[30] in their square-dancing, quilting, tall tales, dulcimer music, and intricately carved wooden deer. When the dying Christy has a vision of Fairlight in heaven, she holds a handmade honeysuckle basket and sings a haunting ballad.

Marshall placed her humble protagonist in a complex world without easy answers. Gandolfo points out the irony of this novel inspiring the Christy Award for excellence in Christian fiction: "Indeed, one wonders whether Marshall's work would be accepted by contemporary evangelical publishers, since the book's minister is a confused young man, ineffectual in his dealings with people, and the novel's authentic spiritual leader is a woman—and a Quaker."[31] Christy's spiritual doubts are realistic and profound, and her main problem is not "fending off the secular world."[32] She struggles to discern the weaknesses in her home church, defend her own faith, and tell the difference between selfishness and altruism. In an evangelical culture that still sends untrained teenagers into regions impoverished by centuries of systemic injustice, Marshall's nuanced portrait of mission work is more important than ever.

"BRAVERY PERSONIFIED": STRONG HEROINES IN *THIS PRESENT DARKNESS*

My university library's copy of Frank E. Peretti's groundbreaking thriller *This Present Darkness* (1986) has been checked out thirty-nine times, and its worn cover and crumbling pages reveal its significance to fans. The

30. Marshall, *Christy*, 62.

31. Gandolfo, *Faith and Fiction*, 113.

32. Gandolfo, *Faith and Fiction*, 114.

novel focuses on intrepid newspaper reporters Marshall Hogan and Bernice Krueger as they uncover a conspiracy in which the shadowy multinational Omni Corporation is buying up the small college town of Ashton and its positions of power. Meanwhile, nondenominational pastor Hank Busche faces a church divided between a faithful flock and hateful parishioners who want to get rid of him. Peretti's innovation was to present these events on two levels, alternating between everyday human life and the supernatural battles of angels and demons. The "New Age" conspiracy, the apostate mainline Protestants, and the godless psychology department now seem like 1980s clichés, but the novel remains interesting due to its female characters. Bernice, Edith Duster, Mary Busche, and Susan Jacobson provide role models for Christian women readers, while the novel also challenges the 1980s masculine ideals of the brawny warrior and prestigious corporate CEO.

Bernice begins the novel as a capable professional with little interest in religion, haunted by her sister's mysterious death in college, determined to use her journalistic expertise to find the murderer, vulnerable to attacks by men and demons, but resilient enough to overcome all challenges through intelligence and force of will. The novel opens with a scene that teeters on the edge of sexist comedy. During the Ashton Summer Festival, Bernie photographs some Omni Corporation executives, so they arrest her as a hooker, and she spends the night in jail: "She was a young, attractive woman in her midtwenties, with unkempt brown hair and large, wire-rimmed glasses, now smudged. She had obviously had a hard night and was presently keeping company with at least a dozen women, some older, some shockingly younger, mostly trucked-in prostitutes."[33] The ongoing jokes about prostitution are insensitive, although the phrase "some shockingly younger" provides a glimpse of compassion, and Bernie comes across as shrill, high-strung, and bossy as she demands her release. Despite this inauspicious beginning, she becomes one of the few Ashton residents to take a stand against demonic activity.

Her masculine nickname and profession aside, Bernie's femininity makes her vulnerable during the many occasions when she works alone. A man brutally attacks her when she enters a low-rent apartment building to find an important witness, and the language breaks into fragments to reflect her point of view: "A rough, dirty hand grabbing a fistful of blouse. A violent, sideways jerk. Tearing cloth, her body reeling. An impact like an explosion in her left ear. A blurred, hate-filled face."[34] Despite her cuts, bruises, and cracked rib, she spends the rest of the novel driving, running, finding

33. Peretti, *This Present Darkness*, 17.
34. Peretti, *This Present Darkness*, 228.

wiretapping equipment, meeting sources, and developing photographs, and her happy ending comes from her decision to follow Christ.

Several minor female characters also turn out to be tougher than they appear. Edith is an elderly widow who overcomes a demonic sickness to attend a church meeting and support Hank. This "wise old matron of the church, former missionary to China"[35] cannot take part in the action sequences, but her formidable prayers make demons drop their swords, upsetting conventional notions of social power. Mary first assumes a childlike role as "the sunny spot in a cloudy sky for Hank, this playful little wife with the melodic giggle,"[36] but when the villains accuse her husband of rape, she confronts the corrupt police chief to demand his release from jail: "Brummel had never in his life seen sweet, seemingly vulnerable Mary Busche so feisty."[37] In a more dramatic character arc, Susan starts out on the demonic side but sees the truth and starts copying records that will give the heroes the evidence they need to destroy the corporation. She joins forces with Bernie, and together they track down the truth about Bernie's sister. At the end of the novel, the State Attorney General tells Susan that she has been very brave. She points at Bernie and says: "You're looking at bravery personified."[38] Both women renounce inappropriate attachments to men, and their friendship replaces the romance plots that dominate Christian fiction.

The novel does contain female villains, including two classic cases of the *femme fatale*. Juleen Langstrat is a psychology professor—graduate of the nefarious UCLA—who seduces students into the demonic world through mind control and brainwashing. Marshall enters her classroom and sees a woman "right out of a lipstick or fashion commercial: long blonde hair, trim figure, deep, dark eyes."[39] Instead of giving pleasure, she fixes Marshall with "a knifelike gaze"[40] and orders him out of the room, leaving him shaken by her evil power. Carmen Fraser is a floozy who dresses provocatively, tries to seduce Hank, and becomes the newspaper's secretary to obtain information. Yet it makes sense that the demons would have women in their clutches, and Juleen and Carmen remain shadowy figures in contrast to our intimate knowledge of Bernie.

---

35. Peretti, *This Present Darkness*, 110.

36. Peretti, *This Present Darkness*, 24.

37. Peretti, *This Present Darkness*, 332.

38. Peretti, *This Present Darkness*, 373.

39. Peretti, *This Present Darkness*, 38.

40. Peretti, *This Present Darkness*, 38.

While the heroines become tougher and more assertive, the heroes discover that human strength is made perfect in weakness. Marshall learns that his high-powered career has led to overwork and neglect of his family, and Hank learns that the Strongman and his Omni Corporation are no match for the spiritual forces supporting a young pastor and his prayer team. The conventional action hero traits of physical brawn and fighting prowess are reserved for the angelic warriors, but Peretti has also pulled back from the macho confidence of spiritual warfare. When Radosh met him at a Christian bookstore many years after *This Present Darkness* and questioned his demonization of liberals, Peretti grew quiet and troubled, acknowledging that he lashed out in his early books. Radosh had imagined him "thumping a Bible with one hand, casting off demons with the other, and throttling a gay abortionist with his feet,"[41] so he cannot shake off "the unnerving experience of finding out that liberal-baiting author Frank Peretti was a reasonable and considerate human being."[42] This is less surprising to a sympathetic reader of *This Present Darkness* or Peretti's memoir *The Wounded Spirit*, which describes a childhood disability that led to severe bullying and lifelong trauma. Peretti should be commended for owning up to his novels' limitations, but he need not be ashamed of female characters that are far superior to those in the *Left Behind* series that built on his success.

"SHO 'NUFF!": *THE SHACK*'S MAMMY STEREOTYPES

In 2007, it seemed like everyone was reading William P. Young's *The Shack*. My Bible study leader said it had transformed his view of God, it showed up in a syllabus in my department, and I could easily borrow a copy when I wanted to see what all the fuss was about. The novel tells the story of Mack Phillips, whose daughter is murdered by a serial killer. When Mack receives a note from God telling him to return to a shack in the wilderness where the police found his daughter's blood, he thinks that the note comes from the killer and travels alone with a gun, hoping for revenge. He enters a supernatural world in which God is a black woman named Papa, Jesus is a Middle Eastern man, and the Holy Spirit is an Asian woman. Young clearly intended to disrupt the white male perspective that informs most Christian imagery, but he stumbled into one of America's most enduring racist stereotypes. The "mammy"—the black woman who lives with a white family, nurtures the children, and never mentions her own needs—emerged before

41. Radosh, *Rapture Ready!*, 118.
42. Radosh, *Rapture Ready!*, 235.

the Civil War and appears in popular culture from 1930s films like *Imitation of Life* and *Gone with the Wind* to (until recently) the boxes of Aunt Jemima pancake mix in supermarkets. *The Shack* falls squarely into this unfortunate literary tradition in which black domestic workers do not feel mistreated or angry but happy to be "part of the family."

Mack meets Papa in a chapter called "Guess Who's Coming to Dinner," an allusion to the 1967 film in which liberal white parents come to accept their daughter's black fiancé. In *Screen Saviors: Hollywood Fictions of Whiteness*, Hernán Vera and Andrew M. Gordon argue that this outwardly progressive film "turns out to be a rather tame, self-congratulatory liberal melodrama that actually expands the white self by announcing, 'Look how tolerant we are!'"[43] This is an uncannily accurate description of *The Shack*, which also "ends by reaffirming the wisdom, power, and tolerance of the white patriarch as he adapts successfully to changing times."[44] Mack initially responds to Papa with disbelief: "Am I going crazy? Am I supposed to believe that God is a big black woman?"[45] Papa explains that she took on this persona to break down his stereotypes: "For me to appear to you as a woman and suggest that you call me Papa is simply to mix metaphors, to help you keep from falling so easily back into your religious conditioning."[46] Since Mack had always imagined God as a white-haired grandfather like Gandalf in *The Lord of the Rings*, he needs to embrace the feminine side of God—maybe even the feminist side, as Papa denounces male headship in marriage and gets so frustrated with Mack's lack of emotion that she mutters: "Men! Such idiots sometimes."[47] This view of God seems so progressive that many of my colleagues have been surprised that I would associate it with racism.

Yet in his efforts to undermine the stereotype of the white man as God, Young reinforces the stereotype of the black woman as mammy. Papa quickly establishes herself as Mack's substitute mother: "With speed that belied her size, she crossed the distance between them and engulfed him in her arms, lifting him clear off his feet and spinning him around like a little child."[48] She smells like his mother, introduces herself as "the housekeeper and cook,"[49] and spends much of her time barefoot in the kitchen. She is so

---

43. Vera and Gordon, *Screen Saviors*, 85.
44. Vera and Gordon, *Screen Saviors*, 86.
45. Young, *Shack*, 88–89.
46. Young, *Shack*, 93.
47. Young, *Shack*, 192.
48. Young, *Shack*, 82.
49. Young, *Shack*, 86.

content with servitude that when Jesus drops a bowl, she jokes: "You just can't get good help around here."[50] Right after she tells Mack that she's appearing as a woman to disrupt his religious conditioning, she provides a different reason: "And after what you've been through, you couldn't very well handle a father right now, could you?"[51] Apparently God has been showing his feminine side only as a temporary accommodation to Mack's childlike grief. Whereas Christy Huddleston, Marshall Hogan, and Bernice Krueger fought relentlessly for their communities and overcame their spiritual immaturity, Mack simply needs to relax and let God care for him.

Near the end of the novel, Mack wakes up in the morning to find that God has transformed into a man: "The man standing next to him looked a bit like Papa; dignified, older, and wiry and taller than Mack. He had silver-white hair pulled back into a ponytail, matched by a gray-splashed mustache and goatee. Plaid shirt with sleeves rolled up, jeans, and hiking boots completed the outfit of someone ready to hit the trail."[52] We cannot tell the man's race, but the "silver-white hair" recalls the image of God as an old man with a white beard. As God tells Mack a few pages later, "We are coming full circle."[53] In the end, Young seems to represent God as a black woman not to draw attention to the ways in which oppressed people reflect the divine character but to support a white man through a painful journey. Once Mack has overcome the worst of his grief, God becomes that silver-haired man again. Despite Young's good intentions, *The Shack* exemplifies the harm that can be done when Christian authors rely on racial stereotypes as shortcuts to an emotional connection with readers.

Fortunately, Octavia Spencer's dignified portrayal of Papa in the 2017 film version reduces the mammy stereotype. She came to this part with an Academy Award for Best Actress in a Supporting Role for *The Help* (2011) and nominations for *Hidden Figures* (2016) and *The Shape of Water* (2017). In a new scene in the opening frame narrative, she plays a kind neighbor who comforts Mack, providing a psychological explanation for why he would later picture God in the form of a real woman from his childhood. The film replaces Papa's dialectical sayings like "Guess that's jes' the way I is" and "Sho 'nuff!"[54] with the standard English "Guess that's just the way I am" and "Well, sure." When Papa turns into a man, he is played by Native Canadian actor Graham Greene, expanding the multicultural mosaic rather than

50. Young, *Shack*, 105.
51. Young, *Shack*, 93.
52. Young, *Shack*, 218.
53. Young, *Shack*, 221.
54. Young, *Shack*, 119.

coming "full circle" to a white male image. After a short time, Papa turns back into Octavia Spencer. The film retains many of the novel's aesthetic and theological shortcomings, but as we will see with *The Chronicles of Narnia* and *Left Behind*, sometimes a strong actress goes a long way toward improving a problematic female character.

THIS BOOK'S APPROACH

Like the brief examples above, the following six chapters examine mainline Protestant and evangelical portrayals of racial minorities, impoverished and working-class people, and vulnerable young women, with an emphasis on the groups most relevant to each text. While some scholars include texts like *The Da Vinci Code* with theological themes but secular worldviews, I include those with Christian artists in prominent roles and many Christian fans. This eliminates a television series like *American Idol*, in which secular producers maintain power over Christian contestants (I described this phenomenon in the article "Jesus, Take the Wheel"). While *Duck Dynasty* also had secular producers, they quickly discovered the considerable power wielded by their evangelical stars. These criteria also eliminate literary fiction like the novels of Marilynne Robinson, which do not have a mass following outside the academy. Except for the Narnia novels that were published in the 1950s but recently made into feature films, I focus on texts produced between 1990 and 2020 that have received less scholarly attention than is warranted by their cultural influence. Since I grew up in Methodist and Congregational churches in Vermont, attended an Episcopal church in Iowa, and now serve as a Catholic professor at a Mennonite Brethren university in California, I have an ecumenical view of the popular culture landscape and have chosen texts that engage a variety of denominations. In some cases, this led me to investigate works that had never appealed to me, like *Redeeming Love* and *Left Behind*, while in other cases I was already a fan, as with the Narnia and Sherwood films.

As an English professor, I focus on novels, movies, and television rather than advertising, collectibles, music, or painting. However, since successful products tend to spawn franchises, I analyze seven *Chronicles of Narnia* novels and three films; the secular and Christian editions of *Redeeming Love*; fourteen Mitford novels, the Mitford cookbook, the *Mitford Bedside Companion*, and the Hallmark film; the first *Left Behind* novel and its two film versions; six Sherwood Baptist Church films; eleven seasons of *Duck Dynasty*, one *Duck Dynasty* cookbook, and ten other Robertson family books. Theological issues and aesthetic considerations arise only when relevant to sociopolitical concerns. It is tempting to discuss Karon's portrayal of the Episcopal Church during a time of denominational conflict or Tim LaHaye's dispensationalism, but my approach privileges those elements that would be most relevant to the wider community of popular culture scholars.

The first three chapters highlight female issues, authors, and audiences. Chapter 1, "Whiner or Warrior? Susan Pevensie's Role in the Novel and Film Versions of *The Chronicles of Narnia*," argues that Lewis's abrupt dismissal of Susan offends many readers, but Walden Media worked hard to create a well-rounded character whose spiritual downfall unfolds over three films. Chapter 2, "The Prostitute in the Fairy Tale: Objectifying Women in *Redeeming Love*," claims that Rivers treats prostitution with sensitivity but romanticizes the hero's violent control over the heroine. Chapter 3, "'But This Is the *South*': Race, Class, and Southern Identity in Jan Karon's Mitford Novels," traces Karon's evolution from the comforting early novels to an explicit discussion of racism that outraged many fans. The next three chapters focus on male artists and include masculine gender roles. Chapter 4, "'He Hoped She *Was* Gone': A World without Christian Women in *Left Behind*," observes that the rapture of pious women liberates the novel's macho heroes, while the two film versions provide stronger heroines. Chapter 5, "From Sidekicks to Protagonists: Black and Latino Characters in the Films of the Sherwood Baptist Church," examines the progress of minority characters from supporting to main roles. Chapter 6, "Lil' Will and Boomerang Becca: Racial Others on *Duck Dynasty*," looks at the marginalization of Hispanic, black, and Asian characters on the reality television hit. The conclusion considers the five most recent texts by these artists and reveals an overall positive trajectory, suggesting that Christian writers have paid attention to wider cultural concerns about social responsibility, although the limitations of the *Duck Dynasty* spin-off *Jep & Jessica* indicate that crossover popular culture still has room for improvement.

Not all of these authors, filmmakers, and television personalities are champions of social justice, but it is time to move beyond the era when critics of "Christian" popular culture used scare quotes to undermine their spiritual or artistic integrity. Romanowski's *Eyes Wide Open* laments that too much "'Christian' popular art either proclaims the faith or leaves people with a warm fuzzy feeling."[55] This generalization fails to account for classics like *The Chronicles of Narnia* or *The Lord of the Rings*, and it has become harder to support with the crossover success of nuanced Christian works in recent years. When Barack Obama was elected the first black President in 2008, heroic archer Katniss Everdeen appeared in *The Hunger Games*, Susan

---

55. Romanowski, *Eyes Wide Open*, 80.

Pevensie plunged into battle in the *Prince Caspian* film, African American volunteer Ken Bevel played a loyal family man in *Fireproof*, and black gospel singer Mandisa's album, *True Beauty*, was nominated for a Grammy. None of these examples are perfect; the film versions of *The Hunger Games* and *Prince Caspian* can be critiqued for their heroines' preoccupation with romance and the exceptional beauty of actresses Jennifer Lawrence and Anna Popplewell, and Bevel plays the limited role of "black best friend" to the white protagonist. Yet none of them can be reduced to a warm fuzzy feeling, and they deserve the same critical attention that Romanowski recommended for other mass culture. We must distinguish between texts whose stereotypes would appall many nonbelievers and those in which Christian artists are leading the way toward a sensitive portrayal of groups who have been abused by the entertainment media for too long.

Chapter 1

WHINER OR WARRIOR?

Susan Pevensie's Role in the Novel and Film Versions of The Chronicles of Narnia

While Walden Media prepared to release its film version of C. S. Lewis's *The Lion, the Witch and the Wardrobe* in December 2005, critics and fans responded by publishing over twenty books on the Narnia Chronicles during that year alone. Some scholars presented themselves as guides to those who were (re)discovering the books, such as Leland Ryken and Marjorie Lamp Mead in *A Reader's Guide through the Wardrobe*: "As a new movie version of the story is released, likely even more adults will find themselves interested in revisiting a classic tale from their childhood, while some who have never read this story will be attracted to it for the first time."[1] In *Not a Tame Lion*, Bruce L. Edwards defended the books against potential Hollywood exploitation: "The literary premises and spiritual principles that most animated Lewis as he depicted them imaginatively within the Narnian landscape could be lost in translation as the stories migrate from text to big screen."[2] Despite these concerns, this film and its sequels *Prince Caspian* (2008) and *The Voyage of the Dawn Treader* (2010) turned out to be thoughtful, carefully crafted, and a rich source of discussion about one of the books' most controversial female characters. Susan Pevensie starts out as a fairly positive heroine, but she disappears from later books, and her siblings have only harsh things to say about her when she is absent from heaven in the final pages. While Lewis's portrayal of Susan strikes many

---

1. Ryken and Mead, *Reader's Guide*, 9–10.
2. Edwards, *Not a Tame Lion*, xiv.

readers as incomplete and misogynistic, the Walden Media films transform her into a powerful warrior whose distractions by romance and beauty become a feminist cautionary tale.

"NO ONE CARED ANYTHING ABOUT SUSAN NOW": HER RISE AND FALL IN THE NOVELS

When we meet the four Pevensie children in *The Lion, the Witch and the Wardrobe*, each has a crucial role to play. Peter and Susan struggle with adult-like problems, such as taking responsibility for others and making hard decisions, while Edmund and Lucy face childhood problems of being overshadowed and teased. Colin Manlove argues that we can view the children "not just as four individuals, but also potentially as four parts of the one spirit,"[3] while Natasha Giardina claims that "Susan is motherly, while Peter is a born leader, and taken together, the four of them appear like a microcosm of the idealized 1950s family."[4] Lewis wrote in "Membership" that everyone in a family is irreplaceable: "If you subtract any one member you have not simply reduced the family in number, you have inflicted an injury on its structure."[5] Critics have a tendency to judge Susan's struggles in the early books in the harsh light of her tragic ending in *The Last Battle*, but this does not reflect the experience of many readers who become attached to her early on. Though Susan gets emotionally overwhelmed at times, her maternal role in the family and compassion for Aslan in his suffering give her the potential to become a compelling figure of gentleness and mercy.

Susan's motherly role and Edmund's resentment are established on the first page, making her already ambiguous in the reader's mind. Due to the bombing of London during World War II, the children have been evacuated to the home of an old Professor in the country:

> "We've fallen on our feet and no mistake," said Peter. "This is going to be perfectly splendid. That old chap will let us do anything we like."
> "I think he's an old dear," said Susan.
> "Oh, come off it!" said Edmund, who was tired and pretending not to be tired, which always made him bad-tempered. "Don't go on talking like that."
> "Like what?" said Susan; "and anyway, it's time you were in bed."

3. Manlove, *Chronicles of Narnia*, 35.

4. Giardina, "Elusive Prey," 35.

5. Lewis, "Membership," 34.

"Trying to talk like Mother," said Edmund. "And who are
you to say when I'm to go to bed? Go to bed yourself."[6]

Edmund does not take issue with Peter's masculine "old chap" but with Susan's feminine "old dear," which is significant foreshadowing if we know that
Susan is condemned in later books for acting too grown-up. Doris T. Myers
links Susan's affected speech here to the fact that she "is never perfectly sincere" and will ultimately be excluded from heaven, even though her footnote
acknowledges that Lewis had not yet planned any sequels.[7] This seems like
an overly harsh interpretation of the early Susan, who seems very sincere
when she encourages Edmund on a rainy day by pointing out the wireless
and books, examines the back of the wardrobe when Lucy claims that it
leads to Narnia, stops Peter and Edmund from fighting, and takes a leading
role when she and Peter seek advice from the Professor.

Susan is responsible for the children's entry into Narnia as a family and
first recognizes that they are in the forest. She thinks of the "very sensible
plan" of wearing the fur coats from the wardrobe.[8] When they see Tumnus's
cave wrecked by the White Witch's secret police and realize that Narnia is a
dangerous place, she is concerned for everyone's welfare: "I mean, it doesn't
seem particularly safe here and it looks as if it won't be much fun either.
And it's getting colder every minute, and we've brought nothing to eat. What
about just going home?"[9] Devin Brown reads this as evidence that Susan
is always "a somewhat reluctant adventurer,"[10] but she changes her mind
when Lucy appeals to her compassion for Tumnus. She's the first to spot Mr.
Beaver and wants to follow him, responds with joy to Aslan's name, compli-
ments the Beavers' dam, and protests when Mr. Beaver says that there's no
point in looking for Edmund. Her weakness is a tendency to despair: "Oh,
how I wish we'd never come."[11] While the other children also show fear in
dangerous situations, Susan's desire to leave altogether makes her seem less
sympathetic.

Perhaps Father Christmas has Susan's protective and helping roles in
mind when he presents her with a bow and arrows: "'You must use the bow
only in great need,' he said, 'for I do not mean you to fight in the battle. It
does not easily miss. And when you put this horn to your lips and blow it,

6. Lewis, *Chronicles of Narnia*, 111–12.

7. Myers, *C. S. Lewis in Context*, 127.

8. Lewis, *Chronicles of Narnia*, 135.

9. Lewis, *Chronicles of Narnia*, 136–37.

10. Brown, *Inside Narnia*, 98.

11. Lewis, *Chronicles of Narnia*, 148.

then, wherever you are, I think help of some kind will come to you."[12] These gifts seem to represent a balance between active warfare and passive calls for help, but she ends up using only the latter in this book. While Peter's sword and Lucy's healing cordial save lives in battle, Susan uses the horn to save herself when she is attacked by a wolf. Readers may wonder why she is given the bow with such ceremony if she is not going to use it. When Father Christmas gives Lucy a dagger but tells her that "battles are ugly when women fight," it seems clear that the weapons are given to the girls only as a last resort.[13] This will be contradicted in later books when Lucy and Jill Pole fight nobly in battle, presenting a challenge for filmmakers who want to maintain a consistent narrative. At this point, Susan seems correct in focusing on her helping role since that is what Father Christmas advised.

Susan's presence at Aslan's death and resurrection gives her a theological significance akin to the Virgin Mary or Mary Magdalene. Paul A. Karkainen misses this possibility when he compares the other children to Jesus' male followers but claims that "Susan does not really show her true colors in this book. She seems the soul of sensibility and compromise, a girl who generally displays a cool, mature manner."[14] He hesitates to claim sensibility, compromise, and maturity as apostolic qualities and suggests that they are not her "true colors." Donald E. Glover seems more accurate when he describes "Lucy and Susan as the two Marys."[15] Yet Lewis obscures these connections by making Susan the one to question the necessity of Aslan's death: "Can't we do something about the Deep Magic? Isn't there something you can work against it?"[16] Aslan's stern response makes it clear that this is a blasphemous question. Edwards claims: "Such a sentiment, though understandable in the passion of the moment, is ill-thought and reflects Susan's naïveté and limited judgment."[17] It would have been logical for Lewis to give these words to Peter, since his name and status as High King link him to the biblical Peter who denies the necessity of Jesus' death. Instead, Lewis gives the line to Susan to emphasize that weighty theological matters should be handled by male disciples and not by females who have received less teaching and are not being groomed for leadership. Rather than making

---

12. Lewis, *Chronicles of Narnia*, 160.

13. Lewis, *Chronicles of Narnia*, 160.

14. Karkainen, *Narnia Explored*, 16.

15. Glover, *Art of Enchantment*, 139.

16. Lewis, *Chronicles of Narnia*, 176.

17. Edwards, *Not a Tame Lion*, 127.

Peter a flawed hero, all the blame falls on Susan and mitigates her Marian significance.[18]

When Susan and Lucy travel with Aslan to the Stone Table, however, they prove much more faithful than the male disciples who fell asleep at Gethsemane and abandoned Jesus before his journey to Golgotha. On the night of Aslan's death, Susan lies awake and considers Aslan's behavior: "'There's been something wrong with him all afternoon,' said Susan. 'Lucy! What was that he said about not being with us at the battle? You don't think he could be stealing away and leaving us tonight, do you?'"[19] After Susan spots Aslan walking into the wood, she begs: "Please, may we come with you—wherever you're going?"[20] Even her tendency to despair is redeemed by the tragic nature of these scenes, for example her sobbing when the Witch's rabble ties Aslan to the table. In the morning, Susan represents the women who find the empty tomb and the disciples who are taught the meaning of the resurrection. When Aslan's body disappears, she cries: "What does it mean?"[21] She asks if the risen Aslan is a ghost, and he licks her forehead in a child-friendly version of Jesus inviting Thomas to feel his wounds. She asks again: "But what does it all mean?"[22] prompting Aslan to explain the Deeper Magic just as Jesus taught the disciples on the road to Emmaus. Like the Virgin Mary in the Gospels and Acts, Susan plays a dual role as grieving mother and questioning disciple.

Susan has no part in the battle at the end of the novel, since it ends a few minutes after she and Lucy arrive on the scene, but we learn of her compassion for Edmund when she decides not to tell him that Aslan died for his treachery. After the coronation, "Susan grew into a tall and gracious woman with black hair that fell almost to her feet and the kings of the countries beyond the sea began to send ambassadors asking for her hand in marriage. And she was called Queen Susan the Gentle."[23]

18. Protestant Lewis rejected the Catholic veneration of Mary "because it seems utterly foreign to the New Testament" (*Collected Letters*, 2:646), so it is not surprising that he avoids characterizing Susan as a Marian figure.

19. Lewis, *Chronicles of Narnia*, 178.

20. Lewis, *Chronicles of Narnia*, 179.

21. Lewis, *Chronicles of Narnia*, 184.

22. Lewis, *Chronicles of Narnia*, 185.

23. Lewis, *Chronicles of Narnia*, 194.

Laura Hollingsworth's fan art painting *Queen Susan* **captures many readers'**
admiration of the gentle queen. Copyright © 2020 by Laura Hollingsworth.
Used by permission. All rights reserved.

The reference to Susan's long hair echoes Mary Magdalene wiping Jesus' feet with her hair, while the reference to foreign kings seems innocent since Lucy inspires similar devotion. It does not seem fair to interpret this happy ending in light of future events, as Mark Eddy Smith does in his analysis of the final scene when the children rediscover the wardrobe and return to England: "Susan alone balks from following the stag past the lamppost, though they all intuit that their fortunes will change drastically if they do. I think it's possible that Susan never gets over her disappointment at returning to Earth, where she isn't a queen, where her clothes, however stylish, will never quite measure up."[24] This is obviously speculation. Susan quickly changes her mind when Lucy and Edmund argue against her: "'Then in the name of Aslan,' said Queen Susan, 'if ye will all have it so, let us go on and take the adventure that shall fall to us.'"[25] Susan did not have to become a negative character in future books, but she could have learned courage just as Peter learns leadership and Edmund justice. Her fate was not yet determined.

Most contemporary readers next encounter Susan in *The Horse and His Boy*, where Lewis foregoes her Marian potential and portrays her as an unredeemed Magdalene whose attraction to the evil Prince Rabadash and then rejection of him almost destroys two countries.[26] Cathy McSporran notes that Susan is the only friend of Narnia to consider marriage: "The whole business, of course, ends in disaster. Susan ends up as a Helen-of-Troy figure, whose rejection of one man leads hundreds of others to war."[27] Although Susan shows great kindness to the motherless Corin, she cannot recognize a cruel suitor who is prepared to take her by force: "'I am the cause of all this,' said Susan, bursting into tears. 'Oh, if only I had never left Cair Paravel.'"[28] Just as Edmund's nasty comments first caused us to doubt her virtue, we are influenced by Rabadash's exclamation: "'The false jade, the—' and here he added a great many descriptions of Queen Susan which would not look at all nice in print."[29] The "false jade" links Susan to the White Witch Jadis, although she has much less power since Rabadash plans to "swing her into the saddle, and then, ride, ride, ride back to Anvard,"[30]

24. Mark Eddy Smith, *Aslan's Call*, 27.

25. Lewis, *Chronicles of Narnia*, 196.

26. Peter J. Schakel describes HarperCollins's 1994 decision to publish all editions in chronological order based on the events in Narnia and the debate about whether this is preferable to the original publishing order (*Way into Narnia*, 13–21). The decline of Susan's character is more gradual in Lewis's publishing order, since we see her stumble on the road of discipleship in *Prince Caspian*, go to America in *Dawn Treader*, and disappear for the length of *Silver Chair* before encountering her as an adult obsessed with romance in *Horse and His Boy*. In the current order, we move abruptly from her largely positive role in *Lion* to a preview of her foolish and destructive adult behavior in *Horse and His Boy*, giving a more negative cast to the childhood and adolescent struggles to come. The Walden Media films avoid this problem since they follow Lewis's publishing order.

27. McSporran, "Daughters of Lilith," 200.

28. Lewis, *Chronicles of Narnia*, 238.

29. Lewis, *Chronicles of Narnia*, 256.

30. Lewis, *Chronicles of Narnia*, 258.

an image out of a stereotypical movie Western in which Susan is completely abject and helpless.

Moreover, the narrator seems to blame her for not taking part in the climactic battle, which contradicts Father Christmas's suggestion that women fight only as a last resort and Aslan's decision to keep the girls out of battle in the earlier novel. As the Narnians prepare for war, Corin explains that Susan stayed behind: "She's not like Lucy, you know, who's as good as a man, or at any rate as good as a boy. Queen Susan is more like an ordinary grown-up lady. She doesn't ride to the wars, though she is an excellent archer."[31] Susan seems to be the victim of rapidly changing standards. What happened to "battles are ugly when women fight?" She is absent for the rest of the book, and this picture of her as damsel in distress overshadows her compassionate presence at Aslan's death and her reign as Queen Susan the Gentle.

In *Prince Caspian*, Susan plays the maternal role when the Pevensies arrive in Narnia, pointing out that they should make plans for dinner, hold onto their shoes, and save the sandwiches. She recognizes the orchard and the castle courtyard and finds the chess piece that confirms that they are in Cair Paravel. In the treasure chamber, she finds her bow from Father Christmas and we learn: "Archery and swimming were the things Susan was good at."[32] In fact, this uniquely martial novel will provide Lewis's only image of Susan as a warrior. They discover Telmarine soldiers in a boat, preparing to drown something that seems to be alive:

> Peter now saw that it was really alive and was in fact a Dwarf, bound hand and foot but struggling as hard as he could. Next moment he heard a twang just beside his ear, and all at once the soldier threw up his arms, dropping the Dwarf into the bottom of the boat, and fell over into the water. He floundered away to the far bank and Peter knew that Susan's arrow had struck his helmet. He turned and saw that she was very pale but was already fitting a second arrow to the string.[33]

Lewis gives Peter's perspective rather than presenting Susan's own thoughts, but her heroism in stopping the soldier without killing him continues when she swims to rescue the Dwarf.

When the Dwarf Trumpkin doubts that the Pevensies can help to defeat the usurping King Miraz, Susan puts on armor alongside the others to convince Trumpkin of their value. After Edmund beats Trumpkin in a

31. Lewis, *Chronicles of Narnia*, 290.

32. Lewis, *Chronicles of Narnia*, 328.

33. Lewis, *Chronicles of Narnia*, 330–31.

swordfight, Susan challenges him to an archery competition and "his eyes brightened, for he was a famous bowman among his own people."[34] Trumpkin condescendingly calls her "lass" and suggests an easy target, but she chooses a challenging one that he narrowly misses: "She was not enjoying her match half so much as Edmund had enjoyed his; not because she had any doubt about hitting the apple but because Susan was so tender-hearted that she almost hated to beat someone who had been beaten already."[35] She easily hits the apple, and Trumpkin protests when she comes up with a false excuse for her victory. He also catches himself soon after when he calls her and Lucy "little girls,"[36] realizing that they are truly queens of Narnia. It seems that Susan has found the right approach to Father Christmas's gift, developing into an excellent archer but using her skills only for emergencies like saving Trumpkin's life and feats of athletic prowess.

After this heroic beginning, Susan shows her worst side on their hike through the woods, complaining so much that her siblings are always chastising her. Edmund calls her "a wet blanket" and makes the sexist jab that girls "never carry a map in their heads."[37] Even Lucy reproaches her for "rotten" comments when Peter realizes they are lost.[38] Though nobody except Edmund believes Lucy when she sees Aslan, Susan is blamed for her tendency to "talk like a grown-up"[39] and for using "her most annoying grown-up voice."[40] We see the dark side of her maternal role as she repeatedly commands Lucy to go to sleep and calls her "downright naughty."[41] In case we didn't notice, the narrator states that "Susan was the worst."[42] We also learn that Lucy was "trying not to say all the things she thought of saying to Susan,"[43] reinforcing the idea from *The Horse and His Boy* that Susan's faults cannot be named in polite company. She complains about hiking down the gorge and is the last of the children to see Aslan.

Susan does apologize to Lucy, with an attention to grammar that is the mark of a true Narnian hero: "But I've been far worse than you know. I really believed it was him—he, I mean—yesterday. When he warned us

---

34. Lewis, *Chronicles of Narnia*, 364.

35. Lewis, *Chronicles of Narnia*, 364–65.

36. Lewis, *Chronicles of Narnia*, 365.

37. Lewis, *Chronicles of Narnia*, 370.

38. Lewis, *Chronicles of Narnia*, 372.

39. Lewis, *Chronicles of Narnia*, 373.

40. Lewis, *Chronicles of Narnia*, 381.

41. Lewis, *Chronicles of Narnia*, 383.

42. Lewis, *Chronicles of Narnia*, 384.

43. Lewis, *Chronicles of Narnia*, 384.

not to go down to the fir wood. And I really believed it was him tonight, when you woke us up. I mean, deep down inside."[44] Karkainen is not convinced: "Her technique is like that of Satan in the Garden of Eden. Satan questions whether or not God really told Eve to eat of every tree save one, and Susan questions whether or not Lucy really saw Aslan."[45] He goes on to call her "hateful" and a "perfect little beast."[46] Yet Glover reminds us that three people voted against Lucy, "Trumpkin out of ignorance, Susan from sloth, Peter from pride or expedience."[47] Aslan doesn't seem terribly angry, simply telling her to overcome her fears and breathing on her so that she can be brave again.

Susan is rarely mentioned again as the boys engage in battle and the girls accompany Aslan to the bacchanalian feasts, although she does make the crucial observation that she wouldn't feel safe around Bacchus without Aslan. She demonstrates mature acceptance when Aslan tells her and Peter that they won't be returning to Narnia, and her only encounter with Caspian emphasizes her generosity and manners as well as the significance of the horn that has become her symbolic voice: "And of course Caspian offered the Horn back to Susan and of course Susan told him to keep it."[48] Although Susan is forgiven, most of her actions were so negative that they leave us with the sense that her Marian potential has come to nothing.

Perhaps it is not surprising that Lewis dismisses Susan with one sentence at the beginning of *The Voyage of the Dawn Treader*: "Grown-ups thought her the pretty one of the family and she was no good at school work (though otherwise very old for her age) and Mother said she 'would get far more out of a trip to America than the youngsters.'"[49] Peter studies for an exam with Professor Kirke, and Lucy and Edmund travel to Narnia, but Susan spends the holidays in a place that seems to offer much less spiritual insight. What could be more damning from a conservative British point of view than the idea that one might enjoy a trip to America?

Even in her absence, Susan has a negative influence when Lucy is tempted to perform a spell in the magician's book to make herself beautiful. Magical pictures entice Lucy, while subtly echoing Susan's role in *The Horse and His Boy*:

44. Lewis, *Chronicles of Narnia*, 386.
45. Karkainen, *Narnia Explored*, 45.
46. Karkainen, *Narnia Explored*, 48.
47. Glover, *Art of Enchantment*, 146.
48. Lewis, *Chronicles of Narnia*, 418.
49. Lewis, *Chronicles of Narnia*, 426.

> She saw herself throned on high at a great tournament in Calormen and all the Kings of the world fought because of her beauty. After that it turned from tournaments to real wars, and all Narnia and Archenland, Telmar and Calormen, Galma and Terebinthia, were laid waste with the fury of the kings and dukes and great lords who fought for her favour. Then it changed and Lucy, still beautiful beyond the lot of mortals, was back in England. And Susan (who had always been the beauty of the family) came home from America. The Susan in the picture looked exactly like the real Susan only plainer and with a nasty expression. And Susan was jealous of the dazzling beauty of Lucy, but that didn't matter a bit because no one cared anything about Susan now.[50]

Aslan's face appears in the book to stop her from saying the spell, but we get the sense that her sinful fantasies are not far from the truth. When she sees Aslan a few minutes later, "she looked almost as beautiful as that other Lucy in the picture,"[51] and we know that all the princes wanted to marry her when she was queen. Susan has also conveniently disappeared from the Chronicles, leaving Lucy as the center of attention. Why is Lucy's vanity passed over so lightly, while Susan's vanity will later exclude her from heaven? Aslan does have a special bond with Lucy based on her extraordinary faith, but readers may wonder why he never took the time to give Susan the lesson that may have saved her soul. We are left to conclude that Lewis simply lost interest in Susan and chose to portray her as the most destructive kind of teenage girl rather than the ideal mother that she had the potential to become.

Susan's fate becomes clear at the end of *The Last Battle*, when the friends of Narnia reunite in Aslan's country after their deaths. Tirian stands in for the reader when he asks about the other sister whom he has read about in the chronicles:

> "My sister Susan," answered Peter shortly and gravely, "is no longer a friend of Narnia."
>
> "Yes," said Eustace, "and whenever you've tried to get her to come and talk about Narnia or do anything about Narnia, she says 'What wonderful memories you have! Fancy your still thinking about all those funny games we used to play when we were children.'"
>
> "Oh, Susan!" said Jill. "She's interested in nothing nowadays except nylons and lipstick and invitations. She always was a jolly sight too keen on being grown-up."

50. Lewis, *Chronicles of Narnia*, 495–96.
51. Lewis, *Chronicles of Narnia*, 498.

"Grown-up, indeed," said the Lady Polly. "I wish she *would* grow up. She wasted all her school time wanting to be the age she is now, and she'll waste all the rest of her life trying to stay that age. Her whole idea is to race on to the silliest time of one's life as quick as she can and then stop there as long as she can."

"Well, don't let's talk about that now," said Peter. "Look! Here are lovely fruit trees. Let us taste them."[52]

That's the last we hear of Susan. The friends have a surprisingly callous attitude toward someone who once played a central role in their adventures.

Many readers' shock and dismay compelled Lewis to point out that there is still hope for Susan, since she did not die in the train wreck that killed her family. In a January 22, 1957 letter to a young reader, he wrote: "She is left alive in this world at the end, having by then turned into a rather silly, conceited young woman. But there is plenty of time for her to mend, and perhaps she will get to Aslan's country in the end—in her own way."[53] Yet this explanation does not satisfy many fans, since we never get to *see* Susan go through the kind of conversion experience that so many other characters have in Narnia.

Critics have debated the "problem of Susan" ever since, with some arguing that she deserves this fate and that not every character can have a happy ending. Walter Hooper upholds Lewis's view in *The Great Divorce* that "those who have chosen Hell shall not be allowed to veto the joys of Heaven."[54] Karkainen compares Susan to characters who participate actively in Narnia's destruction: "Susan is not a shrewd person, but she, like the dwarfs and Ginger, has a warped sense of values."[55] Paul F. Ford claims that "a careful rereading of her story shows that her fall is much better prepared for than some critics think."[56] Karla Faust Jones calls her "a self-limiting character,"[57] and Adam Barkman supports Lewis's conservative gender roles: "Lewis's point is not that Susan is too feminine, but that she is not truly feminine enough."[58] Peter J. Schakel argues that Lewis uses Susan "to make the point that some people abandon their faith and will not reach heaven."[59] Alan Jacobs notes that Lewis was simply a man of his

---

52. Lewis, *Chronicles of Narnia*, 741.

53. Lewis, *Collected Letters*, 3:826.

54. Hooper, *Past Watchful Dragons*, 127.

55. Karkainen, *Narnia Explored*, 182.

56. Ford, *Companion to Narnia*, 414–15.

57. Karla Faust Jones, "Girls in Narnia," 16.

58. Barkman, "All Is Righteousness," 429.

59. Schakel, *Way into Narnia*, 159.

time: "And if every negative female character an author creates is evidence of that author's misogyny, then few writers can escape censure."[60] Monika B. Hilder concludes: "Susan's problem is not that she has grown up, but that she has chosen a narcissistic form of young adulthood as the ideal human condition."[61] However, these critics would not need to defend this passage unless others were outraged that Susan is condemned for normal traits of female adolescence.

The fact that the characters' language about Susan is so informal, impatient, and uncharitable—"She always was a jolly sight too keen on being grown-up" and "I wish she *would* grow up"—indicates that Lewis may be venting his frustrations with young women rather than presenting the tragic conclusion of a carefully constructed character arc. For David Holbrook, this ending exemplifies Lewis's emotional immaturity and fear of female sexuality, "so that he can only be spiteful of his own girl character once she becomes a woman."[62] Candice Fredrick and Sam McBride argue that Lewis sees women as more prone to temptation and resistant to sanctification: "Of course, the idea that women are more likely than men to experience eternal damnation has no precedent in the Bible or in Christian tradition."[63] Jacqueline Carey bluntly states: "I resent the implication that a fondness for invitations and lipstick can render one no longer a friend of Narnia. Poor Susan got shafted!"[64] Laura Miller asks: "What makes these amusements so much worse than pipes and beer and 'bawdy' with your buddies at the pub?"[65] Karin Fry links Susan's beauty to that of the witches: "Perhaps the real reason that Susan cannot survive in Narnia is that she has some feminine power through her beauty and is secretly a threat to the prevailing power structure. Though she never uses her beauty for gain, she is condemned nevertheless."[66] If Lewis believed that a 1950s woman should find a husband and raise a family, then it seems unfair that Susan should be condemned for wanting to look attractive and go to parties.

Others note that Lewis treats Susan with less compassion than equally flawed male characters and that her siblings are dismissive rather than mourning the injury to their family structure. McSporran points out that Edmund and Eustace have committed greater sins than Susan and have

---

60. Jacobs, *Narnian*, 261.

61. Hilder, *Feminine Ethos*, 145.

62. Holbrook, *Skeleton in the Wardrobe*, 201.

63. Fredrick and McBride, *Women among the Inklings*, 149.

64. Carey, "Heathen Eye," 163.

65. Miller, *Magician's Book*, 132.

66. Fry, "No Longer a Friend," 162.

been redeemed, but they do not express remorse about Susan or beg Aslan to pardon her. Even Jill and Polly insult Susan: "Little sense of sisterhood exists in Narnia."[67] Mark Eddy Smith adds: "It seems unthinkable that someone like Susan, who had actually been to Narnia, who had lived for years and years as a queen in Narnia, should turn her back on it in the end."[68] Finally, Susana Rodriguez sums up many feminist complaints: "In allowing Edmund salvation despite the gravity of his crime but depriving Susan for a lesser fault, the texts underscore their bias in the male protagonists' favor while disempowering and damning the females for performing conventionally feminine roles that they were groomed for from the beginning."[69] This leaves the filmmakers with a challenge if they want to remain faithful to Lewis's storyline: How do they present Susan as a positive character who can be a role model for young female viewers but later rejects Aslan?

THE VISUAL RHETORIC OF NARNIA

Pauline Baynes's illustrations strengthen our early impression of Susan as a sweet, caring girl but do not prepare us for her later disgrace.[70] Lewis's "Outline of Narnian History" clarifies that Susan was twelve when she first entered Narnia,[71] and Baynes portrayed her as a young girl with braids. Her four-color book jacket for the 1950 first edition of *The Lion, the Witch and the Wardrobe* portrays Susan and Lucy riding on Aslan's back, with Susan's long, black braids flying straight out behind her. The girls' Mary Jane shoes suggest childhood innocence, like those worn by Alice in Sir John Tenniel's illustrations for *Alice's Adventures in Wonderland*. The 1959 full-color book jacket portrays Susan and Lucy playing with Aslan, swirling a garland of flowers around him. Susan still has long, black braids tied with ribbons and now has bright pink cheeks; she wears a yellow top, green skirt, short socks, and Mary Janes. She and Aslan are looking at each other, while Lucy is below them looking up toward Susan. Both images place Susan in a privileged position in relation to Aslan and capture her best moment in the series: her faithfulness to the risen savior. Susan wears the same girlish outfit

---

67. McSporran, "Daughters of Lilith," 203.

68. Mark Eddy Smith, *Aslan's Call*, 98.

69. Susana Rodriguez, "Boy-Girls and Girl-Beasts," 191.

70. Although my quotes throughout this chapter are from the one-volume *Chronicles of Narnia* included in the bibliography, my analysis of the Baynes illustrations is based on the full-color collector's edition released for the novels' fiftieth anniversary in 2000.

71. Hooper, *Past Watchful Dragons*, 41–44.

in the illustration of her talking to the Professor, where her clasped hands and concerned expression emphasize her maternal protection of Lucy. In subsequent illustrations, Susan holds Lucy's hand and looks back at her as they approach the Beavers' dam, looks intently at Mrs. Beaver while they learn about the prophecy, calls out for Edmund, huddles with Lucy as the Witch's creatures leave the Stone Table, cries over Aslan's dead body, looks toward the lamppost that they rediscover as adults, and tumbles behind her siblings out of the wardrobe.

In *Prince Caspian*, Baynes does not show Susan's full face until the last page, leaving the reader with few visual cues to help interpret her varied behavior. In the first illustration, she turns to help Lucy climb a hill, but their faces are obscured by distance. The next shows the children from the back as they gaze at the ruins of Cair Paravel, with Susan standing close to Lucy. The bows on her braids continue the childlike motif, but brown shoes and full-length stockings suggest a turn toward adolescence. We see Susan again from the back or side as she shows a chess piece to the others, holds her arm over Lucy's shoulders as they look into the treasure chamber, sits in the fishing boat, gazes at the river gorge, and crawls away from the Telmarine arrows. In an illustration that resembles the first edition cover of *The Lion, the Witch and the Wardrobe*, Susan rides on Aslan's back with her braids flying backwards as they approach the river-god, and we see her face finally as the children return to the train platform. Combined with the image of an adult Susan dancing joyfully with Tumnus in *The Horse and His Boy*, these illustrations portray her in a positive light while gradually removing her point of view.

The films allow for much richer visual information about Susan, and her embodiment in the beautiful fifteen-year-old actress Anna Popplewell lends her more maturity and substance. While Baynes showed her face eight times in *The Lion, the Witch and the Wardrobe*, the film version includes ninety-five shots in which her face is the only or most prominent feature, allowing us to identify with her range of moods from skepticism and terror to joy and relief. Her makeup is not noticeable, but her full lips may be a visual nod to the character's eventual obsession with "lipstick and invitations." She wears a fashionable 1940s hair style, parted on the side and curling down below her shoulders. Her English outfits include blouses, cardigans, and plaid skirts, while in Narnia she wears flowers in her hair and dons a long, close-fitting, green dress with slashed sleeves for battle; a long, blue cape with embroidered edges for Aslan's death; and a long, blue velvet dress and cape for the coronation. Overall, she looks lovely in an innocent, virginal manner highlighted by Popplewell's freckles. While there is nothing erotic about her appearance in this film, it is easy to imagine such an attractive teenager succumbing to the temptation of becoming a flirtatious woman. We also get to see her crowned as queen, reminding the viewer that she grows to adulthood twice—in Narnia and in England—which may help explain her ultimate turn away from childish things.

While Susan's full face appeared in only one illustration from *Prince Caspian*, the film includes forty-four close-up shots that reveal more prominent makeup and more elaborate costumes than in the previous film. She quickly exchanges her English school uniform for a lavender Narnian dress with a gold flower pattern and ruffles on the bodice, vertical stripes on the sleeves and skirt, and a blue underskirt. For the battle sequence, she changes to a mail shirt, black bodice with silver decorations, and red skirt that stands out against the grays and neutrals of the battlefield and ties her visually to the red tunics of Aslan's army. She wears a red dress with gold sleeves for the victory procession and a silver-blue dress for the final scene, visually echoing her coronation. Peter also wears blue, linking them to the Telmarine color palette of blue and silver and foreshadowing their return to the human world with the Telmarines. These beautiful costumes do more than lend visual interest to the big screen; they signal Susan's gradually increasing focus on her appearance. By the time she appears briefly in the film of *The Voyage of the Dawn Treader*, she will represent the kind of woman that Lucy must not become.

TARGET PRACTICE: CALLED TO BATTLE IN *THE LION, THE WITCH AND THE WARDROBE*

Andrew Adamson's film, which opened to rave reviews and made $745 million worldwide, follows the novel's plot with heightened excitement and suspense that give Susan more reasons to panic but offer more justification for her doing so. Her character development is also more complex, as the filmmakers transform her weakness and fear into a very relatable struggle to abandon reason and common sense enough to believe in the supernatural. A. O. Scott of the *New York Times* claims that "Lucy and Peter, the eldest, are the more virtuous, while Edmund and Susan have darker, more complicated personalities."[72] Jeffrey Overstreet notes that Susan "will learn that logic and 'too much thinking' can prevent her from apprehending miracles,"[73] while Maitland McDonagh adds that "Popplewell is admirably sympathetic as the stick-in-the-mud who must respond to marvels."[74] The viewer is also

72. Scott, "Two Wars of Good and Evil," para. 8.

73. Overstreet, Review of *Lion*, para. 12.

74. McDonagh, Review of *Lion*, para. 2.

encouraged to see Susan as a powerful heroine since the movie poster and DVD cover show the three oldest siblings in battle, with Susan poised to shoot an arrow. While the filmmakers exaggerate Susan's struggles during the first part of her adventure in Narnia, they strengthen her role as a warrior in the final battle to leave us with a more well-rounded and redeemed character.

The film begins with a wartime sequence that expands on Lewis's reference to the air-raids and justifies Susan's instincts to protect her younger siblings in a life-threatening situation. As German planes drop bombs over London, Susan pulls Lucy out of bed and huddles with her in the bomb shelter. At the train station where the children are being sent to the country, Susan fights her tears and attempts to smile when Mrs. Pevensie tells her to "be a big girl." When Peter is distracted by a group of soldiers, Susan grabs the tickets out of his hand, takes the lead as the children board, and is the first to put her head out the window to find their mother in the crowd. When they arrive at the Professor's house, Susan again takes the lead as the children walk upstairs and returns to her maternal role at bedtime by encouraging Lucy:

> SUSAN. Wars don't last forever, Lucy. We'll be home soon.
> EDMUND. Yeah, if home's still there.
> SUSAN. Isn't it time you were in bed?
> EDMUND. Yes, *Mum.*

This dialogue resembles the first page of the novel, but the stakes are higher, and we have greater compassion for the teenager who is trying to keep the family together.

The following day, we learn that Susan is an intellectual who will face ridicule for her tendency to respond to the magic of Narnia with reason and logic. Before the children decide to play hide-and-seek, Susan sits with a giant dictionary and encourages her siblings to guess definitions: "Come on, Peter. Gastrovascular." Edmund snidely asks if it's Latin for "worst game ever invented," and Peter gently mocks her until she gives up. But her leadership and logic reappear when the children run into the Professor in the middle of the night. Peter tries to drag her out of the office after a brief apology and then claims: "It's nothing. We can handle it." Susan insists on explaining Lucy's story about Narnia and even attempts to use logic, which Lewis's Professor chastised the children for failing to do: "Logically, it's impossible." But the Professor mocks her: "If she's not mad and she's not lying, then logically, we must assume she's telling the truth." He concludes by challenging them to act like a family, in contrast to the novel in which he suggests that they all "try minding our own business."[75] In both cases, the Professor is stern with the children, but in the film we see him fault Susan for coming to a reasonable conclusion and failing to care for her family, both of which seem obviously unfair.

Once all four children arrive in Narnia, the dialogue increases Susan's complaints and downplays her better moments. Lewis's Susan starts out with a sense of adventure, asking "what do we do next?"[76] and encouraging the others to wear the coats. Here she says "maybe we should go back," and Peter suggests wearing the coats, even using the occasion to make fun of her again: "If you think about it logically, we're not even taking them out of the wardrobe." Susan takes last place as they hike and as they enter Tumnus's cave, where she strongly argues for going home and refuses to help the faun. In further departures from the book, Susan argues against following Mr. Beaver, does not compliment the dam, claims that the prophecy "doesn't really rhyme," points out that the children were sent away to avoid war, stands and announces her intention to go home before learning that Edmund is missing, shouts at Peter that this is all his fault, and joins in with Mrs. Beaver's frivolous packing instead of hurrying her.

Susan even protests when Father Christmas arrives, but the filmmakers draw attention to the mixed messages that the girls receive about the weapons in the books and give more approval for using them. Father Christmas begins with Lucy in this version, replacing "battles are ugly when women fight" with "battles are ugly affairs." When Susan receives her bow and arrow, Father Christmas just says: "Trust in this bow, and it will not easily miss." Readers who have noted the contradictions in the books can sympathize when Susan asks: "What happened to 'battles are ugly affairs'?" The children quickly lapse back into their previous roles in a scary sequence that is original to the film. Susan hesitates to cross an icy river, asking Peter to take time to think, but he retorts, "You're trying to be smart, as usual," supported by the suspenseful music and howling wolves on the soundtrack. When the wolves attack and Maugrim tells Peter to surrender, Susan says: "Maybe we should listen to him!" Maugrim replies: "Smart girl," further associating her intelligence with betrayal and cowardice. She goes on to denigrate Father Christmas's gift and Peter's role in Narnia: "Look, just because some man in a red coat hands you a sword, it doesn't make you a hero!" Meanwhile, Mr. Beaver shouts at Peter to keep fighting, clearly the right and brave response. Susan then blames Peter when they temporarily lose Lucy in the river: "What have you done?" She takes her caregiving role to such

75. Lewis, *Chronicles of Narnia,* 132.
76. Lewis, *Chronicles of Narnia,* 135.

an extreme that she becomes a liability, almost a traitor. Although Susan whines in the book, she never suggests that the children should surrender to the Witch's side for their own safety.

Meeting Aslan seems to do Susan even more good in the film than in the book. When Peter admits that he was partly responsible for Edmund's betrayal, the film adds Susan's supportive gesture and her confession, "We all were." She later apologizes to Lucy for her behavior, remembering the fun they used to have together and playing in the water before they are attacked by Maugrim. The film enhances Susan's bravery as she throws a cloth at the wolf in order to reach the horn, calls out warnings to Peter from the tree instead of nearly fainting, and jumps to the ground before it is clear that the wolf is dead. Since Lucy is also attacked, we see Susan as the protector more than the damsel in distress. In a new scene, Peter tells the others that they should go home to avoid the battle, but when the younger children protest, Susan picks up her bow and heads to target practice. We see the girls prepare for battle alongside the boys, as Susan shoots an arrow near the center of the target and Lucy's dagger hits the bull's eye. The film cuts the line in which Susan asks Aslan if he can avoid the Deep Magic but retains the girls' presence at Aslan's death with all of its biblical echoes. New sections emphasize Susan's reestablished maternal role, for example when she gently tells Lucy that it's too late to heal Aslan with her cordial and when she takes the initiative to send the news to the army.

Of course, in the fantasy tradition exemplified by Peter Jackson's *The Lord of the Rings*, the film includes the entire battle sequence rather than the last few minutes that the girls witness in only three paragraphs of the book. The scene begins with the camera zooming into a hand-drawn map that resembles Baynes's maps of Narnia before cutting to the live-action battlefield, suggesting that we are entering into the world of the book; ironically, most of this scene will be invented for the film. Susan still arrives at the very end of the battle, but subtle changes emphasize her warrior status. While Lewis described the battle and its aftermath from Lucy's point of view with constant references like "Lucy heard," "Lucy saw," and "Lucy remembered,"[77] the film places Susan in the front line when Aslan's party arrives, followed quickly by a close-up of her face with bright red arrows over her shoulder. After Aslan kills the Witch, Susan asks: "Where's Edmund?" and we see a close-up of her concerned face before they find him lying wounded on the ground with a Dwarf raising his ax to kill him. Susan cries "Edmund!" and the camera cuts between an over-the-shoulder shot of the Dwarf from her point of view, a low-angle shot of her drawing her bow and shooting,

77. Lewis, *Chronicles of Narnia*, 191–92.

another over-the-shoulder shot of the Dwarf falling, and a shot of Susan running to Edmund's side. Her part in the battle takes only two minutes, but it allows her to combine her maternal instincts with a deadly use of archery that even Father Christmas would approve of. By the time she is crowned Queen Susan the Gentle, it is difficult to imagine a day when she will be "no longer a friend of Narnia." Even her hesitation to follow the White Stag is removed. Yet the filmmakers have managed to portray her as an appealing heroine within this film while sowing the seeds for her later downfall.

Critics of the film object to the fast-paced action that turns Lewis's classic fairy tale into a thrilling Hollywood blockbuster. Megan Stoner critiques the heightened tension between the siblings and their greater reluctance and moral ambivalence: "While this allows for a more modern feel, and certainly provides more action-packed excitement for modern audiences, it sacrifices the very foundational elements of Lewis' *Narnia*: belief, salvation, and destiny."[78] Paul Tankard also questions why bickering siblings are deemed more appropriate to a contemporary audience and why Adamson needed to make the film into an "epic" with chases and big battles: "The sense of wonder which Lewis takes trouble to convey is replaced by excitement."[79] Greg and Jenn Wright praise the film overall but claim: "From the time Edmund disappears from the Beavers' home, Adamson treats his audience to little more than a prolonged chase, inventing X-Box-friendly tunnel-run and ice floe sequences."[80] Lance Weldy agrees that "the timeless human values embedded in C. S. Lewis' text are lost amid the Hollywood Transformation."[81] However, Hugh H. Davis praises the film's Stone Table sequence[82] and Katherine A. Fowkes believes it "succeeds admirably"[83] in creating visual images of fantasy elements like the portal to a magical world and talking animals. Focusing on the gender roles allows us to appreciate how the filmmakers establish Susan's character not only as a whiner who represents feminine weakness but as a logical thinker and brave warrior.

78. Stoner, "Lion, the Witch, and the War Scenes," 78.

79. Tankard, "Lion, the Witch and the Multiplex," 91.

80. Wright and Wright, "C. S. Lewis and Media," 272.

81. Weldy, "Treason of Peter and Susan Pevensie," 177.

82. Hugh H. Davis, "Sing, My Tongue," 77.

83. Fowkes, *Fantasy Film*, 152.

"IT WOULD NEVER HAVE WORKED ANYWAY": DISTRACTED BY ROMANCE IN *PRINCE CASPIAN*

Adamson's next film departs significantly from the novel, but this is understandable given claims that Lewis's *Prince Caspian* is poorly written with inappropriate pagan imagery. Glover argues that the novel is slow and tedious, with less engrossing themes than the first one: "Neither the risks nor the triumphs are as great, and we leave the work feeling a bit let down."[84] Manlove agrees that the novel "does admit to some weakness of inspiration."[85] Critics question Lewis's positive portrayal of Bacchus, with Schakel pointing out that "the Greeks, recognizing the harmful potential of wine, characterized Bacchus by drunken frenzy and cruelty as well as by release and mirthmaking."[86] Holbrook asks: "In what possible sense can the image of Christ be reconciled with a Bacchanalian sacred indulgence in wine and 'wild girls'—belonging in any case to a civilization in which the sexual orgy would have a fertility meaning?"[87] To avoid these pitfalls, the filmmakers rearranged the structure and replaced the bacchanalian imagery with character-driven plots in which Peter struggles with pride while Caspian and Susan fall in love. Yet the focus remains on battle. *New York Times* reviewer Scott notes that Caspian "exchanges some long, half-smoldering looks with Susan. In spite of this hint of romance, what ensues is basically a war movie."[88] Ella Taylor of the *Village Voice* characterizes the dynamics: "A dab hand with the bow and arrows in a tight squeeze, Susan briskly repels the longing glances cast at her by Caspian."[89] The combination of battle and romance enables the filmmakers to present Susan as an admirable heroine who is nonetheless beginning her journey toward the "nylons and lipstick and invitations"[90] that will keep her out of Aslan's country in the end.

After the exciting opening scene in which Caspian flees from Miraz and blows Susan's horn in a desperate call for help, the sound transition to a blaring car horn emphasizes the contrast between her protective power in Narnia and her adolescent vulnerability in London. At the train station where the children are returning to school, Susan rejects a boy's advances, although her noticeable eye makeup suggests that she may be interested in

---

84. Glover, *Art of Enchantment*, 147.
85. Manlove, *Chronicles of Narnia*, 44.
86. Schakel, *Way into Narnia*, 58.
87. Holbrook, *Skeleton in the Wardrobe*, 138.
88. Scott, "Out of the Wardrobe," paras. 5–6.
89. Taylor, "*Prince Caspian* Loses Some Magic," para. 3.
90. Lewis, *Chronicles of Narnia*, 741.

attracting boys overall, and chastises Peter in true motherly form when he gets into a fight. Her comments suggest that she is becoming more comfortable in England than in Narnia: "I think it's time to accept that we live here. It's no use pretending any different." This line introduces a major new theme of the filmmakers: the older children's struggle to reconcile their unpredictable movements between a land where they are powerless and a land where they rule. In a subtle but important sense, this sets up and helps to explain Susan's later rejection of Narnia in the books: none of us can live in the fantastic past, but we must adapt to the real future that we do not always choose. Susan's eventual focus on attracting men could be interpreted more positively as a variation of this line: "I think it's time to accept that we live here. It's no use pretending any different."

The filmmakers thus anticipate Laura Măcineanu's defense of Susan along with Petunia Dursley from J. K. Rowling's *Harry Potter* novels. Many condemn these characters for failing to believe, but Măcineanu notes that magical worlds are closed to them by powers beyond their control. Petunia was born without magical powers, and Susan is banned from Narnia at the end of *Prince Caspian*: "Petunia and Susan were still at a young and impressionable age when they realised they would never again be part of a world of infinite adventures, a world to which their siblings were still invited to go."[91] We can admire their inner strength in choosing "to take control of their lives"[92] by pursuing marriage and family in England. The filmmakers take a similar approach, reminding us that Susan is already growing out of Narnia in this film. Can we blame her for not wanting to become too attached?

Despite her ambivalence, Susan embraces Narnia as soon as the children receive the call from the horn. Susan tells everyone to hold hands and Edmund complains, unlike the book in which Edmund has the idea. When they find the ruined castle, Susan figures out where they are in one minute of screen time. They stand in the throne room in the same positions in which they were crowned in the previous film, the composition of the shot showing that they've returned to their royal roles without a lot of exposition. Even Susan's eye makeup is gone. While Lewis narrates her shooting of the Telmarine soldier from Peter's perspective and notes her very pale face, here she shoots confidently, prepares another arrow, and yells "Drop him!" Although the film drops the archery contest between Susan and Trumpkin, she is clearly established as the warrior from the previous film.

Nor does Susan complain when they travel in the woods, and although she does balk at killing the bear, no one blames her for it. Peter says that girls

91. Măcineanu, "Consciously Rejecting the Magic," 81.
92. Măcineanu, "Consciously Rejecting the Magic," 82.

can't carry a map in their heads at a much slighter provocation, Susan's comment that "I don't remember this way." The focus is on Peter's bad behavior as he fights with Trumpkin over the directions. Susan's one know-it-all comment is a joke on Peter, when they discover the river at the bottom of a gorge and she explains: "You see, over time, water erodes the earth's soil." When Lucy sees Aslan, Susan stays out of the conflict. Peter is the one who asks: "So where exactly do you think you saw Aslan?" and Lucy accuses them all of "trying to sound like grown-ups." Later Susan and Lucy lie awake in a new scene reminiscent of the night of Aslan's death. Though Susan has not spoken a single word against Lucy, she still feels remorse: "Why do you think I didn't see Aslan?" Lucy suggests that she didn't want to see him, and Susan explains: "I finally just got used to the idea of being in England," while the eye makeup that she wears again here and the low neckline that emphasizes her cleavage indicate that she might have romance in mind. When Lucy asks if she is happy to be in Narnia, she responds: "While it lasts," continuing the theme of Susan feeling torn between two worlds. She meets Caspian soon after this, since the film brings everyone together to fight Miraz instead of keeping the boys and girls separate. The camera takes on Caspian's point of view as he looks at Susan with obvious attraction, while she looks down shyly and says nothing.

In a new scene in which Peter argues that they should attack Miraz's castle, Susan is the only character in the shots with Caspian, standing behind him and then coming forward as she supports his argument: "If we dig in, we could probably hold them off indefinitely." Her tendency to be practical is linked to a power struggle between the men as Peter gives her a betrayed look. In the attack, Susan fights alongside Peter and saves Edmund's life, but she sides with Caspian when he wants to find Doctor Cornelius and rushes to defend him when he is fighting Miraz and Prunaprismia (even she gets to use a weapon in the film). Far from a damsel in distress, Susan chastises the emotional prince: "Caspian, this won't make things any better." She also chastises Peter when he insists on continuing the fight after Miraz has sounded the alarm: "Peter, it's too late. We have to call it off while we can." Even as she begins her role as Caspian's love interest, the filmmakers emphasize her voice of reason in the midst of the men's vainglory. During the retreat, a centaur swings Susan onto his back and gallops away while she calls out for Caspian, continuing her role as his protector while she is rescued by a stronger male. When the defeated army returns to Aslan's How, Peter and Caspian clash swords in the foreground while Susan stands between them in the background. But the presence of a horrified Lucy and a weeping centaur woman emphasize the feminine perspective and the human cost of battle in a way that Lewis rarely does. Susan's role as moral center is strengthened after Peter and Caspian are tempted by the White Witch. They turn to see Susan standing between them, shaking her head in contempt as we see Caspian from her point of view in contrast to their first meeting. Clearly not every handsome prince is a good catch.

Susan takes on a more stereotypically feminine role in her relationship with Caspian in a new plot development in which she and Lucy go to the woods to look for Aslan while Peter buys time fighting Miraz in single combat. This links the girls to Aslan and gives them an active spiritual role, but Susan turns into a flirtatious schoolgirl when Caspian offers her the horn: "Why don't you hold onto it? You might need to call me again." This draws attention to her role as Caspian's rescuer, but it also sounds coy due to the modern meaning of "call me" and Lucy's teasing. When Susan is attacked by mounted Telmarine soldiers, she sends Lucy away and shoots four of them in a row before she is knocked to the ground and freezes as a soldier attacks her with a sword. The filmmakers seem to be exploiting Lewis's convention that limits girls to archery while boys engage in sword fighting. Caspian swoops in and routs the Telmarine, then looks down at Susan and teases: "Are you sure you don't need that horn?" He then lifts her onto his horse and rides away, as Rabadash once dreamed of doing.

While this gratuitous scene of male dominance is frustrating, the film goes on to show them fighting together as leaders in the climactic battle, a seventeen-minute sequence that greatly extends her brief battle scene in the previous film. Susan is armed and ready when the battle begins, standing with Trumpkin and other Narnian archers on Aslan's How. She calls out instructions as Miraz's army approaches: "Archers to the ready," "Take your aim," and "Now!" A slow-motion shot follows the arrows through the sky and cuts to them landing on the soldiers. When Telmarines attack the How with catapults, Susan yells: "Brace yourselves!" The next sequence builds suspense with ten rapid cuts as Susan falls from the How, holds on to Trumpkin by one hand, and slips away down the rocky precipice. A cut to Peter and Caspian suggests that they might rush to save her, but she lands on her feet in a reversal of damsel-in-distress expectations. She then joins the men as a fellow warrior running into battle; one aerial shot of the battlefield shows her shooting four arrows and hitting another Telmarine with her bow. When the children greet Aslan after the battle, there is no need for Susan to apologize, since her behavior has been consistently courageous and moral.

The film ends with the older Pevensies explaining that they will not return to Narnia. Susan's curled hair, eye makeup, and off-the-shoulder gown give her a traditionally feminine appearance as she tells Caspian: "It would never have worked anyway. I am thirteen hundred years older than you."

She then turns back and kisses him. In an interview with *Christianity Today*, Lewis's stepson Douglas Gresham put this into perspective for disgruntled fans:

> You've got a beautiful woman and a handsome guy in an adventure together. Let's face it: They are going to make eyes at each other. And of course they kiss goodbye in the last scene, because here's this woman that Caspian's become attached to and he's never going to see her again. End of story. I don't regard that as a romance. I agree that it shouldn't have been in the movie; I think it was nonsense. But it wasn't something I was going to dig my heels in and scream and bite the carpet about.[93]

In fact, there are several twists on this clichéd romantic ending. Susan remains the older, wiser protector of Caspian as she leads the conversation and initiates the kiss, more empowered in Narnia than in England where she is pursued by a boy who doesn't know her name. Nonetheless, the seeds have been sown for a sequence in the next film in which Aslan warns Lucy not to follow Susan down the path of feminine wiles.

"SHE'S QUITE A LOOKER": SEDUCED BY BEAUTY IN *THE VOYAGE OF THE DAWN TREADER*

In the third film, director Michael Apted portrays the younger children struggling with the same issues that plagued the older ones: Edmund clashes with Caspian over status while Lucy worries about whether she is attractive to men. Both of Lewis's passages about Susan are greatly expanded into a cautionary tale about women who focus on outward beauty rather than following Aslan's will for them, with a more positive message for young girls than Lewis provided. The sentence about Susan's poor school work is replaced with a letter that she writes to Lucy from America, giving her a voice but also warning us about her priorities. As her voiceover begins, we see her looking pretty but not seductive in a pink dress and subtle makeup. A photograph of the four children and a little silver lamppost on the desk suggest her continuing allegiance to family and Narnia as she writes: "It's been such an adventure, but nothing like our times in Narnia. America is very exciting, except we never see Father. He works so very hard." We cut to Lucy reading the letter aloud: "I was invited to the British Consul's tea party this week by a naval officer, who happens to be very handsome. I think he fancies me." Susan's voice ends when her attachment to handsome men and

93. Moring, "Narnia Policeman," para. 18.

parties begins, leaving us with an ominous sense that America is having a negative effect, while her reference to the British Consul reminds us of Eustace's attempts to find one in Narnia. Lucy then goes to the mirror and asks: "Do you think I look anything like Susan?" Long before she encounters the magician's book, she envies Susan's beauty and romantic adventures.

When Lucy finds the spell that promises to make her beautiful, she looks into a mirror in the book and sees Susan's reflection instead of her own. She tears out the page and waits until a stormy night on the ship to recite the spell. Again, her reflection in the cabin mirror transforms into Susan, with bright red lipstick standing out in the pale light. The mirror turns into a door that leads to America, where a band plays "In the Mood" in a subtle reference to sexual desirability. "Susan" walks smiling past a line of soldiers as one says: "She's quite a looker." But Lucy soon realizes that this side of the mirror represents an alternative world in which she has never been born and her siblings have never heard of Narnia. In a nod to Frank Capra's classic film *It's a Wonderful Life*, Lucy has become a latter-day George Bailey who needs supernatural intervention to see the importance of every person who feels worthless. Back in the cabin, Aslan admonishes: "You wished yourself away, and with it much more." Lucy's jealousy of Susan has blinded her to more important inner qualities: "You doubt your value. Don't run from who you are." These words seem too clichéd and secular to come from Lewis, and it is unfortunate that Susan loses her intelligence and courage as she is reduced to a pretty face. Yet this warning about focusing too much on beauty is a welcome change from the Disney Princess phenomenon, making it seem fitting that *Dawn Treader* is the only film not associated with Disney. The film's addition of the younger girl Gael strengthens Lucy's identity as a role model and gives her act of burning the spell a larger significance. No one knows what might happen to Susan in a future film of *The Last Battle*, but Adamson and Apted provide the necessary backstory for Lewis's ending and still leave us with a compelling and relatable character.

While Narnia fans and scholars have been anxious from the beginning about their beloved books being transformed for the big screen, the Walden Media films do not shy away from Christian themes. At the end of the *Dawn Treader* film, Aslan speaks the words that most explicitly identify him with Jesus in the Chronicles: "In your world, I have another name. You must learn to know me by it. That was the very reason you were brought to Narnia, that by knowing me here for a little, you may know me better there." This is not surprising given Gresham's collaboration with Philip Anschutz, the evangelical Christian owner of Walden Media, and his insistence on retaining theological messages. The filmmakers also made significant efforts to address critical concerns about the novels, from the role of Bacchus to the fate of Susan to the lack of female characters on the *Dawn Treader*.

The differences between the 1950s novels and the 2000s films clearly reflect the gap between Lewis's conservative beliefs and the liberal atmosphere of Hollywood after the second-wave feminist movement. Writing as a conservative Christian soon after World War II, Lewis would have believed that a young woman's proper role was to marry and have a family, which requires maturity, unselfishness, and commitment to the welfare of others. Susan started out as a positive character insofar as she acted as a substitute mother for her younger siblings, but Lewis used her increasing skepticism and selfishness to warn readers that women can get stuck in the exciting and personally gratifying stage of "nylons and lipstick and invitations" instead of settling down to hard work and taking up their roles in the family as wives and mothers. His failure to elaborate on this point may reflect his assumption that readers shared his worldview. In the early twenty-first century, with its emphasis on "girl power" and widespread cultural investment in providing strong female role models, the filmmakers are more interested in portraying Susan as a teenager who can hold her own alongside the boys. They share Lewis's concerns about vanity and boy-crazy behavior that distract girls from more important endeavors (no longer limited to marriage), but they strive to create a more developed character arc. In order to avoid the appearance of sexism, the films provide a balanced picture of Susan in both traditionally feminine and masculine roles and clearly explain where she goes wrong as she turns away from Aslan.

The future of the Narnia films has been uncertain since Walden Media's rights expired after *The Voyage of the Dawn Treader*. In October 2018, Netflix announced that it had purchased the film rights: "Under the terms of a multi-year deal between Netflix and The C. S. Lewis Company, Netflix will develop classic stories from across the Narnia universe into series and films for its members worldwide."[94] History is now repeating itself as Narnia fans worry about how the novels will fare as a multimedia fantasy franchise. This seems like an appropriate time to evaluate the positive aspects of the Walden Media trilogy. Overall, the filmmakers' attempts to translate Lewis's vision for the twenty-first century seem appropriate and valid, and their complexity and thoughtfulness make them worthy of more scholarly attention than they have yet received.

Rather than assuming that Lewis's books are the perfect source to which no filmmaker could do justice, we need to remember that he often expressed his views of women in uncharitable and unhelpful ways. Mary

---

94. Netflix Media Center, "Netflix to Develop Series," para. 1.

Stewart Van Leeuwen testifies that Lewis was a role model in her conversion experience but "at the same time a major stumbling block to my acceptance of Christianity"[95] due to his claims that women could never experience an intellectual life with fellow believers. As we will see in the next chapter with Francine Rivers's *Redeeming Love*, it can be very hard for conservative Christians to uphold biblical gender roles without sliding into the secular world's destructive patterns of misogyny and violence. While Lewis portrayed a middle-class girl who devolves into a frivolous woman, Rivers raises the stakes with an orphaned girl who is forced into prostitution. The problem with Narnia is that Susan never gets to be saved, but the problem with *Redeeming Love* will be how Angel's "salvation" unfolds.

95. Van Leeuwen, *Sword between the Sexes?*, 28.

Chapter 2

THE PROSTITUTE
IN THE FAIRY TALE

Objectifying Women in Redeeming Love

The cover of my copy of *Redeeming Love* is disturbing. A woman in a scarlet Victorian dress stands alone against a cream background. The viewer's eye is drawn to the dress by several details: parts of the design, especially the bodice, are raised to create texture, and the skirt flows beyond the front cover across the spine and onto the back cover. The woman's mouth and nose are visible, but the image abruptly ends at the top of the book, cutting off her face below the eyes. Romance novel covers are notoriously sexist, but this one is surprising given Francine Rivers's main point that we should not be so quick to judge women like her prostitute heroine. The epigraph to the Christian edition of the novel is from John 8:7: "Let anyone among you who is without sin, be the first to throw a stone at her."[1] This cover is the first of many ironies, paradoxes, and tensions that await the reader of this popular Christian romance. The cover image of the blind, brainless heroine also foreshadows the result of a feminist reading that I attempted to perform with an open mind. While Rivers deserves credit for condemning the sex industry and refusing to blame its victims, Michael Hosea's use of force and deception to "redeem" Angel misses the point of the Hosea allegory and the ideal biblical relationship between husband and wife.

---

1. Rivers, *Redeeming Love* (1997), 8.

A TALE OF TWO EDITIONS: THE HISTORY OF
REDEEMING LOVE

The front matter of the 1997 Multnomah edition reveals an intriguing mystery and suggests that the top of the heroine's head is not the only thing missing here. The copyright page includes this note: "This is the 'redeemed' version of Redeeming Love, published by Bantam Books in 1991. The original edition is no longer available."[2] In the acknowledgments, Rivers thanks her editor "for her belief in this book, and her help in redeeming it for the Christian reader."[3] The back cover states: "Francine Rivers wrote for the general market for a number of years before becoming a Christian. Since then, she has used her writing as a means of drawing closer to the Lord."[4] The cover design makes multiple connections between author and heroine.

The cover of *Redeeming Love* cuts off the top of the heroine's head, foreshadowing her lack of vision and intellectual agency.

2. Rivers, *Redeeming Love* (1997), 4.
3. Rivers, *Redeeming Love* (1997), 7.
4. Rivers, *Redeeming Love* (1997).

On the front cover, the blonde heroine wears a low-cut red dress, turning her half-head slightly away from the viewer's gaze while revealing her entire body. On the back cover, the blonde Rivers wears a modest red turtleneck, smiling directly at the camera without showing her body below the shoulders. Together, Rivers's head and the heroine's body make one complete figure. Just as Rivers worked as a secular novelist in an industry often associated with pornography, the back cover tells us that Angel has all too much sexual experience: "Sold into prostitution as a child, she survives by keeping her hatred alive."[5] The framing documents and images thus create a triple parallel: Rivers, the heroine, and the book have all been "redeemed."

Like any good literary detective, I found a copy of the "no longer available" 1991 Bantam edition, with a pink lily on the cover that ironically looks more "Christian" than the scarlet dress. Yet the Bantam book reveals its ties to the mainstream romance genre. It is a mass market paperback, with small dimensions and low-quality paper, costing $3.99. The front cover identifies Rivers as "bestselling author of *Rebel in His Arms*," and the back cover claims that "Angel must face—and conquer—the darkest demon of her past."[6] The first page is a teaser from the novel in which Angel is "shaking violently" while Michael tells her: "I knew the day I saw you that you belonged with me."[7] The back pages advertise romances like *The Flames of Vengeance*, *Scandal*, *Brazen Virtue*, and *Sacred Sins*.[8] In contrast, the Multnomah trade paperback costs $14.99, and the back cover calls it "a life-changing story of God's unconditional, redemptive, all-consuming love."[9] It begins with evangelical endorsements and a Bible epigraph and ends with an account of Rivers's conversion and a Bible study guide.

Beyond these surface features, what changed between the secular and "redeemed" editions? Since Rivers was already a Christian when she wrote the Bantam edition inspired by the biblical Hosea, this is not a secular book being transformed into a Christian book, but a book for the secular market being transformed for the Christian market. The plot is the same, but many curses like "damned" and "bitch" are removed, and "whore" becomes "prostitute" or "soiled dove." Explicit sex scenes are removed or softened. For example, in the secular edition, Cleo is aroused by her lover: "The place between her legs was moist and tingling. When Merrick put his hand beneath

---

5. Rivers, *Redeeming Love* (1997).

6. Rivers, *Redeeming Love* (1991).

7. Rivers, *Redeeming Love* (1991).

8. Rivers, *Redeeming Love* (1991).

9. Rivers, *Redeeming Love* (1997).

the table, she parted her thighs."[10] In the Christian version, we see this from a child's point of view: "She seemed to be having a good time, and she kept staring at Merrick and smiling."[11] The secular edition describes Angel trying to seduce Michael: "Her satin wrap had opened even more, exposing two perfect rose-tipped breasts. She crossed her legs, and the wrap fell open there as well. *God.*"[12] In the Christian version, Michael does not take the Lord's name in vain: "Her satin wrap had opened a little. He knew she was toying with him."[13] The Christian version also has Angel give her life to Jesus during an altar call and makes the voices of God and Satan more prominent and clearly distinguished by having God speak in bold italics and Satan in bold. The most problematic aspects did not change: Michael compels Angel to marry him against her will and keeps her captive for much of the novel. She is largely powerless, suicidal, filled with shame and self-hatred, and relentlessly compelled to return to a man whose violence is always justified in the name of love.

A brief plot overview reveals that *Redeeming Love* is a decidedly old-school romance, more akin to Samuel Richardson's eighteenth-century bestseller *Pamela* than the egalitarian romances typical of the 1990s. "Child of Darkness" describes Angel's history as the daughter of a prostitute who dies and leaves her to be sold into the sex industry at eight years old. "Defiance" begins ten years later in 1850, with Angel working in a brothel in the gold rush town of Pair-a-Dice, California, where Michael Hosea sees her on the street and decides that she is the one God wants him to marry. Angel repeatedly refuses, but Michael marries her while she is semi-conscious after being beaten nearly to death by the brothel's bodyguard. He drugs her and brings her to his farm, which she cannot escape because it is thirty miles from the nearest town. She finally has sex with Michael's brother-in-law Paul for a ride to Pair-a-Dice. In "Fear," Michael forcibly brings her home and invites the newly arrived Altman family to homestead nearby, creating a community that Angel grows to love despite her longing to escape. In "Humility," Michael finally lets her go, and she moves to San Francisco and founds an agency that trains prostitutes for the legal workforce. When Paul shows up three years later and evokes her duty to Michael, she returns, and the epilogue describes their sixty-eight years of marriage.

Redeeming Love contains many elements that concern feminist romance critics: a weak heroine at the mercy of a violent hero, a reduction of

10. Rivers, *Redeeming Love* (1991), 17.

11. Rivers, *Redeeming Love* (1997), 25–26.

12. Rivers, *Redeeming Love* (1991), 52.

13. Rivers, *Redeeming Love* (1997), 63.

the heroine's point of view, rape, captivity, and the idea that marriage is the only happy ending. In the early 1980s, Tania Modleski critiqued Harlequins in which "the heroine of the novels can achieve happiness only by undergoing a complex process of self-subversion, during which she sacrifices her aggressive instincts, her 'pride,' and—nearly—her life,"[14] and Kay Mussell argued that romances "make triumphant a climax that annihilates rather than transcends or fulfills."[15] Janice A. Radway claimed that the genre cannot explain how "each individual heroine is able to translate male reticence and cruelty into tenderness and devotion"[16] and identified elements of the romance plot such as the hero's punishment of the heroine, in which even rape can be justified by his frustrated desire.[17] *Redeeming Love* never goes this far, but Michael has an unrealistic ability to become violent without losing control. He grabs Angel and drags her around, but he always reverts to his "true" nature of tenderness and devotion, a combination that does not usually appear in real men. While Angel enjoys brief career success, the moral seems to be that any paid work by a married woman is morally equivalent to adultery.

Redeeming Love also lacks the genre's more feminist attributes, like an intelligent heroine who freely chooses the hero. The readers that Radway interviewed saw their favorite stories "as chronicles of female triumph"[18] in which heroines rebel against traditional gender roles and "refuse to be silenced by the male desire to control women."[19] Even inexperienced heroines can tame the experienced or promiscuous heroes. Carol Thurston argued that erotic novels by the late 1980s were focusing on "the full development of the heroine as an individual in her own right,"[20] and Jayne Ann Krentz focuses on the empowerment of the heroine winning her battle with the hero: "With courage, intelligence, and gentleness she brings the most dangerous creature on earth, the human male, to his knees."[21] Pamela Regis contrasts earlier heroines who were constrained by highly patriarchal societies with the modern heroine who has "the freedom she needs to pursue her own ends; the rights she needs to possess her own property, as well as, often enough, the skills requisite to acquire that property herself; and a right to

14. Modleski, *Loving with a Vengeance*, 29.
15. Mussell, *Fantasy and Reconciliation*, 189.
16. Radway, *Reading the Romance*, 128.
17. Radway, *Reading the Romance*, 134–43.
18. Radway, *Reading the Romance*, 54.
19. Radway, *Reading the Romance*, 124.
20. Thurston, *Romance Revolution*, 7.
21. Krentz, "Introduction," 5.

companionate marriage."[22] Because current heroines are "in command of their lives,"[23] they focus on taming or healing the hero. Yet *Redeeming Love* reverses all of the conventions that lead to female empowerment. Michael is the innocent virgin who tames and heals, while Angel is the fallen woman with the manipulative sexuality of the conventional female rival. Rivers's combination of the nineteenth-century heroine's struggle for survival and the twentieth-century romance's focus on the hero leaves no room for vicarious enjoyment of Angel's triumph over him or anything else.

Nor does *Redeeming Love* conform to typical Christian standards. In "Hope, Faith and Toughness: An Analysis of the Christian Hero," Rebecca Barrett-Fox argues that this hero retains "the rugged individualism, toughness, and power of secular heroes but combines this traditional masculinity with gentleness, patience, and attention to female needs."[24] While this model can be dangerous for readers who expect their husbands to behave this way, it has liberating potential since it "places emotional responsibility at least partly on men."[25] Michael seems like an extreme version of this Christian hero, swinging back and forth from gentleness and patience to horrifying violence. *Redeeming Love* has even less in common with the Amish romances that Valerie Weaver-Zercher describes as "chaste texts about chaste protagonists living within a chaste subculture."[26] While Amish novels allow readers to escape from their hypersexual world, Rivers compels her readers to confront the role of sexual exploitation throughout American history.

Despite all this, *Redeeming Love* is one of the most popular Christian romances. In *Romancing God: Evangelical Women and Inspirational Fiction*, Lynn S. Neal interviews fans who see it as "the 'ultimate romance,' as it celebrates the power of unconditional love."[27] As in much inspirational fiction, "Instead of an angry judge or a distant relative, God emerges in the novels as a pivotal figure who would never stop loving these women."[28] While one woman struggled because her husband didn't measure up to Michael's example,[29] most readers felt that Michael's love for Angel accurately portrays God's love for them. Anita Gandolfo claims that *Redeeming Love* was the favorite novel among Amazon readers that she studied and that it

22. Regis, *Natural History of the Romance Novel*, 110–11.
23. Regis, *Natural History of the Romance Novel*, 111.
24. Barrett-Fox, "Hope, Faith and Toughness," 97.
25. Barrett-Fox, "Hope, Faith and Toughness," 101.
26. Weaver-Zercher, *Thrill of the Chaste*, 13.
27. Neal, *Romancing God*, 158.
28. Neal, *Romancing God*, 164.
29. Neal, *Romancing God*, 165.

represents "Christian fiction at its best,"[30] although she later acknowledges that Michael's moral certitude is most inspiring to "a relatively unsophisticated reader."[31] Weaver-Zercher observed similar unsophisticated reading patterns in a Christian women's book club discussion of an Amish romance: "The first half hour or more of the book discussion includes scant reference to the novel."[32] The discussion guides encourage this approach, since "readers are invited to make explicit connections between literature and life much more frequently than to critique or analyze."[33] The study guide in *Redeeming Love* follows this pattern, with questions encouraging personal application rather than critique.

The Multnomah edition's claim that the novel represents "God's unconditional, redemptive, all-consuming love" has likely influenced readers' interpretations, but the word *unconditional* seems misleading on the levels of plot and theology. Michael has plenty of conditions, demanding that Angel live on his farm, do her chores, and follow his rules. Of course, God's insistence on righteous living is clear in the book of Hosea and the reality of final judgment. With a simple view of Michael and God as examples of "unconditional love," readers may be indulging in comforts and reassurances that are not beneficial to them as wives or Christians. Before examining these aspects of the novel, however, we will begin with the realistic elements that seem both unusual and admirable in a Christian romance.

REALISM IN *REDEEMING LOVE*: RIVERS'S CONDEMNATION OF THE SEX INDUSTRY

As a historical romance, *Redeeming Love* vacillates between a realistic depiction of nineteenth-century America and a fantasy element common to the genre. In the opening section, "Child of Darkness," Rivers focuses on realism. It is suspenseful and thrilling to read about a girl whose father abandons her, mother dies, and mother's boyfriend sells her to a brothel, but there is little sense of escaping to a simple or pure Victorian past. By refusing to sugarcoat the realities of prostitution, Rivers exemplifies Hsu-Ming Teo's claim that women's historical novels "present an unsettling view of the past which forces the reader to think about past gender and social orders which limited women's lives and condemned them to silence, preventing

---

30. Gandolfo, *Faith and Fiction*, 70.

31. Gandolfo, *Faith and Fiction*, 147.

32. Weaver-Zercher, *Thrill of the Chaste*, 108.

33. Weaver-Zercher, *Thrill of the Chaste*, 108.

their stories from appearing in the historical record."[34] Many Christians have never read a book that focuses on prostitution or seriously considered its role on the American frontier. In the Christian edition, "A Note from the Publisher" recommends discretion with younger readers: "If this book were a movie, it would be rated PG-13."[35] Rivers presents an "unsettling view of the past" and critiques a patriarchal system that continues to traffic in young women.

The novel's first page juxtaposes fantasy and realism. The epigraph from Shakespeare's *King Lear* ("The prince of darkness is a gentleman") signals the archetypal qualities of the villain who is about to appear and hints that the story will contain more tragic elements than are typical for the romance genre. Then the historical marker "New England, 1835" locates the reader in a place and time.[36] As Radway claims, "Such deliberate use of the conventions of the realistic novel thus denies that the romance is only a timeless fairy tale existing solely within the reader's imagination or between the pages of a book."[37] The first paragraph invokes the cliché of the tall, dark, handsome hero, only to reverse expectations by revealing that he is the heroine's father: "Alex Stafford was just like Mama said. He was tall and dark, and Sarah had never seen anyone so beautiful. Even dressed in dusty riding clothes, his hair damp with perspiration, he was like the princes in the stories Mama read. Sarah's heart beat with wild joy and pride. None of the other fathers she saw at Mass compared to him."[38] The reader is plunged into a maze of unclear relationships. If the handsome prince is her father, why is Sarah meeting him for the first time? How does the child Sarah relate to the adult Angel? Because the section is told from a child's point of view, the reader is also plunged into irony as we recognize ugly truths that she cannot understand. The reading experience is demanding and horrifying rather than comforting or escapist.

The second paragraph foreshadows Sarah's life as a child prostitute and introduces the theme of incest: "He looked at her with his dark eyes, and her heart sang. She was wearing her best blue frock and white pinafore, and Mama had braided her hair with pink and blue ribbons. Did Papa like the way she looked? Mama said blue was his favorite color, but why didn't he smile?"[39] These lines seem especially eerie on a second reading, since

34. Teo, "Bertrice teaches you," 25.

35. Rivers, *Redeeming Love* (1997), 2.

36. Rivers, *Redeeming Love* (1997), 11.

37. Radway, *Reading the Romance*, 204.

38. Rivers, *Redeeming Love* (1997), 11.

39. Rivers, *Redeeming Love* (1997), 11.

we know that Sarah will be dressed in similar clothing to appeal to the perverted tastes of Duke, the dark, handsome man who buys her a few years later, and that Angel will have sex with her father when she is a teenager to get revenge on him for abandoning her. The creepy role of her "best blue frock and white pinafore" also introduces Rivers's refusal to indulge her readers' love for period costumes. According to Lisa Fletcher, "The heroine descending the stairs, or flouncing into a room, laced, frilled, and beribboned, circulates as *the* image of popular historical romance,"[40] and while these costumes are not always empowering to the heroines, they are often described to bring readers pleasure and help them escape into the novel's desirable world. Rivers radically changes this convention, since Angel's beautiful outfits are associated with prostitution, while Michael dresses her in plain clothing and even rags. This Victorian world offers few pleasures other than those of Gothic suspense.

The confusing family relationships are explained a few pages later, when Sarah overhears Alex reveal the truth: "I have enough children by my wife. Legitimate children. I told you I didn't want another."[41] When I first read the novel, I had to reread the first chapter to understand fully that the heroine was being rejected by her father, a married man who was angry that his mistress did not have an abortion. The 1991 edition makes the parents' sinfulness more obvious from the beginning. The first three paragraphs are the same, but then the point of view switches: "Alex saw the hope in his mistress' eyes and frowned darkly. He was tired of being pressed from all directions. He had ridden four hours to get here and he had but two to stay. He wanted Mae in bed, warm and willing. He didn't want to waste time on a child, even one of his own breeding, rotten luck that it was."[42] This version is clearer and more realistic, as it switches between the adults' cynical points of view and Sarah's innocence. However, the 1997 version provides a different kind of unsettling experience with its own merits. From Sarah's perspective, we read about her mother sending her to the seashore with the servant Cleo, where Sarah waits in a rat-infested hallway while Cleo has sex with an old boyfriend and then listens to her drunken rants about the evils of men. The revisions to make the book more "Christian" by avoiding explicit language end up placing greater demands on the reader to make sense of the plot and creating stronger identification with the child heroine.

The descriptions become even more painful when Sarah's mother becomes a prostitute and drinks herself to death. Rivers includes some

40. Fletcher, *Historical Romance Fiction*, 66.

41. Rivers, *Redeeming Love* (1997), 15.

42. Rivers, *Redeeming Love* (1991), 3–4.

sentimental language: "She died in the morning, the first sunlight of spring on her face and her rosary beads in her dead-white hands."[43] Yet most details are realistic: Sarah screaming for the men not to handle the body, her mother's boyfriend Rab pressing her against his foul-smelling shirt, a man chatting with his friends as he sews up the shroud, Rab taking Sarah to be dressed for her "adoption." The mother's death supports Radway's psychoanalytic argument about the appeal of romance novels: "When she is plucked from her earlier relationships and thrust out into a public world, the heroine's consequent terror and feeling of emptiness most likely evokes for the reader distant memories of her initial separation from her mother and her later ambivalent attempts to establish an individual identity."[44] If women are drawn to romances to fulfill their subconscious desire to be reunited with the nurturing mother, this may help to explain the tremendous appeal of *Redeeming Love*. This scene also begins Sarah's role as a Cinderella figure. The Grimms' "Cinderella" begins: "The wife of a rich man fell sick, and as she felt that her end was drawing near, she called her only daughter to her bedside and said, 'Dear child, be good and pious, and then the good God will always protect thee, and I will look down on thee from heaven and be near thee.' Thereupon she closed her eyes and departed."[45] Like Cinderella, Sarah is left with an ineffective father figure, whose attempt to find her a new family makes her the victim of unspeakable cruelty.

The section ends with the chilling scene of Duke taking sexual ownership of Sarah, and his actions eerily foreshadow Michael's treatment of her years later. Duke washed the makeup off her face, just as Michael will prepare her bath. When she was too scared to look up, Duke "tipped her chin back" and demanded: "Look at me, little one."[46] Michael does this many times, culminating in the final love scene: "When he tipped her chin up, she had no choice but to look into his eyes again."[47] When Duke asked her name, she was too scared to answer, but he responded: "It doesn't matter. I think I'm going to call you Angel."[48] Michael refuses to call her Angel and makes up a series of other names for her. Rather than contrasting Duke's evil actions with Michael's loving ones, these parallels hint that both men approach Angel as an object that they demand to possess.

---

43. Rivers, *Redeeming Love* (1997), 35.
44. Radway, *Reading the Romance*, 138.
45. Grimm and Grimm, *Grimm's Fairy Tales*, 73.
46. Rivers, *Redeeming Love* (1997), 44.
47. Rivers, *Redeeming Love* (1997), 461.
48. Rivers, *Redeeming Love* (1997), 44.

FANTASY IN *REDEEMING LOVE*: FORCE, DECEPTION, AND THE FAIRY TALE

"Defiance" begins with the historical marker "California, 1850" and a decidedly unglamorous portrait of the Mother Lode as Angel pushes back a tent flap and smells the stench. Yet the first chapter introduces several new fairy-tale motifs: the brothel is called the Palace, the madam is the Duchess, and the bodyguard is "a woman-hating giant."[49] Like the Grimms' Rapunzel with her "magnificent long hair, fine as spun gold,"[50] Angel spends most of her time trapped in her upstairs room, brushing "her long, golden hair."[51] Some feminists argue that fairy-tale motifs in romance novels can be empowering; Jennifer Crusie Smith in "This Is Not Your Mother's Cinderella" claims that while "the Grimms' Cinderella is pretty much a passive wimp,"[52] the new variety "shows the reader an acceptable version of 'what to do'—not sit in the ashes but be active and aggressive and demand satisfaction in her life."[53] Linda J. Lee agrees that romances gain feminist energy when they incorporate motifs from tales like "Beauty and the Beast": "Fairy tales have been interpreted as encapsulating collective fantasies and providing a way for women to subvert and resist patriarchal norms."[54] As usual, *Redeeming Love* falls on the least empowering end of the spectrum. Since Rivers draws on tales with relatively passive heroines like Cinderella, Rapunzel, Sleeping Beauty, and Snow White, the fairy-tale elements reconcile readers to Angel's helplessness and her need to be rescued by Prince Charming.

After reading an entire section that focuses on Angel's perspective and critiques male sexual exploitation, we find ourselves suddenly in a male point of view, looking at Angel as an object of desire. Michael is unloading vegetables from his wagon when he sees her walking down the street and hears the voice of God (in bold italics):

> Michael couldn't take his eyes off her. His heart beat faster and faster as she came near. He willed her to look at him, but she didn't. He let out his breath after she passed him, not even aware that he had been holding it.
> ***This one, beloved.***

---

49. Rivers, *Redeeming Love* (1997), 48.
50. Grimm and Grimm, *Grimm's Fairy Tales*, 34.
51. Rivers, *Redeeming Love* (1997), 51.
52. Jennifer Crusie Smith, "This Is Not Your Mother's Cinderella," 54.
53. Jennifer Crusie Smith, "This Is Not Your Mother's Cinderella," 60.
54. Linda J. Lee, "Guilty Pleasures," 62.

Michael felt a rush of adrenaline mingled with joy.[55]

Since most romances follow the heroine's struggle to discern how she feels about a man, or which man to choose, Michael's instant recognition of Angel as his future wife departs from convention in two important ways: the *man* is the one who makes the choice, and he does so without a moment of doubt. Regis points out that love at first sight "is largely a male phenomenon,"[56] which privileges a woman's appearance over her inner character.

Even more troubling is the conflation of Michael's lust with God's voice. The 1991 edition focuses on Michael's thoughts: "She's the one I've been looking for. His reaction was so strong he could not be mistaken."[57] The Christian version juxtaposes Michael's desire for a woman he has never met with God's will for his marriage. This seems like dangerous thinking, since most sexual feelings in real life do not receive instant divine endorsement. Michael gets to experience joy on his first page of the novel, in contrast to Angel's fifty pages of suffering. Even after learning that she is a prostitute, Michael only pretends to protest. "'Lord, this isn't exactly what I had in mind.' But he knew he was going to marry that girl anyway."[58] If Michael has no choice because he is submitting to God, why doesn't Angel have a choice?

Michael pays to visit Angel's room several times to persuade her to marry him, and Rivers shifts rapidly between their points of view, violating Angel's boundaries even on a narrative level. Feminist elements are still present, as we learn about her physical abuse by the bodyguard Magowan and her profound misery. Yet there is an ominous contrast between Michael's confidence that she will marry him and Angel's fear and confusion. Her first impression of him is unromantic: "He was taller and older than most, and well-muscled. Other than that, she noticed nothing special about him."[59] His refusal to have sex unnerves Angel, removing the power that she normally has over men, while he still looks at her body as an object of desire. Michael states the main problem clearly: "How was he going to make her understand he was different from the other men who came to her when he came by the same way they did?"[60] This question is never resolved in a satisfying way.

55. Rivers, *Redeeming Love* (1997), 53.
56. Regis, *Natural History of the Romance Novel*, 60.
57. Rivers, *Redeeming Love* (1991), 42.
58. Rivers, *Redeeming Love* (1997), 56.
59. Rivers, *Redeeming Love* (1997), 60.
60. Rivers, *Redeeming Love* (1997), 63.

Perhaps a fairy-tale heroine like Rapunzel does not ask her rescuer a lot of questions, but Angel is a realistic character with no reason to trust him. His control of the situation seems sinister when he refuses to call her Angel and names her Mara: "It means bitter."[61] He does not feel the need to woo her, but simply explains during their first meeting: "You're going to marry me, and I'm going to take you out of here."[62] When she refuses, Michael resorts to emotional bullying that is more upsetting to her than prostitution. He scares her by losing his temper and slamming the door, with an edge in his voice as he makes demands. He wants her emotional consent rather than a relationship from "the neck down,"[63] an ironic reference to the novel's cover that portrays her from the nose down, but he still treats her as a product that he paid for rather than a person. Angel panics and asks the Duchess for her money so that she can leave. Like the witch who imprisons Rapunzel, the Duchess refuses to let her go, calling her "a princess up here"[64] and sending Magowan to teach her a lesson.

One of the novel's most striking features is the couple's marriage in the first quarter of the book. Early marriages are not unusual in romance novels, and Radway notes that they occur in seven of her readers' twenty ideal romances.[65] Regis also describes the "marriage of convenience" in which the couple falls in love after the wedding.[66] The unusual aspect is that Angel has been beaten so severely that she is delirious, lying in a trance like a Sleeping Beauty who does not awaken to the prince's kiss or celebrate a public marriage "with all splendour."[67] She doesn't recognize the voice of the man asking to marry her, so her "consent" is an act of desperation: "She would agree to wed Satan himself if it would get her out of the Palace. 'Why not?' she managed."[68] She feels someone slip a ring on her finger and give her laudanum so that she will sleep on the way back to the farm: "Angel wanted to ask who she had married, but what did it matter?"[69] Modleski

---

61. Rivers, *Redeeming Love* (1997), 64.

62. Rivers, *Redeeming Love* (1997), 65.

63. Rivers, *Redeeming Love* (1997), 80.

64. Rivers, *Redeeming Love* (1997), 92.

65. Radway, *Reading the Romance*, 123.

66. Regis, *Natural History of the Romance Novel*, 30.

67. Grimm and Grimm, *Grimm's Fairy Tales*, 119.

68. Rivers, *Redeeming Love* (1997), 100.

69. Rivers, *Redeeming Love* (1997), 100. A comparison to Janette Oke's groundbreaking novel *Love Comes Softly* (1979) reveals the extent to which Rivers builds on and departs from the Christian romance tradition. Oke's novel also takes place on the nineteenth-century frontier and features an unchurched heroine in tragic circumstances marrying a Christian hero whom she barely knows. Grief-stricken widow

writes about similar plots in which the hero becomes aroused by a sick or unconscious heroine: "It is hard not to laugh at this near necrophilia, but it does reveal the impossible situation of woman: to be alive and conscious is to be suspect."[70] Angel's role has evolved from Cinderella losing her mother, to Rapunzel brushing her hair, to Sleeping Beauty in the tower, to Snow White, presumed dead in her glass coffin, with the prince taking home her beautiful corpse.

Since Angel marries Michael when she is symbolically dead, Rivers collapses two conventional elements of the romance plot: the point of ritual death and the betrothal. Regis describes the usual order of events: "a *definition of society*, always corrupt, that the romance novel will reform; the *meeting* between the heroine and hero; an account of their *attraction* for each other; the *barrier* between them; the *point of ritual death*; the *recognition* that fells the barrier; the *declaration* of heroine and hero that they love each other; and their *betrothal*."[71] Regis notes that elements can happen in any order and might be repeated, but the escape from ritual death typically provides "fundamental release from inhibition to action, from constraint to choice, from bondage to freedom."[72] Angel wakes from ritual death only to find herself in bondage to Michael, and the novel lingers on this stage of suicidal thoughts and self-hatred for the next 350 pages until Angel's recognition and declaration in the last ten pages.

Scholars debate whether heroines are empowered or harmed by the romance convention of their captivity by the hero. Kate McCafferty examines the feminist elements of historical novels in which Native American men introduce their captives into a more egalitarian world than the vicious realm of white patriarchy, and Anne K. Kaler argues that the captivity involves a reversal of traditional gender conventions as "the female undertakes the journey of the hero and the male undertakes the spiritual awakening."[73] Robin Harders agrees that a white woman's captivity by a savage "Other"

Marty Claridge marries Clark Davis just hours after her husband's funeral because the preacher is only in town for the day: "She must have uttered her own responses at the proper times, for the preacher's words came through the haze, '. . . now pronounce you man and wife'" (*Love Comes Softly*, 24). The striking parallel to Angel's semi-conscious state during her wedding suggests an ambivalence about marriage—or the wedding industry—among Christian women. Yet unlike Michael Hosea, Clark shows only consideration and gentleness to his vulnerable young wife. *Love Comes Softly* may not be as aesthetically sophisticated or psychologically complex as *Redeeming Love*, but its hero seems more biblical in his approach to marriage.

70. Modleski, *Loving with a Vengeance*, 43.

71. Regis, *Natural History of the Romance Novel*, 14 (italics original).

72. Regis, *Natural History of the Romance Novel*, 56.

73. Kaler, "Conventions of Captivity," 86.

can be subversive, as she chooses him over a European man, breaks down racial stereotypes, and forms a hybrid identity: "In the captivity romance, the heroine is allowed to desire and to choose, and once she chooses love, her adventure is often one that marks a significant cultural challenge or change."[74] However, Emily A. Haddad critiques Orientalist romances in which captivity prepares women for marriage by subduing their independence: "In each of these novels, captivity initially promotes the expression of freedom as an ideal, as the heroines rebel against their imprisonment. When they fall in love, however, their attraction to their future husbands becomes more compelling than freedom. Bondage gives way to bonding."[75] Since Angel's captor is a white man, her captivity seems to function according to Haddad's description, as a training ground for marital submission rather than a subversive interracial bond.

Michael's devotion to nursing Angel back to health makes this captivity seem benign. In keeping with Radway's theory, Michael is a clear mother substitute during Angel's first days on the farm. He feeds her when she is bedridden, and the 1991 edition includes the detail that she is too weak to use the chamber pot: "He had to slide a tin basin under her and hold her while she relieved herself."[76] In the later edition, when she first gets out of bed, Angel stands at the cabin window, weak and naked, whispering "Oh, Mama," and Michael comes home, places a blanket around her, and holds her "in his arms like a child."[77] Yet Michael combines tenderness with control. In one example, the couple is fighting late at night, and he rips off the bedcovers: "'Get up. Now. You're going whether you like it or not.' Angel was frightened of him as he loomed over her. She could sense him trying to rein in his temper."[78] He demands that they walk outside whether dressed or naked; when she tries to return to bed, he catches her arm and spins her around. He pulls her through the darkness and sits her down on a hill with the reminder: "You're not going to have it your way. It's got to be my way or not at all."[79] It eventually becomes clear that he has brought her to see the sunrise, an unrealistic ending to this display of dominance. The novel insists that although he may be angry, and she may be afraid, he always has her best interests at heart.

---

74. Harders, "Borderlands of Desire," 149.

75. Haddad, "Bound to Love," 49.

76. Rivers, *Redeeming Love* (1991), 91.

77. Rivers, *Redeeming Love* (1997), 112.

78. Rivers, *Redeeming Love* (1997), 136.

79. Rivers, *Redeeming Love* (1997), 138.

Michael is portrayed as a nurturing mother, but he also takes on the role of Cinderella's scheming stepmother. Rather than changing Ella to Cinderella, he changes her name to reflect his mood: Mara, Amanda, Tirzah. He claims that a "farmer's wife doesn't wear satin and lace"[80] and gives her worn clothing that falls into rags and makes her ashamed. He prevents her from leaving his property, where she spends a lot of time cooking over the fire. Cinderella's stepmother keeps her at home by making her pick lentils from the ashes, and Michael makes her pick black walnuts: "It was a mean, low trick, but the result would keep her on the homestead for a couple more weeks."[81] She works until her "back was a mass of pain"[82] only to discover that the black dye won't come off her hands, linking her to the slaves on the plantation where Michael's father taught him how to deal with women. Angel works as hard as Cinderella, not only performing housework, but trying to escape from a character who combines the stepmother and the prince.

Like Cinderella, Angel runs away from her prince three times. Cinderella escapes after the first two nights of the ball by going through a pigeon-house and climbing a pear tree. The third night, "Cinderella wished to leave, and the King's son was anxious to go with her, but she escaped from him so quickly that he could not follow her."[83] The prince traps her shoe by spreading pitch on the stairs, then pursues her throughout the kingdom by asking women to try on the shoe. Angel is not as quick, and her first escape attempt is short-lived. She gets lost trying to find the road and drops her shoes along the way; like Cinderella's prince, Michael finds the shoes and follows them to her. He gives her an ultimatum: she can walk thirty miles, or she can stay, "and we're still playing by my rules."[84] She returns bitterly, knowing that she can't walk that far. He washes her feet in an act of Christian love but reveals his view of women as either open or closed to his demands: "A woman is either a wall or a door."[85] Rivers changed "girl" to "woman" for the Christian edition, but the sentiment still rankles.

Her second escape attempt has tragic consequences, as Michael's brother-in-law Paul demands sex in exchange for the ride. In Rivers's defense, there are no rape fantasies in this novel; Angel is traumatized and vomits afterwards. She then discovers that the Palace has burned down, her money is gone, and she has no choice but to return to her old trade at

---

80. Rivers, *Redeeming Love* (1997), 113.
81. Rivers, *Redeeming Love* (1997), 146.
82. Rivers, *Redeeming Love* (1997), 147.
83. Grimm and Grimm, *Grimm's Fairy Tales*, 77.
84. Rivers, *Redeeming Love* (1997), 162.
85. Rivers, *Redeeming Love* (1997), 164.

a saloon. Michael shows up and drags her away with acts of violent machismo: "Before she was fully clothed, he yanked her off the bed, opened the door, and shoved her into the corridor. He hadn't even allowed her to put her shoes on."[86] He fights off every man in the saloon, picks her up, and tosses her into the wagon. When she jumps off and runs in terror, he pins her down and barely stops himself from further violence: "If he had hit her back once, he would have killed her."[87] This behavior surely compromises his ability to represent God's "unconditional love." Ironically, Satan is the only one who recognizes the fairy-tale symbolism. Just as the wicked Queen orders Snow White to be killed and "thought she had eaten the heart,"[88] Satan warns Angel, **"He'll cut your heart out and carve it up for dinner,"**[89] and she is afraid of her growing attraction to Michael.

In her third escape attempt, she hitches a ride with kind-hearted salesman Sam Teal, the first of many benevolent male helpers who are too old to be potential suitors. She discovers her talent for sales and earns her first honest money, then travels to Sacramento and works at the mercantile of Michael's friend, Joseph Hochschild. Michael arrives to put an end to her newfound independence in the scene that served as the teaser for the 1991 edition. In the Christian edition, when she begs him to leave her alone, "He yanked the bag from her hand and sent it bouncing off the back wall."[90] However, her sexual desire has become leverage for him as he draws her into his arms: "'I couldn't stop thinking about you,' she said miserably, pressing closer, inhaling the sweet scent of his body. She had missed this feeling of safety that only came when she was with him. He was so determined to have her. Well, why not let him?"[91] As Modleski claims, "If you can't lick them, you might as well love them."[92] Ecstatic sex scenes might reconcile Angel to her situation (like the two long and explicit scenes in this chapter in the 1991 version), but it is odd that she associates Michael with "this feeling of safety that only came when she was with him." She has been much safer with Sam and Joseph, who protect her and treat her with respect.

Meanwhile, Angel's life on the farm is entangled in three interwoven love triangles: (1) Michael's brother-in-law, Paul, becomes a serious rival for Michael's attention and a serious threat to Angel, (2) beautiful Miriam

86. Rivers, *Redeeming Love* (1997), 192.

87. Rivers, *Redeeming Love* (1997), 195.

88. Grimm and Grimm, *Grimm's Fairy Tales*, 125.

89. Rivers, *Redeeming Love* (1997), 280.

90. Rivers, *Redeeming Love* (1997), 307.

91. Rivers, *Redeeming Love* (1997), 308.

92. Modleski, *Loving with a Vengeance*, 36.

Altman also becomes a rival for Michael's attention, and (3) Paul denies his love for Miriam because he thinks she belongs with Michael. No wonder Angel keeps trying to escape: she must compete with both male and female rivals for a man she never chose. Paul's role is highly complex from the moment that he arrives from the gold fields, where he made a futile attempt to overcome his grief over his wife Tessie's death. Since Angel is wearing Tessie's old clothes, one would expect a conventional love triangle in which Paul sees her as a double of his late wife, falls in love with her, and fights with Michael for her favor. This could have been empowering for Angel, as it was in a similar plot in Catherine Marshall's *Christy*, where Dr. MacNeill becomes attracted to Christy because she resembles his late wife—even borrowing his wife's old clothes during a storm—and he ends up overthrowing Christy's much less appealing love interest.[93] Carole Veldman-Genz argues that a heroine's choice between two men "expresses a confident and determining female gaze and a knowing, autonomous subjectivity."[94] What happens to Angel is more bizarre, since Paul does not fight with Michael over her, but with her over Michael.

Instead of a romantic suitor, Paul becomes a symbolic female rival. He is feminized when he first embraces Michael upon his return, "Paul almost wept at the feel of those strong, sure arms," "he had to fight back unmanly tears," and "his hair had grown long."[95] Profoundly jealous when he learns that Michael is married, he becomes obsessed with getting rid of Angel. Eve Kosofsky Sedgwick argues in *Between Men* that the classic love triangle takes the form of a male homosocial bond as two men fight over a woman,[96] and here the homoerotic bond is exposed as Paul openly strives for Michael's attention. Angel states this directly to Paul during her second escape attempt: "Now that I'm gone, you can have Michael to yourself all

---

93. *Christy* is a much better romance than *Redeeming Love*, even though the love story is only a subplot to Christy's work as missionary schoolteacher. There are two eligible men in Christy's life, handsome young minister David Grantland and ornery widower Dr. Neil MacNeill. David initially seems like every evangelical woman's dream man, but clues slowly reveal that his faith is superficial and that his attraction to Christy is merely physical. Meanwhile, MacNeill has an honest and challenging relationship with Christy rooted in her resemblance to his first love. While any reader of Jane Austen's *Sense and Sensibility* will recognize the John Willoughby/Colonel Brandon love triangle and the inevitability of Christy ending up with the older and more substantial MacNeill, the heroine has to work hard to discern which man to marry. In *Redeeming Love*, Angel does not need to discern anything, only to submit to God/Michael's will.

94. Veldman-Genz, "More the Merrier?," 111.

95. Rivers, *Redeeming Love* (1997), 167.

96. Sedgwick, *Between Men*, 21.

winter long."[97] Paul responds with fury: "Was she making some sort of foul insinuation? Did she doubt his manhood?"[98] The 1991 version makes this more explicit: "Was she making some sort of foul insinuation about his sexual preferences?"[99] In the later version, Paul rapes Angel as an act of homophobic panic, switching from female rival to male villain: "He was rough and quick, his sole desire to hurt and degrade her."[100] We get a sense of the novel's unconventional qualities when we consider that Angel is raped by her "female" rival. Since Angel has no other romantic prospects, her final return to Michael feels less like a free choice. This plot forces her to choose not between two legitimate suitors, but between independence and marriage. We know that independence is the evil choice because Satan's bold-faced words constantly recommend it, and the fact that Angel is already married to Michael allows Rivers to cast any other choice as a betrayal.

The second love triangle is equally humiliating to Angel, as she believes that she should leave Michael so that he can marry the virginal Miriam and have the children that Angel cannot give him. Veldman-Genz claims that triangles in which heroines have to compete with other women for the hero have a patriarchal flavor: "This doubling of women into opposites—good/bad, virgin/whore, sane/mad—functions as a zoning method that circumscribes women antithetically, thereby perpetuating female rivalry."[101] To make matters worse, Rivers flips the conventional pattern so that *Miriam* takes the "good" role of the sane virgin and *Angel* takes the "bad" role of the crazy whore. Not only does this provide Angel with dozens more chances to feel unworthy, but she is completely wrong, showing her lack of discernment. The reader knows that Michael has no interest in Miriam and that Miriam is in love with Paul, so the triangle is a figment of Angel's tortured imagination.

Miriam is more assertive than Angel, and her subplot with Paul provides a glimpse of the spunky heroine who tames her wild beast, representing a new generation of California women who make their elders seem like doormats in comparison. Miriam's mother Elizabeth represents the wifely submission that Angel must learn, which is probably why Michael does not even consult with Angel before inviting the entire Altman family to stay in the cabin for the winter. Elizabeth lost a child and mother on the Oregon Trail, and Angel suspects that she never wanted to leave home, but when

97. Rivers, *Redeeming Love* (1997), 184.

98. Rivers, *Redeeming Love* (1997), 184.

99. Rivers, *Redeeming Love* (1991), 161.

100. Rivers, *Redeeming Love* (1997), 185.

101. Veldman-Genz, "More the Merrier?," 112.

Elizabeth looked at her husband John "there was no resentment in her expression."[102] John does not even tell Elizabeth when he buys the land next door to Michael, builds a cabin, then loads up the wagon and tells her that they are moving to Oregon. The practical joke seems downright cruel, but when the wagon stops at their new home, "Elizabeth wept and threw herself into John's arms, telling him he was a wretch and she adored him."[103] Miriam jokes that she should apologize for being so angry in the wagon, and nobody finds it inappropriate for a husband to make a major decision without telling his wife. Yet Miriam demands a more equal relationship, despite her elements of the fairy-tale heroine who dreams "about her Prince Charming."[104] Miriam finally compels Paul to marry her by going to his cabin and getting into his bed like the biblical Ruth. Through her determination and sexual magnetism, she overcomes Paul's grief and guilt, transforming him into a good husband. What kind of romance novel has a female rival that seems more appealing than the heroine?

Angel's imaginary rivalry with Miriam motivates her to leave Michael for the last time, and Michael finally seems to have learned the lesson that "if you love something, let it go." Angel's initial experiences in San Francisco continue the helpless misery that we have experienced for 375 pages. She works in a café with another kind male helper, Virgil Harper, who guides her through hell like Dante's Virgil. In typical fashion, the café burns down, and our Cinderella finds herself digging "through the ash and rubble."[105] Like Charlotte Brontë's famous Victorian heroine Jane Eyre after she leaves Edward Rochester, Angel has a supernatural connection with Michael, who dreams that she is calling out to him in the midst of a fire.[106] Unlike Jane Eyre, who works as a teacher, reunites with her family, and inherits enough money to be independent, Angel finds herself back in the clutches of Duke, who pursues her to California and locks her in his new brothel. Duke's sadism makes Michael's loving bondage seem benign, and Angel dreams that Michael stands before her with a flame burning over his heart: "Then the light separated from Michael and came the last few feet toward her. It was a man, glorious and magnificent, light streaming from him in all directions."[107] She asks his name, and he gives her a series of names for God.

102. Rivers, *Redeeming Love* (1997), 248.
103. Rivers, *Redeeming Love* (1997), 265.
104. Rivers, *Redeeming Love* (1997), 255.
105. Rivers, *Redeeming Love* (1997), 384.
106. Rivers, *Redeeming Love* (1997), 390.
107. Rivers, *Redeeming Love* (1997), 399.

When Michael releases her from bondage, she quickly begins to see him as a Christ figure.

In the last fifty pages, Angel finally achieves her long-desired independence, becomes a Christian, and begins a satisfying career. Jonathan Axle, another male helper, rescues her from the brothel, and his spunky daughter Susanna becomes her first female friend that is not a rival. Susanna teaches Angel to read, which Michael never bothered to do during those long winter nights in the cabin, encourages her Christian conversion, and becomes her business partner when she founds the House of Magdalena. Finally, the reader gets to experience the feminist elements of modern romance: the female friendship, the career, the sense of freedom. When Miriam sends Paul to find Angel three years later, he enters her office where books and papers are strewn over the desk. No longer the desperate woman who submits to Paul's rape and then vomits in the woods, Angel is calm and collected. He asks: "Whose house is this?" She responds with a powerful word: "Mine."[108] This female triumph seems too little and too late.

Rivers suggests that Angel's career is a form of adultery that she must renounce. She must first acknowledge that Paul's rape was her fault because she chose to leave Michael: "She couldn't cast blame on anyone but herself. The choice had been hers. She had never even thought of consequences. The repercussions had been like a stone flung into smooth water."[109] The metaphor of the stone echoes the novel's epigraph and indicates that she is casting the first stone at her adulterous self. Paul argues that returning to Michael is her duty, regardless of the value of her charitable organization: "No matter how good a cause, it's just an excuse now."[110] This idea reflects Rivers's own experience that she described in the author's note at the end of the novel. Just as Angel always longed for her own cabin where she would be free from the demands of men, Rivers once put her career before her family: "I frequently contemplated how much easier it would be to live by myself in a cabin away from everyone, with an electric typewriter as my only company."[111] Rivers may have been right to fulfill her commitment to the family that she chose, but it seems unfair to expect Angel to do the same when she was married without her consent. Rivers also continued working after her conversion, with *Redeeming Love* as one product of that career, whereas Angel must choose between her San Francisco office and Michael's farm a hundred miles away. Although the epilogue notes that "she returned

---

108. Rivers, *Redeeming Love* (1997), 445.
109. Rivers, *Redeeming Love* (1997), 449.
110. Rivers, *Redeeming Love* (1997), 454.
111. Rivers, *Redeeming Love* (1997), 465.

for one week each year to the House of Magdalena,"[112] her first priority must be her marriage.

When Angel returns to Michael for their final reunion, she literally strips off the vestiges of her independence. She walks toward the field where he stands, removing her clothing: "Oh, if she could only be Eve again, a new creature in Paradise. Before the Fall."[113] She slowly strips for five paragraphs before approaching Michael in humble nakedness. While this may have a certain Edenic resonance, there is something disturbing about a woman removing her clothes outdoors, where anyone could see. This reminds the reader of the many times that Michael undressed her or did not allow her to dress, so that she is naked a lot throughout the book. Rivers removed many of the erotic descriptions of Angel's body from the 1991 edition, including more than twenty-five references to her breasts, but this final striptease objectifies her just as much.

The ending also lacks a key convention of romance fiction. Fletcher argues that saying "I love you" is the most basic speech act that characterizes romance,[114] but *Redeeming Love* denies readers this pleasure since Angel is struck dumb by remorse: "All her carefully planned words fled. So many words to say a simple, heartfelt thing: *I love you, and I'm sorry*. She could not even speak."[115] Even though Angel was basically kidnapped and could be seen as justified for leaving Michael, her final action is to beg his forgiveness: "Weeping, Angel sank to her knees. Hot tears fell on his boots. She wiped them away with her hair. She bent over, heartbroken, and put her hands on his feet. 'Oh, Michael, Michael, I'm sorry. . . .' *Oh, God, forgive me*."[116] The ellipses connect Michael to God, as does the tradition that Mary Magdalene was the sinful woman who approached Jesus "and began to bathe his feet with her tears and to dry them with her hair" (Luke 7:38 NRSV). Michael forgives her, but neither says "I love you." She finally tells him her real name, Sarah, he receives a sign from God that she will have children, and he lifts her into the air. In comparison, the Grimms' Cinderella has admirable control and dignity during her final reunion with the prince:

> She first washed her hands and face clean, and then went and bowed down before the King's son, who gave her the golden shoe. Then she seated herself on a stool, drew her foot out of the heavy wooden shoe, and put it into the slipper, which fitted like

112. Rivers, *Redeeming Love* (1997), 463.

113. Rivers, *Redeeming Love* (1997), 460.

114. Fletcher, *Historical Romance Fiction*, 41.

115. Rivers, *Redeeming Love* (1997), 461 (italics original).

116. Rivers, *Redeeming Love* (1997), 461 (italics original).

> a glove. And when she rose up and the King's son looked at her face he recognized the beautiful maiden who had danced with him and cried, "That is the true bride!"[117]

Like Angel, Cinderella first "bowed down" before the hero and then "rose up." However, she rises by herself, she does not weep, and she gets to keep her clothes on.

The last paragraph before the epilogue is an italicized message to the reader that summarizes the moral of the story: *"Stand against the darkness, and love. That's the way back into Eden. That's the way back to life."*[118] The 1991 edition included one additional sentence: "Oh, Cleo, Cleo, wherever you are, I pray you seek the truth."[119] This reference to a character that we have not seen for almost 400 pages is unexpected, but there is a poignancy in ending the book with Angel thinking of another woman whose bitterness threatened to destroy her life. The 1997 edition focuses less on the heroine's private thoughts than on the narrator's moral, which is strengthened for the reader who continues to Rivers's story about her need to place marriage before career. Rivers also claims: "Everything in *Redeeming Love* was a gift from the Lord: plot, characters, theme. None of it is mine to claim."[120] This gives the book an almost scriptural authority, but it raises the question: If the plot, characters, and theme were gifts from the Lord, why did they need to be revised for a Christian audience?

HOSEA AND BEYOND: THE ROLE OF THE BIBLE IN *REDEEMING LOVE*

Much of the novel's strangeness comes from its attempt to map the book of Hosea, a prophetic message to Israel in the eighth century BC, onto a mass-market romance in the twentieth century AD. Two more different rhetorical situations could hardly be imagined. Yet Neal claims that many Christians see romance novels as windows into the Bible: "Reading evangelical romance prompts thinking about, features verses from, and applies principles of the Bible, but often it replaces actual study of the Bible."[121] The introduction to Hosea in *The New Oxford Annotated Bible* uses the phrase

---

117. Grimm and Grimm, *Grimm's Fairy Tales*, 78.

118. Rivers, *Redeeming Love* (1997), 462.

119. Rivers, *Redeeming Love* (1991), 412.

120. Rivers, *Redeeming Love* (1997), 467.

121. Neal, *Romancing God*, 153.

"redeeming love" twice, but the biblical book bears little resemblance to the novel.[122]

Hosea is a public figure who marries Gomer to make a political and religious statement: "When the LORD first spoke through Hosea, the LORD said to Hosea, 'Go, take for yourself a wife of whoredom and have children of whoredom, for the land commits great whoredom by forsaking the LORD'" (Hos 1:2 NRSV). Gomer has three children, presumably with other men, and he gives them symbolic names: "God sows," "Not pitied," and "Not my people" (Hos 1:4–9 NRSV). Hosea stands in for the Lord and Gomer for Israel as the speaker threatens her with punishments: he will strip her naked, take back his grain and wine, uncover her shame, put an end to her mirth, lay waste to her vines and fig trees (Hos 2:3–13 NRSV). Yet the tone changes to forgiveness: "And I will take you for my wife forever; I will take you for my wife in righteousness and in justice, in steadfast love, and in mercy" (Hos 2:19 NRSV). In chapter 3, Hosea buys Gomer back again, telling her that she shall abstain from sex just as Israel will be deprived of its kings and sacrifices. The very short account of Gomer never includes her point of view, justifying Angel's question: "Maybe she just wanted to be left alone. Did the prophet ever think of that?"[123] In transforming this indictment of Israel's idol worship into a romance novel, Rivers must turn a brief religious allegory into a realistic love story that teaches Christian women how to be good wives. The moral changes from "return to God" to "return to your husband."

Yet the book of Hosea was never meant to be a marriage manual. Hosea's marriage was a drastic step to make a point, not something that men should emulate on a wide scale. The same is true of fairy tales, which make little sense as marriage guides (the prince falls in love with Snow White in her coffin) but work well as allegories of divine love (the prince represents Christ bringing us from death to life). To make Michael and Angel into role models, Rivers must bend over backwards to justify their non-Christian behavior by dwelling on his calling from God and her terrible childhood. Angel's inability to have children changes the primary metaphor from wanton fertility to barrenness, allowing Rivers to avoid the unwholesome task of describing Angel having children with other men and connecting Angel to the biblical barren women who are healed by God.

Rivers evidently succeeded in turning Hosea and Gomer into contemporary realistic characters for many readers, and Michael could have followed the same plotline with a gentler approach. St. Paul tells husbands

---

122. Metzger and Murphy, *New Oxford Annotated Bible*, 1148 OT.

123. Rivers, *Redeeming Love* (1997), 134.

to love their wives as Christ loves the church: "In the same way, husbands should love their wives as they do their own bodies. He who loves his wife loves himself. For no one ever hates his own body, but he nourishes and tenderly cares for it, just as Christ does for the church, because we are members of his body" (Eph 5:28–30 NRSV). Michael shows tenderness toward his wife, but he also disciplines her using barely constrained violence and mind games. We don't see this behavior in the biblical Hosea, and it has no place in a Christian marriage.

Rivers compares Michael to several biblical characters besides Hosea, always in a flattering context, like when his Jewish friend Joseph describes him: "A man like Noah. A man like the shepherd-king, David. A man after God's own heart."[124] Joseph does not compare David's lustful and deceptive behavior toward Bathsheba to Michael's behavior toward Angel, but he exonerates Michael and "prayed Angel wouldn't rip that heart out of him."[125] When Michael tells Angel that her walls are coming down, she wryly comments: "Joshua blowing his horn."[126] Characters rarely question his actions, which makes sense given that Michael is the name of a warrior archangel, and Hosea means "salvation" or "deliverance."

On the other hand, Angel is compared to biblical women that parallel her sinfulness as well as her potential redemption. Soon after meeting her, Michael names her Mara after the bitter mother-in-law from the book of Ruth. During their first sexual encounter, he calls her Tirzah after the beautiful city in the Song of Solomon, demanding that she say his name while refusing to use hers. Paul notes that she is beautiful "like Salome and Delilah and Jezebel,"[127] women who manipulate men with their sexuality. Michael asks, "How was Angel any different from Hosea's wife, Gomer, sold to the prophet by her own father? A child of prostitution. An adulteress."[128] While this is a compassionate moment, Gomer does not live in Judeo-Christian memory as a female role model.

Michael teaches Angel about biblical women's sinfulness and sexuality, beginning with Eve and the mistake that he is determined not to make with his wife: "Adam was weak and went along with what she said rather than follow what God had told him."[129] When Michael takes Angel to church, and she leaves in humiliation, he tries to comfort her by telling her about

124. Rivers, *Redeeming Love* (1997), 223.
125. Rivers, *Redeeming Love* (1997), 223.
126. Rivers, *Redeeming Love* (1997), 232.
127. Rivers, *Redeeming Love* (1997), 171.
128. Rivers, *Redeeming Love* (1997), 213.
129. Rivers, *Redeeming Love* (1997), 217.

women in the lineage of Christ: "Rahab was a prostitute. Ruth slept at the feet of a man she wasn't married to, on a public threshing floor. Bathsheba was an adulteress. When she found she was pregnant, her lover plotted the murder of her husband. And Mary became pregnant by Someone other than the man she was betrothed to marry."[130] These descriptions focus on the women's supposedly illicit sexuality rather than their heroism. Rahab saved the lives of Joshua's spies and paved the way for the Israelites to enter the promised land (Josh 2). Ruth slept at the feet of her kinsman, the most appropriate person to marry her after her husband's death (Ruth 3). Bathsheba was a rape survivor who became the mother of King Solomon (2 Sam 11–12), and Mary submitted to a miraculous conception and gave birth to Christ (Luke 1). Michael's response to Angel's birth name is the most positive biblical comparison: "A wanderer in foreign lands, a barren woman filled with doubt. Yet Sarah of old had become a symbol of trust in God and ultimately the mother of a nation."[131] However, the connection focuses on Michael's desires, as he looks forward to the day when Sarah will *give him* a child.

Why do so many Christian women see this as their favorite novel? Since *Redeeming Love* is such an unconventional romance, the answers must lie at least partly in its departures from convention: its unflinching portrayal of traumatic and exploitative sex and its invocation of biblical allegory to portray its hero as God. The novel may evoke women's suspicion or experience that sex is not always blissful and that it can make them feel used and ashamed; maybe thousands of young, virginal readers can identify with a prostitute so easily because all women feel like prostitutes sometimes. At the same time, many women are attracted to the "alpha male," and the novel offers them a much racier story than they would normally read. It may also address readers' frustrations with the power of God, the church, and men, serving as an extended apology for male headship. The historical setting distances the novel from readers and allows its fantastic elements to perform the work of the fairy tale: facing fears, overcoming trials, and experiencing catharsis. This explanation accounts for the popularity of *this* romance, among the hundreds of relatively sweet, pure, sentimental ones. Apparently this fairly explicit text allows many Christian women to work through their simultaneous resentment of and desire for patriarchal control, a biblical reality with which we all must come to terms. The danger lies in a woman's fantasy that she will meet a man just like Michael Hosea, since no

130. Rivers, *Redeeming Love* (1997), 228.
131. Rivers, *Redeeming Love* (1997), 462.

flawed human being can ever be God. Most men who drag women outside in the middle of the night are not taking them to see the sunrise.

It is troubling that Christian texts like C. S. Lewis's *The Chronicles of Narnia* and *Redeeming Love* contain graphic stories of beautiful women whose sexual attractiveness places them in mortal peril and threatens their salvation. As we saw in the previous chapter, Prince Rabadash is enraged when Susan Pevensie declines his proposal in *The Horse and His Boy*, still shrieking in the final pages: "Let the earth gape! Let blood and fire obliterate the world! But be sure I will never desist till I have dragged to my palace by her hair the barbarian queen."[132] Michael Hosea also becomes furious when Angel refuses to marry him, expressing his frustration in prayer: "*She doesn't want what I'm offering. What am I supposed to do? Drag her out of here by her hair?*"[133] These references to dragging women by their hair are a disturbing departure from biblical standards in which a woman's long hair is "her glory" and "given to her for a covering" (1 Cor 11:15 NRSV). Such similar threats by a comical pagan villain from a children's story and a serious Christian hero from an evangelical romance reveal that violence against women is a part of our world that we cannot escape. Susan and Angel are young women separated from their mothers trying to navigate the confusing terrain of guarding their sexuality and resisting evil men. Both authors blame them for their missteps, with Lewis ultimately declaring Susan "no longer a friend of Narnia" and Rivers making Angel grovel at her husband's feet for his forgiveness. In the next chapter, we turn to the novels of Jan Karon, which belie their reputation as sentimental escapism by including one rape nearly as graphic as anything in *Redeeming Love*. However, since Karon often portrays strong, complex, admirable women, we will turn to the tensions of race and class that haunt her idyllic Southern community.

---

132. Lewis, *Chronicles of Narnia*, 307.

133. Rivers, *Redeeming Love* (1997), 76 (italics original).

Chapter 3

"BUT THIS IS THE *SOUTH*"

Race, Class, and Southern Identity
in Jan Karon's Mitford Novels

The fourteen novels in Jan Karon's Mitford series—beginning with *At Home in Mitford* (1994) and ending with *To Be Where You Are* (2017)—focus on a small town in North Carolina and its Episcopal priest, Father Tim Kavanagh. Mitford is a bucolic village with streets named Lilac Road and Wisteria Lane, resembling nineteenth-century British fiction more than present-day North Carolina. Yet Karon occasionally insists on the Southern nature of her stories, even suggesting that a common term or practice is unique to the South. When Father Tim claims that Anglican burial tradition does not include talking about the departed person, Olivia Harper responds: "But this is the *South!*"[1] Since everyone talks about the deceased during funerals, Olivia's comment seems like an overcompensation for the books' departure from regional conventions—or a hint that Southerners have a unique talent for mourning. In fact, the South that Karon tends to affirm is also passing away, the victim of consumerism, bad taste, and urban sprawl. Karon seems ambivalent both about being understood as a regional writer and about whether the South can be celebrated. In 2005, she attempted to end the Mitford series and start a new one that exposed Southern racism in a relatively graphic manner. What seemed like a positive new direction[2] led to such fan outrage that Karon ended up folding that novel into the original

---

1. Karon, *These High, Green Hills*, 289.

2. For an optimistic reading of this new direction published ten years ago, see Nickel, "But This Is the *South*."

series and continuing as before. Despite Karon's attempts to try something new, the Mitford series tends to land in a Southern worldview that is all too familiar, filled with nostalgia for a lost world of white Southern gentility while portraying many poor white and black characters as caricatures of Confederate pride and devoted servitude.

IN THE SOUTH, BUT NOT OF IT?

In "Making Mitford Real," Karon describes returning to her native North Carolina after living in New York and San Francisco. Her nostalgia for the South includes regional characteristics such as pimiento cheese and lower-class dialect: "I longed to return to the uncommon music of common speech in our foothills and mountains, to hear 'ain't' for *aren't*, and 'tote' for *carry*."[3] Yet she goes on to insist that "I've found Mitford in Milford (Michigan), in Manteo (North Carolina), in Montrose (California), and even in certain neighborhoods of Manhattan. There are Mitfords everywhere!"[4] The same tension occurs twelve years later in *Bathed in Prayer*, where she begins the introduction by describing a childhood attempt to write a Civil War novel inspired by *Gone with the Wind* and ends by asserting that "Mitford is everywhere."[5] When I surveyed thirty-six devoted Mitford readers from around the country in 2008, they often reminded me that Mitford is a state of mind rather than a specific location. All but three readers knew that Mitford is in North Carolina, but one respondent called my question about its location "sneaky," since "I have heard Ms. Karon say, and would agree, that the spirit of Mitford, of loving and caring about our neighbors and friends, is alive and well all over the place." When readers were asked to rank eight possible reasons for enjoying the books, the Southern setting came out next to last, placing well below Christian values and "the chance to experience a simpler, more caring world."[6]

3. Karon, *Mitford Bedside Companion*, 30.

4. Karon, *Mitford Bedside Companion*, 31.

5. Karon, *Bathed in Prayer*, 7.

6. I conducted the survey after *Home to Holly Springs*. Twenty-five readers responded to the survey posted on the Mitford Books Bulletin Board on *MitfordBooks. com*, while eleven surveys were mailed to Mitford readers recommended by friends and family, including a Mitford book group affiliated with a Foursquare Gospel Church. There were fourteen respondents from the South (Arkansas, Florida, Georgia, Maryland, Missouri, North Carolina, Tennessee, and Virginia), six from the Northeast (Massachusetts, New York, and Vermont), six from the Midwest (Illinois, Indiana, Michigan, Minnesota, and Wisconsin), and ten from the West (Arizona, California, Colorado, and Oregon). All but one were women, with an average age of fifty-six. They had read an average of eight out of nine Mitford novels and most had read companion texts like the

Critics of Southern literature have been quick to agree with Karon that she is not really a "Southern writer." She is not mentioned in the massive volume *The History of Southern Women's Literature* edited by Carolyn Perry and Mary Louise Weaks. Sharon Monteith begins her discussion of contemporary Southern women writers by eliminating those who do not fit her criteria: "Karon's novels are popular with readers who seek a soft-focus South; the narratives exemplify a white housewives' utopia that exudes bland and sweet didacticism and lacks the irony that peppers Southern fiction."[7] Ted Olson includes Karon in a list of best-selling authors writing about Appalachia but claims that the novels "hold little pretense of being anything other than popular page-turners."[8] Christopher D. Geist distinguishes Karon from the Southern literary legacy: "Old southern issues of the burdens of history, racial tensions, and poverty seem far away in this new popular literature coming from the region."[9] While Scott Romine devotes several pages to the Mitford novels, he uses them as a point of contrast to texts that he considers "more complex."[10] His astute observation that the series "preserves its pastoral integrity by marginalizing African American characters" is relegated to a footnote.[11]

Yet Karon's denial that she is a "Southern writer" may be her most Southern quality, since Richard Gray reminds us that "denying regional affiliation is in itself a venerable Southern tradition."[12] Karon resembles earlier authors who claim to uphold universal ideals but whose class and race prejudices are deeply rooted in the South. Like the writers of plantation fiction, she cloaks racist representations with nostalgia for an era in which privileged whites reigned peacefully. This pastoral literature "posits a world innocent of politics—because innocent of the conflicts that generate politics—but continually endangered by a surrounding world of political and

---

cookbook and *Mitford Bedside Companion*. They were sympathetic readers, with only four claiming they had "disagreed with or been offended by anything in the books" (all involving a character or plot event that they did not like, none concerning race or the South). Seventy-five percent believed that the books were "realistic." I created a list of eight possible reasons for enjoying the books and the respondents ranked them in the following order of enjoyment: characters; Christian values; the chance to experience a simpler, more caring world; humor; writing style; escape from everyday life; Southern setting; and sharing/discussing the books with other readers.

7. Monteith, "Recent and Contemporary Women Writers," 537.

8. Ted Olson, "Literature," 177.

9. Geist, "Popular Literature," 124.

10. Romine, *Real South*, 157.

11. Romine, *Real South*, 257.

12. Gray, *Southern Aberrations*, 399.

economic corruption."[13] In Mitford, these dangers still come from Yankees and liberals, as well as Florida developers who would destroy the village's close-knit community. Rather than chivalric masters and contented slaves, we have benevolent employers and loving African American servants who speak in dialect, for example when Louella Baxter Marshall insists on down-home cooking: "Low-fat? Pass it on by, honey, you can *skip* this chile!"[14] Lisa Cohen Minnick advises readers to pay close attention to an author's motives for using black dialect, but she notes that "there seem to be far fewer examples today of white-authored representation of African American speech. Perhaps this is the result of increased sensitivity to the complications inherent in attempting to render black voices authentically, given the troubling history of these renderings."[15] Karon's comical black dialect contributes to a racist literary tradition, whether it stems from an attempt to celebrate black voices or a failure to recognize the dialect's "troubling history."

Karon's small-town Christian fiction also upholds the values of the Agrarian movement that formed at Vanderbilt University in the 1920s and 1930s and remained a source of lively debate among Southern critics during the publication of the Mitford novels. Religious faith was deeply important to Agrarians such as John Crowe Ransom, the son of a Methodist minister, and Allen Tate, a convert to Catholicism. Tate's ideal of a modern world "that included England, France, and Italy as well as the American South"[16] foreshadows the central role that all three countries play in Mitford as repositories of high culture. Even Karon's denial that Mitford is uniquely Southern finds its counterpart in the New Criticism that followed the Agrarian movement, with its doctrine that literature should transcend its region and "constitute an extension of reality rather than a reflection of it."[17] In the words of contemporary Agrarian defender Mark Royden Winchell, "they decided to construct an ideal of what the South might become from an image of what they imagined it to have been."[18] Readers who told me that they strive to recreate Mitford in their own towns suggest that Karon has successfully presented the South to them as a model for the nation.

Michael Kreyling's *Inventing Southern Literature* analyzes the methods of "keeping history at bay"[19] in Southern conservative thought, providing a

---

13. Grammer, "Plantation Fiction," 58.

14. Karon, *Out to Canaan*, 194.

15. Minnick, *Dialect and Dichotomy*, 27.

16. Bryant, *Twentieth-Century Southern Literature*, 50.

17. Bryant, *Twentieth-Century Southern Literature*, 61.

18. Winchell, *Reinventing the South*, 109.

19. Kreyling, *Inventing Southern Literature*, xii.

context for the sense of timelessness that causes many readers to think that the Mitford novels are set in the distant past. Like other writers, Karon appears to view the South as the world's "cultural salvation,"[20] while "New York is the familiar image of the place where the nefarious forces of destruction nest."[21] Kreyling reminds us that despite the move toward parody and irony in Southern literature, "a strongly conservative minority still dedicates itself to preserving the South as a cultural refuge from the excesses and wrong turns of modern life."[22] Gray describes a broader trend in which we can place Mitford: recent movies and advertisements often present the South "as a desirable other, one potential, purchasable release from the pressures of living and working in a world governed by the new technologies and international capital."[23] Karon is not the only writer who has marketed the South as an escape from the supposedly more fast-paced and heartless states, although her popularity with Southern readers proves that the region is not immune to the same stresses. John Mort's *Christian Fiction: A Guide to the Genre* places Mitford in the Nostalgia section with books that "bring the golden past into the present."[24] The books are hard to define generically, but this categorization doesn't reflect Father Tim's struggles with email and cell phones or the fact that "there is heartache to be found, even horror"[25] in the Mitford world.

Feminist discussions of Southern women's literature resonate with Karon's work, even if her conservatism makes other popular novels seem remarkably progressive, like Bobbie Ann Mason's *In Country*, Fannie Flagg's *Fried Green Tomatoes at the Whistle Stop Café*, and Rebecca Wells's *Divine Secrets of the Ya-Ya Sisterhood*. Published in the same year as the first Mitford novel, Linda Tate's *A Southern Weave of Women* argues: "Only when all southern women's voices are heard do we begin to understand the South itself."[26] While Karon has little in common with the subversive writers that Tate discusses, she shares their "points of connection—family, race, history, sense of place, and women's voice."[27] In their introduction to *Haunted Bodies: Gender and Southern Texts*, Anne Goodwyn Jones and Susan V. Donaldson acknowledge: "The stories of southern bodies have been structured in

20. Kreyling, *Inventing Southern Literature*, 23.
21. Kreyling, *Inventing Southern Literature*, 47.
22. Kreyling, *Inventing Southern Literature*, 166.
23. Gray, *Southern Aberrations*, 356.
24. Mort, *Christian Fiction*, 232.
25. Mort, *Christian Fiction*, 233.
26. Tate, *Southern Weave of Women*, 6.
27. Tate, *Southern Weave of Women*, 6.

large part by the interlocking logics of dichotomy—masculine and feminine, white and black, master and slave, planter and 'white trash,' Cavalier and Yankee—that have characterized the dominant public written discourse of the South."[28] While these dichotomies remain fairly solid in Mitford, Tim's anxious memories of his Mississippi childhood remind us that "ambiguities always threaten to reassert themselves."[29] If we read Karon carefully, even a middle-class, white, male preacher suffers from identity crisis. Her immense popularity also demands a closer look. Though her politics may not be appealing to academics, our refusal to engage them makes it impossible for us to recognize the full range of writing that millions of Americans use to imagine "the South."

"MORBID DECLINE": RUINS OF THE OLD SOUTH

There are two mansions in Mitford, both falling into ruins at the beginning of the series, which represent the ongoing decline and reinvention of the Old South: built with Victorian architecture in the 1910s and 1920s, they are renovated to serve the needs of the white middle class of the twenty-first century. The Porter Place on Main Street was once the pride of the village, but we learn in *At Home in Mitford*: "The stone benches with carved angels' heads were crumbling to dust. Many of the shutters lay in the grass where they had fallen."[30] The current owner is the elderly Miss Rose Watson, a vicious schizophrenic whose bizarre outfits deconstruct the styles of a Southern belle, for example "a green taffeta evening gown, a moth-eaten plaid velvet cummerbund, elbow-length satin gloves, a World War II officer's cape, and saddle oxfords without laces."[31] Her working-class husband Billy seems incapable of keeping up the house. True to a class system that props up the rich at the expense of the poor, the town pitches in to save the property, turning it into a museum with an apartment for its former owners. A way of life that has degenerated into "morbid decline"[32] is restored and subsidized by the working and middle classes.

The community fundraising seems democratic and patriotic; the Mitford Museum Festival in *A Light in the Window* includes barbering, manicures, hot dogs, and the mayor kissing a pig. The unveiling of Willard Porter's statue focuses on his service in World War II, with a brass band

28. Jones and Donaldson, "Haunted Bodies," 2.

29. Jones and Donaldson, "Haunted Bodies," 6.

30. Karon, *At Home in Mitford*, 35.

31. Karon, *At Home in Mitford*, 144.

32. Karon, *At Home in Mitford*, 286.

playing "God Bless America."[33] Yet the mayor persuades Percy Mosely from the Main Street Grill to donate a valuable historic jukebox to the museum,[34] revealing how the lower-middle-class business owner sacrifices his profit to help people who never helped him. When Percy retires, the diner that served Mitford for generations will be replaced with a shoe store and its legacy will disappear except for one artifact that embellishes the Porter Place, where Rose and Billy continue to live in the back rooms, surrounded by stacks of old newspapers that symbolize the weight of forgotten history.

Miss Sadie Baxter's mansion Fernbank has a more rural setting, located among apple orchards on the edge of town, and more clearly represents nostalgia for an era when devoted black servants ministered to their white employers. In *At Home in Mitford*, the elderly, unmarried Sadie tells Father Tim a long story of her childhood, and her descriptions of another local mansion seem like a modern version of plantation fiction: "Oh, we all loved Boxwood! It had so many servants hurrying about, and they all seemed so happy in their work. Miss Lureen was good to her people. Why, when her Packard wore out, do you know who she gave it to? Her chauffeur!"[35] The narrative does not question Sadie's assertion: "Life was better in those days, Father, it really was."[36] Even when falling apart, Fernbank serves the town as a symbol of luxury and retreat from the modern world. *A Light in the Window* shows how even the dark side of the Southern past can be reimagined as an ideal when Sadie finds her illegitimate sister's birth certificate: "It had been a family of secrets, a life of secrets."[37] Yet this does not destroy the notion that life "was better in those days," as Sadie discovers that fellow churchgoer Olivia Davenport is her grand-niece and spends a fortune to restore the ballroom for Olivia's wedding reception. This event seems as democratic as the Museum Festival, with townspeople from all walks of life entering a space that had always been inaccessible: "Quite a few had never been on the lawn at Fernbank and had only seen the rooftop over the trees."[38] Yet the space does not belong to them, and their awe at the ballroom's beauty reinforces the class structure that normalizes money being spent on a painted ceiling while people in Mitford live in poverty or labor in the canning plant in Wesley.

33. Karon, *Light in the Window*, 371.

34. Karon, *Light in the Window*, 335.

35. Karon, *At Home in Mitford*, 305.

36. Karon, *At Home in Mitford*, 307.

37. Karon, *Light in the Window*, 44.

38. Karon, *Light in the Window*, 360.

A Donna Kae Nelson illustration in *These High, Green Hills* evokes a utopian world in which townspeople lionize Miss Sadie due to her elite status rather than any personal relationship. The drawing appears at the head of the chapter "And Many More" in the context of Sadie's ninetieth birthday party at the church.[39]

Children of several races celebrate Mitford's richest white citizen. Illustrations by Donna Kae Nelson; from THESE HIGH, GREEN HILLS by Jan Karon, copyright © 1996 by Jan Karon. Used by permission of Viking Books, an imprint of Penguin Publishing Group, a division of Penguin Random House LLC. All rights reserved.

Five suspiciously multicultural children hold a banner saying "Happy Birthday Miss Sadie": three appear to be white and blond, one is marked as Asian by dark hair and slanted eyes, and one is marked as African American by dark hair, full lips, and a backwards baseball cap. Even in a black-and-white drawing, Nelson uses widely circulating racial markers to insert Asian and black families into the Mitford community—despite their absence in the narrative—for the purpose of celebrating a philanthropic but reclusive representative of old money.

Like the Porter Place, Fernbank ends up in public hands when Sadie leaves it to the church after her death. When the Miami Development Group offers to convert it into a spa, Tim tries to convince himself to do the practical thing: "Surely he was trying to hold on to what was vanished and

39. Karon, *These High, Green Hills*, 225.

gone, to another way of life that had been vibrantly preserved in Miss Sadie's engrossing stories."[40] But the narrative affirms Tim's nostalgia when he sells the property to Andrew Gregory, who makes it into an expensive Italian restaurant. Tim acknowledges that Sadie would not like Lucera's yuppie atmosphere, but he accepts it as a reasonable substitute for the Old South that she remembered—perhaps because it is inaccessible to most of the town. People continue to call the restaurant "Miss Sadie's,"[41] and the map in each novel continues to label the house as Fernbank.

A third crumbling Southern mansion reinforces the image of the Old South as "vanished and gone," with the power to generate nostalgia despite elements of the bizarre and grotesque. When Tim visits Whitecap Island on the North Carolina coast in A New Song, he ventures into the overgrown yard of a mansion called Nouvelle Chanson. The sole inhabitant is a nasty, reclusive cripple, ironically named Morris Love. Just as Miss Rose's schizophrenia reflects the Old South's mixed motives and divided loyalties, his Tourette's syndrome reflects its unpredictable and erratic actions. Yet Morris will be redeemed by becoming the organist at the local Episcopal church, and even his house is not entirely ruined:

> There was definitely a musty smell, but everything looked
> clean and orderly. Ornately carved armchairs stood on either
> side of a heavy mirror in which he was startled to see himself.
> On the floor, a pattern of black and white tiles, and to the right,
> a curving stairwell and a vast, lighted oil painting on the high
> wall. The painting was of rolling countryside, somewhere in
> Europe, perhaps, with a church spire and a procession of people
> in a lane.[42]

Tim is startled to see his reflection, perhaps recognizing that he has been searching for his own Southern identity in these old houses all along. The painting of "a church spire and a procession of people in a lane" mirrors the Penguin cover illustration of a white church with a steeple and a procession moving toward the door. By reading A New Song, Karon implies that we can inhabit the carefully guarded space of Southern wealth represented by Nouvelle Chanson. Since Miss Rose, Miss Sadie, and Morris Love are all childless, their wealth conveniently leaves the old aristocracy and becomes available for middle-class refashioning and consumption.

This familiar plotline moves to the Deep South in Home to Holly Springs, when Tim returns to a childhood home evocatively named "Whitefield" and

40. Karon, Out to Canaan, 94.

41. Karon, Shepherds Abiding, 220.

42. Karon, New Song, 287.

finds it being restored by its white owner's brother and his black helper, Ray Edwards, who lives over the garage. Whitefield was a slave plantation, and the novel takes for granted that black history disappears while white history is renovated. The black servant Peggy's cottage is ruined: "The tin-sheathed roof had collapsed, cedars grew through the rotting floor of the kitchen, and honeysuckle was taking care of the rest."[43] The slave cabins have caved in, their brick salvaged for the new steps and path. Ray describes going back to Memphis and finding his childhood home gone, "Wit' th' wind,"[44] ironically using a film about plantation owners to describe his loss. He calls Tim "a lucky man" to find his homeplace still standing,[45] but racial and economic realities seem more relevant than luck. Whitefield's twelve-foot ceilings and Doric columns are restored by a working-class white and black man who cook for Tim in the nurturing tradition of slaves and servants. Karon's investment in restoring the mansions of privileged white families contradicts her claim that Mitford can be found in Manhattan or California. The books become vehicles for appreciating a Southern past that might appear repellent on the surface but which always turns out to be valuable enough to preserve.

"IT AIN'T DOLLYWOOD": POOR WHITE CHARACTERS AND SPACES

Mitford contains an elaborate class hierarchy with detailed examples on every level: the impoverished inhabitants of the Creek; shiftless poor whites like Clyde Barlowe; the respectable working classes like Tim's housekeeper Puny Bradshaw Guthrie; the lower-middle classes like Percy Mosely and Fancy Skinner, who speak in dialect but own small businesses; middle-class professionals with college degrees like Tim and Cynthia Kavanagh; upper-middle-class professionals like Dr. Harper and Andrew Gregory; and the upper classes like Edith Mallory and Sadie Baxter, who make charitable donations out of their millions. With Father Tim as the primary point-of-view character, the series is biased toward the desires of the middle class. Karon often approaches poor whites with humor or horror, but she gives the most attention to foster children Dooley Barlowe and Lace Turner as they transform into upwardly mobile professionals who continue the cycle by adopting a poor white child of their own.

43. Karon, *Home to Holly Springs*, 70.
44. Karon, *Home to Holly Springs*, 96.
45. Karon, *Home to Holly Springs*, 96.

Karon frequently undercuts the more educated characters' sentimental language with humor about working-class Southern pride. In *A New Song*, Coot Hendrick, the hillbilly descendent of the town founder, claims that his great-great-granpaw shot and buried five Yankee runaways during the Civil War.[46] Even before they find the graves, people debate whether this should be a source of local pride. A Wesley College professor argues for preserving the site "so that residents and visitors can understand and enjoy our mountain frontier heritage."[47] Beulah Mae Hendrick embellishes this heritage by singing a folk song to the Town Council:

> Shot five Yankees
> a-runnin' from th' war
> Caught 'em in a cornfield
> Sleepin' by a f'ar
> Now they'll not run no more, oh
> They'll not run no more![48]

When archaeologists find the graves, the town plans a historical site with a marker and walking trail.[49] The Kavanaghs' servants at Meadowgate—Pansy, Iris, Lily, Rose, Arbutus, Delphinium, Violet, and Daisy Flower—provide similar comic relief when Tim sees a Confederate flag waving from Del's antenna.[50] Karon's reliance on poor white characters to express Confederate pride disassociates her from a white supremacist ideology while rendering it harmless.

References to food in *At Home in Mitford* associate the poorer characters with uniquely Southern tastes. Russell Jacks likes to "cook me a mess of greens and fry out some side meat,"[51] church members bring Homeless Hobbes ham biscuits, collards, grits, and sausage dressing,[52] and Coot dumps peanuts in his Coke.[53] Tim and Cynthia consume bouillabaisse and cabernet, their cosmopolitan tastes reinforcing their superiority to the rednecks. Yet *Jan Karon's Mitford Cookbook & Kitchen Reader* presents wealthy and middle-class white women as the authentic regional cooks. Karon describes editor Martha McIntosh's Southern credentials, "not the least of which is that she was born in Mississippi, just down the road from Father Tim, and is

46. Karon, *New Song*, 23.

47. Karon, *New Song*, 199.

48. Karon, *New Song*, 255.

49. Karon, *In This Mountain*, 378–79.

50. Karon, *Light from Heaven*, 279.

51. Karon, *At Home in Mitford*, 108.

52. Karon, *At Home in Mitford*, 157.

53. Karon, *At Home in Mitford*, 205.

wise in the ways of all the things he loves. A classic Southern ambrosia? She grew up on it. A totally scrumptious chicken pie? She learned this secret at her grandmother's knee."[54] The recipes include Southern dishes (sweet tea, cornbread, ham biscuits, livermush, grits, spoon bread, fried chicken, sweet potato pie, fried okra) and dishes that would be served anywhere in America (apple pie, pork roast, green beans, scalloped potatoes). However, the recipe credits show that most contributors are from the South: Alabama, Georgia, Mississippi, North Carolina, South Carolina, Tennessee, and Virginia.

This listing of states invokes a kinship of Southerners throughout the region, but the novels' symbolic geography privileges middle-class Mitford over poor areas of town and many other Southern states. Every book contains a detailed map of the town in which the top right corner is covered by the word "Mitford." Readers know this to be the location of the Creek, an impoverished community associated with crime. When drug dealers from the Creek steal Tim's dog in *At Home in Mitford*, police officers call them "low-down snakes"[55] and "scumheads."[56] Tim does not see the Creek for himself until the third novel, *These High, Green Hills*, from the distance of a private airplane: "Then he saw the open sore on the breast of the creek bank—ramshackle, unpainted houses, tin-roofed sheds, houses that had burned and stood in their rubble, rusted trailers and vehicles abandoned in the weeds or sitting on blocks."[57] Tim converts the poverty to a natural metaphor, an open sore on a breast, to remove himself from responsibility. When his pilot points out: "It ain't Dollywood!"[58] he invokes the country music attraction as the epitome of high class. Yet the reader senses that both Dollywood and the Creek appear at the bottom of Tim's hierarchy of Southern spaces.

Homeless Hobbes lives in idealized poverty on the edge of the Creek and becomes the sole recipient of the town's nominal charity. As Caryn D. Riswold notes, "The town seems to have its limits, both in the almost obligatory Thanksgiving food delivery to the token homeless person, and in its ignorance of others worse off than him beyond its immediate border."[59] These "town limits" are more firmly established than Riswold acknowledges, since Hobbes is not really homeless; he left an advertising career to return to his Southern roots, just like Karon herself. "The split between inside and

---

54. Karon, *Jan Karon's Mitford Cookbook*, xi.

55. Karon, *At Home in Mitford*, 358.

56. Karon, *At Home in Mitford*, 376.

57. Karon, *These High, Green Hills*, 112.

58. Karon, *These High, Green Hills*, 112.

59. Riswold, "Four Fictions," 141.

outside of Mitford is clearly distinguishable, with one being highly preferred over the other. This fails to live out the general ideal of Christian engagement with the world—the church as a prophetic presence."[60] Despite some ministry attempts by Tim and other pastors, the Creek is finally converted into a shopping center and erased from the Mitford landscape, just as it has always been erased from the map.

Western Appalachia does not fare any better. In *Out to Canaan,* the *Mitford Muse* newspaper lists the recipients of funds from a church rummage sale with characteristically poor spelling as "Bosnia, Croatia, Ruwanda" and "Harlan County, Kentucky,"[61] equating the needs of entire nations with the imagined need of a single Kentucky county. Tennessee always seems to be associated with lowbrow comedy or terrifying poverty. In *A New Song,* Joe Ivey confesses that he left Memphis because he saw Elvis mowing his yard at Graceland,[62] and a diner owner in Whitecap responds viscerally to her husband's proposal that they retire there: "Tennessee! The very thought gave her the shivers. All those log cabins, all those grizzlies stumbling around in the dark, plus moonshine out the kazoo."[63] When Tim and Cynthia plan to do missions work in Tennessee, Tim has a nightmare that links his fear of this environment to his buried Mississippi childhood: "He sat in a straight-back chair in a small, empty room with a dirt floor. It was the same cool, hard-packed floor of his grandmother's potato cellar."[64] The room fills with silent children who "looked at him, searching for something he had no ability to name or to deliver."[65] Soon after, he goes into a diabetic coma that nearly kills him, closing off any possibility of missions. Clearly, Tennessee is divided from Mitford by more than a state line. This portrait of the area as nightmarish and potentially fatal to visitors contradicts Karon's claim that there "are Mitfords everywhere" and implies that Mitford is an elite space surrounded by the horrors of most Southern life.

Appalachian poverty receives better coverage in *Light from Heaven,* when Tim revives an old church thirty minutes from Mitford. Like Catherine Marshall in *Christy,* Karon paints a nuanced portrait of the rural area's poor whites. Just as Tim relied on Homeless Hobbes as cultural liaison to the largely inaccessible Creek, he relies on missionary Agnes Merton as his

---

60. Riswold, "Four Fictions," 141.

61. Karon, *Out to Canaan,* 300.

62. Karon, *New Song,* 12–13.

63. Karon, *New Song,* 383.

64. Karon, *In This Mountain,* 80.

65. Karon, *In This Mountain,* 80–81.

guide to "the poorest county in the state."[66] Some residents are humorous, like Jubal Adderholt, a toothless old man who eats squirrel brains and keeps a pet groundhog in his shirt. Some are horrifying, like the mentally ill Fred Lynch, who shoots at imaginary rabbits in a surreal scene that sat in Tim's stomach "like bile."[67] Many are humble, honest, and admirable: talented woodcarver Clarence Merton, selfless caregiver Granny Meaders, skilled mason Lloyd Goodnight, mechanic Robert Prichard, and seventeen-year-old Donny Luster, who works numerous jobs to support his sister. This community that is largely ignored by the outside world takes care of its own and meets enormous obstacles with dignity.

The most multifaceted poor white characters are Dooley and Lace, whose story extends over fourteen novels and twenty years of real time as they progress from impoverished waifs to the upper-middle-class Dr. and Mrs. Kavanagh. Yet this long narrative reinforces the myth that higher classes always know what is best for the poor and can make choices on their behalf for the greater good. Laura Briggs argues in *Somebody's Children* that "simple, heroic narratives of rescued orphans" mask the power imbalance between poor birth parents and wealthier adoptive parents: "Adoption may sometimes be the best outcome in a bad situation, but it is always layered with pain, coercion, and lack of access to necessary resources, with relatives (usually single mothers) who are vulnerable."[68] Karon's adoption narratives are not always simple or heroic, but she never depicts poor whites as loving parents who need a better way to earn a living; their moral unfitness demands that children are removed from their care. Dooley appears in *At Home in Mitford* as the grandson of Russell Jacks, the Lord's Chapel sexton, who has taken over for the boy's absent father and alcoholic mother. When Father Tim sees the "barefoot, freckle-faced, red-haired boy in dirty overalls," he quickly transforms him into a character from Southern fiction: "I declare, thought the rector. Tom Sawyer!"[69] When Russell becomes too ill to care for him, Tim informally adopts him and struggles to teach him middle-class behavior while Dooley clings to his identity. Throughout this heartbreaking battle, the narrative always unfolds in a way that justifies the intervention.

As the last representative of Mitford's elite, Miss Sadie insists on sending Dooley to boarding school in *A Light in the Window*, and Russell and Dooley submit with resignation. Russell is fixing an alarm clock when Tim

---

66. Karon, *Light from Heaven*, 90.
67. Karon, *Light from Heaven*, 314.
68. Briggs, *Somebody's Children*, 4.
69. Karon, *At Home in Mitford*, 81.

proposes the idea: "Russell studied two small clock springs in the palm of his hand, silent."[70] The broken clock poignantly symbolizes the little time Russell has left with his grandson, which he sacrifices because he cannot care for the boy. When Dooley hears the news, he simply "stared at the book in his lap."[71] Despite Dooley's resistance, he ends up thriving in his Virginia school and spends the summers at Meadowgate, the farm outside Mitford owned by veterinarian Doc Owen. Both settings remove him from the narrative for most of his teens, so his painfully slow ascent to a higher social class takes place largely offstage.

Father Tim becomes the benefactor of the entire Barlowe family, reinforcing the idea that poor whites need middle-class guidance to lead functional lives. When Pauline Barlowe turns up in Mitford with severe burns from a fire at the Creek, she allows Tim to keep Dooley and begs him to find the other children whom she has abandoned. Over several novels, Tim pulls them out of horrifying poor white spaces—a trailer in the Creek, a garbage-strewn house in Florida, a trailer near Holding—and delivers them to the working-class family formed by Pauline and her new husband, Buck Leeper, a construction superintendent. The children's father, Clyde, is one of Mitford's few irredeemable characters; Tim runs him off the Meadowgate property with threats in *Light from Heaven*, and he dies in *To Be Where You Are* without fanfare and without mourning. Nobody seriously challenges Tim's right to make decisions about and for these children. The end justifies the means: Dooley becomes a veterinarian with a thriving clinic at Meadowgate, and his siblings slowly overcome their emotional trauma to become productive citizens.

Lace follows a parallel trajectory as a girl from the Creek who crosses paths with Father Tim and finds a home with the wealthy Doc and Olivia Harper. In *These High, Green Hills*, Tim finds her stealing ferns from Fernbank, trespassing on elite space: "The ways and means of making a living in these mountains had never been easy, he knew that, but let an incident like this go by, and Fernbank could be stripped of the very resource that inspired its name."[72] Whereas he placed Dooley into a category that he could understand ("Tom Sawyer!"), he has a hard time categorizing Lace. He first thinks that she is a boy, then compares her to a wild rabbit, and when she later comes to his house, "she had been beaten so brutally that her face made little sense to him."[73] Her parents are quickly disqualified as caregivers: her

70. Karon, *Light in the Window*, 255.
71. Karon, *Light in the Window*, 314.
72. Karon, *These High, Green Hills*, 119.
73. Karon, *These High, Green Hills*, 178.

mother is bedridden and later dies, and her father Cate is an abusive drunk, an irredeemable character, just as the Creek is an irredeemable community. Although Lace is furious when she is removed from her home—"It took two social workers to stop her and hold her"[74]—Karon presents this as the only option for a good future. Sadie's grand-niece adopts Lace and assimilates her into the family from which she once stole ferns.

The story gains complexity when Dooley and Lace forge a relationship despite their emotional and physical scars. Their rescue from poverty remains largely unquestioned, but Karon does not shy away from the painful aspects of upward mobility. Lace attends a school called "Mrs. Hemingway's,"[75] a foreboding name given that Ernest Hemingway divorced three wives and the fourth found his body after his suicide, proving that wealth does not bring happiness. In *A Common Life*, a flashback to Tim and Cynthia's wedding years earlier, Karon leaves Tim's point of view to explore other characters, including a young Dooley who remembers stealing food to feed his siblings and being threatened by the store manager. The poignant segment ends with a glimpse into his secret life when he is alone with the dog: "Barnabas would never tell anyone that he was crying and couldn't stop."[76] Lace drives a BMW during *In This Mountain*, but her "fear and anger are an old axe blade, buried deep."[77] When Miss Sadie leaves Dooley over a million dollars, Tim procrastinates for six novels before telling him about his inheritance, reluctant to give full independence to his adopted son. In *Light from Heaven*, both Sadie's ghost and Louella chastise Tim for his selfishness, and Dooley finally gains the power to make his own financial decisions at the end of the original series.

When Karon returned to the Mitford books, she devoted much attention to Dooley and Lace's continuing journey. In *Come Rain or Come Shine*, Lace believes that she cannot have children due to her father's abuse, so the couple fosters a four-year-old boy. We first meet him in a segment limited to his perspective, since later novels often depart from Tim's point of view: "Jack Tyler was wearing a dark blue suit too large for his frame, with a dingy dress shirt and beat-up gym shoes. He carried his sole possessions in a black plastic bag with a tie—it appeared pretty empty—and held on tight to a stuffed kangaroo."[78] He feels nauseous as he drives into Meadowgate with a social worker, remembering his grandmother's harsh words and fearing the

---

74. Karon, *These High, Green Hills*, 293.

75. Karon, *New Song*, 58.

76. Karon, *Common Life*, 87.

77. Karon, *In This Mountain*, 240.

78. Karon, *Come Rain or Come Shine*, 149.

barking dogs. He thinks of Dooley and Lace as "the dad" and "the mom" and stiffens his body to avoid mistakes. This is a big improvement from the first novel in which Dooley appears only through Tim's eyes, but not everything has changed. In Mitford—as in the rest of America—the adoption plot tends to unfold in ways most convenient to the middle class. Jack Tyler's parents are long gone, and his grandmother does not love him, so there is little struggle between biological and adoptive parents. Dooley and Lace's story inspires readers to have compassion for impoverished children and to wonder how many others from the Creek could have gone to college, but Karon never dwells on the injustice of the American class system or the serious hardships of the working poor.

"SLAVERY DONE BEEN OVER ALL THESE YEARS": AFRICAN AMERICANS IN THE MITFORD WORLD

In the same year that Karon published *At Home in Mitford*, Patricia A. Turner published *Ceramic Uncles & Celluloid Mammies*, describing a resurgence of popular interest in the smiling, overweight black mammy who faithfully serves a white family. Turner asks: "What does the present fascination with mammy images reveal about contemporary society? What price has been exacted from the real black women who have been forced to make their way in a culture that pays homage to a distorted icon?"[79] The only African American in Mitford, Louella Baxter Marshall, clearly embodies the mammy stereotype, with her dark skin, buxom figure, broad dialect, fabulous cooking, and passionate devotion to her mistress. She was born to a servant at Fernbank and has lived and worked there for much of her life, apparently without pay. In *At Home in Mitford*, Louella returns to Fernbank after living with her grandson in Georgia. Tim's first response to her skin color reveals his fantasy that she will nurture the white church community: "It was inspiring to see Louella's broad, mahogany face smiling at him these days from the gospel side. Her presence brought something nourishing to the spirit of the congregation, like raisins added to bread."[80] Louella quickly falls back into domestic servitude, reinforcing Monteith's claim in *Advancing Sisterhood?* that "black women characters have not yet been liberated from the kitchens of white women in contemporary fiction."[81] When Tim visits Sadie, Louella rings a bell to say that lunch is ready and refuses to join

---

79. Patricia A. Turner, *Ceramic Uncles & Celluloid Mammies*, 43.

80. Karon, *At Home in Mitford*, 214.

81. Monteith, *Advancing Sisterhood?*, 102–3.

them: "I'm eatin' right here in this kitchen."[82] At different times, Louella sleeps in the sewing room and on the sofa at the foot of Sadie's bed.

Numerous symbolic episodes reinforce Louella's role in the community. In *A Light in the Window*, Sadie and Olivia are trying on the late Mrs. Baxter's hats, classic Southern belle styles with wide brims and organdy sashes. They force Louella to join them, not understanding her resistance to this act of reverse minstrelsy, in which she must dress up in her white employer's clothes just as Sadie used to dress her up as a baby. In a rare moment of protest, Louella refuses to play along: "Slavery done been over all these years . . . an' some folks act like it still goin' on."[83] Yet a classic mammy stereotype puts her back in her place. The men tell her that she looks terrific in the hat, and she breaks "into one of her huge smiles."[84] A Hal Just illustration in *Out to Canaan* depicts Louella at the nursing home where she moves after Sadie's death.[85] She sits in the foreground, dwarfing Tim who sits like a child on a footstool in the background; although the text describes her as dressed "to the nines,"[86] the drawing reflects the mammy's full lips, obese body, and plain dress. By *Light from Heaven*, Louella spends her days watching soap operas, reminding Tim that "I never liked to fool with money"[87] to explain why she did not inherit Sadie's millions.

In *A New Song*, Karon introduces another black domestic servant who devoted her life to her mother's white employers—this time with the unsubtle name of Mamie. In superficial ways, Morris Love's housekeeper defies the buxom, overweight, unintelligent mammy stereotype. Tim observes that she is slender, graceful, elegant, and genteel, with a tidy house and a husband, but as soon as he learns her identity, the stereotypes flood in: "You're Mamie,' he said, noting her carefully braided hair and the printed scarf tied round like a headband."[88] Tim feels so drawn to this woman that he haunts the area around her house "as if he'd found someone who'd been lost to him for many years."[89] Mamie admits that she did not intend to devote her life to servitude, but she assures Tim that she has no regrets: "Noah and I raised a fine son. He's a doctor in Philadelphia."[90] Like Louella, Mamie chooses to

82. Karon, *At Home in Mitford*, 310.

83. Karon, *Light in the Window*, 56.

84. Karon, *Light in the Window*, 56.

85. Karon, *Out to Canaan*, 162.

86. Karon, *Out to Canaan*, 164.

87. Karon, *Light from Heaven*, 129.

88. Karon, *New Song*, 360.

89. Karon, *New Song*, 361.

90. Karon, *New Song*, 364.

live near her white employer in an all-white town rather than with her own relative. When Tim asks if she was born on the island, she responds: "My people washed up on shore like timbers from the old ships. We think our wreck happened sometime around 1860."[91] This story of a shipwreck right before the Civil War erases the entire history of slavery, as if black people "washed up on shore" just in time to be liberated by the North. Although Mamie is slender, married, and articulate, she does not conflict with Karon's other portraits of black women.

We finally discover why Tim has such a powerful reaction to Mamie when we learn about his own mammy in a flashback in *Shepherds Abiding*. As with Louella, Peggy's dialect signals her race before an explicit reference to her skin color. Her first words are rendered in eye dialect: "Miz Kavanagh, is it all right t' give Timothy some of this candy fruit?"[92] Her skin is then compared to food, "exactly the color of gingerbread."[93] Ironically, Peggy uses her dialectical speech to teach Tim the correct pronunciation of *bûche de Noël*, raising the question of how she can pronounce perfect French but says "yo" instead of "your." In later flashbacks, we glimpse the Kavanaghs' "big white house in the stand of oaks," the cottage where Peggy feeds him cornbread and sweet potato,[94] and "her head wrapped in a red kerchief" as she corrects his grammar, although she continues to speak in dialect.[95] In *Light from Heaven*, Tim reveals that Peggy vanished when he was ten: "It occurred to him as he sat here, more than a half century later, that he'd looked for Peggy for most of his life."[96] This explains his childlike adoration of Louella and Mamie and his fondness for his working-class white maids. Tim feels a familial affection for both black and white domestic workers, but Karon rarely depicts them in their own homes.

In *Clinging to Mammy*, Micki McElya explains the ongoing appeal of this cultural icon: "The myth of the faithful slave lingers because so many white Americans have wished to live in a world in which African Americans are not angry over past and present injustices, a world in which white people were and are not complicit, in which the injustices themselves . . . seem not to exist at all."[97] This myth seems pervasive among the readers that I surveyed, who made no references to race or racism when asked open-ended

---

91. Karon, *New Song*, 365.

92. Karon, *Shepherds Abiding*, 88.

93. Karon, *Shepherds Abiding*, 90.

94. Karon, *Shepherds Abiding*, 165–66.

95. Karon, *Shepherds Abiding*, 246.

96. Karon, *Light from Heaven*, 145.

97. McElya, *Clinging to Mammy*, 3.

questions like: "Have you ever disagreed with or been offended by anything in the books?" and "Do you think that the Mitford books are realistic?" In a follow-up interview in which I brought up the issue directly, one liberal, white New England reader explained how she overcame her initial annoyance that Louella has to wait on Sadie just because she is black: "I think the reader is transferred to a magical 'other' place, almost like reading about a foreign culture. In a foreign culture, we have been schooled not to judge or feel superior. It makes the black question seem to be one outside our realm, not triggering our call to action about black stereotypes and inequalities of all kinds." If Mitford can be found "everywhere," it also turns out to be nowhere, a "magical 'other' place" where racism becomes invisible.

To her credit, Karon rejected the mammy stereotype when she ended the initial series. My Penguin paperback calls *Light from Heaven* the "Final Novel in the Beloved Mitford Series," and my Viking hardcover calls *Home to Holly Springs* the "First of the Father Tim Novels." With a new appearance and publishing imprint, this book offers a jarring contrast to Karon's previous portrayals of the South. It is no surprise that one reader told the Mitford Bulletin Board that she threw the book in the trash without finishing, since it refuses to offer the comfortable pleasures that drew readers to Mitford. Karon's dedication to the novel explains how she originally chose Tim's hometown based on its name on a map. *Home to Holly Springs* compelled her to "visit this gem of the Deep South"[98] and face the unmistakable presence of black people. As Tim drives into town, he passes a strip mall where "two black men in shirts and ties washed a funeral home hearse,"[99] foreshadowing the stories that he will hear connecting black men to danger and death. Memories of racial strife come flooding back: the burning of Rust College, "th' hope of th' coloreds,"[100] his mother forbidding him to say "nigger,"[101] his grandfather shooting a black man.[102] Clearly, we're not in Mitford anymore. When Tim questions his friend's nostalgia for their childhood—"But were they really the good old days, do you think?"[103]—he questions his cherished assumptions about the past.

On this journey, Tim learns some surprising things that transform the Peggy of Mitford into the more well-rounded character Peggy Lambert Winchester. In one graphic flashback, Tim remembers sitting in a tree and

---

98. Karon, *Home to Holly Springs*, ix.

99. Karon, *Home to Holly Springs*, 13.

100. Karon, *Home to Holly Springs*, 8.

101. Karon, *Home to Holly Springs*, 76.

102. Karon, *Home to Holly Springs*, 110.

103. Karon, *Home to Holly Springs*, 115.

seeing two white men chasing Peggy: "And then he saw them in the clearing—two men, one fat and one scrawny, and a dark woman racing ahead of them as if everything under heaven depended on it, the screams not stopping."[104] When the men throw her onto the ground and begin to rape her, Tim shoots at them, and they run off: "Peggy lay in the stubbled field naked and weeping, he had no idea what to do about Peggy being naked, he was burning with shame and fear, his heart pounding in his throat."[105] This coming-of-age experience opens Tim's eyes to white male violence against women of color, even while he enjoys the role of savior. Halfway through the novel, Tim reunites with the now elderly Peggy and sits on a stool at her feet, just like he does with Louella. Yet while Louella speaks sparingly and often humorously, Peggy tells her story for two chapters: growing up in a turpentine camp, escaping from a brothel, having an affair with Tim's father, and getting pregnant with his half-brother Henry Winchester. Tim is shocked: "He felt as if he'd been injected with a paralyzing drug; he could not move his mouth nor avert his gaze from hers."[106] Peggy forces him to confront his family's complicity in racism alongside his responsibility to a brother who is dying of leukemia and needs him to donate stem cells.

When Peggy shows Tim the scars hidden beneath the mammy's typical head covering, Karon demonstrates her willingness to explore themes "of flesh that has been ruptured or riven by violence, of fractured, excessive bodies telling us something that diverse southern cultures don't want us to say."[107] Two long scars form a perfect cross: "'This longest one'—she ran her forefinger over it—'is where th' woods rider got me for bringin' Daddy a cup of water. An' this one's where th' Devil himself got me th' time you saved my life.'"[108] Tim reacts selfishly, planning to buy off Henry with stem cells and keep him a secret: "If he gave Henry what Henry needed, well, then, they were done, it was over."[109] It would be easy to reprise his role as white savior and forget everything he learned. As he gets to know his soft-spoken brother, who reads Latin and quotes Paul Laurence Dunbar and Langston Hughes, Tim learns that he must explore their relationship further. The cover of Home to Holly Springs conflates Tim's mother figures by showing the back of a slender caregiver in nylon stockings who could be either Peggy Lambert Winchester or Madelaine Howard Kavanagh, but the novel makes

104. Karon, Home to Holly Springs, 142.
105. Karon, Home to Holly Springs, 145.
106. Karon, Home to Holly Springs, 239.
107. Yaeger, Dirt and Desire, xiii.
108. Karon, Home to Holly Springs, 253.
109. Karon, Home to Holly Springs, 264.

it clear that both women endured more than Tim realized, and Peggy is the one who survived.

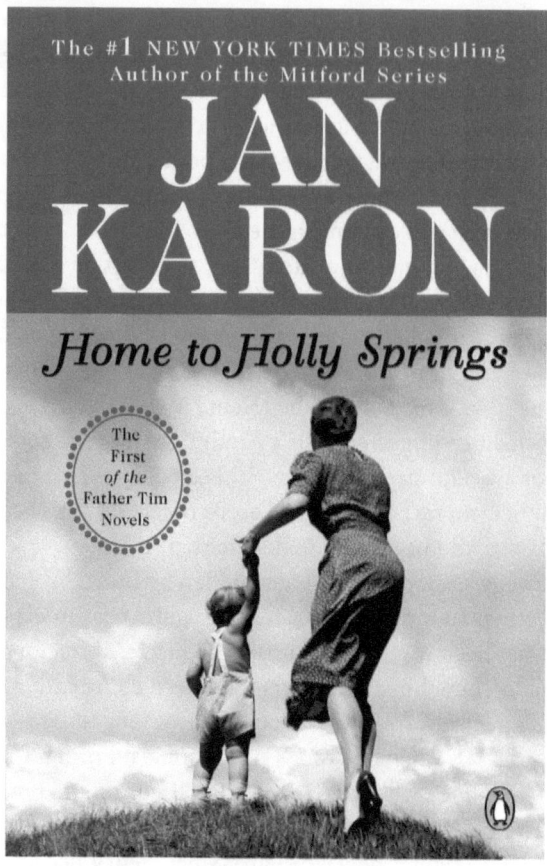

The cover of *Home to Holly Springs* reflects the book's subtlety about racial identity, showing the back of a woman who could be either Tim's white mother or black servant.

Even though the racist incidents were largely confined to Father Tim's childhood, many readers rejected this novel because it was too shocking to associate with a Mitford character. Karon's next novel *In the Company of Others* moved to Ireland, making good on previous hints that Tim and Cynthia would someday visit the land of his ancestors and moving as far as possible from the racial politics of the American South. This would have been an easy place for Karon to bury her critique of racism and never raise it again, but the echoes of Holly Springs continue to sound. Tim and Cynthia read the 1860s journal of their innkeeper's ancestor who condemns "the horrific tyranny of slavery" and describes an uncle who freed his slaves.[110] Karon follows this entry with Tim's interest in the Mass Rock on the property, where Catholics worshipped in times of persecution, subtly connecting the sufferings of African Americans and Irish Catholics.[111]

Father Tim continues to have childhood flashbacks: Peggy corrects his English "in the voice that never sounded like Peggy,"[112] an example of her strategic code-switching between standard English and black dialect. He remembers feeling the ghostly presence of slaves at Whitefield, smelling their fires and hearing their laughter.[113] He dreams about his brother:

> And the dream of Henry, of looking into a bathroom mirror while shaving and seeing Henry's face. It was his own reflection, he knew, yet it was Henry's face in dark contrast to the white shaving foam. So he, Timothy, was actually a black man? How had he kept this knowledge from himself these many years? What did it mean and how was he to go forward? Was he both Henry and himself in one, or had he become Henry altogether? He felt the fear rising in him, leaned closer to the mirror, looked into his brother's eyes. Why had no one mentioned this, made him see it? In the dream, something broke in him and he wept, and then the smell of coffee, and the notion that Peggy must be perking it on the stove.[114]

This paragraph appears between two unconnected ones: he walks downstairs, and he notices that the innkeeper looks worried. The initial fragment leaves open the connection between his exploration of Irish heritage and his attempts to accept his biracial brother. His comforting metaphor of domestic servants being "like family" is strained to the breaking point by the recognition that there is no clear genetic border where one family ends and another begins.

When Karon returned to Mitford with *Somewhere Safe with Somebody Good*, and the previous two novels were relabeled as Mitford Novels 10–11,

110. Karon, *In the Company of Others*, 134.

111. This novel provides a welcome note of ecumenism in a series that denies the presence of Catholics and suggests that they are not true believers. Unlike many real Southern towns, Mitford has no Catholic church, and the only significant Catholic character is the French Hélène Pringle, who has no personal relationship with Jesus until she prays a Protestant sinner's prayer. The Irish novel ends with a family reconciliation centered on the sacrament of confession and presided over by a likeable Catholic priest (*In the Company of Others*, 429–34).

112. Karon, *In the Company of Others*, 144.

113. Karon, *In the Company of Others*, 282.

114. Karon, *In the Company of Others*, 323.

she used two tactics to explore Southern racism without alienating read-ers. First, she sublimates the story of Father Tim and his brother into two plots about white characters: Father Henry Talbot attempts suicide, echoing Henry Winchester's name and near-death experience,[115] while Irene Mc-Graw discovers that she has a twin sister and the *Mitford Muse* prints an article about their reunion.[116] This is an ironic parallel to Karon's second tactic, a subplot in which Tim writes and calls Henry but is afraid to tell anyone about him. Henry's leukemia keeps him in Mississippi, as physically weak and nonthreatening as Louella in her nursing home. Karon maintains his safe distance from Mitford while pointing to the racism that might make him unwelcome there, just as he was unwelcome to many readers of *Home to Holly Springs*.

The scene in which Tim confesses his secret to Louella reveals Karon's increasing nuance in portraying racial dynamics. After he arrives at the nursing home and finds Louella asleep, the point of view shifts to Louella planning to be cremated to use less of Sadie's money. While this self-denial is a classic mammy attribute, Louella wants some of her ashes to be scattered "in th' ol' part of th' buryin' ground where some of my people are at,"[117] a fleeting reference to Mitford's former black community. The point of view switches back to Tim and the "primordial consolation" that he feels with Louella based on his memories of Peggy, but as he "had a moment of yearn-ing for those days,"[118] Louella wakes up and tells him that she was dreaming about her childhood when people called her "that bad word we don' use no more."[119] Tim blurts out that he has a brother from his father and the woman who helped raise him. "Black like me," Louella clarifies, "Happen all th' time."[120] Her complete lack of surprise refashions Tim's shocking secret into a mundane racist occurrence. Even so, he cannot bring himself to tell his white friends.

Father Tim never has the courage to invite Henry to Mitford, so Henry finally appears in *Come Rain or Come Shine* on his own initiative, announc-ing that he's attending a convention nearby on the weekend of Dooley's wedding and would like to visit. Cynthia calls this "the perfect example of what southerners call a rock and a hard place,"[121] again pretending that a

115. Karon, *Somewhere Safe with Somebody Good*, 258.

116. Karon, *Somewhere Safe with Somebody Good*, 514.

117. Karon, *Somewhere Safe with Somebody Good*, 54.

118. Karon, *Somewhere Safe with Somebody Good*, 55.

119. Karon, *Somewhere Safe with Somebody Good*, 55.

120. Karon, *Somewhere Safe with Somebody Good*, 56.

121. Karon, *Come Rain or Come Shine*, 103.

common idiom is uniquely Southern and deflecting Tim's guilt for not inviting Henry first. Yet Karon stresses that Tim's reluctance to acknowledge
his brother stems from entrenched racism: "He despised his fear, so deeply,
viscerally rooted that he could not gouge it out."[122] This fear turns out to be
unfounded when Dooley offers Henry "Miss Sadie's place at the table,"[123]
filling the empty chair that symbolized the lost world of white gentility with
the present reality of biracial kinship. The wedding guests are surprised but
polite, and two sequences from Henry's point of view focus on his joy and
gratitude. Karon pushes back against readers' rejection of *Home to Holly
Springs* by introducing Henry into Mitford, but the integration of the nearly
all-white town is temporary and limited. Louella's advanced age keeps her
away from the wedding, although she sends food that stands in for her presence. Mitford still does not allow people of color to congregate.

"TOTAL HALLMARK AND NOT AT ALL KARON": MITFORD ON THE SMALL SCREEN

We can see Hollywood's limited interest in Christian content when a bestseller like *At Home in Mitford* is not made into a film for over twenty years,
and the one finally released by Hallmark Channel in 2017 is so unlike the
novel. Nancy M. Tischler once placed the Mitford books "in the warm and
fuzzy Hallmark tradition,"[124] but the banal Hallmark version ironically
throws Karon's explorations of Southern identity into greater relief. The film
was shot in British Columbia, and Father Tim is played by Canadian actor Cameron Mathison, but the prominent American flags evoke Anytown,
USA. Only North Carolina license plates suggest a Southern setting. Though
executive producer and star Andie MacDowell is from South Carolina and
once had such a strong accent that one of her performances was dubbed,[125]
nobody in this film uses Southern dialect. The entire cast is middle class,
with no impoverished Creek or wealthy Miss Sadie. Dooley is no longer a
foster child traumatized by poverty but a middle-class child whose parents
are deployed in the military. This adaptation of Tim and Cynthia's courtship
removes Mitford's only black resident and the Christian message that was
central to millions of fans.

---

122. Karon, *Come Rain or Come Shine*, 104.

123. Karon, *Come Rain or Come Shine*, 104.

124. Tischler, *Encyclopedia of Contemporary Christian Fiction*, 176.

125. Newman, "Some Call for a Voice," para. 5.

The film's eighty-four minutes do not allow for many Mitford characters, but it is disappointing that the screenwriters replace Louella with African Americans in minor roles. In keeping with the Hallmark formula of women leaving the city to find love in the country, the first scene takes place in Cynthia's Boston office with its view of the city skyline. A black man wearing a maroon blazer and name tag says the first line: "Your car's all packed and waiting at the curb, Miss Coppersmith." She apologizes for overpacking, and he laughs. He does not seem to be a chauffeur since she later drives her own car, so he might be a doorman, his generic servanthood part of the urban trappings that Cynthia eschews for a simpler life. There are a few black extras in Mitford; her publisher and Dr. Harper also look African American but are only onscreen for a few minutes. This seems like a missed opportunity, since a talented actress could have improved on Louella's portrayal in the book, as Octavia Spencer did with her role in the film version of *The Shack* released the same year.

The glamorous stars and formulaic romance plot aggravated readers who appreciate Karon's flawed characters and Christian values. Of the twenty-eight *Internet Movie Database* reviews, twenty-two are negative, with most giving one to three stars out of ten and using phrases like "Artistic Dishonesty," "Weak as Pond Water," "A Travesty," "Not the Real Mitford," "Not Even Close," "Disappointing," and "Shame on You!"[126] One reviewer points out that "Father Tim is turning 60 in the beginning of the Mitford series, thinning and receding hair and somewhat overweight and diabetic."[127] No wonder fans balked at Tim and Cynthia being played by an *All My Children* star who once appeared on the cover of *Playgirl* and a L'Oréal spokesmodel whose most acclaimed movie was *Sex, Lies, and Videotape*. Karon's pudgy senior citizens with everyday struggles have been transformed by a romantic comedy that one reviewer rightly calls "total Hallmark and not at all Karon."[128] The reviews on Amazon.com are more polarized, with thirty-eight positive and twenty-seven critical, possibly because many of them bought the DVD. Eighteen reviewers gave the movie one star, with several wishing they could give zero or negative stars, and titled their reviews with phrases like "A Total Miss," "Don't Bother," and "Utter Disappointment."[129] They were also annoyed by departures from Karon's realistic characters: "Father Tim was an older gentleman that had thinning hair and carried some weight around his middle. Cynthia was a petite woman who wore curlers in

126. "*At Home in Mitford* User Reviews."
127. "*At Home in Mitford* User Reviews."
128. "*At Home in Mitford* User Reviews."
129. "*At Home in Mitford* Customer Reviews."

her hair."[130] However, positive reviewers appreciated the sweet, wholesome romance, and one commented: "I thought that the hero being a pastor was going to be weird and that there would be too heavy of a religious undertone, but I didn't find that to be the case at all."[131] While many Mitford fans were turned off by the film, it seems to have pleased many Hallmark fans who were looking for a light, entertaining, and not overly religious story.

The film reduces the Christian message as much as possible given that Father Tim is still an Episcopal priest. He only wears his collar occasionally, and he and Cynthia eat ice cream in the pews of Lord's Chapel. In a new plotline, Cynthia restores two paintings in the church, one of Christ walking on water and one of modern-looking men in a boat. Cynthia assures a nosy parishioner that she is Episcopalian, and Tim jokes: "I'm sure even if she was Protestant it would probably be fine," which reveals the screenwriters' lack of religious knowledge because Episcopalians are Protestants.[132] When Tim and Cynthia talk in the chapel, the nonspecific painting of the men in the boat is prominent in every shot of her, while a stained glass window of Jesus remains out of focus in the reverse shots of him. Tim's story of vocation includes few Christian distinctives: "I lost my father when I was a kid, and I became very shut down. And it was this place, this church that brought me back. Everyone here rallied around me. My mother and I realized that family isn't only blood, it's community, it's congregation, and I knew that I needed to be that for people, the same way that they saved me."[133] This is much simpler than the painful journey that brought Karon's Father Tim from Mississippi to Mitford. The film's Cynthia echoes his claim that the congregation "saved me" when she calls him "a kind priest who comes in and saves us all."[134] Tim enters the pulpit only to make announcements and thank Cynthia for working on the paintings. People are the source of salvation in this film, which makes no claims about the truth or value of the Christian faith.

The contrast between this forgettable television movie and Karon's compelling novel *To Be Where You Are*, both released in 2017, draws attention to her growth over twenty-three years. I will discuss the latest novel at more length in the conclusion, but Karon's willingness to enter working-class points of view moved me to tears. The Mitford books, fractured by the original ending and bandaged back together with new editions into an

130. *"At Home in Mitford* Customer Reviews."

131. *"At Home in Mitford* Customer Reviews."

132. *At Home in Mitford.*

133. *At Home in Mitford.*

134. *At Home in Mitford.*

unbroken series, reveal how much Southern authors struggle to overcome entrenched stereotypes due to their own biases and the limits of what readers will accept. Like other popular writers, Christian novelists are constrained by the market, and Karon deserves credit for testing the boundaries of how much reality Christian readers can withstand. When we turn to *Left Behind*, another long-running and best-selling series, we leave behind much of this subtlety and enter a world in which the authors' prejudices often reinforce those of their audience.

Chapter 4

"HE HOPED SHE *WAS* GONE"
A World without Christian Women in Left Behind

Imagine a world without Christian women. Does it look the same, but with fewer potluck suppers and inspirational novels? Have feminists gained power, no longer held back by their conservative peers? Or is everyone just relieved to be free from the nagging? *Left Behind* creators Tim LaHaye and Jerry B. Jenkins focus on the last scenario. Although all children are taken up with born-again adults in the rapture, removing the need for childcare, one might expect the men left behind to be crippled by the loss of their helpmeets. Yet instead they seem to be liberated. They have been released from the discomfort caused by their wives' moral superiority and can now assume their God-given roles as leaders of the church. The main female characters left behind are not angry feminists but women who depend on them for survival and salvation. Like *The Chronicles of Narnia*, the *Left Behind* series portrays women in limited and troubling ways that filmmakers saw the need to change. The *Left Behind* franchise includes sixteen novels, four films, and a spin-off series for kids, but this chapter will focus on the first novel and its two film versions starring Kirk Cameron (2000) and Nicolas Cage (2014). The novel's Rayford Steele and Buck Williams are invigorated by their newfound leadership over damsels in distress Hattie Durham and Chloe Steele, but the first film transforms Hattie into a competent professional, and the second film traps the men in an airplane while Chloe saves the day.

THE RAPTURE AS MALE FANTASY: SCHOLARLY
RESPONSES TO *LEFT BEHIND*

While largely ignoring Francine Rivers and Jan Karon, many scholars have analyzed *Left Behind*'s controversial depictions of the end times and challenged LaHaye's premillennial dispensationalism, indicating that critics find masculine apocalyptic narratives more significant or more irksome than feminine domestic ones. Gary DeMar's *End Times Fiction* refutes the belief that biblical prophecies refer to a future age culminating in a rapture and tribulation rather than to events of the first century, while Carl E. Olson's *Will Catholics Be "Left Behind"?* discusses anti-Catholicism in the novels and in LaHaye's nonfiction. Bruce David Forbes and Jeanne Halgren Kilde's *Rapture, Revelation, and the End Times* compares the authors' views to other possibilities in the Bible and Christian tradition. Joanne M. Swenson describes eschatological popular culture's move "From Dogma to Aesthetica," with nonfictional doctrines replaced by aesthetic experiences from *Left Behind*'s urgency to Thomas Kinkade's romanticism. Glenn W. Shuck's *Marks of the Beast* analyzes the novels' future tribulation in light of evangelicals' present struggles, especially their uneasy relationship to network culture, and Wesley J. Bergen distinguishes the series from early Christian apocalyptic literature due to its terrestrial focus and claim to be interpreting the Bible, although contemporary evangelicals share their ancestors' sense of crisis and concern for purity.

Scholars also discuss the novels' right-wing politics and potential ideological effects. Darryl Jones highlights their attacks on liberals and socialists, calling one LaHaye magazine article "the unhinged right-wing ranting of a crazy old coot."[1] Anita Gandolfo fears that naive readers will be influenced by the "propaganda disguised as fiction"[2] and "blatantly antagonistic and intolerant tone."[3] Johann Pautz relates the novels to other far-right apocalyptic fiction influenced by militia movements and the John Birch Society, and Albert H. Tricomi relates them to earlier American missionary novels that "mark out America as a nation chosen by God to play a major role in the destiny of humankind"[4] and reinforce attitudes like distrust of international organizations and speculation that Barack Obama is the Antichrist. Peter Swirski laments that this approach "eliminates the political middle ground and the presumption of vectoring a collective impulse, and with them the

1. Darryl Jones, "Liberal Antichrist," 104.
2. Gandolfo, *Faith and Fiction*, 103.
3. Gandolfo, *Faith and Fiction*, 108.
4. Tricomi, *Missionary Positions*, 183.

culture of collaboration and compromise."[5] Marnie Jones claims that the books and videogame represent a failure of imagination among evangelicals whose children cannot read *Harry Potter* but can take part in "spiritual warfare" while playing *Left Behind: Eternal Forces*. Dan Mathewson calls the series "Death Pornography," and Christian Lundberg adds that it holds out "The Pleasure of Sadism." Since the popularity of the *Left Behind* books surged after the 9/11 terrorist attacks, their tendencies to provoke feelings of revenge or empathy seem especially relevant.

Yet Jennie Chapman reminds us that millions of diverse fans will not have identical worldviews: "As it can hardly be argued that every reader of the franchise is a right-wing, homophobic, misogynistic zealot (with a poor taste in literature at that), we must look to other explanations in our analysis of the complex and apparently confounding popularity of *Left Behind*."[6] Crawford Gribben's *Writing the Rapture* looks at the wide range of products, parodies, critiques, and alternatives that the franchise inspired: "Left Behind products cannot be understood in totalizing terms. Little more than a decade after its beginning, the brand is losing its coherence and is spiraling out of its creators' control."[7] Mathew Guest questions whether readers are easily duped: "*Left Behind* is not simply a vessel for evangelical ideas, as often proclaimed by its critics, but is one site for the expression and negotiation of evangelical tensions, forged out of an ongoing confrontation with Western modernity."[8] Like many popular Christian texts, *Left Behind* is far too complex for one-dimensional reading.

For example, the novels' sincere efforts to promote multiculturalism and support Israel break down upon closer examination into many racial, religious, and class stereotypes. Melani McAlister argues that "LaHaye and Jenkins exhibit a genuine but awkward embrace of diversity and yet a none-too-subtle racism,"[9] for example erasing Palestinians from the narrative. Sherryll Mleynek deplores their solution to the "Jewish problem" through conversion to Christianity and their refusal to acknowledge the historical significance of the Holocaust. Andrew Strombeck calls attention to "their devotion to free-market capitalism,"[10] despite their claims to be on the margins of society, surface attempts at multiculturalism, and moments of compassion for refugees and disaster victims. Jonathan Freedman shows

5. Swirski, "'To Sacrifice One's Intellect,'" para. 59.

6. Chapman, "Selling Faith," 152.

7. Gribben, *Writing the Rapture*, 132.

8. Guest, "Keeping the End in Mind," 485.

9. McAlister, "Prophecy, Politics, and the Popular," 791.

10. Strombeck, "Invest in Jesus," 162.

that they project antisemitic stereotypes onto the antichrist, like the power to brainwash people through the media and control the banking system. Lisa Lampert-Weissig notes that they also associate the antichrist with the Nazis, so that the Holocaust haunts the novels as a foreshadowing of the coming Apocalypse. Evelyn Stiller identifies sexist and racist elements in the videogame *Left Behind: Eternal Forces*; female characters are restricted to the roles of friend, influencer, and healer while being denied "the male-only options of builder, advanced builder, foreman, soldier, spy, Special Forces, sniper, disciple, evangelist, and missionary."[11] In a male-dominated video-game industry, game designers have less reason than filmmakers to appeal to women.

While critics are fascinated by the gender roles, studies indicate that readers are less interested in the topic. Paul C. Gutjahr's study of Amazon reviewers shows that half the readers were men, but all readers' favorite characters were Buck and Rayford: "Relational issues are downplayed as world events, harrowing escapes, rescue missions, and various murder plots are foregrounded."[12] Only nine of eighty-three reviewers chose Chloe as their favorite character, and no other women made the list.[13] This is a series written by men, in which the male heroes are better developed. In *Rapture Culture*, Amy Johnson Frykholm finds that readers engage with characters based on beliefs and actions: "Readers often say, 'My mother is like Hattie' or 'I am like Rayford,' but these identifications do not necessarily follow gender lines. Overwhelmingly, male and female readers alike identify themselves with Buck."[14] Frykholm notes that many women are hostile to Hattie and concludes that readers looking for entertainment and edification do not consider abstract ideological issues. In "The Gender Dynamics of the *Left Behind* Series," Frykholm adds that the authors updated earlier rapture fiction to accommodate mainstream popular culture, making the gender roles more familiar and less noticeable. "Worldly Man" Rayford is more sensitive and emotionally available, while "Prodigal Daughter" Chloe is more assertive and adventurous. However, by saving the Worldly Man rather than condemning him, "*Left Behind* makes a far greater case for male domination and female submission."[15] Chloe still dies in the penultimate novel of the original series, while the men continue their adventures.

11. Stiller, "Gaming Armageddon," 318.

12. Gutjahr, "No Longer Left Behind," 221.

13. Gutjahr, "No Longer Left Behind," 233.

14. Frykholm, *Rapture Culture*, 91.

15. Frykholm, "Gender Dynamics," 281.

Several scholars critique Rayford and Buck's "paramilitary" or "brut-ish" masculinity. Rebecca Barrett-Fox compares them to the Promise Keepers: "'Paramilitary' because they often take on the rhetoric of a hero physically battling and suffering in the protection of those in his realm of responsibility, these tales romanticize leadership and death in an appeal to what their creators see as an intrinsic element of masculinity—the need to defend one's clan."[16] Kristy Maddux compares them to the genteel William Wilberforce in *Amazing Grace* and the submissive Jesus in *The Passion of the Christ*: "This masculinity is particularly brutish, prizing strength, instinct, and courage over rationality and intellect."[17] Even the strongest woman, Chloe, cannot perform dangerous missions as well as the men, leaving her to die and to be remembered as a devoted wife and mother. Yet in "Rapture Fiction and the Predicament of Christian Male Leadership," Frykholm ob-serves that machismo can never defeat the antichrist: "No Christian man can ultimately be a superhero. He cannot prevail against the world anymore than he could prevail against Christ. Getting saved by someone else turns you, the muscular Christian, into the damsel in distress, the one in need of a saviour."[18] Rayford struggles with leadership, Buck struggles to overpower a lesbian colleague, and neither can save Chloe from being captured and killed.

Chapman's *Plotting Apocalypse* argues that the authors punish Chloe for transgressing gender expectations, along with Rayford's college girl-friend Kitty Wiley, his almost-lover Hattie, his fellow believer Leah Rose, and his second wife Amanda White—everyone except the perfect home-maker Irene Steele. While female characters may be strong, independent, and intelligent, "acts of female agency must ultimately be punished within the texts to reconstitute the sacred imperative of female submission on which the stability of God's order relies."[19] The violent martyrdoms of fe-male characters are a form of gynocide that purges undesirable elements from the Christian community.

The rapture liberates men from Christian women and from Mother Church. Gribben's *Rapture Fiction and the Evangelical Crisis* addresses "signs of serious theological decay"[20] in the novels' descriptions of conversion, the church, and Christian life, such as overly romantic language about faith, weak understanding of God's sovereignty, belief that the "Sinner's Prayer"

16. Barrett-Fox, "Hope, Faith and Toughness," 95.

17. Maddux, *Faithful Citizen*, 110.

18. Frykholm, "Rapture Fiction," 19.

19. Chapman, *Plotting Apocalypse*, 138.

20. Gribben, *Rapture Fiction*, 10.

guarantees salvation, and reliance on human leaders rather than Scripture. Gribben later describes the individualism of the post-rapture world: "These new believers are not baptized and are not invited to participate in the Lord's Supper: in line with traditional Dispensationalism, they are not part of the Church, the body of Christ, and so are not in a position to benefit from the sacraments."[21] The series contains few examples of formal worship, pastoral authority, fasting, or service, thus freeing up believers to follow the action. Christians have worried about the feminization of the church since the nineteenth century, so it makes sense that freedom from choir practices and Christmas pageants might be among the rapture's utopian elements. Frykholm "began to understand rapture fiction as a genre of male fantasy"[22] when its heroes vanquish enemies and save damsels. I will explore another side of male fantasy that frees men from social niceties and church responsibilities while providing plenty of blood, gore, and adventure.

"HE DIDN'T ENJOY GOING HOME": AMBIVALENCE ABOUT MARRIAGE IN THE NOVEL

The back of my *Left Behind* book advertises LaHaye's *How to Be Happy Though Married*, an ambiguous title implying that happiness can occur *despite* marriage. Writing in 1968, LaHaye described eroding values and rising divorce rates: "One of the most common causes of emotionally disturbed people today is the average American home."[23] He promoted traditional gender roles: the husband should lead the household and handle the finances, while the wife should stay home with children and spend thirty minutes on her appearance before her husband returns from work. With syntax that echoes the previous quote, LaHaye claimed: "One of the great hindrances to a happy home today is the false notion that a woman does not have to subject herself to her husband."[24] However, the book also contained advice for husbands, including women's right to orgasm. LaHaye expressed qualified optimism about marriage, yet the *Left Behind* books published over twenty-five years later seem more ambivalent. Rayford and Pastor Bruce Barnes feel liberated by their wives' disappearances, even though the rapture functions as a divine *Good Housekeeping* Seal of Approval on their homemaking skills.

Left Behind begins with Rayford contemplating an affair because his wife does not fulfill his needs: "Irene was attractive and vivacious enough,

21. Gribben, "Piety and Polemic," 486.
22. Frykholm, "Rapture Fiction," 22.
23. LaHaye, *How to Be Happy*, 8.
24. LaHaye, *How to Be Happy*, 105.

even at forty. But lately he had found himself repelled by her obsession with religion."[25] Irene is attractive *enough, even* at forty. Rayford feels guilty for kissing another woman at a party when Irene was nine months pregnant, but he recalls a conversation about her faith in which she was "not amused" by his jokes and "cold" when he kissed her, leaving him "rejected and vulnerable in his own living room."[26] Rayford's marital problems clearly stem from his selfish demand for pleasure, but his negative portrait of Irene lingers because we never meet her for ourselves, as the book's point of view alternates between Rayford and Buck.

Rayford assumes that Irene has vanished in the rapture, but he seems remarkably nonchalant about confirming her fate. He finds a care package in his mailbox at O'Hare, but instead of tearing open this last message from his wife, "He slipped the envelope into his case and went looking for Hattie Durham."[27] When he learns that his first officer committed suicide, "For the first time the enormity of the situation became personal,"[28] as if his wife vanishing was not personal. When he arrives home, he describes "his trophy house" as "sepulchral" and Irene's housekeeping as "fastidious,"[29] implying that she failed to make it warm and welcoming. He delays opening the door, then hangs up his coat, puts away his bag, turns off the coffee pot and radio, opens the drapes, listens to his messages, checks the garage, and gazes at family photos before going upstairs. "For her sake, if this was the Rapture, he hoped she *was* gone,"[30] but his delay reveals his fear of finding her at home. When he uncovers his son's empty pajamas and socks, "He sat on the bed and wept, nearly smiling at Irene's harping about Raymie's not wearing socks to bed."[31] He is *nearly smiling* at the memory of Irene's *harping*, which could indicate nostalgia or liberation. He notes the girliness of the "frilly" master bedroom before the moment of truth: "Her flannel nightgown, the one he always kidded her about and which she wore only when he was not home, evidenced her now departed form."[32] Jenkins interrupts the discovery of Irene's disappearance with seventeen words about her unappealing nightgown, the sentence structure echoing Rayford's delays and criticisms

25. LaHaye and Jenkins, *Left Behind*, 1.

26. LaHaye and Jenkins, *Left Behind*, 4–5.

27. LaHaye and Jenkins, *Left Behind*, 49.

28. LaHaye and Jenkins, *Left Behind*, 53.

29. LaHaye and Jenkins, *Left Behind*, 66.

30. LaHaye and Jenkins, *Left Behind*, 67.

31. LaHaye and Jenkins, *Left Behind*, 74.

32. LaHaye and Jenkins, *Left Behind*, 75.

of his wife.[33] Would sexier lingerie have made him love her more? He immediately opens the care package and finds her homemade cookies. Irene nurtures him even after the rapture, turning the focus away from his need for repentance.

Rayford's memories remain ambivalent during the following days. He pulls a bottle of bourbon from the high cabinet where Irene made him hide his liquor, drinks three inches, but then feels guilty and throws it away. He recalls being relieved by the deaths of his elderly parents, officially contrasting but subtly comparing that loss to his current bereavement. He admits that "he didn't enjoy going home"[34] during Irene's difficult pregnancy and gives a detailed account of his preference for "an old-fashioned affair" over "something as tawdry as paying for sex,"[35] as if on some level considering his new options as a widower. Most people grieving the sudden loss of a spouse would not linger on memories of the hard times. Even the delicious cookies "had become painful reminders."[36] Meanwhile, Buck's segments mirror this ambivalence as the bachelor journalist feels sorrow about the disappearances and excitement about the career opportunities that they afford.

Bruce also describes his wife's saintly behavior alongside his liberation from the restrictions of family life. When the rapture occurred, he was reading a sports magazine in bed even though she was trying to sleep, and he confesses to lying about money, sneaking to movies, and looking at pornography. Only days later, Bruce looks "exhausted but happy" and claims that God "has blessed me beyond anything I could have imagined."[37] He instantly becomes the senior pastor and gives the same message repeatedly to overflow crowds. He tells Buck that they can talk until midnight: "I have no family responsibilities anymore."[38] Rayford and Bruce regret their misbehavior, which should encourage male readers to take a good look at their own marriages, but Jenkins also taps into readers' boredom and heightens their anticipation for a world where they no longer have to focus on the family.

Rayford's conversion develops the spiritual side of the male fantasy: he sits alone in front of the TV, watching a tape made by Irene's head pastor

---

33. Since LaHaye provided ideas and outlines for the books while Jenkins was the main writer, I will often refer to Jenkins as the author of specific wording.

34. LaHaye and Jenkins, *Left Behind*, 143.

35. LaHaye and Jenkins, *Left Behind*, 144.

36. LaHaye and Jenkins, *Left Behind*, 146.

37. LaHaye and Jenkins, *Left Behind*, 221–22.

38. LaHaye and Jenkins, *Left Behind*, 425.

before the rapture. The novel would unfold very differently if Irene left him a letter or tape and became his post-rapture spiritual director. But the notes that she leaves in her Bible, such as the word "Precious,"[39] offer little help and send him looking for male leadership. His private conversion demonstrates both the evangelical emphasis on a personal relationship with Jesus and the appeal of a "man cave": he gives his life to Christ but retains control of the remote. After Chloe goes to bed, "Rayford settled in front of the television and popped in the video."[40] Despite the casual word *popped*, he is convinced by the pastor: "He was alone with his thoughts, alone with God, and he felt God's presence."[41] Rayford kneels, pushes play, and prays along with the tape. While two different churches and Irene failed to convince him, he responds to the invitation given by an absent man through the comforting distance of technology, ironically reinforcing the antichrist's continual evocation of "brotherly love."[42] He begins his new life in a man's world.

"TOO DITZY TO FIGURE IT OUT": HATTIE IN THE NOVEL

Rayford lusts after his senior flight attendant in the first sentence: "Rayford Steele's mind was on a woman he had never touched. With his fully loaded 747 on autopilot above the Atlantic en route to a 6 a.m. landing at Heathrow, Rayford had pushed from his mind thoughts of his family."[43] The "fully loaded 747" and sexy stewardess evoke pornography more than Christian fiction. Daniel Radosh jokes, "That's right, Buck Williams and Rayford Steele. There's also Steve Plank, Bruce Barnes, and Dirk Burton. Apparently, having a porn star name is enough to keep you from getting raptured."[44] The first sentences of Earl Lee's parody *Kiss My Left Behind* exaggerate this connection: "Captain Ramrod Steel leaned back in his pilot seat and closed his eyes. He tried hard to imagine what the slim, blonde flight attendant would look like wearing his pilot's cap and not much else."[45] Hattie Durham is not a porn star name, but "Hattie" links her to fashion and the Mad Hatter while "Durham" ironically evokes Durham Cathedral and Durham University in England and the prestigious Duke University in Durham, North Carolina.

39. LaHaye and Jenkins, *Left Behind*, 123.

40. LaHaye and Jenkins, *Left Behind*, 208–9.

41. LaHaye and Jenkins, *Left Behind*, 215.

42. LaHaye and Jenkins, *Left Behind*, 245.

43. LaHaye and Jenkins, *Left Behind*, 1.

44. Radosh, *Rapture Ready!*, 77.

45. Earl Lee, *Kiss My Left Behind*, 1.

None of these highbrow associations fit our ditzy character. Rayford's lust may be sinful and destructive, but Hattie's foolishness, helplessness, immorality, and spiritual weakness imply that a successful professional woman in her late twenties cannot survive without his leadership.

We first meet Hattie in her panic following the rapture. While Rayford usually enjoys her flirtatious touching, during this nonsexual encounter her "fingers felt like talons,"[46] the metaphor linking her to a bird of prey. Yet Jenkins calls attention to her physical and emotional weakness as she shudders, buckles, squeals, buries her head in Rayford's chest, sobs, kneels whimpering in the corner, and screams when she finds a colleague's clothes. When Rayford tells her that she needs to do her job, "She nodded, her eyes vacant."[47] She manages to take charge of the terrified passengers and confronts Buck about dismantling the phone to go online. He calls her "beautiful Hattie," and she snaps back: "Don't patronize me, sir,"[48] a valid response that shows some strength of character. Buck takes her hand and offers to call her family, and she soon devolves back into weeping. He later tells her that he works for *Global Weekly*: "And you were going to send me to my room for tampering with the phone."[49] He portrays Hattie as a damsel in distress and an interfering mother like Irene.

Hattie's sexist colleagues overpower her just as easily when they arrive at the airport. She asserts herself when Rayford urges her to ride to the terminal with the elderly and infirm rather than walk with the crew: "Just because I can't fly the thing doesn't mean I don't feel some ownership. And don't treat me like a little woman."[50] He claims that he would never do that, but a helicopter pilot resists taking her home because she is just a flight attendant and then asks: "What do you weigh, doll?"[51] She sits on Rayford's lap like a child, while he notes that his attraction has drained away: "She was beautiful and sexy and smart, but only for her age."[52] Often called a "girl" like most women in the novel, she is really twenty-seven. She quivers in fear before leaving Rayford, and he watches her "trotting toward her condominium,"[53] the horse metaphor joining the bird of prey metaphor to render her subhuman.

46. LaHaye and Jenkins, *Left Behind*, 16.
47. LaHaye and Jenkins, *Left Behind*, 19.
48. LaHaye and Jenkins, *Left Behind*, 32.
49. LaHaye and Jenkins, *Left Behind*, 41.
50. LaHaye and Jenkins, *Left Behind*, 44.
51. LaHaye and Jenkins, *Left Behind*, 51.
52. LaHaye and Jenkins, *Left Behind*, 53.
53. LaHaye and Jenkins, *Left Behind*, 54.

Buck and his companions also condescend to women airport workers. One female attendant asks a doctor not to bandage Buck's head in a public area, and he says "I promise to clean up, hon,"[54] and tells her to worry about the drinks and nuts. Soon after, Buck yells at a woman who asks him to unplug his extension cord. Jenkins's first adjectives to describe Buck's coworkers Marge Potter and Lucinda Washington are "matronly"[55] and "fiftyish,"[56] defining them by sexual undesirability rather than professional skill. Buck recalls teasing his older black colleague by calling her "Lucy" and playing a practical joke on her that she easily forgave.[57] Even after the rapture, women try to cramp men's style by asking them to follow rules, but the crisis allows men to ignore them even more pointedly than before.

Hattie calls Rayford and Buck more than ten times during the following weeks, as if she has nowhere else to turn in her fear and loneliness. An inverted "love triangle" unfolds that connects the men through annoyance rather than desire. Rayford and Buck do not meet until the last quarter of the novel, but Jenkins often transitions between their points of view by focusing on their only mutual acquaintance, and Hattie becomes an object of exchange between them in one such sequence. She calls Rayford, but he snubs her with his usual ambivalence: "He was sorry about that, but not sorry that he had gotten rid of her for the time being."[58] She calls Buck, who rolls his eyes and plans to remove his home number from his business card: "Didn't she have any girlfriends to unload on?"[59] When Buck hangs up, she calls Rayford again. The men later exchange her in person in New York, when she meets Buck in the morning, meets Rayford in the afternoon, introduces them, and dines with them both. Her obnoxious presence links the men's separate stories until they meet and Chloe becomes their eroticized connection.

In the second half of the novel, both men treat Hattie so insensitively that they push her into the arms of Nicolae Carpathia, the antichrist. When Hattie complains about the downturn at her sister's abortion clinic due to the rapture of the unborn, "Rayford had to admit he had never found Hattie guilty of brilliance," and he concludes, "What kind of lunacy was this? He shouldn't waste his energy arguing with someone who clearly didn't have

54. LaHaye and Jenkins, *Left Behind*, 60.

55. LaHaye and Jenkins, *Left Behind*, 61.

56. LaHaye and Jenkins, *Left Behind*, 78.

57. LaHaye and Jenkins, *Left Behind*, 78–79.

58. LaHaye and Jenkins, *Left Behind*, 147.

59. LaHaye and Jenkins, *Left Behind*, 148.

a clue."[60] Behind Hattie's back, Rayford denies her requests to work on his flights, avoiding and deceiving her as he once did with Irene. She finally stops calling him, but he becomes determined to evangelize to her with the forceful conviction of his new spiritual authority.

Rayford still has not learned to listen; the women in his life want understanding, but he keeps offering them salvation. Like Michael Hosea from *Redeeming Love*, he refuses to hear her side of the story: "I'm not here to argue with you or even to have a conversation. There are things I must tell you, and I want you just to listen."[61] As if this was not clear enough, Jenkins adds numerous references to Hattie being forbidden and then unable to talk. Rayford says that he doesn't want a dialogue; he is frustrated when she argues with him; she puts her hand over her mouth; she promises not to interrupt again; she keeps her pledge of silence; he allows her to break her silence temporarily; she nods, unable to speak; she tries to speak but cannot regain her composure.[62] He bluntly tells her that he never loved her and that his only interest was physical, which brings her to tears. He won't let her speak freely but demands her forgiveness. She ultimately submits to this treatment, returning from the bathroom "as if ready for more punishment"[63] and concluding that he is sweet and that she appreciates him. Between her experience in a chauvinistic airline industry and Rayford's version of evangelism, she is perfectly primed to meet the antichrist.

Buck introduces Hattie to Carpathia because he sees her as a "diversion," the same word that Rayford uses for his former relationship with her,[64] but he doesn't exactly talk her up to the new head of the United Nations:

> "I just wanted to apologize for bringing this girl up to meet you. She's just a flight attendant, and—"
>
> "Nobody is just anything," he said, taking Buck's arm. "Everyone is of equal value, regardless of their station."
>
> Carpathia led Buck to the door, insisting he be introduced. Hattie was appropriate and reserved, though she giggled when Carpathia kissed her on each cheek. He asked her about herself, her family, her job. Buck wondered if he had ever taken a Carnegie course on how to win friends and influence people.[65]

60. LaHaye and Jenkins, *Left Behind*, 267.

61. LaHaye and Jenkins, *Left Behind*, 367.

62. LaHaye and Jenkins, *Left Behind*, 368–71.

63. LaHaye and Jenkins, *Left Behind*, 375.

64. LaHaye and Jenkins, *Left Behind*, 328.

65. LaHaye and Jenkins, *Left Behind*, 335–36.

Jenkins portrays the antichrist's pretense of egalitarianism as more harmful than typical male selfishness: Rayford and Buck are rude to her, but at least they don't sleep with her. Carpathia gives Hattie a phone number that exposes his secret position with the United Nations, but Buck dismisses this to a colleague: "Maybe he's assuming this Durham woman is too ditzy to figure it out."[66] Calling Hattie "this Durham woman" and characterizing her as "ditzy" reduces Buck's responsibility for introducing her to an evil genius.

When Carpathia's intentions toward Hattie turn sexual, she does not think twice. Buck refuses to bring Hattie to him—"What am I now, a pimp?"[67]—and tells her that "you don't strike me as that kind of girl."[68] She takes offense at the word *girl*, which draws her closer to the antichrist's spurious feminism. Buck meets her again at the United Nations, where her nameplate says "Personal Assistant"[69] and she "seemed to melt in Carpathia's presence."[70] Even when Carpathia puts a gun to his colleague's head and tells Hattie to slide her chair back to avoid soiling her outfit with brain matter, she obeys with "fingers trembling."[71] She falls victim to his brainwashing, whereas Buck's faith allows him to see the truth. Hattie began the novel in terror after the rapture, and she ends in terror after the murder: "Hattie shivered in her seat and appeared to try to emit a scream that would not come."[72] Being Carpathia's "Personal Assistant" is worse than being Rayford's mistress, and Jenkins blames her for rejecting the gospel and ignoring the men's advice. Even her friendship with Chloe fails to bear fruit, since they spend their time in the beauty salon and the women's room.

"THAT MADDENING INTELLECTUAL GRID": CHLOE IN THE NOVEL

The novel's only heroine is Rayford's twenty-year-old daughter Chloe, a Stanford University student who drops out after the rapture to bond with her father, learn about Jesus, and fall in love with Buck. Chloe never refers to her major or anything that she learned at Stanford, a prestigious university

66. LaHaye and Jenkins, *Left Behind*, 340.
67. LaHaye and Jenkins, *Left Behind*, 417.
68. LaHaye and Jenkins, *Left Behind*, 437.
69. LaHaye and Jenkins, *Left Behind*, 446.
70. LaHaye and Jenkins, *Left Behind*, 451.
71. LaHaye and Jenkins, *Left Behind*, 457.
72. LaHaye and Jenkins, *Left Behind*, 458.

that currently boasts over 16,000 students and 2,000 faculty.[73] Jenkins depicts them as an amazingly godless community that had lost only "ten students and two profs"[74] during the first reports of the rapture. Rayford knows it will be hard to convert her because she is independent like him: "She was competitive, a driver, someone who had to be convinced and persuaded."[75] While intellectual rigor might be desirable for a college student, Rayford must overcome it to bring Chloe into the kingdom, which he sees as his primary postrapture responsibility.

Chloe spends the first third of the novel traveling home to Chicago, and we see little evidence of the skeptical academic when we finally meet her in person and she wails: "Oh, Daddy!"[76] The segment ends three short paragraphs later, cutting off the first opportunity to develop her character. In Rayford's next segment, he reveals his expectation that women will nurture him: "He had secretly hoped she would be of comfort to him,"[77] but she barricades herself in the house, going through her mother's and brother's things. She calls him "Daddy" ten times in this segment and sits on his lap like Hattie: "Her father took her hand, and she rose and sat in his lap, hiding her face and sobbing. His heart aching for her, Rayford rocked her until she was silent. 'Where are they?' she whined at last."[78] Chloe vacillates between childish dependence and adolescent rebellion: she complains that Rayford treats her like a little girl, but he mocks her by "switching to a babyish voice"[79] and admires Bruce for telling her not to interrupt his testimony. No wonder Chloe delays becoming a Christian for so long.

Due to the novel's male points of view, we never see Chloe alone or with friends. Jenkins notes briefly that she attended a church service, and the previous owner of my book wrote in the margin: "Why no coverage of that scene?" Rayford dismisses her religious struggles as immaturity, even though he had just converted a few days earlier: "Had he been this pseudo-sophisticated at that age? Of course he had. He had run everything through that maddening intellectual grid—until recently, when the supernatural came crashing through his academic pretense."[80] If Hattie is too dumb to be a Christian, then Chloe is too smart. Like Susan Pevensie in the Narnia

73. Stanford University, "About Stanford," lines 1–8.

74. LaHaye and Jenkins, *Left Behind*, 48.

75. LaHaye and Jenkins, *Left Behind*, 103.

76. LaHaye and Jenkins, *Left Behind*, 155.

77. LaHaye and Jenkins, *Left Behind*, 159.

78. LaHaye and Jenkins, *Left Behind*, 163.

79. LaHaye and Jenkins, *Left Behind*, 188.

80. LaHaye and Jenkins, *Left Behind*, 237.

books, she finds no real hearing for her doubts. Rayford "had to keep himself from slapping his own daughter" when she astutely questions his motives for inviting Hattie to dinner,[81] and she rejects godly womanhood when she hopes that "you don't expect me to cook or something sexist and domestic like that."[82] As with Hattie, her ongoing dependence on men renders her feminist protests unconvincing and ineffectual. She runs to a neighbor when burglars break into the house and accompanies her father to church because she is afraid to stay home alone. These weaknesses overwhelm her insightful moments, like when she is the first to identify Carpathia as the antichrist.[83]

On a trip to New York, Chloe meets Buck, who is ten years older, and they develop an instant romance in which she continues to play a childlike role. In another echo of Michael Hosea, Buck falls in love at first sight: "He loved Chloe's name, her eyes, her smile. She looked directly at him and gave a firm handshake, something he liked in a woman. So many women felt it was feminine to offer a limp hand. *What a beautiful girl!* he thought."[84] We hear about this from Buck's perspective, and he falls for Chloe's beauty before she speaks. His rejection of "a limp hand" conveys his admiration of strong women (and perhaps homophobia), but then they eat cookies and Buck wipes chocolate from her mouth. Buck interrupts when she starts to explain her father's theory of the disappearances because he plans to interview Rayford later: "Buck held up a hand. 'Oh, I'm sorry, don't tell me. I want to get it fresh from him.'"[85] He doesn't want her own ideas because his article wouldn't use two people from the same family, and he exaggerates their age difference: "I'd buy you another cookie, little girl, but I don't want to spoil your appetite."[86] She is strongly attracted to him nonetheless.

After Rayford and Buck finally meet, Chloe replaces Hattie as the erotic center of their homosocial bond. Like *Redeeming Love*, the romance in *Left Behind* bears out Eve Kosofsky Sedgwick's theory that "in any erotic rivalry, the bond that links the two rivals is as intense and potent as the bond that links either of the rivals to the beloved."[87] Jenkins previously created a narrative bond between Rayford and Buck through their annoyance with Hattie, and he now turns the love triangle upright and makes them "rivals"

81. LaHaye and Jenkins, *Left Behind*, 237.
82. LaHaye and Jenkins, *Left Behind*, 249.
83. LaHaye and Jenkins, *Left Behind*, 275.
84. LaHaye and Jenkins, *Left Behind*, 364–65.
85. LaHaye and Jenkins, *Left Behind*, 372.
86. LaHaye and Jenkins, *Left Behind*, 373.
87. Sedgwick, *Between Men*, 21.

for Chloe. When all four characters have dinner together, Jenkins links the male points of view through their mutual admiration of Chloe. Buck's segment ends: "Chloe was radiant, looking five years older in a classy evening dress. It was clear she and Hattie had spent the late afternoon in a beauty salon."[88] Rayford's segment begins: "Rayford thought his daughter looked stunning that evening, and he wondered what the magazine writer thought of her."[89] The homosocial desire begins as Buck admires the older man: "He realized he had seen a lot of Rayford in Chloe,"[90] displacing his attraction into more acceptable channels. He gets chills when listening to the pilot's testimony: "Buck focused on Captain Steele, his pulse racing, looking neither right nor left. He could not move. He was certain the women could hear his crashing heart."[91] Their bond marginalizes Hattie and Chloe, who go to the bathroom for much of this conversation.

The men's relationship continues to unfold according to romantic conventions. While Rayford had to enforce Hattie's silence earlier that day in order to give his testimony, the same message renders Buck "speechless" with conviction.[92] Yet Rayford worries that he isn't getting through to the journalist, echoing the dramatic irony of the romance novel in which the heroine doubts the hero's obvious attraction. Buck foolishly says that he'll get back to Rayford before using his quotes "only to give himself a reason to reconnect with the pilot."[93] The postrapture world of "brotherly love" draws Buck to Rayford, but Chloe is the appropriate object of his romantic desire.

Rayford's powerful effect on Buck spills over onto Chloe, her spiritual direction mirroring that of her future husband: "Buck was putting his equipment away when he noticed Chloe was crying, tears streaming down her face. What was it with these women?"[94] Despite this dismissive remark, Buck secretly books the seat next to Chloe's on the return flight to Chicago, and when he boards the plane and finds her turned away, he doesn't speak. He spies on her while she finally breaks down and prays, not alone in a TV room, but on a crowded plane with her future husband watching from inches away. Her conversion stems from the men's influence rather than being alone with God. Rayford has been praying for her: "Again he felt deeply impressed of God, as if the Lord were speaking directly to his spirit,

88. LaHaye and Jenkins, *Left Behind*, 381.
89. LaHaye and Jenkins, *Left Behind*, 381.
90. LaHaye and Jenkins, *Left Behind*, 383.
91. LaHaye and Jenkins, *Left Behind*, 385.
92. LaHaye and Jenkins, *Left Behind*, 386.
93. LaHaye and Jenkins, *Left Behind*, 387.
94. LaHaye and Jenkins, *Left Behind*, 388.

Patience. Let her be."[95] As in *Redeeming Love*, we overhear God talking to men about women. When she finishes praying and turns toward Buck, she acts like a clichéd romantic heroine: "She folded her hands and drew them to her mouth, her eyes filling. Then she took his hand in both of hers. 'Oh, Buck,' she whispered. 'Oh, Buck.'"[96] She prayed for a sign that God cares about her, and he responded by sending her a husband. However, Chloe has no luck trying to convert Buck, since evangelism is now male territory, and he delays a decision until he can see Bruce.

Further scenes develop the erotic entanglements in which Rayford's rapturous bond with Buck transforms Chloe into his Christian wife. Rayford comes into the cabin and hugs Chloe after her conversion, telling the staring passengers that she is his daughter. One woman retorts: "And I'm the queen of England."[97] By mistaking father and daughter for lovers, the woman calls attention to the love triangle that connects them both to Buck, who watches this scene in a segment devoted to his point of view. When Buck visits Bruce to learn about the rapture, he fears that the pastor will "pop the question"[98] and ask him to accept Christ, the marriage metaphor highlighting the tensions between "brotherly love" and romantic desire. Buck then starts playing hard to get. He coyly declines to tell Bruce and Rayford that he plans to attend church, arrives late, and leaves a note for Chloe explaining why he left without talking to her: "It isn't that I didn't want to say good-bye. But I don't."[99] Huh? The grammar of romance breaks down completely under the weight of male ambivalence.

In a parallel to Rayford's "man cave" conversion, Buck converts in a men's room at the United Nations, emphasizing that men need physical distance from women to feel the presence of God for the first time. Before the meeting in which Carpathia murders his colleagues, Buck finally realizes that he needs the protection of Christ. After he locks the door, he finds it easy to surrender: "Buck backed up against the door, thrust his hands deep into his pockets, and dropped his chin to his chest, remembering Bruce's advice that he could talk to God the same way he talked to a friend."[100] After Buck resists brainwashing, the novel ends with him reuniting with Chloe, Bruce, and Rayford, the group that Chloe names the Tribulation Force.

95. LaHaye and Jenkins, *Left Behind*, 399.

96. LaHaye and Jenkins, *Left Behind*, 401.

97. LaHaye and Jenkins, *Left Behind*, 409.

98. LaHaye and Jenkins, *Left Behind*, 425.

99. LaHaye and Jenkins, *Left Behind*, 439.

100. LaHaye and Jenkins, *Left Behind*, 446.

The "world without Christian women" does not last long. In *Tribulation Force*, Rayford marries Amanda and Buck marries Chloe in a double wedding in Bruce's office (apparently the rapture liberates men from big weddings). In *Soul Harvest*, Amanda goes missing, and evidence suggests that she may be a spy. Rayford searches for her body and the truth, and the most vivid scene about Amanda is when he dives into a river and finds her bloated corpse. He later learns that she was not a spy, as if the authors included her only to revisit their ambivalence about marriage. Hattie appears in seven novels as a damsel in distress who must be rescued from her own destructive behavior before finally converting and quickly dying as a martyr in *Desecration*, followed by Chloe, who dies by guillotine in *Armageddon*. The last chapter of *Glorious Appearing* echoes the first chapter of *Left Behind*: "Rayford Steele's mind was on a woman he had not touched in more than seven years."[101] The original series began with his desire to touch Hattie and ends with his desire to touch Irene, who appears in her glorified body and reassures him about marrying Amanda. After seven years of tribulation, Rayford's beliefs about gender roles have not changed, but he has slept with another woman and gotten away with it.

"ONE OF US HAD TO MAKE A MOVE": A STRONGER HATTIE IN *LEFT BEHIND: THE MOVIE* (2000)

The *Left Behind* books were the product of collaboration between two men, and the first film was produced by two men, Peter and Paul Lalonde of Cloud Ten Pictures, but the movie is also linked to a Christian celebrity couple. Kirk Cameron played teen heartthrob Mike Seaver on the sitcom *Growing Pains* (1985–1992) and Chelsea Noble played his girlfriend; they married in real life in 1991. In the DVD special feature "The Making of *Left Behind: The Movie*," Cameron explains that they got involved with this project after Chelsea slapped him late at night and told him: "'Oh, my gosh, this is the greatest book. You've got to read this. It's a fantastic book, and they need to make this into a movie,' and she said, 'And I would love to play the role of Hattie.'" Cameron went back to sleep, but Noble was determined to locate the film rights. As an experienced Christian actress, Noble was not content to play a dumb blonde who becomes the antichrist's arm candy. The film portrays Irene as a wronged woman and Chloe as a rebellious young adult who grows up quickly after the rapture, while it transforms Hattie into a competent professional with a life apart from Rayford and his fantasies.

101. LaHaye and Jenkins, *Glorious Appearing*, 327.

Left Behind: The Movie anticipates Jenkins's prequel novels (2005–2007) by depicting Irene's life before the rapture, struggling with a defiant child and straying husband. The novel began with Rayford's frustration with his nagging wife, but the film invites us into the home where she lovingly prepares her son's birthday party. Irene (Christie MacFadyen) appears slim and youthful, with a short haircut that strengthens her resemblance to her daughter, in contrast to Jenkins's description of her as attractive enough "even at forty." She kisses Rayford (Brad Johnson) as he leaves, driving home his guilt for going to see Hattie. When he returns to the house after the rapture, he does not invent reasons to hang around downstairs. He calls out for Irene, rushes upstairs, and finds Raymie's empty bed in one minute of screen time. He finds his wife's silky pink pajamas—no flannel nightgowns here—throws her Bible at the mirror, and confronts his shattered reflection. Since the first shot of Ray was his reflection in the mirror in his pilot's uniform, this cinematic cliché illuminates the loss of his playboy identity. In later scenes invented for the film, Rayford watches a video of Raymie's birthday party and visits his empty classroom, where he finds his homework stating: "I want to be a pilot like my dad." These dramatic scenes have greater impact in the 95-minute film than Rayford's occasional regrets in the 468-page novel. He does not become a Christian in his TV room but in the church with Bruce, revealing a commitment to leave his selfish habits and fight for the greater good.

Chloe (Janaya Stephens) also appears for the first time during the birthday party scene. The film does not mention Stanford, and her jeans and nose ring make her look like a teenager. According to *Internet Movie Database*, teen star Lacey Chabert was the first choice for the part, which would have made Chloe even younger.[102] Chloe asks Raymie, "Do you always do as you're told?" He responds, "You should try it sometime." She refuses to help decorate and declares: "Never having kids." Rayford greets her with sarcasm: "Nice touch with the nose ring, Chloe. Why not just shave your head and get it over with?" This adolescent rebellion allows for a greater character arc when she loses the mother that she took for granted.

The novel's Chloe wallows in grief and refuses to leave the house after the rapture, but this Chloe rushes to help others in crisis and seek the truth about the disappearances, foreshadowing the extremely active Chloe in the 2014 version. She is driving, listening to music and talking on her cell phone, when she comes upon a major accident. She bravely rushes into the scene, comforts an injured man, opens the door of a truck to find the driver gone, then shoulders her backpack and walks away when her car is

---

102. "Left Behind: The Movie Trivia," para. 9.

stolen. She returns home to find a man sleeping on her couch and threatens him with a vase: "Hold it right there. Don't move." She then recognizes him from television: "Buck Williams, what are you doing in my house?" Buck (Kirk Cameron) puts his hands up and responds: "Hoping you're not going to brain me with that vase." This is far more egalitarian than a first date in which they eat cookies and he wipes her mouth. She cries and Buck comforts her, but she insists on taking him to a private pilot: "I'll go mad if I just sit here and do nothing." Since Cameron is only four years older than Stephens, they do not appear to have a ten-year age gap.

Chloe removes her nose ring, the symbol of her rebellion, and her conversion happens quietly. She rejects Rayford's faith because he was such a bad father, and when she overhears him taking to Hattie, she asks: "Is that why you never had time for us?" Yet she gets out her *Teen Devotional Bible* (another signal of her age) and watches the rapture tape. Her conversion at the church happens simultaneously with Buck's conversion in the men's room; the same song plays as the camera cuts from Buck saying "All of it's true!" to Chloe kneeling before the cross with her father. However, the music fades while Buck prays aloud, whereas we do not hear Chloe speak. Buck confronts his reflection in an echo of Rayford's mirror scene, while Chloe imitates Rayford by folding her hands in prayer. She remains very much his child, especially since the film limits the romance to Chloe and Buck hugging in the final scene.

The film portrays Hattie as a successful career woman from the beginning. She walks through the plane, attending to the children, and we learn about her previous professional relationship with Buck when she tells him about her new job at the United Nations. Since many Christian viewers know that "Hattie" and "Buck" are married in real life, this brief filmic encounter shimmers with connotations of a modern partnership that balances marriage, children, and two careers. In the cockpit, Hattie informs Rayford coolly: "I'm taking a job at the UN. Tonight's my last flight." When he protests, she explains: "One of us had to make a move. . . . I'm tired of waiting, tired of the looks, the flirting, waiting for you to give me a reason why I should stay." He kisses her, indicating that their relationship has gone further than in the novel, but the camera cuts to the cabin where the rapture has just occurred. Her declaration of independence suggests that she will be liberated from Rayford by the rapture, not the other way around. Like Chloe, Hattie remains fairly calm about the disappearances: "I am not nuts, Ray. Go look for yourself." She has weak moments, begging Rayford not to leave her at the airport: "Stay with me, please. I'm so scared." She later goes to his house and leaves crying when he brandishes a Bible and asks forgiveness for their illicit relationship, but she doesn't call him after that with pathetic appeals for attention, and we next see her working at the United Nations.

Hattie landing this job before the rapture makes a lot more sense than the book's idea that a flight attendant could meet with a world leader simply because she is attracted to him. The novel insinuates that the antichrist did not choose his "personal assistant" for her clerical skills, but the film contains no sexual overtones. She clearly admires Carpathia but does not appear as his mistress. She does not panic during the murders, although she does submit to the brainwashing afterwards. Buck tries to warn her: "Hattie, you are in such . . ." and she interrupts: "I know, a privileged position. I intend to do whatever I can to help Nicolae. He's a great man." Nicolae approaches and puts his hand on her shoulder, then she follows him down the hall. Like Susan Pevensie in the Narnia films, Hattie remains a sympathetic nonbeliever who invites the viewer to empathize with her downfall rather than condemn her brainless flirtation.

Responses to the film bemoan its aesthetic, theological, and commercial failures, which Jenkins predicted in the novel. Buck watches a newscast of the destruction and thinks: "If somebody tried to sell a screenplay about millions of people disappearing, leaving everything but their bodies behind, it would be laughed off,"[103] and Ken Ritz claims that "millions of people all over the world disappearing into thin air sounds like a B movie."[104] The most expensive Christian film ever made with a budget of $17.4 million, it was a box office disappointment, and the two sequels went straight to video. Stephen Holden of the New York Times claims that it was "written and filmed in the clunking kitsch style of a 1970's made-for-television disaster movie. But the dialogue won't stop making bizarre thudding sounds."[105] Desson Howe of the Washington Post calls it "a blundering cringefest, thanks to unintentionally laughable dialogue, hackneyed writing and uninspired direction."[106] Scholar Heather Hendershot argues that Peter Lalonde is out of touch with secular audiences who "think that the Rapture is baloncy,"[107] although she also cites Cloud Ten's ill-advised marketing strategy of releasing the film on video before it appeared in theaters and a legal dispute which prevented them from using the book authors' names in advertising. Christopher Powers claims that the trilogy's blockbuster format makes it impossible to address genuine issues of faith, and in 2011, John Walliss argued that the

103. LaHaye and Jenkins, *Left Behind*, 110.
104. LaHaye and Jenkins, *Left Behind*, 120.
105. Holden, "Biblically Inspired Tale," para. 3.
106. Howe, "'Left Behind,'" para. 2.
107. Hendershot, *Shaking the World for Jesus*, 207.

trilogy's failure ended the rapture film trend. Little did he know that three more years would bring the Lalondes' second attempt at *Left Behind*. While this was not a great success either, it explodes the books' male fantasy by making Chloe the heroine.

"I FOUND A PLACE WHERE YOU GUYS CAN LAND": A STRONGER CHLOE IN *LEFT BEHIND* (2014)

In the latest film, the most famous actor plays a different character. Instead of the boyish Kirk Cameron as Buck, we have the middle-aged Nicolas Cage as Rayford. Quite a departure from the first film's brawny pilot played by a Marlboro Man, Cage is best known for playing dysfunctional or morally ambiguous characters in R-rated action, adventure, crime, drama, and thriller films. He won an Academy Award for playing a suicidal alcoholic in *Leaving Las Vegas*, and a nomination for playing self-loathing and dim-witted twins in *Adaptation*. He gained popularity as a terrorist in *Face/Off*, an ex-con in *Con Air*, and a historian evading the FBI in *National Treasure*. He rescued damsels in distress in three movies right before *Left Behind*: his kidnapped daughter in *Stolen*, a teen prostitute in *The Frozen Ground*, and a prospective rape victim in *Joe*, while he tried to avenge his daughter's killer in *Rage*. Audiences go into a Nicolas Cage film expecting action and adventure, which explains their bewildered response when he does nothing but slowly decide to believe in Jesus, and his inaction recalls his most celebrated roles as a pathetic loser. The film covers only the book's first two chapters: there is some new backstory, a much longer version of the opening airplane sequence, and new material in which Rayford struggles to land in apocalyptic New York City. Because Rayford and Buck (Chad Michael Murray) spend most of the movie trapped on the plane, the film heightens their frustration and denies them liberation, replacing male fantasy with mid-life crisis. In this feminist action movie, Chloe clears a runway and saves the passengers while her father and love interest look on helplessly from a broken cockpit symbolizing impotence.

The pre-rapture backstory again emphasizes Rayford's guilt. The film begins with Chloe (Cassi Thomson) arriving in New York for his birthday, but when she calls from the airport, Irene (Lea Thompson) tells her that he has to work. The previous film began with Rayford ditching his son's birthday, and now he ditches his own birthday to attend a concert with Hattie in London. We never see him at home, where Irene talks on the phone in the kitchen, the towels under her arm accentuating her homemaking role. As in the previous film, Irene looks like her daughter, this time with blonde hair, hoop earrings, necklace, and stylish top. She lovingly discusses her faith with Chloe: "This is important to me. And so are you." Chloe storms out of the house, leaving Irene watching sadly in the window. Yet one later glimpse of Irene's life reveals the "iron and steel" that makes her name symbolic in the novels. After the rapture, Chloe opens Irene's Bible to a prayer list marking the "Song of Moses" from Deuteronomy. The shot includes phrases like "I kill, and I make alive," "whet my glittering sword," and "make mine arrows drunk with blood." While her husband was away, Irene was a leader in the army of God. Chloe takes over Rayford's role in the earlier film by throwing the Bible through the window.

Irene gets the moral high ground, but Hattie (Nicky Whelan) is not developed much beyond the novel. The first shots of Hattie exaggerate the male cinematic gaze: close-ups of her hand reaching into her bag, pulling out lip gloss, and uncapping it, then her lips in the rearview mirror as she applies the gloss. We briefly see her eyes in the mirror before she puts on sunglasses. After a point-of-view shot in which she watches Rayford's car approach, the camera cuts to her spike heels and long, bare legs emerging from the car. A similar sequence repeats in Rayford's car, with a close-up of his hand removing his wedding ring, then shots of him leaving the car and walking toward Hattie. She coyly asks, "Going my way?" Although the film leans heavily on Rayford's unworthiness as a husband, Hattie remains merely an object of temptation.

After the rapture, Rayford can control his emotions while Hattie cannot. She cries and whimpers, "Ray, I'm scared. Aren't you?" He responds: "I will be, as soon as I have time." Yet this version lessens her guilt because she is furious when she discovers that Rayford is married: "You lied to me about your wife. You lied to your wife about this trip. You even lied to your own daughter. It seems that you're able to lie to just about everybody in your life, and now you're asking me to find God?" The film retains the theme that Rayford ruins his evangelistic credibility by failing to take responsibility for the broken relationship. In the DVD's "Behind the Scenes Featurette," Whelan states: "It's too easy just to come in and play this nasty girl that's having an affair with the captain. She doesn't know that he's married."

Hattie Durham (Nicky Whelan) learns that Rayford Steele (Nicolas Cage) is married in *Left Behind* (2014). The human figures are dwarfed by the edges of a cockpit symbolizing male angst and entrapment. Courtesy of Stoney Lake Entertainment.

This allows Hattie to redeem herself through her work: "She's going to help save everyone and their lives, and she really puts her priorities right." Both movie versions of Hattie gain our sympathy far more than the novel character who knew that Rayford was married and remains obnoxious for eight books before she finally dies. Since this movie ends with the plane landing, Hattie does not become the mistress of the antichrist.

Chloe emerges as the protagonist of this story, which reverses the typical scenario in which heroic male action rescues the trapped and passive female. In an early airport scene, Chloe defends Buck when he is harassed by an overbearing Christian woman, the type that the novelists and filmmakers find most annoying. The woman purchases Buck's book *Acts of God* and then confronts him when he is signing autographs: "Can I ask you a question, Mr. Williams? Do you read the Bible?" He demurs, and she continues: "Matthew 24, verse 7, says that there shall be famines, pestilence, and earthquakes in diverse places. All of these things, the disasters, the wars, they are all signs." What thoughtful evangelist combines a hostile tone with the word "diverse?" The viewer cannot help but take Chloe's side when she challenges the woman about why God allows natural disasters, setting up her preoccupation with the problem of evil. Like Susan Pevensie in the Narnia films, Chloe has a clear and relatable reason to resist the gospel message and remains sympathetic despite this resistance. She captures Buck's interest by "rescuing" him from a Christian woman that is obnoxious even to evangelical filmmakers.

The egalitarian romance unfolds as Buck joins Chloe at her table, says "I enjoyed your speech," and knocks over her jacket as he introduces himself. Murray is twelve years older than Thomson, increasing the book's age gap, but Buck's nerves undercut his professional experience. He notices the UCA Bears logo on her jacket—Chloe has been downgraded from Stanford to the University of Central Arkansas—but she holds her own in their banter:

> BUCK. So you're in college?
> CHLOE. Wow, that investigative journalism really pays off.
> BUCK. I just wanted to say thank you for rescuing me from that
> 　　　nutty lady.

Rather than getting cookie on her face like in the novel, she declines his offer to buy her coffee, and they discuss her frustration with her parents. She leaves the table to confront Rayford when he arrives, asking about his wedding ring as he lamely pretends that he doesn't know Hattie. Chloe then asks Buck why a loving God would not save people from earthquakes and tsunamis. This scene belies Hendershot's generalization: "No unsaved character in evangelical film or fiction ever resists for complicated political or theological reasons."[108] The problem of evil is a complicated issue that many viewers could understand as a barrier to faith for a thoughtful and compassionate person. Chloe is not just a brat rebelling against her mom.

The rapture occurs when Chloe and Raymie are shopping at the mall, allowing her to take on the role of the panicking "mother" whose child disappears. The camera cuts from Chloe holding Raymie's empty clothes, to a mother at the mall holding up her arms, to Hattie offering Rayford coffee on the plane, to Shasta Carvell (Jordin Sparks) seeing her daughter's empty seat and screaming. The rapture first affects women and families, not Rayford and Hattie. As we cut between the mall and the plane, Shasta cries out "Have you seen my daughter?," while Chloe yells "Raymie!" Chaos breaks out in the mall, beginning the action sequences in which Chloe fights for survival on the mean streets of postrapture New York City. The novel barely covered her trip home from Stanford, but the film extensively covers her trip home from the mall.

---

108. Hendershot, *Shaking the World for Jesus*, 202.

Chloe Steele (Cassi Thomson) narrowly avoids a plane crashing into the mall parking lot in *Left Behind* (2014). Courtesy of Stoney Lake Entertainment.

She dodges a small plane that crashes into her parked car and catches fire, watches a school bus crash into a river, runs from a man pointing a gun at her, breaks a hospital door, and crawls through broken glass. The genre switches from action to horror as she arrives home, wields a baseball bat, and searches the rooms more bravely than her father did in the book. She hears the shower running, echoing the most famous scene of *Psycho*, opens the door, and sees her mother's jewelry on the floor. Rather than Rayford slowly uncovering his wife's nightgown, the film focuses on Chloe realizing that she is alone in a life-threatening situation.

Meanwhile, all is not well in the cockpit, where the filmmakers invent numerous terrors to make the hours in the plane exciting and to drive home the theme of beleaguered masculinity. Donna Peberdy identified this trend three years earlier in *Masculinity and Film Performance: Male Angst in Contemporary American Cinema*: "I suggest that two 'events' in the late 1990s and early 2000s—the introduction of Viagra onto the marketplace and the mass retirement of the 'baby boom'—brought the aging male to the fore."[109] In the 1995 novel, Rayford had no technical difficulties with the plane and contacted another pilot fairly quickly. In the 2014 film, Rayford's birthday makes him feel old, his first officer disappears, the plane starts to dive, and he can't contact anyone. Despite nearly twenty years of technological progress,

109. Peberdy, *Masculinity and Film Performance*, 14.

he calls desperately into his headset: "Come on, there has to be someone out there!" Rayford collides with an unmanned aircraft, his plane starts leaking fuel, and he loses the elevators: "Looks like we've begun our descent into New York about two hours early." Rayford's plane has become impotent and the only direction that he can travel is down. He is much slower to recognize the rapture than in the novel, and the filmmakers give tiny clues that are difficult to follow. One close-up of the missing first officer's watch seems to have great significance, but it is hard to see the miniscule "John 3:16" in the center. It is slightly more understandable when Rayford finds a Bible study in a missing flight attendant's planner. He learns that all the runways are closed, and he cries from his death trap: "I need some room!"

Reviewers reserved their greatest sarcasm for Cage's melancholy performance, revealing how much the male fantasy has been stripped away. The *Los Angeles Times* quips, "To say he sleepwalks through this one would be an insult to sleepwalkers."[110] The *New York Times* claims that "Cage keeps his jaw set on resolute and his body language on weary,"[111] the *Washington Post* that he delivers "one of the lowest-energy performances of his career,"[112] the *Hollywood Reporter* that he "seems virtually sedated,"[113] and *Variety* that "he simply looks tired."[114] RogerEbert.com describes him as "oddly inert as the movie's voice of reason. Looking distractingly rubbery with a helmet of fake, dark hair, he seems to have been Photoshopped into the film. His presence is so strangely awkward and unconvincing."[115] The *Chicago Tribune* jokes that of the film's $16 million budget, "roughly $15 million appears to have gone to Cage on a dare that he maintain a straight face."[116] *LA Weekly* speculates, "Perhaps Cage flipped a coin before Armstrong called 'Action!' and decided to play this role straight."[117] Cage's performance stems from a script that traps him in a chair with no opportunities to change his life or enjoy the freedoms of the tribulation.

While Rayford and Buck worry about landing the plane, the first-class passengers form a community with the women as damsels in distress. There is a senile old woman and a blonde drug addict who panics and sleeps a lot, although she talks about the rapture that she learned about in summer

---

110. Goldstein, "'Left Behind' Is a Disaster," para. 3.

111. Catsoulis, "Flight Was Fully Booked," para. 2.

112. Michael O'Sullivan, "'Left Behind' Movie Review," para. 4.

113. Scheck, Review of *Left Behind*, para. 10.

114. Barker, "Film Review: 'Left Behind,'" para. 7.

115. Lemire, Review of *Left Behind*, para. 5.

116. Phillips, "Review: 'Left Behind,'" para. 2.

117. Nicholson, "*Left Behind* Is Sinfully Boring," para. 7.

camp. The script provides few clear names, although the credits identify Christian singer Jordin Sparks's character as Shasta. She irrationally believes that her husband has kidnapped her daughter and waves a gun around before turning it on herself. Buck soothes her by telling a story about his mom dying: "I came home from school one day, and I found her. She was lying there, still. Don't you do that to Katie. Now, we may not know what happened here today, but it is not Katie's fault. Do you hear me?" Bad motherhood continues to be a major theme as men protect women from their own weakness and destruction.

While the passengers slowly plummet toward their deaths, Chloe climbs a bridge at sunset and looks across the water like a Statue of Liberty, with an orange light standing in for the flaming torch. Yet we learn that she may be suicidal when we see the note that she wrote to Rayford: "Today is the saddest day of my life." On the soundtrack, the Dani and Lizzy song "Dancing in the Sky" questions whether heaven is really peaceful and free. Chloe looks up and tells her mom that she is sorry, and a high-angle shot of her looking down suggests that she is about to jump when Buck calls. She learns that there is nowhere for the plane to land, climbs down, and turns into an action hero, complete with fast-paced music and unrealistic details. She instantly finds an abandoned motorcycle, sitting there many hours after the rapture with its headlight on, and rides off to find a runway.

Rayford, Buck, and Chloe stay in touch while she clears a strip of highway that was closed for construction. In an eerie reminder of 9/11, Rayford warns that if he can't find a runway, "I'll be flying a 400-ton missile right into Queens." This explains the film's change of setting from Chicago to New York and implies that Chloe can single-handedly prevent another 9/11. At the construction area, she jumps into a truck, drives over a barrier, and calls Buck: "Put me on speaker! I think I found a place where you guys can land. The new east-west highway near the mall. No one's out here. I think I can clear enough room." She slams through barriers, opens a compass app and reads coordinates, swerves around a "Men Working" sign, and moves a road roller, as Rayford makes the Freudian aside to Buck: "I'm going to need every inch she can get us." She performs a traditional female role by giving the men space, but she saves their lives by moving heavy construction equipment. She clears nine-tenths of a mile before the plane approaches, but the men hold a condescending private conversation with Buck saying there's not enough room and Rayford responding: "If there isn't, I don't want her to think it was her fault." Yet Chloe is determined to create enough light for them to see the runway. She pours gasoline over the road equipment, throws a lighter on it, and drives off. Magically, the plane flies over her and lands inches away from a tank full of flammable material. Chloe runs after the plane while Hattie opens the door and throws down the landing chute, tell-ing everyone: "Let's go!" The women move, while the men remain trapped.

The film returns to conventional romantic imagery as Chloe and Buck embrace, the same image that ended the 2000 film. This time, he thanks her for saving his life and says: "Looks like the end of the world." Chloe gets the last line: "I'm afraid this is just the beginning." Over the closing credits, Jordin Sparks sings Larry Norman's "I Wish We'd All Been Ready," featured in the 1972 rapture film *A Thief in the Night*. This ties the film to its "Jesus Freak" forebears and signals a subtle departure from the books. Radosh observes that "there is no sense in the *Left Behind* books that the au-thors *actually* wish we'd all been ready. They're far more invested in having someone around to get their asses kicked."[118] Yet the song does not seem out of place in the film, which lingers on the initial crisis that brings the world together. Norman's gentle lyrics match a final scene in which Chloe saves a plane full of nonbelievers, in contrast to the books in which they are brutally destroyed by wars and plagues.

The *Left Behind* franchise has many limitations, but the changes in women's roles reveal the complexity of gender ideology and the ways in which filmmakers try to broaden their audiences by appealing to women. Like Susan from *The Chronicles of Narnia* and Angel from *Redeeming Love*, Hattie and Chloe are beautiful young women in crisis whom the authors punish for their lack of submission to male authority but whom the film-makers portray more sympathetically. The films also incorporate racial di-versity. In the DVD special feature "The Making of *Left Behind: The Movie*," Clarence Gilyard stated that although Bruce wasn't black in the script, "God just decided that I would play this character." Bruce becomes the wise men-tor who shows Rayford the rapture video in which Pastor Vernon Billings is also black. The sequel *Left Behind: World at War* stars Academy-Award-winning black actor Louis Gossett Jr. as President Gerald Fitzhugh, and the tradition continues in the 2014 version, filmed in Baton Rouge, Louisiana, with Bruce played by New Orleans native Lance Nichols. These roles an-ticipate the Sherwood Baptist Church films discussed in the next chapter, in which Kirk Cameron returns, but the complexity of black and Latino characters will far exceed anything in *Left Behind*.

118. Radosh, *Rapture Ready!*, 84 (italics original).

Chapter 5

FROM SIDEKICKS TO PROTAGONISTS

Black and Latino Characters in the Films
of the Sherwood Baptist Church

The Sherwood Baptist Church of Albany, Georgia has become famous for creating Christian films with mainstream success far beyond the church basement. Written and directed by brothers Stephen and Alex Kendrick, with church members participating in the acting, music, set design, and camera work, the films have exceeded box office expectations. The first film, *Flywheel,* cost $20,000 and showed in a few local theaters, but the fifth film, *War Room,* cost $3 million and grossed over $67 million in the USA.[1] While Christian films are often cheesy and unrealistic, Sherwood Pictures handles topics such as business ethics, infertility, divorce, pornography, gang violence, childhood death, and adultery. The films began with black characters in minor roles and have become increasingly sophisticated in their depiction of race relations in twenty-first-century Georgia. The limited characters in the early films represent the "sincere fictions" that Hernán Vera and Andrew M. Gordon describe in *Screen Saviors: Hollywood Fictions of Whiteness*: "Sincerity refers to our remaining unaware of alternative aspects we could have incorporated into these fictions. To be sincere implies honestly believing in something, although one could also be sincere out of repression, denial, naïveté, or simple ignorance."[2] Yet the Kendricks did not remain unaware of these concerns. Whereas Jan Karon made a radical change in her racial portrayals, the Kendricks have improved them

1. "War Room."
2. Vera and Gordon, *Screen Saviors,* 16.

gradually without alienating their fans. From *Flywheel* to *War Room*, the films progressed from using the black buddy as comic relief to portraying black and Latino protagonists whose strength and wisdom overcome profound challenges.

"A BLACK MAN IN A BLACK MAN'S BODY": BUDDY COMEDY IN *FLYWHEEL* AND *FACING THE GIANTS*

In the "buddy film," two men from different races bond while fighting mutual enemies. Although the interracial comradeship seems progressive, the films reinforce white supremacy by placing the white buddy in a leadership role, denying racism, and depicting the villains as racial stereotypes. In "The Buddy Politic," Cynthia J. Fuchs argues that filmmakers bury racial differences "under a collective performance of extraordinary virility."[3] In *American Anatomies*, Robyn Wiegman agrees that the buddy narrative "transforms the historical contestations between black and white men into the image of democratic fraternity."[4] In *Toms, Coons, Mulattoes, Mammies, and Bucks*, Donald Bogle analyzes interracial buddies from Bing Crosby and Louis Armstrong to Frank Sinatra and Sammy Davis Jr.:

> In essence, all these teams have been wish-fulfillment fantasies for a nation that has repeatedly hoped to simplify its racial tensions. The movie relationships have usually been frauds, refusing to explore the complex and often contradictory dynamics of real interracial friendships. Such movie friendships have usually held to one dictum: namely, that interracial buddies can be such only when the white buddy is in charge.[5]

Brian Locke critiques the Orientalist buddy film in which black and white protagonists draw together before an Asian threat, "a fantasy that denies rather than resolves the long-running and ongoing practice of white supremacy."[6] The first two Sherwood films follow these patterns by placing the white buddy in a superior role and avoiding the subject of racism, although they do not indulge in the typical Hollywood violence.[7]

3. Fuchs, "Buddy Politic," 195.

4. Wiegman, *American Anatomies*, 118.

5. Bogle, *Toms, Coons, Mulattoes*, 271–72.

6. Locke, *Racial Stigma*, 9.

7. In another common reading of the buddy film, the male bond is haunted by potential homosexual attraction that must be denied by inserting wives and girlfriends into the plot. Fuchs claims that "these films efface the intimacy and vulnerability associated with homosexuality by the 'marriage' of racial others, so that this

Alex Kendrick explains in the DVD introduction that the church created *Flywheel* (2003) as a local ministry, and they were shocked when it made its way to video stores nationwide and several television networks. Kendrick plays Jay Austin, a dishonest used car salesman who is indifferent to his pregnant wife Judy (Janet Lee Dapper) and his son. The film begins with Jay buying a classic car—a white Triumph—that clearly evokes white privilege, but the first lines of dialogue establish that it doesn't run, just as the owner's life is broken almost beyond repair. On the verge of financial ruin, Jay finds God and begins an ethical life. An undercover journalist reports his fair prices, saving his business and allowing him to reimburse customers that he cheated. *Flywheel* introduces the main theme of the first four Sherwood films: white masculinity in crisis. The ordinary people and mundane activities exemplify Donna Peberdy's claim that "cinematic performances of male angst, and male identity in general, are intricately and intimately connected to performances of male social roles in everyday life."[8] Jay's employee Sam Jones (Marc Keenan) and customer Katie Harris (Rutha Harris) are minor black characters who call out his shortcomings and introduce him to a higher moral standard in a humorous and supportive manner.

Sam first appears as a minor background character, washing his hands in the kitchen behind the office and shaking his head in judgement over Jay's shady business deal. Like generations of black domestic servants before him, Sam stays in the back and keeps his opinions about his boss to himself. This scene provides the full names of white salesmen Bernie Meyers (Tracy Goode) and Vince Berkley (Treavor Lokey), repeating Bernie's name five times and Vince's three times, but we do not learn Sam's name for another

---

transgressiveness displaces homosexual anxiety" ("Buddy Politic," 195). Mark Simpson makes a similar argument about buddy war films, in which men pay the ultimate price for their emotional bonds: "Classically, the moment when the buddy lies dead or dying is the moment when the full force of the love the boys/men feel for one another can be shown. And, for all the efforts of the conscientious film maker, the deadliness is thus attached not so much to *war* as to the queer romance of it all" (*Male Impersonators*, 214). Wiegman adds that "the homosocial bond's assertion of a stridently undifferentiated masculine space can function to veil its simultaneous rejuvenation of racial hierarchies" (*American Anatomies*, 125). While the Sherwood films do not discuss homosexuality openly, *Fireproof* and *Courageous* address the temptation for men to linger in an all-male workplace at the expense of their families. The *Fireproof* special feature "Firegoofs" includes a Freudian slip in which Kirk Cameron starts to tell his black buddy: "Michael, I have been married to you for five years," rather than "I have worked with you for five years." Male bonding becomes destructive when it replaces marital bonding. Despite their buddy film parallels, the Sherwood films cover women's struggles and defend women's right to emotional support from their husbands far more than mainstream action movies.

8. Peberdy, *Masculinity and Film Performance*, 15.

fifteen minutes. He seems to have a custodial job, since we later see him polishing cars. He wears a backwards baseball cap, jeans, and the same sweatshirt that he wears in all of his scenes. When Jay leaves the office after telling a male customer that girls will love his new car, Sam jokes: "I know that's what my woman always wanted: a 1988 wrecked Honda." Thus far he seems like a typical black buddy who will provide comic relief without challenging the viewer's worldview.

Yet Sam's disapproval of his boss undermines the stereotypical "tom" that Bogle traces back to *Uncle Tom's Cabin*: "Always as toms are chased, harassed, hounded, flogged, enslaved, and insulted, they keep the faith, n'er turn against their white massas, and remain hearty, submissive, stoic, generous, selfless, and oh-so-very kind."[9] Despite his low status in the workplace, Sam is more ethical than the white salesmen. His reference to "what my woman always wanted" gives little information about his personal life, but he seems to care about his partner more than Jay cares about Judy. We next see Sam watching the obese Bernie and Vince squeeze out of a Miata. He shakes his head at their laziness and gluttony and compares them to marshmallows getting out of a Hot Wheel. We learn his name when Bernie says: "That's not funny, Sam!" His responsibility separates him from Bogle's description of the unreliable "coon"[10] and his mild manner from the "brutal black buck."[11] He may not strike most viewers as significant, but he is a relatable person rather than a destructive stereotype.

Sam proves his moral fiber thirty minutes later, when Jay informs the staff that he has decided to run an ethical business. The scene begins with banter as Bernie describes himself as "a hard-working man trapped in a lazy man's body" and Vince as "a tan body-builder trapped in a chubby white man's body." Jay asks Sam what they should know about him, and Sam retorts: "I'm just a black man in a black man's body, working with a bunch of *strange* white boys." This line denies Southern racism by presenting black men's physicality as natural and uncomplicated, but Sam also sets himself apart and "washes his hands" of the others, as he did literally in the opening scene. Sam nods approvingly when Jay tells them to set honest prices; when Bernie and Vince storm out, Sam says: "I told you those were strange white boys," linking their greed and dishonesty to their outraged sense of white privilege. Sam gets promoted to salesman, shows talent, and outsmarts a customer who tries to take advantage of him. In his few minutes on screen,

9. Bogle, *Toms, Coons, Mulattoes*, 4–6.
10. Bogle, *Toms, Coons, Mulattoes*, 7–8.
11. Bogle, *Toms, Coons, Mulattoes*, 10.

he sets the precedent for later portrayals of black men as defenders of Christian faith.

Katie is another comical black character who exposes Jay's self-righteousness after his conversion. When Jay returns money to former customers, one young black woman cries and says, "This is an answer to my prayer," and a black businesswoman hugs him. This seems like a "white savior" scenario, in which beneficent whites provide for people of color. According to Vera and Gordon, "The messianic white self is the redeemer of the weak, the great leader who saves blacks from slavery or oppression, rescues people of color from poverty and disease, or leads Indians in battle for their dignity and survival."[12] In *The White Savior Film*, Matthew W. Hughey describes "the genre in which a white messianic character saves a lower- or working-class, usually urban or isolated, nonwhite character from a sad fate."[13] *Flywheel* complicates this trope because Jay *caused* the characters' hardship by overcharging them for the cars, and he provides financial restitution rather than charity. He tells Judy, "I thought I'd have to eat crow," linking his abuse of power to the Jim Crow era.

We realize that the filmmakers are setting up Jay for a fall, evoking the "white savior" only to make Vera and Gordon's point that "messiah fantasies are essentially grandiose, exhibitionistic, and narcissistic."[14] The fall comes when Katie responds with anger rather than gratitude: "You cheated me? So you think you can waltz right in with a twelve-hundred-dollar check and expect me to accept what you've done?" Her black relative chimes in with phrases like "That's right!" When Jay tries to get a word in edgewise, Katie says: "Don't you interrupt me!" She whacks him repeatedly over the head with the check as she finishes her tirade: "I'm tired of the lies, the deceit, the confessions, and everything else." Jay leaves in shame while Katie says: "Now get out of here and go get right with God, before I get you right with him." Then she happily exclaims: "Oh, sweet Jesus! Twelve hundred dollars!" We cut to Sam laughing at Jay: "So you were getting kind of cocky, weren't you?" His comment links the two black characters who judge Jay's moral progress.

Katie wraps her outrage in humor and conforms to Bogle's description of the mammy as "big, fat, and cantankerous."[15] Yet she is a far cry from the self-sacrificing Aunt Delilah in *Imitation of Life* or Louella Baxter Marshall in *Mitford*, who decline money from their employers. Katie takes Jay's money because she knows it rightfully belongs to her. In the DVD special feature

12. Vera and Gordon, *Screen Saviors*, 33.

13. Hughey, *White Savior Film*, 1.

14. Vera and Gordon, *Screen Saviors*, 34.

15. Bogle, *Toms, Coons, Mulattoes*, 9.

"The Making of *Flywheel*," Kendrick explains that he was filming volunteer actress Rutha Harris in her home, and her sister Rosetta was watching. He suggested incorporating her into the scene: "What if she's responding to her sister as if she's preaching a sermon? So all I did was turn the camera to her and ask her, 'Would you do me a favor? And would you mind me filming you saying just one word here or there like "Amen!" or "Tell him!" or "That's right!"' And she said sure. And so she was already sitting there, you know, eating a snack. I did nothing to prep her." Despite Kendrick's claim that "all I did was turn the camera to her," his enthusiasm for black preaching as a form of humor clearly shaped the scene, as we will see again in *Facing the Giants*.

But the scene's magic is due to the hilarious performances of the Harris sisters. Mark Moring's *Christianity Today* article "A Black & White Production" places Rutha Harris in the center of civil rights history:

> When Martin Luther King Jr. led a civil rights march into Albany, Georgia, in December 1961, racial tensions were boiling. Jim Crow laws were still in effect, the Ku Klux Klan was a threat, and most whites were serious about keeping blacks in their place.
>
> As one of the original Freedom Singers, Rutha Harris marched alongside King, singing songs like "Ain't Gonna Let Nobody Turn Me Around," while whites lined the streets, harassing the passing activists. "Those songs gave us hope," says Harris, 70, who still lives in Albany. "They filled the voids that segregation brought into our lives."[16]

Moring describes the city's intense racism and the ground-breaking partnership of the mostly white Sherwood Baptist Church and the mostly black Mt. Zion Baptist Church in providing social services and collaborating on the films. The Kendricks state later in the DVD commentary that Rutha appeared in the choir in *The Preacher's Wife*, so this scene combines the talents of an experienced actress with the details of her real home (not a white set designer's idea of a black woman's home) and her interactions with her real sister.[17] The scene has an important message for white Christians: don't think you're a hero for doing the right thing.

Katie reappears to rescue Jay after a conniving television reporter forces him to admit that he used to cheat customers, and he cannot prove that he has changed. After a lengthy montage of white characters praying,

16. Moring, "Black & White Production," 55.

17. Unless otherwise stated, all statements about the films from Stephen and Alex Kendrick come from the DVD commentaries. Since their words often overlap, I will refer to them simply as "the Kendricks."

Katie arrives as the answer to their prayer, balancing the earlier scene when Jay was "an answer to my prayer" for a black customer. A shot of Katie's black vehicle prefigures her appearance as God's messenger, echoing previous shots of Jay's white vehicle pulling into the lot after significant acts of God. Katie marches up and tells the reporter that Jay gave her money back: "This story ain't over until you report that." We find out her name on the caption of the news broadcast when the reporter interviews her. Katie then points a finger at Jay: "Now I have rebuked you. I have defended you. Now it's time for you to stand up and be a godly man worth defending. Do you understand me?" Like Sam, Katie stands up for old-fashioned morals, although she can be more aggressive because a middle-aged black woman is less threatening than a young black man. She is a maternal figure who cares for the white hero, but she insists on getting the money that he owes her, refuses to act grateful, and tells him what she thinks of him. She does not stay in the background but walks confidently into a live interview and speaks her mind to the whole region. This film does not include serious discussion of racism, and it ends with the white Triumph running smoothly, but Sam and Katie undercut the tom and mammy stereotypes by criticizing a white man with power over them.

Facing the Giants (2006) follows a recognizable plot formula: the underdog sports team that wins the state championship. Grant Taylor (Alex Kendrick) is a Shiloh Christian Academy football coach with a losing record who renews his faith and trains the players to follow God. The film participates in the cinematic trend of men whose "failure to live up to the perceived expectations of male social roles is key to their downfall and angst."[18] The Kendricks did not downplay Christian themes as they reached mainstream box office success, since this film has more obvious biblical parallels than *Flywheel*. David Childers (Bailey Cave), the small kid who befriends his teammate Jonathan and beats the rival team the Giants, echoes the story of David and Goliath from 1 Samuel 17. Assistant Coach J. T. Hawkins (Chris Willis) expands on Sam's role as the black buddy whose gentle humor reveals his boss's mistakes.

J. T. first appears in Grant's office, looking serious, shaking his head, and wearing a wedding ring, echoing Sam's moral judgment and subtle connection to family. Whereas Sam had a minor role compared to white sidekick Bernie (played by Tracy Goode), J. T. has equal status with Assistant Coach Brady Owens (also played by Goode). They break the news to Grant that another player transferred to a rival team, and Brady jokes: "Nobody wants to be on TV going, 'We're number six!'" Like Sam, J. T. waits

---

18. Peberdy, *Masculinity and Film Performance*, 89.

until his boss leaves, then says: "Just had to go there, didn't you?" In the next office scene, Brady makes fun of J. T.'s bald head, and J. T. responds: "No, see, when a black man goes bald, he still looks good. Look at Michael Jordan, George Foreman, Samuel L. Jackson. Classy-looking brothers. Who you got? Kojak?" The Kendricks note that Willis shaved his head for this line, requiring him to embody the convention that he gently mocks, while the numerous bald black men in their films reinforce the stereotype. J. T.'s expression of racial pride echoes Sam's claim that "I'm just a black man in a black man's body," supporting the idea that black male physicality and identity are simple and unproblematic.

The Kendricks hired Willis despite his lack of acting experience: "We wrote those lines hoping we would find a young, black, Christian George Jefferson, and Chris nailed that role." Yet television scholars have critiqued the sitcom *The Jeffersons* (1975–1985) and the buffoonish character that Gerard Jones calls "a retrograde bigot, a domestic tyrant, a social idiot."[19] Robin R. Means Coleman and Charlton D. McIlwain state about *The Jeffersons*, "Blackness was represented as sassy and rude, barely tolerable, and hardly useful."[20] In *Prime Time Blues*, Bogle notes that George "seemed an update of the exaggerated comic coon,"[21] but many black viewers liked his confident racial identity and zest for life. Presumably, the Kendricks wanted J. T. to resemble George Jefferson in his witty one-liners, rather than his bigotry, foolishness, rudeness, or snobbery.

Indeed, J. T. is more than a buffoon. Like Sam, he serves as a moral touchstone for his white boss, following his example by using the Bible to teach football skills. J. T. encourages David to kick the ball into the center of the goal by preaching from Matthew 7: "'Narrow is the gate and straight is the way that leads to life, and few there be that find it.' Anybody could kick it wide left or wide right. My momma can kick it wide left and wide right. But that ain't what's gonna get you home." The upbeat music, Brady respond-ing "Come on!" and "Oh, my word!," and J. T.'s pronounced dialect evoke a black church sermon and black stand-up comedy that uses the phrase "my momma." The Kendricks explain that they wrote this scene early in the pro-cess, and it was one of their favorites. Like Karon, they defend the humor as uniquely Southern: "Our test audiences—the Southern audiences—loved it. Some of the Northern ones don't get it. They don't understand; they've never been in a black church; they don't know how this works. Everybody should attend an African American church where you have this response from the

---

19. Gerard Jones, *Honey, I'm Home!*, 220.

20. Means Coleman and McIlwain, "Hidden Truths," 130.

21. Bogle, *Prime Time Blues*, 212.

audience when they agree with the minister. You've got to do that at least once." This form of ethnic borrowing uses black preaching for comic effect, and the Kendricks encourage viewers to attend black churches as tourism, but they extend appreciation for them in a region still haunted by racist violence.

J. T. remains funny and encouraging when he discovers the new truck that a player's father donated to the coach. J. T. has been complaining that Grant never uses the plays he suggests, but then he finds the note on the vehicle and joyfully proclaims: "Somebody done gave you a truck!" Dramatic music swells and Grant's eyes fill with tears, but J. T. undercuts the sentimentality: "Is this just 'cause you head coach? 'Cause I'm assistant coach. You'd think I'd get a moped out of this or something." J. T. plays the "tom" by supporting his boss, but he resembles Katie Harris in expressing his desire for the payment that he deserves. The truck's "Jay Austin Motors" license plate reinforces the connection to *Flywheel* and suggests that Kendrick's previous character has progressed to selling expensive new vehicles. The two white characters are greatly blessed, while we never see J. T. in his own car or home.

A locker room scene demonstrates the subtle dynamics of interracial banter. The assistant coaches are cleaning helmets when J. T. tells Grant that Stan Shultz called him, inspiring an extended verbal prank on their boss when he moves offscreen:

> BRADY. Stan Shultz. Isn't that the cartoonist?
> GRANT. That's Charles Schulz.
> J. T. No, I thought Charles Schulz was that man that flew across the ocean in the *Spirit of St. Andrew*.
> GRANT. That's Charles Lindbergh, and it was the *Spirit of St. Louis*.
> BRADY. No, Lindbergh is a cheese.

The dialogue continues with the assistants claiming that Limburger is "that blimp that blew up," Hindenburg is "where you go skiing in Tennessee," and Gatlinburg is "the country music group." Unlike the racist vaudeville routine in which the black man played the fool, this joke is on the white man's failure to recognize that his employees are only feigning ignorance. Clearly, J. T. is not as stupid as Grant thinks. This is the last extended scene between the three men, since the road to the championship leaves J. T. and Brady on the sidelines. Neither of the buddy characters plays a role in the film's drama, but this will change with the next production.

"THE REAL DEAL": THE BLACK MENTOR IN *FIREPROOF* AND *COURAGEOUS*

Fireproof (2008) marked a new level of professionalism as the church hired Kirk Cameron from *Left Behind* to play Caleb Holt, a firefighter who saves his marriage to Catherine (Erin Bethea) with a book called *The Love Dare*.[22] The main cast includes four African Americans, in addition to minor characters like the Turner family whose daughter is rescued from a house fire by Caleb. The Kendricks divide the roles of comic buddy and moral conscience between rookie firefighter Terrell Sanders (Eric Young) and veteran firefighter Michael Simmons (Ken Bevel). Catherine's colleagues, Latasha Brown and Deidra Harris (real sisters Renata and Dwan Williams), echo Katie Harris's humorously uncensored observations. Many familiar black roles return in *Fireproof*, but now a black mentor plays a significant role in the drama.

Chubby sidekick Terrell engages in comic banter and pranks at the firehouse with white fellow rookies Eric and Wayne, although a few references to his atheism gesture toward serious character development. He is the only black male character in the films with an ethnic name, and his first scene has dramatic potential as he rebukes Eric for abandoning him during a fire: "This ain't no game. You playin' with people's lives." Yet he quickly walks offscreen, and Caleb continues his speech for him. Terrell later sweeps the firehouse kitchen and tells Wayne that marriage is "a lot harder than you think," but his home life remains as undeveloped as those of Sam and J. T.

22. Two fascinating studies examine *Fireproof*'s surprising box office success, grossing over $33 million. James Russell argues, "At first glance, *Fireproof* seems to be a quintessential independent Evangelical release, but in fact the film was the product of a complex arrangement established between Sherwood Pictures and the larger machinery of Hollywood" ("Evangelical Audiences," 392). Despite the Kendricks' emphasis on their independence from the mainstream film industry, the Sony distributor Provident Films paid for the entire theatrical release. Russell concludes that "we can begin to understand the significance of a film like *Fireproof* if we view Sherwood Pictures as a filmmaking 'brand' that has been acquired and then carefully developed by a major Hollywood studio" ("Evangelical Audiences," 406–7). Gillian Frank analyzes the bestselling book *The Love Dare* as an astute cross-promotional tactic that allowed film viewers to apply the dare to their own marriages and write about their experiences on the book's website. However, most participants did not get beyond day ten, and many who persevered could not save their marriages, supporting Frank's argument "that the consequences of readers striving to love in the manner prescribed by the Kendricks—unconditionally—perpetuate non-reciprocal, non-egalitarian, unloving, and sometimes abusive relationships" ("'Ideals of Stability,'" para. 4). Although Frank does not articulate the situation this way, women are socialized to value and invest in relationships, so it stands to reason that a husband like Caleb is more likely to win back his wife than a wife to win back her husband.

Only in deleted scenes does Terrell argue with Michael about God and ask Caleb for advice about his broken marriage. In the final cut, Terrell serves primarily to lighten the mood when the drama becomes too serious.

Caleb's best friend Michael is better developed than any previous black character, with a seemingly perfect marriage and hidden scars. The Kendricks point out that volunteer actor Ken Bevel was a Marine who left for Kuwait and Iraq after filming, so "Ken really is Michael." Michael displays his muscular physique while risking his life for others, but he also provides wise counsel about domestic life. Caleb first asks him for advice in the firehouse weight room, the most masculine space in an all-male environment. Michael admits that his marriage went through hard times, but he took responsibility: "I realized that it wasn't my marriage that was broken. I just didn't know how to make it work." He advises counseling with a mildly sexist metaphor: "Catherine does need to respect you. But just remember, a woman's like a rose. If you treat her right, she'll bloom. If you don't, she'll wilt." The comedy returns when Caleb asks where he got that, and Michael answers wryly: "Counseling." Later scenes develop the contrast between the two husbands when Caleb screams at Catherine and Michael holds hands with Tina. In the firehouse kitchen, Michael further demonstrates his fondness for cheesy metaphors: "Salt and pepper are completely different. Their make-up is different, their taste and their color, but you always see 'em together," making an explicit point about the indissoluble marriage bond and a subtle reference to interracial relationships.

Michael's Christian faith emerges after the firefighters risk their lives in a dramatic rescue of two women trapped in a wrecked car in the path of an oncoming train. He thanks God and says that he is not afraid to die: "I know where I'm going." When Terrell rejects the concepts of heaven and hell, Caleb admonishes: "You might not agree with Michael, but you and I both know he's the real deal." The perfect husband and bravest firefighter, Michael seems like the idealized result of white filmmakers trying to be politically correct. Yet he later confesses that he divorced a woman before Tina, lending him more credibility as he urges Caleb not to make the same mistake. Like Terrell's atheism, this backstory undermines the positive stereotype that African Americans naturally follow Christ without the struggles and doubts of the white characters.

Of course, the "black best friend" has become just as ubiquitous and limiting as the "black buddy" of the action film. Vera and Gordon explain, "The story of the white man whose best friend is a man of another color is nothing new in American popular culture."[23] The *Guardian*'s Maurice

23. Vera and Gordon, *Screen Saviors*, 155.

Mcleod describes the stereotype: "BBFs often have very little life of their own and seem to exist to be black and to be friends with the hero. They often speak and act in a hyper-racialised way and provide the comedy which is a break from all of the serious heroic stuff the main character does."[24] Michael does "serious heroic stuff" in his own right, but his wife only visits the firehouse once, and we never see him at home or meet his children. Mcleod jokes: "If you are a regular character in a show but your name is just letters or a 'street name,' you might be a BBF,"[25] highlighting the conventionality of J. T. in *Facing the Giants* and his doppelgänger T. J. in *Courageous*. Ralina L. Joseph analyzes how whites depicted Barack Obama as their "black best friend" in the 2007–2008 presidential campaign that took place while *Fireproof* was filmed and released: "In postraciality, people of color like Obama become the special, safe minority. He does not make Whites uncomfortable by bringing up issues of race, racialized difference, or racialized inequality; that is, he does not play the race card. He is a token who is valuable for his mere presence."[26] Michael shares Obama's charisma, and Joseph's comment that the black best friend's "controlled masculinity additionally serves to distance him from stereotypes of threatening Black masculinity"[27] prefigures Bevel's role in *Courageous*.

Latasha and Deidra depart from the female "black best friends" that Sarah E. Turner describes as sassy and outspoken but unfailingly wise, loyal, and nonthreatening, symbols of "racial harmony" who suggest "that all is right with the world."[28] Latasha and Deidra are sassy, outspoken, and loyal, but the Christian viewer must decode their behavior as unwise when they gossip about a handsome doctor's interest in Catherine and encourage her to leave Caleb, their black dialect racializing their destructive rhetoric of "girl power." Latasha urges: "You got to get out. He don't deserve you." Deidra adds: "A real man's got to be a hero to his wife before he can be to anybody else, or he ain't a real man." The scene cuts to Caleb ranting to Michael, and the cross-cutting grows increasingly humorous as husband and wife blame each other. Caleb says, "I can see 'em all right now, crying, having some sort of group hug," and we cut to the girlfriends having a group hug. They play a more devastating role when Caleb tries to win Catherine back, and they claim that he's buttering her up for a divorce. Catherine's white colleague gives her sound advice, but Latasha and Deidra remain

24. Mcleod, "Why the Black Best Friend," para. 9.
25. Mcleod, "Why the Black Best Friend," para. 11.
26. Joseph, "Imagining Obama," 399.
27. Joseph, "Imagining Obama," 399.
28. Sarah E. Turner, "BBFFs," 251–52.

shallow women motivated by selfishness rather than sincere feminism. By depicting them as likeable and funny but immoral, the Kendricks reveal the emptiness of nurture that simply supports whatever the white hero does. Turner describes the female BBF's popularity "as seemingly symptomatic of American culture's continuing unease with black masculinity,"[29] but we see the opposite in the cross-cutting sequence that juxtaposes their bad advice with Michael's good advice. Building on Michael's positive role, the next film will show the black best friend at home with his family, facing problems unrelated to the white hero.

Courageous (2011) focuses on four deputies in the Albany Sheriff's Office—Nathan Hayes (Bevel), Adam Mitchell (Alex Kendrick), Shane Fuller (Kevin Downes), and David Thomson (Ben Davies)—and their friend Javier Martinez (Robert Amaya). This ensemble cast demonstrates that "the definition of masculinity is essentially a collective process whereby men compete with other men for validation and confirmation."[30] The main cast includes three black and two Latino characters. Nathan and his wife Kayla (Eleanor Brown) struggle to raise two sons and teen daughter Jade (Taylor Hutcherson), while Nathan fights black criminals like gang leader T. J. (T. C. Stallings). Javier takes over the comical sidekick role that the black characters seem to have outgrown, yet we see an extended portrait of his home life with his wife Carmen (Angelita Nelson) and their two children. *Courageous* does not simply replace the black buddy with a Latino buddy but treats Nathan and Javier as protagonists alongside the white hero.

Courageous takes up the national concern about men's abandonment of their families, which Barbara Ehrenreich examined as early as 1983 in *The Hearts of Men: American Dreams and the Flight from Commitment*. When relaxed moral standards and divorce laws made it easier for men to leave their breadwinning roles, Ehrenreich hoped that it was still possible "to give new strength and shared meaning to the words we have lost—responsibility, maturity and even, perhaps, manliness."[31] In 1995, David Blankenhorn proclaimed in *Fatherless America: Confronting Our Most Urgent Social Problem*: "Our society's conspicuous failure to sustain or create compelling norms of fatherhood amounts to a social and personal disaster. Today's story of fatherhood features one-dimensional characters, an unbelievable plot, and an unhappy ending,"[32] prefiguring the Kendricks' desire to create a fatherhood film with multidimensional characters, a believable plot, and a happy

---

29. Sarah E. Turner, "BBFFs," 250.
30. Peberdy, *Masculinity and Film Performance*, 106.
31. Ehrenreich, *Hearts of Men*, 182.
32. Blankenhorn, *Fatherless America*, 4.

ending. Deborah Lupton and Lesley Barclay point out that 1990s sitcoms like *Frasier* and *Seinfeld* showed men delaying or avoiding fatherhood, while films depicted men who end up raising children "through accident or misfortune rather than by choice, and have little idea about what to do when this happens."[33] Peberdy agrees that interrogations of fatherhood reached a new level in the 1990s: "With the endemic image of the deadbeat dad voluntarily shirking his 'responsibilities' as a father and parent, along with the apparent erosion of the marriage institution and the decline of the male breadwinner role, the American father was running the risk of becoming an endangered species."[34] The most diverse film so far, *Courageous* approaches fatherhood from the perspectives of three racial groups in the working and middle classes.

The first scene is a dramatic conflict between Nathan and T. J., the black villain whose name reverses J. T. from *Facing the Giants*. Nathan pulls up to a gas station and leaves his truck at the pump, when the stereotypical gangster with stocking cap, tank top, and bulging muscles jumps in and drives away. Nathan unexpectedly runs after him, grabs the door, and wrestles for the steering wheel as the truck races down the road. This recalls Michael from *Fireproof* risking his life to save a car from an oncoming train, but we don't know why he takes such extreme measures to save his vehicle. When the truck crashes and the gangster escapes, we see Nathan's baby in the back seat. What seemed like ill-advised machismo turns into a display of ideal fatherhood, with the baby played by Bevel's real son. Nathan soon introduces himself as a new deputy who has moved back to Albany for a better life for his children.

This scene places black men in the roles of lawman and outlaw. Wiegman believes that such films deny "the historical supremacy ascribed to the white male,"[35] in this case giving the impression that black men have been released from the bonds of racism and can freely choose whether they want to be the gangster or the loving father. This also assuages the white viewer's fear of racial violence: "By extending a strenuous masculinity to black men, the black cop figure can work to transform his potential subversion of U. S. culture into affirmation, protection, and appeal—through presence and visibility—to democratic enunciations."[36] *Courageous* could have challenged the racial status quo with Nathan confronting a white racist rather than a black criminal. On the positive side, the filmmakers continue to add more

33. Lupton and Barclay, *Constructing Fatherhood*, 71.
34. Peberdy, *Masculinity and Film Performance*, 122.
35. Wiegman, *American Anatomies*, 123.
36. Wiegman, *American Anatomies*, 138.

types of black characters: we have the humorous sidekick, the wise mentor, the positive sassy black woman, the negative sassy black woman, the
devoted father, the heroic lawman, the gangster, and soon the beautiful teen
girl and the vulnerable gang recruit.

Nathan is a much better father than his white colleagues, continuing
the theme of black men as moral exemplars. Adam forgets his daughter's
piano recital and refuses to run in a father-son marathon, Shane only sees
his son on weekends, and David abandoned a child that he fathered in college. Yet Nathan tells Jade that he must approve the boys that she dates, in
keeping with films like *John Q.* and *The Pursuit of Happyness* that combated
political rhetoric in which "African American fathers were scrutinised and
criticised for incompetence, absence and failure to nurture, fuelling the
debate about a 'crisis of black masculinity.'"[37] Nathan's wife is loving and
sympathetic, distinguishing this film from others that promote black fatherhood at the expense of women: "With the wives marginalised or depicted
as deficient or unnecessary and then expelled from the narrative, it is no
longer the father who is dispensable but the mother."[38] The film focuses on
fathers, but it shows only loving mothers.

Like *Fireproof*'s Michael, Nathan gains complexity as we learn about
his hidden scars. He describes his background to the other deputies: "My
dad had six children, from three different women. I was the fifth child.
Before I was born, he had already left. I'm thirty-seven years old, and I've
never met my biological father." When Adam creates a fatherhood resolution, Nathan embraces the concept, and Kayla plans a ceremony presided
over by Nathan's childhood mentor (played by Pastor Daniel Simmons from
Mt. Zion Baptist Church). Nathan recites the resolution first, although it
seems hardly necessary in his case. He does read a letter of forgiveness at the
grave of his father Clinton Brown, whose name ties the failed promises of
a liberal president to the tragic losses of the black community, and he gives
Jade a ring to wear until she is engaged, but his only real challenge is her love
interest Derrick, who is involved in a gang.

The portrayal of black criminals seems fairly balanced, given how
many films represent them as one-dimensionally evil. An early scene
evokes stereotypes, as the deputies enter a black neighborhood to look for
two drug dealers. Adam finds the young men in front of the house suspi-
cious, although they merely saunter away, and a disheveled woman (Renata
Williams, one of the sassy girlfriends from *Fireproof*) answers the door and
proclaims: "I ain't even supposed to be here." The drug dealers run out the

37. Peberdy, *Masculinity and Film Performance*, 140.
38. Peberdy, *Masculinity and Film Performance*, 142.

back door, leading to a chase in which Nathan scolds his partner for getting lost: "Look, man, you gotta learn the streets. I needed you." This echoes the *Fireproof* scene in which Terrell scolds Eric for leaving him in a fire, making it the second film in a row in which a black man reprimands a white man for abandoning him on the job, a subtle nod to workplace discrimination without explicitly mentioning racism. The chase ends when the deputies arrest the drug dealers, in keeping with standard film and television fare.

However, the Kendricks reveal that this scene was complicated because the crew was filming in real Albany streets. The black actors evangelized to the neighborhood kids, while Albany drug dealers got so used to seeing fake cops that Albany cops took them by surprise and busted a real drug deal while this scene was being filmed. On a film set that is also an evangelism rally and a drug bust, in which fake gangsters witness to real kids and fake cops fool real gangsters, it becomes clear that the black criminal is a role like any other. As the Kendricks describe the actors, "They had to act like these thug guys, but in real life they were fantastic young men." The film also complicates the stereotype of black drug dealers when Adam's white partner turns out to be stealing drugs collected as evidence, and a black deputy cuffs him and takes him away in a reversal of the white-cop, black-criminal scenario.

The story of Jade's friend Derrick (Donald Howze) also humanizes the gangster role. Black kids watch through a window as the gang initiates Derrick with a severe beating. He appears much smaller than the menacing thugs around him, and T. J. gives him a speech about loyalty while he lies in pain on the floor, encouraging the audience to sympathize with this teenager looking for a family and suggesting that the older members also started out this way. The Kendricks explain that boys join gangs because they desire protection, and a former Crips gang member helped make the initiation realistic. Derrick seems vulnerable and relatable when he asks Jade on a date, although the viewer's knowledge that he is running drugs makes us relieved that Nathan doesn't let her go. Three deleted scenes focus on Derrick, proving that the filmmakers hoped to include more of his story: gang leader Antoine tells him to respect his grandmother, he gets a perfect score on his economics test, and he gives Jade a bracelet. Derrick is an ordinary kid, despite his gang involvement. The final cut culminates in an interracial shootout, in which Derrick saves Nathan's life and cries in the back seat of the deputy car as he tells Nathan: "I ain't got nobody, man. I just ain't got nobody." Nathan later visits him in jail to read the Bible, holding out hope that he may escape the gang and have a better future.

Javier Martinez is a warm-hearted manual laborer and loving father who bears little resemblance to the film industry's often vicious portrayal of Hispanics. Clara E. Rodríguez challenges her readers: "Chances are you cannot recall the last time you saw a Latino in the movies who was not somehow enmeshed in violence, whether as victim, villain, or cop."[39] Jorge J. Barrueto adds: "When Hollywood has Hispanics as its subject matter, violence and demographic fears are the main narrative signifiers. Hispanic males are invariably drug dealers, violent gangsters and repulsive aliens."[40] Javier's ordinariness distances him from these violent tropes and the stereotypes that Charles Ramírez Berg calls the bandit, the buffoon, and the Latin lover. He is comical without the buffoon's simplemindedness, broken English, or childish emotions.[41] He is funny on purpose, often at the expense of other characters, and we tend to laugh *with* him, not at him. Yet he does fall into the positive stereotypical category of contented workers who "reassure the public of the usefulness of Hispanic labor."[42] The Kendricks present Javier's promotion at the thread factory as the happiest possible ending, but it is still noteworthy for them to include positive Latino characters.

Local church members play many roles in the films, but the Kendricks explain that the Hispanic actors came from Miami and Jacksonville: "This couple was probably one of the hardest to find to cast for the movie, because we wanted them to have a certain look and age, and be able to speak English and Spanish, and just be able to look like that they're married, and also have hearts for the Lord, and be good at acting." Since Albany's population is 72 percent black, 23 percent white, and 2 percent Hispanic or Latino,[43] this search for Latino actors demonstrates their multicultural commitments. They took the actors' advice on how Hispanic people would say the lines: "We have a lot of different cultural viewpoints in this film, and that is intentional. You know, we want to tackle the issue of fatherhood from various angles."

The portrayal of the Martinez family strikes a balance between realism and relatability. Director of Photography Bob Scott filmed the first scene in their home in one shot that lasts nearly two minutes, and the Kendricks note that they wanted the viewer to study the characters. The shot begins with Carmen talking to the kids in Spanish, with subtitles even though the content is trivial. She switches to English, which seems unrealistic, but too many subtitles would create emotional distance from the viewer. The crosses in their home, rather than crucifixes, imply that they are Protestant like the

39. Clara E. Rodríguez, "Keeping It Reel?," 180.

40. Barrueto, *Hispanic Image in Hollywood*, 3.

41. Berg, *Latino Images in Film*, 72.

42. Barrueto, *Hispanic Image in Hollywood*, 11.

43. United States Census Bureau, "QuickFacts: Albany City."

other families. As *Christianity Today* reviewer Steven D. Greydanus notes, "A hint of Catholicism or Pentecostalism in the Latino household might have contributed a bit of realistic diversity,"[44] but the filmmakers seem primarily concerned to build connections for viewers with few Hispanic friends. Javier has just been laid off from a construction job, and he walks to find work so that Carmen can take the car to the store, echoing Nathan's devotion to his children. Lupton and Barclay claim that "in popular film the working-class father is far more often held up as a figure of fun and even contempt, as lacking the skills to relate to his family and win their respect."[45] Although Javier comes close to the Hispanic buffoon in his sidekick role, his loving authority at home distinguishes him from the clownish working-class father represented by Homer Simpson, Al Bundy, and Dan Conner.

The way in which Javier meets Adam both evokes and denies the idea that Latino laborers are interchangeable. Javier walks by Adam's house, praying in Spanish about how to provide for his family. Adam mistakes him for another Javier whom he hired over the phone and invites him to build a shed for $150 per day. This little "white savior" narrative is demeaning in several ways: Adam doesn't care *which* Javier works for him; Adam asks for a "work permit," which implies a question about legal citizenship; Javier is too scared to ask questions; and Adam later praises him for "working like a machine." Yet the film constructs the meeting as providential for both men, and it leads to a close friendship, with Adam helping Javier find a full-time factory job.

Javier's most complex scene juxtaposes serious black gangs and humorous Latino gangs, employing the stereotype of the Hispanic buffoon to mock the stereotype of the Hispanic bandit. Javier is going to lunch with Adam and Shane in the deputy car when they are called to a gang-related incident, and he jokes that he started a gang once: "We were the Snake Kings. We had lots of snakes in our neighborhood, so we would throw rocks at them and try to kill them." The "gang" included his two brothers, and they only killed one snake. This humor distances Latinos from crime but also from serious hardship: the "work permit" is the only veiled reference to immigration, and the Martinez family appears to be poor due to the scarcity of blue-collar jobs rather than racism. In contrast to the deadly serious tone of Derrick's gang initiation, Adam and Javier play a prank on a black gangster, telling him that he must ride in the back seat with a vicious killer from the Snake Kings. The black man becomes increasingly terrified as Javier gives him menacing looks, and Spanish guitar music plays while subtitles

---

44. Greydanus, "Calling for Heroic Commitment," 56.
45. Lupton and Barclay, *Constructing Fatherhood*, 71.

translate Javier speaking in Spanish in a threatening tone: "We are going to lunch. I am getting a chicken sandwich and a lemonade." Javier pretends to wrestle his hands free, and the gangster repeatedly yells, "Stop the car!" as the white deputies laugh in the front seat.

This prank on a black man seems more problematic than J. T.'s prank on a white man in the locker room in *Facing the Giants*, since the film has portrayed the black community as the city's most vulnerable population. In the wake of Rodney King and Black Lives Matter, it is irresponsible to joke about a black man's terror after his arrest by white cops. The deputies use their white privilege to provoke conflict between ethnic groups that struggle with poverty and crime. Why should muscular Nathan grapple violently with gangsters, while chubby Javier plays around with one? Why should Latino gangs be considered a joking matter? Why trivialize the problems that Latinos face in the South, despite Javier's struggle to put food on the table? On the other hand, the scene reinforces the performative nature of masculinity and race that we have seen in the confusion between fake cops and real cops, fake gangsters and real gangsters during filming. Adam plays the angry deputy who threatens the pretend criminal and calls him "Martinez." Javier starts acting like a gangster, and the black man stops acting like one. The gangster's inability to recognize common words like *pollo* and cognates like *limonada* draws attention to many Americans' illogical fear of Spanish and to the cultural misunderstandings that prevent minority groups from making common cause. Films often mock Latinos' broken English, but this joke is on someone who can't understand basic Spanish.

Sabina Sawhney's "The Joke and the Hoax: (Not) Speaking as the Other" describes how postcolonial theorist Gayatri Chakravorty Spivak played a joke by telling people false information about her native culture, shifting the balance of power by mocking the susceptibility of her listeners and refusing to act as "native informant." *Courageous* includes these dynamics, but since this prank is the white filmmakers' idea, and Adam's idea in the diegetic world, it is also a cultural performance to please whites. Sawhney states: "In return for being adopted as a token member and for gaining entry into the privileged group, the representative of the subordinate group must comply with the demands placed on him."[46] Right after this scene, Adam tells his family that the guys like Javier: "We've kind of adopted him in our group," proving that they interpret the joke as charming rather than subversive. Fortunately, that is not the last scene with Javier, who faces a serious ethical dilemma when his white boss offers him a promotion if he will falsify information. Javier agonizes over the decision but sticks to his morals: "It

---

46. Sawhney, "Joke and the Hoax," 210.

would be dishonoring to my God and my family to lie on that report." It turns out that the boss was merely testing him, so Javier has a happy ending in a managerial position.[47]

The film ends with Adam speaking to his church about the importance of fatherhood. The scene was filmed at Sherwood on Father's Day 2010 with Mt. Zion Baptist members in attendance, a utopian vision of an integrated congregation that Albany cannot sustain in reality. The image of Adam, Nathan, and Javier standing together on the platform still represents a leap forward from *Flywheel*, when Sam was onscreen for a few minutes, and we knew nothing about his personal life. Wiegman argues that we should not "entirely dismiss the utopianism that underlies the figuration of interracial bonding. For the dream of the post-colonial, post-segregationist moment, of the possibility of bonding across racial difference, is no politically insignificant wish."[48] Too few Hollywood films even attempt racially diverse ensemble casts, and the project is fraught with problems since characters should be neither idealized nor demonized. *Courageous* undermines the stereotype of black and Latino family dysfunction by portraying whites as the "deadbeat dads" who learn from men of color how to be good fathers.

"I SEE IN YOU A WARRIOR": THE BLACK FAMILY IN *WAR ROOM*

In 2004, Heather Hendershot observed: "African Americans appear as token sidekicks in several Christian movies, cartoons, and sitcoms, but they are never protagonists."[49] *War Room* (2015) breaks this trend with a main cast that is two-thirds African American. The Kendricks move from Sherwood Pictures to Kendrick Brothers Productions, from Georgia to North Carolina, and from white male issues to black female issues. Prayer warrior Clara Williams (Karen Abercrombie) befriends her realtor Elizabeth Jordan (Priscilla Shirer) and discovers that Elizabeth's perfect upper-middle-class

---

47. Amaya reappears in a deleted sequence from the next film, *War Room*, in a comical role as a self-help guru who alarms the community center by screaming during lectures. It is understandable that the Kendricks cut the sequence, which is unconnected to the main plot, but the film represents a lost opportunity to develop their portrayal of Latinos as they have done with African Americans. It would have made a huge difference if Amaya had been given a serious role like the pharmaceutical manager who chooses not to prosecute his black employee for stealing drugs. Alex Kendrick in that role reinforces the "white savior" trope, whereas casting Amaya would have expanded the Latino roles beyond comic relief.

48. Wiegman, *American Anatomies*, 131.

49. Hendershot, *Shaking the World*, 10.

life is a sham. Her marriage to Tony (T. C. Stallings) is falling apart and destroying their ten-year-old daughter Danielle (Alena Pitts). Alex Kendrick takes a supporting role as Tony's boss, appearing in only three scenes. *War Room* breaks new ground by placing black women at the center and exposing the emptiness of American consumerism.

The title *War Room* evokes male military power, and the Kendrick Brothers logo of a shield with a cross evokes medieval knighthood, but Clara's opening voiceover quickly departs from earlier films' white male orientation. According to Vera and Gordon, "Usually, if there is voice-over narrative in a Hollywood film, the white hero narrates and controls the point of view,"[50] but here an elderly black woman speaks wearily over combat footage from Vietnam: "War. It's been a part of humanity in every age. We fight for power, for riches, for rights, or for freedom." Clara mentions "power" and "riches" over shots of machine guns and tanks, "rights" over an exploding bomb, and "freedom" over soldiers carrying their wounded comrade. Clifford G. Christians asserts that redemptive evangelical texts "ought to become sites of struggle against continuities and consensus,"[51] and these juxtapositions between word and image destabilize a patriotic view of male heroism. The cut to the homefront with a 1970s Clara visiting her husband's grave and the slow pan across the graveyard that marks the transition to the present time connect past world events to present domestic struggles. Clara watches a young couple fight and continues: "I find myself amazed that of the many battles we engage in today, be it money, control, or matters of the heart, very few of us know how to fight the right way or understand who we're really fighting against." In this film, women are the soldiers, Satan is the enemy, and neglectful husbands are the disputed ground. Clara will play the wise mentor associated with African American men in earlier films, but she will take a much larger role and will mentor someone of her own race.

50. Vera and Gordon, *Screen Saviors*, 177.
51. Christians, "Redemptive Media," 344.

The Kendrick Brothers took the bold step of centering their fifth film on an African American family. *War Room* © 2015 Faithstep Films, LLC. All Rights Reserved. Courtesy of Sony Pictures Entertainment.

The African American Jordans need salvation as much as the white Austins, Taylors, Holts, and Mitchells of previous films. They are not icons of family values like the equally wealthy Huxtables on *The Cosby Show* (1984–1992). At home, the parents bicker and ignore their daughter, and at church, Tony checks out an attractive woman across the aisle. Their lack of ethnic distinctives makes them relatable to a wide audience, but black protagonists in business attire are still new for the Kendricks. Clara's photo of Martin Luther King links her to civil rights history and adds a subtext of racial uplift to her efforts to save this disintegrating family. She tells Elizabeth, "I see in you a warrior that needs to be awakened," and she challenges her to stop fighting her husband and start fighting Satan on his behalf.

Elizabeth Jordan is a beautiful career woman played by a Christian inspirational speaker, but the Kendricks make her realistic and relatable by showing her with smelly feet, stuffing potato chips into her mouth, and answering the door with messy hair and bad breath. Her large collection of high-heeled shoes symbolizes her discomfort with her professional role, and she struggles as a mother when Danielle asks her questions that she cannot answer: "What jump rope trick did I just learn to do? Who's my new coach? What award did I win last week on my team?" Clara inspires Elizabeth with the Christian paradoxes that victory comes in surrender and that she can take control of her life by submitting to her husband. When

Elizabeth converts her closet into a prayer room, African American gospel singer Vickie Winans sings "Shake Yourself Loose." Getting in touch with God may lead Elizabeth to greater rootedness in black culture.

Tony Jordan, true to the Sherwood tradition of husbands behaving badly, is a smooth-talking pharmaceutical salesman who steals drugs from his company, flirts with women, snaps at his wife, and ignores his daughter. Yet there is a stark contrast between T. C. Stallings's role as T. J. the gangster in *Courageous* and his appearance here in a business suit in a high-end office, allowing the actor to show his range and disconnecting him from any one stereotype. Tony Jordan is an expanded version of the initials T. J., and when he dreams about confronting a criminal who turns out to be himself, he confronts his inner gangster and takes him down a different path. He surrenders to Jesus, returns the stolen drugs, and competes with his daughter in a double-dutch competition. In *The Games Black Girls Play: Learning the Ropes from Double-Dutch to Hip-Hop*, Kyra D. Gaunt describes double-dutch as an expression of black female identity: "Contrary to the racial insinuations of outsiders, double-dutch play among black girls created an arena where race and gender identity moved from the periphery to the center, sometimes embracing and reinterpreting the very epithets that others used to signify inferiority of their race and sex."[52] Gaunt explains how black female expression was policed and controlled when double-dutch became a competitive sport, and the Jordans compete in an upscale, racially integrated community center. Just as Tony lost his job in a white-collar version of inner-city drug dealing, he redeems himself in a white-collar version of an inner-city sport. Yet Stallings' athletic prowess allows him to compete at a high level, and Tony supports the dreams of a daughter that he once belittled for jumping rope.

Alongside the Jordans, we see black characters in supporting roles. Tenae Downing plays Veronica Drake, the beautiful colleague who tempts Tony to commit adultery, with enough nuance to gain the viewer's sympathy. Christian comedian Michael Jr. plays Michael Alexander, Tony's best friend who offers marriage advice at the gym. The Kendricks recycle racial characteristics in the buddy role: like Caleb's best friend in *Fireproof*, he is named Michael, has a bald head, saves people's lives in his job, and provides comic relief and Christian counsel. Yet he now mentors a friend of his own race, detaching the scenes from their interracial buddy movie connotations. Meanwhile, the film shows white characters serving the Jordans: a waitress in Atlanta, a delivery man, and a front-desk receptionist. A white man mugs Clara and Elizabeth, and a black cop takes their statement. This casting

---

52. Gaunt, *Games Black Girls Play*, 138.

reverses the Hollywood norm of white protagonists served and attacked by people of color.

The rhetoric of a "war room" where women pray for their families applies the second-wave feminist mantra "the personal is political" to the spiritual realm, demonstrating the wide-ranging consequences of one woman's actions. *Fireproof* showed a faithful man saving his wife despite her morally bankrupt friends, but *War Room* shows a faithful wife saving her husband with the help of her female colleagues. Elizabeth's boss Mandy—played by Beth Moore, a famous speaker and author of Bible studies for women—articulates the burdens and possibilities of wifely submission. The Kendricks note that Moore improvised the line: "You know what my momma used to say to me? She used to say that sometimes submission is learning to duck so God can hit your husband." Her small role in this film reflects her social media presence in real life. On the day that I was writing this section, Moore posted a tweet about misogyny in Christian culture. While the filmmakers do not go this far, they show Elizabeth becoming increasingly confident and empowered. In the film's turning point, Elizabeth orders Satan to leave her home, reclaiming the domestic space: "Go back to hell where you belong and leave my family alone!" The DVD commentaries and special features include many real women's contributions: the owner of the house used for the Jordan home had lost a son there and encouraged Priscilla Shirer to drive out Satan for real; a cancer survivor asked the Make-A-Wish Foundation to appear in the film and plays a receptionist; ninety-one-year-old Molly Bruno prayed for the film and donated her worn Bible for the final scene.

Social class plays a more nuanced role in *War Room* than in previous films, since the Jordans' upper-middle-class lifestyle contributes to their spiritual malaise. Stephen Kendrick claims that they are "trying to live their American dream but disconnected really from God and from one another." When Elizabeth lists Clara's house for sale, she looks at physical features while Clara focuses on family memories, and a shot of Clara's humble wedding band contrasts a later shot of Elizabeth's huge diamond ring as she eats a tensely silent dinner with her daughter. The Jordans fight about money in a home that is much too large for them; twelve exterior shots of the house gain an ominous quality as we anticipate heartbreak in the following scene. One interior shot frames Danielle behind an iron staircase railing like the bars of a prison cell, and Tony's nightmare shows Elizabeth being mugged in a warehouse full of boxes. After Tony finally prays, "Forgive me, Jesus," the camera cuts to an aerial shot of an affluent subdivision that is not clearly linked to the previous or following scenes; it hovers in the film as a reminder of the spiritual unrest hidden within every picture of prosperity. Aerial shots of Charlotte and Atlanta are even more ominous given the destructive nature of Tony's work; the office scenes feature large, empty spaces, and Tony confesses to stealing from the company in the back of a shot with a large conference table in the foreground.

The film promotes downward mobility as Tony becomes the director of the community center for half his former pay, and Elizabeth responds: "I would rather have a man chasing Jesus than a house full of stuff." Tony gives up his corporate SUV with its "Jay Austin Motors" license plate, the inside joke reversing the symbolism of *Facing the Giants* in which Grant's "Jay Austin Motors" truck was a gift from God. However, the characters' ongoing consumerism undercuts these messages about the entrapment of material possessions. After her conversion, Elizabeth buys leather devotional journals for herself and Danielle online, and even Clara buys a smart phone to download prayer apps and gospel songs. We never see the Jordans leave their trophy house, which seems inevitable given Tony's career change. However, Tony and Danielle competing in the double-dutch competition reminds viewers that family matters most, and it is a nice touch that they win second place in contrast to *Facing the Giants*.

The film ends with another Clara voiceover in which she prays for the nation over a multicultural montage of people praying and reading the Bible, with a shot of the US Capitol when she says: "Raise up a generation, Lord, that will take light into this world, that will not compromise when under pressure." The mounting urgency of the speech and the music, culminating with the film title and Bible verse, echo the ending of *Courageous*, but this film replaces the white man speaking from a pulpit with the black woman speaking from a closet. The credits roll over a world map, completing the political frame established by the opening shots of Vietnam. While *Left Behind* portrayed Christian women as annoying, *War Room* preaches that they can change the world.

In "'Take My Film and Let It Be': Critics and Consecration in Faith-Based Cinema," Rick Clifton Moore acknowledges that the Kendricks' films have fared poorly with mainstream reviewers, whose desire to influence taste and demonstrate cultural capital leads them to prefer aesthetically complex films and reject Christian concepts. Although *War Room* was the box office champion in the week of its release, outperforming *Straight Outta Compton*, "Insiders downplayed the event, by pointing out that it was a 'slow weekend.'"[53] Reviewers objected to Clara's preachiness and Elizabeth's submission, with three reviewers suggesting that the "use of African American

---

53. Rick Clifton Moore, "'Take My Film,'" 151.

actors was a marketing ploy."[54] Yet Moore believes that critics who disliked the rhetoric of wifely submission failed to appreciate that Tony begs his wife's forgiveness, and the film ends with "him on his knees again, washing Elizabeth's feet, a very traditional image of submission from the teachings of Jesus."[55] They also failed to recognize that over one-third of viewers were African Americans, who are more likely than whites to believe in Satan and embrace prayer.[56] Moore makes a convincing case that critics' ideological commitments prevent them from approaching the films with an open mind or recognizing that the Kendricks have responded to their concerns by extending their focus on women and people of color.

From their early days making films with church volunteers to their current international success, the Kendricks have grown in their portrayal of multicultural casts. *War Room* does have utopian, postracial, "colorblind" elements, since the Jordans do not suffer any form of racism and could have been replaced with white characters without altering the screenplay. However, given the small number of films with black female protagonists, the Kendricks deserve credit for expanding their comfort zones and exploring the diversity of the kingdom of God. As they say in the *War Room* commentary, "White, black, Latino, Asian, people of faith praying together in unity, that's what heaven's going to be like anyway." We will see in the conclusion that their latest film *Overcomer* (2019) features a white coach and black female athlete, requiring great finesse to avoid the "white savior" trap. Meanwhile, the next chapter explores *Duck Dynasty*, another Southern franchise with surprising mainstream success, and a conflict between a transracial adoptive family and producers who want to avoid race at all costs.

54. Rick Clifton Moore, "'Take My Film,'" 153.

55. Rick Clifton Moore, "'Take My Film,'" 155.

56. Rick Clifton Moore, "'Take My Film,'" 155–56.

Chapter 6

LIL' WILL AND BOOMERANG BECCA

Racial Others on Duck Dynasty

The A&E reality television series *Duck Dynasty* (2012–2017) has much in common with the films of the Sherwood Baptist Church. Evangelical Christian brothers Jase and Willie Robertson contributed ideas, energy, and humor; family members and local citizens played the characters; and West Monroe, Louisiana provided the real locations and authentic Southern foods, dialects, and churches. The rags-to-riches story of "rednecks" who make millions on their unique duck calls was unexpectedly popular, with Rick Kissell of *Variety* reporting in August 2013: "'Duck Dynasty' kicked off its new season with a whopping 11.8 million viewers—the largest audience ever for a non-fiction cable series."[1] Yet the Robertsons enjoyed much less creative control because the show appeared on a mainstream network that downplayed their faith and portrayed them as clueless bumpkins who spend their days engaging in slapstick antics to amuse the American public. The show includes clean language, respectful children, occasional church events, and family prayers concluding each episode, but it lacks what Heather Hendershot calls "evangelical intensity."[2] The family combated this view with nonfiction books about how they overcame struggles with poverty, alcoholism, adultery, childhood sexual abuse, childhood disability, divorce, and pornography addiction through the salvation of Jesus Christ. While the Sherwood films developed black and Latino characters, A&E preferred to invent or exaggerate the Robertsons' cultural incompetence and largely ignored the diversity in their city and even in their family. From adopted

1. Kissell, "'Duck Dynasty' Premiere," para. 1.
2. Hendershot, *Shaking the World for Jesus*, 7.

son Lil' Will to foreign exchange student Rebecca, people of color remain on the periphery of *Duck Dynasty*, whether they are treated with affection or open resentment.

POPULAR AND SCHOLARLY RESPONSES TO RACE AND RACISM ON *DUCK DYNASTY*

The ideological gap between liberal producers and the conservative Robertsons lies behind the biggest controversy to strike the series. In December 2013, Drew Magary's *GQ* article "What the Duck?" ignited a media firestorm primarily based on Phil Robertson's opposition to homosexuality, although his observations about race were drawn into the fray. The following passage about his childhood appears isolated in a text box, with the ellipses in the original, suggesting that *GQ* chose the words for maximum effect:

> "I never, with my eyes, saw the mistreatment of any black person. Not once. Where we lived was all farmers. The blacks worked for the farmers. I hoed cotton with them. I'm with the blacks, because we're white trash. We're going across the field. . . . They're singing and happy. I never heard one of them, one black person, say, I tell you what: These doggone white people—not a word! . . . Pre-entitlement, pre-welfare, you say: Were they happy? They were godly; they were happy; no one was singing the blues."[3]

Magary's long, nuanced portrait also describes Phil as "welcoming and gracious,"[4] the family as "immensely likable,"[5] and Willie as an advocate for adopting biracial children. Yet the NAACP and the Human Rights Campaign denounced Phil's comments, and A&E suspended him with the statement: "His personal views in no way reflect those of A+E Networks, who have always been strong supporters and champions of the LGBT community."[6] The Robertsons refused to continue the series without Phil, and A&E reinstated him the following week.[7]

Many readers found Phil's views of Southern race relations offensive, but this nostalgic wishful thinking appears in many popular texts, like Jan Karon's Mitford novels, without attracting attention. Matthew W. Hughey calls this postracial rhetoric the dominant mode of racial discourse from

---

3. Magary, "What the Duck?," floating text box.
4. Magary, "What the Duck?," para. 6.
5. Magary, "What the Duck?," para. 16.
6. Yan and Ford, "'Duck Dynasty' Family Stands," para. 10.
7. Yahr, "A&E Retracts Its Suspension."

1999–2011, the years preceding *Duck Dynasty*: "This refined form of color blindness, while based at least in a small part on the notion that race should not matter ideally, also labors to obfuscate the ways that race continues to matter in reality."[8] A&E had always maximized ratings by poking fun at the Robertsons while celebrating them as an exotic Southern alternative to high-tech, urban culture. After all, how many acres of cotton did the media executives hoe during their childhoods? They could have framed Phil's opposition to homosexuality as a common conservative view and his racial comments as based on his own limited experience.[9] But the response to Magary's article required the producers to distance themselves from the family, using the common tactic of displacing racism onto rednecks. Hernán Vera and Andrew M. Gordon explain: "In terms of the sincere fictions of the white American self, the hostile redneck is a lower-class character on whom racism and sexism can be projected. The members of the audience can reassure themselves that they do not resemble this brute, so therefore they must not be racists."[10] Although the producers indulged in racial stereotyping throughout the series, punishing Phil in this moment made them appear blameless.

Nonetheless, the postracial perspective that Phil expressed to Magary and that permeates the Robertson books remains naïve and unrealistic. Working with ghostwriters and collaborators who shaped the colorblind discourse, family members insist that they treat everyone the same way regardless of skin color, advocate transracial adoption, and avoid the subject of racism. The older generation depicts a peaceful relationship between the races when they grew up in the 1950s and 1960s, like Si Robertson's book *Si-cology 101*:

---

8. Hughey, *White Savior Film*, 116.

9. Larry Alex Taunton's article in the *Atlantic*, "The Genuine Conflict Being Ignored in the *Duck Dynasty* Debate," argues that Phil's conservative Christian views shocked nobody except the A&E executives: "As even the most casual viewer of the show can tell you, he claims to be a follower of Jesus Christ. As such, is anyone really surprised to discover that the *Duck Dynasty* star is opposed to homosexuality on moral grounds? Apparently, the brass at A&E found it astonishing. Perhaps they should put down *GQ* and watch their own programming" (para. 4). Taunton cites a recent poll in which 45 percent of Americans believed that homosexual acts were sinful, proving that Robertson's opinion was "hardly anomalous" (para. 7). I would also note the irony that *GQ* deliberately published remarks that many considered anti-gay and racist, indicating that their desire to vilify the Robertsons and generate readership outweighed their commitment to progressive values, politically correct discourse, and the support of LGBT and African American communities. Although Phil made the comments, *GQ* disseminated them nationwide.

10. Vera and Gordon, *Screen Saviors*, 42.

Hey, if you're a Christian, racism is out. God made man-kind from dust and then He made woman. We don't even know what color Adam was. When I was growing up in Dixie, Loui-siana, there were probably only six or seven white kids in the entire town. Most of my friends were African-American. If I had chores to do, I'd get my friends to help me paint a fence, clean the barn, or cut the grass. Then I'd take them to the water hole and teach them how to swim.[11]

The next paragraph tells how the black community helped the Robertsons when his father fell from an oil rig and broke his back: "Momma told some of the ladies in the neighborhood that we weren't going to have a Christmas that year because she didn't have any money to buy us presents. Well, the black families in town took up a donation and raised about two hundred dollars for us."[12] This nostalgic image of collaboration between poor whites and blacks avoids many historical realities, but it is more balanced than *Duck Dynasty* Christmas episodes that portray African Americans only as the grateful objects of the Robertsons' charity.

Phil's memoir, *Happy, Happy, Happy,* acknowledges racial tensions during his time running a rural honky-tonk and presents segregation as a fragile but functional system: "The blacks drove up in the back, and we had their jive going on back there, and the rednecks came through the front. I was in the middle, serving and cooking for everyone, while trying to keep the peace."[13] His second book, *UnPHILtered,* treads more carefully in the wake of the *GQ* debacle. He devotes an entire chapter to racial issues, ac-knowledging the historical documentation of lynchings, beatings, and mur-ders of Southern blacks, but clarifying that he never personally witnessed these things. In the interview, he was trying to express admiration for his black neighbors' strong faith:

> The thing I'll always remember is that many of the African Americans I knew attended church every Sunday and stayed there for nearly the entire day. There was a small church with a tall steeple on the edge of the cotton field, and they piled in there every Sunday morning. I mean they were there from sun-rise to sunset! They often ate lunch and dinner on the church lawn. The reason they worshipped for so long, in my opinion, is that during a time when their civil rights were being trampled,

---

11. Si Robertson, *Si-cology 101,* 218.
12. Si Robertson, *Si-cology 101,* 218–19.
13. Phil Robertson, *Happy, Happy, Happy,* 78.

they embraced the one thing that couldn't be taken away from them—their faith.[14]

While the Robertsons stressed their loving interracial relationships, *GQ* and A&E broadcast their supposed bigotry as part of their controversial and thus lucrative redneck appeal.

Duck Dynasty scholarship highlights the close ties between redneck identity and racism. Shannon E. M. O'Sullivan's "Playing 'Redneck': White Masculinity and Working-Class Performance on *Duck Dynasty*" analyzes the Robertsons' backwoods personas as calculated performances, given their wealth, social and educational capital, and former preppy appearances:

> In short, the most popular reality television program on US cable television to date promotes the dominant myth that the United States is a classless society, in which there are no structural barriers to upward social mobility. It also reinforces the prevailing perception that white, rural, heteronormative men are "real men." Thus, it promotes white, heteronormative male supremacy.[15]

Gwendolyn Audrey Foster's "Consuming the Apocalypse, Marketing Bunker Materiality" compares the Robertsons to families in *Doomsday Preppers* and calls them "a white male fantasy of elitism crossed with redneck masculinity."[16] Holly Willson Holladay's "Reckoning with the 'Redneck': *Duck Dynasty* and the Boundaries of Morally Appropriate Whiteness" recounts interviews with viewers who admire the Robertsons' "family values, faith, and hard work,"[17] but question their working-class authenticity based on their college degrees and suburban homes. While the family's blend of redneck performance and postracial discourse did not convince everyone, the producers must share the blame for the limited representations of people of color in a city that is 35 percent African American,[18] and a family that includes biracial, Asian American, and African American adopted children.

---

14. Phil Robertson, *UnPHILtered*, 94.

15. Shannon E. M. O'Sullivan, "Playing 'Redneck,'" 381.

16. Foster, "Consuming the Apocalypse," 286. Foster misidentifies the Robertsons as "preppers" consumed with preparing for the apocalypse, since the series contains no references to bunkers, stockpiling food, or the End of the World as We Know It. Willie was an executive producer for the 2014 *Left Behind* movie filmed in Baton Rouge, linking him instead to the concept of a pre-tribulation rapture of Christian believers that would preclude the need for bunkers full of supplies.

17. Holladay, "Reckoning with the 'Redneck,'" 256.

18. United States Census Bureau, "QuickFacts: West Monroe."

"IT'S HARD TO FIND GOOD HELP THESE DAYS": LATINOS ON *DUCK DYNASTY*

Sadie Robertson's book, *Live Original,* describes how the family's summer trips to an orphanage in the Dominican Republic have changed her deeply and opened her eyes to the poverty in her home state,[19] and John Luke Robertson's *Young & Beardless* mentions mission trips to the Dominican Republic and Nicaragua.[20] Rather than following the family to Latin America, *Duck Dynasty* prefers sitcom clichés like the Hawaiian vacation in "Aloha, Robertsons!," in which Si continually thinks that he's in Mexico. He responds to a woman saying "Aloha" with "*Hola* to you too, *señorita*" and tells Jase: "I'm trying to speak the native language, *el stupido.*" He asks to see the Mayan ruins, and when everyone says that the Mayans were in Mexico, he insists: "Hey, I know I'm in Hawaii, all right? Home of the burrito." Si still claims that he is the most cultured man in the family because he has been to Vietnam, Germany, Boise, and Shreveport. It's hard to tell if Si really believes that Hawaiians speak Spanish or if this is all played for lowbrow comedy. In the absence of meaningful cultural discussion, these jokes shut out viewers from Mexican and Hawaiian backgrounds.

Much closer to home, "John Luke After Dentist" includes the Robertsons' offensive treatment of a real Hispanic business. Jase needs to discard some rancid meat, but rather than dumping it into the swamp, he heads to El Chile Verde Mexican Restaurant: "Tacos, enchiladas, it's the perfect camouflage." He finds the dumpster locked, so he and younger brother Jep go inside to wait for a manager, eating chips and dancing to mariachi music. The manager initially agrees to let them dump the meat, but when he realizes that it smells like a dead body, he walks away protesting: "*No, no, no muerto.*" We cut to an interview with Phil saying "it's hard to find good help these days," as if the restaurant were obliged to dispose of their rancid meat, and Jase adds: "Facial profiling strikes again." Jase explains this pun on "racial profiling" in his book *Good Call,* claiming that people clutch their children and lock their doors when they see his long beard. He describes a policeman who kept his hand on his gun when he pulled Jase over for speeding, and a staff member at the Trump International Hotel who escorted him outside when he asked for the restroom, although he mentioned this incident on a talk show and Donald Trump's office called to apologize.[21] Whereas victims of racial profiling suffer severe violence due to the skin that they cannot

---

19. Sadie Robertson, *Live Original,* 172–77.
20. John Luke Robertson, *Young & Beardless,* 150.
21. Jase Robertson, *Good Call,* 177–79.

conceal, victims of "facial profiling" suffer minor annoyance due to the beards that they choose to wear. This false analogy portrays the Robertsons as victims of discrimination even as they harass Mexicans.

Duck Dynasty typically refers to racial and ethnic groups in the context of mainstream popular culture, making no distinction between authentic cultural references and offensive ethnic borrowings. Willie and his white assistant quote from *Nacho Libre* with mock Mexican accents,[22] Jase dresses as Zorro for a Renaissance fair although Willie points out that the character is from nineteenth-century Mexico,[23] Si makes *carne asada* a code word but can't pronounce it,[24] and John Luke packs for college wearing a sombrero.[25] As Ted Turnau points out, "Man cannot live on silliness alone. It can be a lopsided diet that leaves us insulated and oblivious to the hurts and problems around us."[26] The stakes are even higher when the Robertson family includes adopted children from the cultures in question.

"SKIN COLOR SHOULD NOT MAKE A DIFFERENCE": LIL' WILL AND OTHER BLACK CHARACTERS

In *The Duck Commander Family*, Korie Robertson explains how a lawyer approached her and Willie "and told us how difficult it was to place biracial children in homes in the South. We were shocked. It was the twenty-first century. We committed to being a part of changing that in our society. Skin color should not make a difference."[27] They adopted Will as a newborn, and the Robertsons describe him as a fun-loving extrovert with great musical talent. In *The Women of Duck Commander*, Korie claims: "Will has a way of capturing the heart of everyone he meets. He makes friends in the toy section of Walmart, on the beach playing in the sand, and in the video game room at the pizza place. He has a great smile and a contagious laugh."[28] Sadie's *Live Original* praises him for warming up her car on winter mornings,[29] and Korie's *Strong and Kind* tells the story of him encouraging

---

22. "Willie's Number Two."
23. "Renaissance Men."
24. "Heroes Welcome."
25. "Toad to Perdition."
26. Turnau, *Popologetics*, 273.
27. Willie and Korie Robertson, *Duck Commander Family*, 144.
28. Kay Robertson et al., *Women of Duck Commander*, 157.
29. Sadie Robertson, *Live Original*, 90.

a biracial five-year-old at his school.[30] The books never mention the issues that arise in a transracial family.

Many white adoptive parents express this colorblind attitude. In *White Parents, Black Children*, Darron T. Smith, et al., note that most white parents are not equipped to help black children develop healthy racial identities or endure racism: "White people tend to understand the world in a way that filters out the realities of race and racism,"[31] but black male youth "experience the highest levels of race-based discrimination, hostility, exclusion, and other forms of microaggressions and mistreatment."[32] The authors point out that the National Association of Black Social Workers recommends placing black children in white homes only as a last resort. White parents must seek training and take deliberate action: "Sensitivity to racial mistreatment, dialogues about it, involvement with the adoptee's birth community, and a search for models from that community are critical to avoid feelings of low self-esteem, depression, acting out, and identity confusion."[33] In the same year that *Duck Dynasty* premiered, Laura Briggs's *Somebody's Children* highlighted the politics of transracial and transnational adoption:

> Stranger adoption is a national and international system whereby the children of impoverished or otherwise disenfranchised mothers are transferred to middle-class, wealthy mothers (and fathers). The relative power of these two groups, and the fact that stranger adoption almost never takes place in the opposite direction, sets the inescapable framework in which adoption is inserted.[34]

Well-meaning parents like the Robertsons often choose transracial adoption without fully understanding its troubled history.

Duck Dynasty avoids the controversy by featuring Will less than his older white siblings. Many episodes follow John Luke and Sadie through mundane situations like dating, learning to drive, and going to the dentist, and special occasions like getting married and going to college, while only three episodes focus on Will. This is partly due to his age—the younger Robertsons star in fewer episodes due to the challenges of filming with children, but even the smallest cousin, River, has a subplot devoted to his seventh birthday. Will was eleven at the beginning of the series and sixteen by the end, and his relative absence reinforces the show's mixture of colorblindness

30. Korie Robertson, *Strong and Kind*, 38–39.

31. Darron T. Smith et al., *White Parents, Black Children*, 4.

32. Darron T. Smith et al., *White Parents, Black Children*, 5.

33. Darron T. Smith et al., *White Parents, Black Children*, 117.

34. Briggs, *Somebody's Children*, 4–5.

and racial stereotyping. He appears in the second episode, "CEO for a Day," as a mysteriously dark figure among the white children. Captions provide the other cousins' names, but his bears the family nickname "LIL' WILL." The adjective and apostrophe set him apart and bear connotations of the black dialect that has haunted white representations since the days of slavery, and he remains in the background throughout the first season. Since we rarely see him and he rarely speaks, viewers are left wondering about his experience in this redneck family.

Like multiracial celebrities Keanu Reeves and Vin Diesel, Will's identity is wrapped in mystery and ambiguity, although his location in Southern reality rather than Hollywood fiction renders him more silent and less seductive, and he never became a star like John Luke and Sadie. Four years before *Duck Dynasty*, Mary Beltrán and Camilla Fojas observed in *Mixed Race Hollywood* that "biracial and multiracial models, actors, and film and television characters seem to be everywhere."[35] Yet Lisa Nakamura argues that they often bear the burden of symbolizing a colorblind future and covering their racial difference, with a neoliberal "don't ask, don't tell" policy requiring minorities "to act blind to their own color."[36] According to this logic, "it is acceptable and sometimes good for an individual to *be* black but unacceptable for them to *perform their blackness*."[37] *Duck Dynasty* never mentions Will's blackness; someone who listened to the audio alone would never know his race.

Season two's "I'm Dreaming of a Redneck Christmas" finally tells Will's adoption story in a way that seems flippant and uncharitable. Will and Sadie bring old albums into the kitchen where the family prepares for dinner, and Korie narrates while photos of Will's first Christmas appear onscreen: "I remember when we went to Baton Rouge and picked you up. You were the cutest thing I've ever seen." *Duck Dynasty* often portrays people of color in photos that distance them from the viewer, and these images both erase Will's history before the Robertsons and replace his present contributions to the family. Briggs concludes *Somebody's Children* with a description that mirrors this television moment: "If adoption has often been a symbol of hopefulness and new beginnings, it is worth noticing that it is also an event in which long histories of inequality and social marginalization are sedimented, frozen in time and then made into family stories."[38] Moreover, Willie keeps interrupting to complain about his hunger: "You know what I

---

35. Beltrán and Fojas, *Mixed Race Hollywood*, 1.

36. Nakamura, "*Mixedfolks.com*," 69.

37. Nakamura, "*Mixedfolks.com*," 69 (italics original).

38. Briggs, *Somebody's Children*, 283.

remember too? Christmas cookies." Willie's voiceover eventually picks up the adoption narrative only to undercut its significance: "Korie and I adopted Will when he was a month old, and it was one of the happiest days of my life, and he's grown up to be a true Robertson. But none of that's gonna change in the next twenty minutes." These jokes prevent the scene from becoming too sentimental, but they imply that Willie doesn't care about the important ritual of remembering an adoption day. Since Will only speaks a few words, the series establishes a pattern of having other people speak for him. He and other black characters stay in the background until another Christmas episode five seasons later.

In season seven's "A Home for the Holidays," the Robertsons buy a house for Theresser Lewis, mother of Willie's high school friend Paul. In *The Duck Commander Family*, Willie remembers the African American Lewises eating possums, turtles, and raccoons,[39] which he finds disgusting even though the Robertsons proudly eat squirrels, frogs, and many other animals that can be hunted in West Monroe.[40] He does not explain whether they ate possum due to hardship, cultural preference, or really bad wilderness skills, simply expressing his characteristic disdain for ethnic or foreign foods. Yet Willie considered himself a virtual member of their community: "I was running around town with Paul all the time. I think it's safe to say I was the only white kid in his neighborhood. We were shooting basketball on

39. Willie and Korie Robertson, *Duck Commander Family*, 52.

40. The contrast between *Jan Karon's Mitford Cookbook & Kitchen Reader* (2004) and *Miss Kay's Duck Commander Kitchen* (2013) highlights the range of white Southern identities from upper-class, refined charm to working-class, redneck pride. The Mitford cookbook's front cover features a pastel illustration of an outdoor picnic; its back cover has a photo of Karon sitting indoors surrounded by flowers and fruit, wearing a silky beige jacket, pearl earrings and necklace, and a ring with a large jewel, holding a rose-colored glass. The Duck Commander cookbook's front cover features a photo of Miss Kay in a red apron, holding a cast iron pot that looks to be full of jambalaya, surrounded by macaroni and cheese, biscuits, and pecan pie; its back cover has a photo of Miss Kay standing outdoors in a flowered apron, holding a pie in an aluminum pan. The Mitford book is decorated with photographs of the food on fine china in elegant place settings, while the text is mostly excerpts from the novels. The Duck Commander book is decorated with photographs of the Robertson family and simpler photographs of the food in plain dishes or sitting on a cutting board or tea towel, while the text contains Miss Kay's reflections on family life. Miss Kay's recipes reveal their working-class roots by relying heavily on processed foods like canned baked beans, liquid smoke, Ritz crackers, cream of mushroom soup, Jell-O, butter-flavored Crisco, Velveeta, Cool Whip, and miniature marshmallows. The food is also proudly Southern, with chapters devoted to "Louisiana at Its Best!" and "Our Cajun Christmas" that include plenty of crawfish, shrimp, and hushpuppies. Of course, given that *Duck Dynasty* is primarily about hunting, there are plenty of recipes for cooking your freshly killed ducks, deer, and squirrels. Despite these stark differences, both books include a personal exhortation to the reader to invest in an iron skillet and describe how to season it.

the square one day, and a cop drove by and called me over to his police car. The cop asked me, 'What are you doing over here? You don't need to be in this neighborhood.'"[41] Willie answered proudly: "I practically live here."[42] After Paul spent time in prison, Willie hired him as warehouse manager: "We helped him get a truck and moved him into a trailer on Phil's land. He was married in Phil's yard, and I was proud to be his best man. He and his wife, Krystle, work for us."[43] In *UnPHILtered*, Phil retells the stories about the police stopping Willie in Paul's neighborhood, Paul's time in prison, the Robertsons helping him, and the wedding.[44] Clearly, Paul became the stereotypical "black best friend," their go-to example to prove their racial tolerance. The Robertsons do not reflect on the paternalistic attitudes that can creep into such a relationship when the white man becomes the boss.

"A Home for the Holidays" features a "white savior" plot, in which the Robertsons proudly help a black family who appear in the final moments to express their gratitude. Hughey describes the popularity of white messianic characters "saving people of color who lack the fortitude, wisdom, resources, or plain old willpower to rescue themselves."[45] The episode begins with the Robertsons exchanging gag gifts, highlighting their excessive wealth, and Willie announces: "We've been family friends of Paul and his mother and their whole family for years, so I want to do something really exciting for her this Christmas." Willie taking the role of their "Secret Santa" reinforces "the myth of a great white father figure whose benevolent paternalism over people of color is the way things not only have been but should be."[46] An old photo of Willie and Paul appears so quickly that I did not notice Paul's race the first time I saw the episode, but I was sure that he would turn out to be black. There is something all too familiar in the ease with which the Robertsons buy and decorate the house without consulting the recipients. Rather than allowing Paul to appear live and speak for himself, Willie narrates: "His mom Theresser was like a second mom to me, but since she's been going through some rough times lately, we thought we'd do something really nice for her. I thought that we could give Paul's mom a new home." He tells his family that the modular home will arrive the next day, and he needs everyone's help getting it decorated. The episode does not mention that Willie practically lived with the Lewis family in high school or raise the

41. Willie and Korie Robertson, *Duck Commander Family*, 52.
42. Willie and Korie Robertson, *Duck Commander Family*, 52.
43. Willie and Korie Robertson, *Duck Commander Family*, 222.
44. Phil Robertson, *UnPHILtered*, 95–96.
45. Hughey, *White Savior Film*, 18.
46. Hughey, *White Savior Film*, 19.

question of why two Duck Commander employees cannot afford a decent home on the salary that Willie pays them.

Despite their good intentions, the Robertsons are not making a financial sacrifice—Willie considered buying a $50,000 racehorse in the previous episode—and they put in little hard labor. "Deck the Halls" plays over a montage of paid workers preparing the ground and putting the house together, and the duck call workers fool around as they build the deck. Jase engages in a subtle echo of blackface minstrelsy by opening his mouth wide to imitate Theresser's response; the Robertsons imagine the Lewises reacting to their philanthropy rather than including them in the project. Phil claims: "Our connection with the Lewis family goes way back, years and years. They literally, in our view, they're just family members." The episode doubles his perspective by cutting from his interview to his comments at the building site: "We've been going to church with Theresser for forty years. She's going to think, 'Boy, the Almighty waited a while before he blessed me, but he finally moved!'" Phil places words in her mouth and frames the Robertsons' gift as an act of God without explaining why they didn't help until now. Meanwhile, some of the Robertsons record the song "Christmas in West Monroe" at a local music studio. Despite this natural opportunity to showcase Will's musical talents, we only hear him rap for a few seconds both in the studio and in the band's final performance.

The episode adopts HGTV formulas for the "reveal" of a new home: Paul and Theresser drive down the road, we cut to commercial, and we watch them approach again. There is a camera in the car, but we can barely hear Paul when he says, "This is your new house, Momma," and there is no caption to identify the woman in the back seat, who is presumably Paul's wife. Theresser wears a Duck Commander T-shirt, advertising the company brand as the focus turns to her much-anticipated gratitude. When she says: "I must've died and went to heaven," the line appears in a subtitle because she and Paul are facing away from the camera, toward the new house and the crowd of friends. Her thankful words are more important than her identity. An interview with Phil begins while she climbs the steps saying "I can't even talk," and he provides the story's moral over shots of her hugging the Robertsons and entering the house in a low-angle shot that cuts off the Lewis family's heads: "Most people just think in terms of money, but it's way more than that. Loving God and loving your neighbor are the two greatest commands in the Bible. This comes under the heading of loving your neighbor. We love 'em. Really, that's what Christmas is all about. It's a good feeling." During the closing prayer, the camera zooms in on Phil as he breaks down in tears and calls Theresser "my sister," while Willie's voiceover emphasizes that "the word 'family' means more than just blood kin. It's also the people we grew up with, the people we go to church with, our neighbors, our friends, and our community." If Paul and Theresser are part of the family, where were they during the first six seasons, and why do they never appear on *Duck Dynasty* again?

Later in season seven, "Friday Afternoon Lights" is the first episode to focus on Will, although it shifts from his football talent and aspirations to his father's incompetence as a coach. Willie's voiceover introduces the plot: "A big part of parenting is encouraging your kids to follow their dreams, and that's not something I take lightly. My son Little Will wants to play college football one day, so today I took him to my old university to get a little taste of the action." Since black adoptees in white families "spoke of being pushed toward sports and entertainment activities in high school, including football,"[47] and since Will has one line in the opening segment, we should ask whether this is really his dream. Willie announces that he's becoming an assistant coach for Will's team, then shows up late for his first day and interrupts the coach's introduction to start harassing the boys. Shots of Will surrounded by white teammates point to the struggles that he must face as "the lone, token representative of the African American community in a largely White environment."[48] He finally challenges his father: "I'm pretty sure I can beat *you* when we're running," but Willie's response is loaded with historical connotations: "Now I knew, when I took this job, sooner or later one of these kids was gonna have to be put in their place." Will easily wins the race, but the humor stems from Jase narrating like a sports announcer as Willie collapses with a leg cramp in slow motion. Will issues a second challenge to Jase, Phil, and Duck Commander employees Martin and Godwin: "I'm pretty sure I can beat y'all too since y'all are kinda old." The adults beat the kids in a football sequence typical of *Duck Dynasty*'s preference for slapstick over skill. Willie claims that he does not take his children's dreams lightly, but the series insists on doing just that.

When the Robertsons dress in period costumes for season nine's "Renaissance Men," Will appears as the court jester. Since he doesn't exactly embrace the role, it seems like someone's failed attempt to place him into one of the stereotypes from Donald Bogle's *Toms, Coons, Mulattoes, Mammies, and Bucks*. Will's mischievous criticism of his parents distances him from the faithful "tom," the colorblind comedy prevents any associations with the "tragic mulatto," and he bears none of the sexual threat of the brutal "buck," but the purple and black jester outfit links him to the coon's role "as

47. Darron T. Smith et al., *White Parents, Black Children*, 7.
48. Darron T. Smith et al., *White Parents, Black Children*, 8.

amusement object and black buffoon."[49] Wearing a pointed hat with bells, Will sits in the cage on the dunking booth under the sign "Dunk the Fool" and refuses to heckle his family members as they throw their balls. Si pokes his cage with a stick, adding to the unintended echoes of a slave auction. Willie eventually dunks him, and a long, multiangle, slow-motion replay of him falling into the freezing water functions as payback for triumphing over his father in "Friday Afternoon Lights."

Will shows more of his personality in season ten's "Father Knows Pest," which begins with him excited about his driver's permit and asking to drive home from his basketball game. He appears on the interview couch for the first time in the series, still captioned as LIL' WILL. Korie explains that Willie teaches the kids to drive, while she reads them books, and Will says: "I never remembered you reading me a book." Korie says that she also cooked for him, and Will makes a choking sound. Will's criticism of his parents ends quickly, and we return to the parking lot, where Will backs out of the space only to have Willie take over and crash into a cart full of basketballs. The family banters with Will's African American coach about how John Luke once hit his car, and we cut to the opening theme song. An interview with Will and his coach would have shown a transracial adoptee interacting with a mentor from his birth community, but the episode follows "Friday Afternoon Lights" as Will challenges the older generation: "I'll get my driver's manual, and I'm gonna see who's best according to the manual." Will gives driving tests to Willie and Si, sitting in the passenger seat and deducting points for every mistake. He has never spoken this much or had this much power over the plot. He concludes that "both of y'all flunked the test" and issues a second challenge: "We could go to Excalibur and go ride the go-carts." However, only Willie and Si compete in the go-cart race. This episode shows Will as a funny and confident teen, but he spends very little time in the driver's seat.

In the final season's "Uneasy Rider," Willie urges Will to buy a practical first vehicle. Will shares an interview with his father, enthusiastically describing the cool car he wants, and this appears to be a typical reality sitcom plot like season two's "Truck Commander," in which John Luke shops for his first vehicle. Yet Will's race creates unacknowledged ironies when they arrive at a seller's home. Will gets excited about two white sports cars in the driveway—symbols of white privilege like the Triumph in *Flywheel*—but the seller explains that they belong to his daughter and shows Will a used police vehicle. Willie croons "Hello, Officer Will" with complete disregard for the Black Lives Matter movement drawing national attention to police

49. Bogle, *Toms, Coons, Mulattoes*, 7.

violence toward black men. Will doesn't mention these connotations, but he says "no" nine times in the following sequence. A few episodes later, "Drive-In Revivin'" begins with Will looking proudly ethnic in his Afro and asking for money to buy a gift for a girl. This suggests that the plot will involve Will going on a date, like John Luke and Sadie before him, but it quickly veers in another direction. His father claims that you don't need money to be romantic, leading to *another* challenge for the older generation in which Willie must plan a free date for Korie. Will disappears until we see him in the background at the end. Perhaps a plot about Will's romance would be too controversial, since a white girlfriend would raise the issue of "interracial" dating, while a black, Hispanic, or Asian girlfriend would introduce another person of color into the mostly white cast.

Will's plots evoke Southern racial tensions only to disavow them, but their legacy appears in subtle forms throughout the series. While "Sharp Dressed Man" was the theme song for the A&E broadcasts, the first five seasons on DVD feature "Workin' Man Zombie" by the white Minneapolis band the 4onthefloor, with its angry working-class lyrics about your blood boiling while you slave your life away. The song's video includes white men in chains, dramatizing the metaphor of blue-collar labor as a form of slavery, but moving the lyrics to Louisiana gives them troubling new connotations. The accompanying images show the Robertsons inheriting Southern white privilege: the men drive a shiny car to an elegant house with white columns that recalls an antebellum plantation. They join their wives, who are dressed in ball gowns, and pose on the tree-lined drive. The song only makes sense as an ironic address to black and working-class viewers: *you* may be slaving your whole life away, but not the Robertsons.[50]

Two episodes contain similar moments in which the producers fail to recognize the viewer's social location as a potential barrier to appreciating the dark humor. In "Master and Duck Commander," Jase chats with a black woman at a gas station, and Si appears in the duck blind on their trailer and pretends to shoot her; she gasps and places her hand on her chest, her laughter not fully covering the threat of racial violence. In "Bachelor Party Blowout," the duck call workers visit a cabin filled with Civil War weapons

---

50. *Duck Dynasty* has a complicated relationship to labor, since the obfuscated labor of filming the show prevents the family from running their business at the same time. We rarely see the women working at Duck Commander or doing housework. Many scenes take place at the warehouse, but it appears to be strangely empty of workers, except for the room where Si, Jase, Godwin, and Martin make the duck calls. We enter this room regularly and watch them work and banter for a while, but then some incident launches the plot, and they leave for a silly escapade. The choice of a theme song about slaving your life away seems quite ironic, which may be why the lyrics were removed for season six and replaced with instrumental music.

and shoot historic rifles and a cannon. Si exaggerates his Southern accent to challenge Martin to a duel, but the soundtrack includes the Union anthem "Battle Hymn of the Republic" rather than the Confederate "Dixie." Slow-motion sequences linger on the firing of each weapon, but the flour sack and barrel used as targets deflect attention from the historical defense of slavery. We never see Will or other African Americans with guns on *Duck Dynasty*, as if black men with guns would threaten the light-hearted tone.

African Americans appear in minor roles in colorblind contexts, like a firefighter at a pancake breakfast,[51] a friend in Miss Kay Robertson's Big Sister Club,[52] and a resident assistant at Liberty University whose ethnic name Willie mocks.[53] The Robertsons' antics often cause problems for black laborers. In "Half in the Bag," Si pursues his dream of bagging groceries, and supermarket manager Leo has to fire him for incompetence. Leo and another black worker then take part in a bagging contest at the warehouse, placing them within the meaningless competition at the center of the series. One running joke is that Si can't remember Leo's name and keeps calling him the more ethnic-sounding "Leon." In "Bingo Star," a Bingo worker asks Willie to call the numbers but has to replace him due to his total disregard for the rules. In "Bro'd Trip," a busy postal employee has to wait for the duck call workers to finish their packages because they have been messing around. None of these trivial scenarios allow black people to express a genuine grievance against the extremely wealthy family.

In the final season's "Good Willie Hunting," the wives and older cousins go to Africa on a mission trip, the first time we see the family interact with people of color outside the US. It is refreshing to see their faith extend beyond the formulaic closing prayer, although the unusual structure suggests that the producers struggled to integrate more heartfelt subject matter into what they continued to see as a comedy series. Most episodes alternate between two plots, but this one begins with fourteen straight minutes of the men playing "manhunt" and then switches to the mission trip for the rest of the episode. To emphasize the geographical distance, a world map appears on the screen, and the camera shifts from Louisiana to Uganda. It is not clear why the African plotline was segregated, given the upbeat tone as the Robertsons visit a school, shop in a market, and see a home they helped build. The producers highlight the family's cultural incompetence through a running gag in which John Luke tries to speak Swahili, only to discover that nobody understands Swahili in this region. Africans speak only a few words

51. "Quackdraft."
52. "Search N' Decoy."
53. "RV There Yet?"

and appear as warm-hearted hosts and grateful recipients of charitable giving. The episode ends by cross-cutting between Sadie praying over a meal in Uganda and Phil praying over a meal in Louisiana, the only attempt to show a global Christian community.

The next episode, "Sleep Cover," also segregates the Louisiana and Uganda plotlines, as if the producers wanted to avoid the cognitive dissonance between the Robertsons' conspicuous consumption and the joyful hospitality of Africans living in relative poverty. The episode begins with Willie and two of the younger children video chatting with Korie in Uganda. When she describes the cute kids there, Willie jokes "bring some home," and she responds "that's okay," trivializing the couple's adoption advocacy. The family asks if she has seen lions and zebras, and she has to explain that she is not on safari. After Bella hosts a sleepover and the men play night golf, the episode ends with the wives and children returning from Uganda, and Si asks if they are "medically cleared." More emphasis on the Robertsons' mission work would have deepened the show's appeal to many evangelicals, even if international cooperation and fellowship are notoriously difficult to achieve in the context of extreme economic inequality.

Many episodes mention African American popular culture in contexts that have been emptied of racial significance. The title "Driving Miss Sadie" alludes to *Driving Miss Daisy*, a controversial Best Picture about a Jewish woman and her black chauffeur, and "Friday Afternoon Lights" to *Friday Night Lights*, a television series that portrays racial tensions in a Texas town. Viewers would not know the race of most celebrities mentioned without outside knowledge: Miss Kay has a turtle named Mr. T,[54] the duck call workers discuss Whoopi Goldberg's role in *Ghost*,[55] Si tells Jase to talk to him "like I'm Oprah,"[56] Jep claims to be the hippest brother because he knows about Dr. Dre and Kris Kross,[57] and Si blows on a bugle and says: "I'm a regular Louis Armstrong."[58] The overall impression is that the modern South contains no racism and no reason for Will to consider his race at all.

---

54. "Scoot Along Si."
55. "Quack O'Lanterns."
56. "Life of Si."
57. "Governor's Travels."
58. "Mo Math, Mo Problems."

"HONORARY ROBERTSON": BOOMERANG BECCA AND OTHER ASIANS

In *The Duck Commander Family*, Korie explains that Rebecca Ann Lo arrived as an exchange student from Taiwan when she was sixteen. Her culture shock was intense: "She had learned some English in school in Taiwan, but with our Southern accents, Rebecca just could not understand us. Somehow she and I figured out how to communicate."[59] The family grew to love Rebecca, and her mother reluctantly allowed her to stay in Louisiana permanently. Willie says that "we are her American mom and dad,"[60] even though he describes a prank in which he convinced Rebecca that he was a former professional baseball player and a business trip in which he rejected strange Taiwanese foods. This passage echoes Willie's description of Paul Lewis, which mocks the family for eating possum but claims that he practically lived in their neighborhood, as if he can enter into meaningful intercultural relationships without understanding the most basic differences. Sadie's *Live Original* combines her fondness for Rebecca with cultural insensitivity: "She loves to laugh and to make others laugh, and she really enjoys telling jokes. The problem with her jokes is that they may be funny in her native language or in the country where she was raised, but they are not funny at all in English or in Louisiana!"[61] Yet Korie boasts that Rebecca graduated "from Louisiana State University in just four years with a degree in fashion design"[62] and describes a bouquet that Rebecca made her for Mother's Day with materials from Taiwan.[63] Just as the show rarely features Will's musical talents, it will downplay Rebecca's skill as a fashion designer and exaggerate her cultural and business incompetence.

The Robertsons' colorblind attitude toward Will's transracial adoption extends to Rebecca's transnational adoption, and again they closely resemble other white parents. Catherine Ceniza Choy's *Global Families* notes that Asian international adoption "has become a powerful way to imagine contemporary U. S. multiculturalism because it shapes one of the most intimate, emotionally laden, and cherished institutions: the family,"[64] but the "specter of American racism and nativism toward Asians haunts

59. Willie and Korie Robertson, *Duck Commander Family*, 155.
60. Willie and Korie Robertson, *Duck Commander Family*, 157.
61. Sadie Robertson, *Live Original*, 7.
62. Kay Robertson et al., *Women of Duck Commander*, 160.
63. Korie Robertson, *Strong and Kind*, 175.
64. Choy, *Global Families*, 2.

the joyous imagery."[65] Kim Park Nelson's *Invisible Asians* describes white parents encouraging Korean children to identify as white: "Forgetting the reality of adoption was a key part of normalizing adoptive families, and, to forget adoption, the most visible sign of difference between parents and children, race, had to be overlooked."[66] Korie comments that "if I ever make the mistake of saying I have only four kids, the rest of our children are quick to point out I have five."[67] Korie not only forgets Rebecca's racial difference, she forgets to include Rebecca as one of her children. Even for adoptees more firmly entrenched in their adoptive families, white parents create a painful situation when they deny or minimize racial discrimination. Park Nelson calls the oral histories of adult Korean American adoptees "exhausting" and "intensely sad,"[68] which may explain why Rebecca rarely appears on this comedy show and becomes one of the "invisible Asians" who are erased from public discourse about immigration and Asian American identity.

Duck Dynasty never mentions Rebecca until the season five premiere, "Boomerang Becca," which draws upon stereotypes of Asians as demanding and pushy but implies that they are acceptable because it's all in good fun. Willie sets up the plot: "Rebecca is an exchange student that Korie and I took in about ten years ago. She spent the last two years interning in the fashion industry, and today she flies back home." He establishes the main conflict when he tells the men: "She's in for a couple days, then she's outta here." His fear that Rebecca might overstay her welcome recalls long-standing notions of "yellow peril" that portray "Asians and Asian Americans as threatening to take over, invade, or otherwise negatively Asianize the US nation"[69] and could easily touch a nerve for immigrant viewers who feel unwelcome in the United States. Willie holds up a photo as he describes Rebecca's presumption in seeing herself as part of the family: "Here we are at the beach, taking a family portrait. There's Rebecca." Jase adds: "You remember what happened the first time. She's like, 'Yeah, I'm going to be an exchange student for a year.' Ten years later, she's now part of the family." It is unclear whether Rebecca is part of the family in the official sense of John Luke and Sadie, or in the metaphorical sense of Theresser and Paul Lewis. Just as Willie undermined Will's adoption story with his impatience to have dinner, he undermines Rebecca's story with his impatience to turn her room into a man cave.

65. Choy, *Global Families*, 3.

66. Park Nelson, *Invisible Asians*, 4.

67. Kay Robertson et al., *Women of Duck Commander*, 160.

68. Park Nelson, *Invisible Asians*, 27.

69. Ono and Pham, *Asian Americans*, 25.

The Duck Commander Family described Rebecca as an adopted child two years earlier, but when she appears waiting at the airport with her luggage, the caption identifies her as "REBECCA: Honorary Robertson." This word choice evokes a painful history of racial exclusion. Mia Tuan's *Forever Foreigners or Honorary Whites?* claims that "Asian ethnics are often portrayed in extreme and simplified terms, either as perpetually foreign or as honorary members of an exclusive party hosted by whites."[70] Rebecca greets the Robertsons warmly and begins to talk about her experiences in Los Angeles, but Willie is distracted by watching John Luke wrestle the bags into the truck, and she has to ask: "Are you listening to all this?" The scene cuts back to the interview, where Willie tells the viewer what he was too polite to say at the airport: "Look, I hate to ruin the moment by asking, 'How long are you gonna stay?' But once I see a dog and all that luggage, I can't help but think, 'How long are you gonna stay?'" This cut-to-interview structure places a barrier between Rebecca and the viewers, encouraging us to identify with Willie's perspective rather than hers. She does not get to complain about having to wait on the curb or express frustration with her adoptive father's lack of hospitality.

Another structural feature of *Duck Dynasty* is the highly produced short sequence that takes place between longer segments, usually featuring the characters interacting with props. After the airport scene, there is a slow-motion sequence of Rebecca throwing her luggage at John Luke until he crumbles to the ground, confirming Willie's notion that she is selfish, spoiled, and making unreasonable demands, a symbolic representative of immigrants who drain America's resources. While Korie prepares a surprise party for Rebecca, Willie grills her about her job options and asks bluntly: "Do you plan on living with us till you're thirty?" He backs down when she mentions her business plan, but he later interrupts the surprise party segment by asking the audience if she should pay rent because she's twenty-four. During the closing prayer, he asks God to bless Rebecca and her career: "The good news is in the Robertson family, someone will always be there to help, with open arms and unconditional love." The partygoers watch slide shows of family photos including Rebecca, once again distancing her from viewers and freezing her in time as a family member welcomed "with open arms" despite Willie's treatment of her throughout this episode.

In season ten's "Wild Wild West Monroe," Rebecca's preparations to bring her American fiancé to Taiwan uncover more stereotypes about Asians speaking broken English, participating in meaningless cultural rituals, and eating strange food. Early in the episode, Rebecca video chats with

70. Tuan, *Forever Foreigners?*, 19.

her mother and invites the Robertsons to say hello, but Willie complains that "she only speaks Chinese." Rebecca retorts: "Well, you should have learned some by now." As Tuan explains, "Language, one of the most obvious symbols of cultural difference, has historically been an easy target for nativist resentment."[71] Rebecca then appears in her first interview, sitting between her adoptive parents, identified onscreen as "Willie's Daughter." Korie explains her history and that "we didn't officially adopt her, but we are her American family," and Willie undercuts the emotion with a joke: "It was for tax reasons." There is a sentimental moment when Rebecca says: "Korie is my American mom, and my dad passed away when I was younger, so Willie is really kind of like my only father figure," but the producers mock her slight mispronunciation with a subtitle that reads "Father fuger." She laughs and says: "I knew I could not say that!" This reflects Tuan's description of Asian Americans using a "self-mocking strategy in order to make themselves less threatening to their white friends,"[72] which leads to hidden injuries and loss of dignity. Back at the house, Willie interrupts the video chat by loudly saying goodbye, and when Rebecca's mother continues to wave from the screen, he says: "Close it, Rebecca. Close it. Close it. Just close the computer." Sadie closes the laptop, ending this rare instance of someone on *Duck Dynasty* speaking a language other than English.

Korie's idea of helping Rebecca and John Reed practice the traditional Taiwanese engagement ceremony marks the first time that we have seen the Robertsons connect with an adopted child's cultural heritage. Yet Willie mocks the ceremonial handwashing: "This ritual means, we like you, but, just saying, don't know where your hands have been." He then opens a ceremonial red envelope and finds that John Reed is offering him three dollars and an ice cream gift card to marry his daughter. This seems like innocent humor except for the broader context in which "mimicry and mockery are common media frames used to represent Asians and Asian Americans" and clarify "who has the power to name and regulate appropriate and inappropriate behavior."[73] Fortunately, Rebecca expresses her emotions in an interview, which shows great improvement over "Boomerang Becca" five seasons earlier: "I'm really impressed with how John Reed gets along with my family here, but it's also important to know the other side of me that's in Taiwan." In the alternate plot that inspired the episode title, Jase and Jep decide to have a cowboy shooting competition, and a short sequence follows in which offscreen guns shoot red paper lanterns that are hanging above two

71. Tuan, *Forever Foreigners?*, 109.

72. Tuan, *Forever Foreigners?*, 84.

73. Ono and Pham, *Asian Americans*, 102–3.

duck decoys dressed as bride and groom. The sequence ties together two plots—shooting contests and wedding preparations—through the violent destruction of Rebecca's home culture. When the couple leaves for the airport, Korie presents Rebecca with a red dress for the ceremony, but Willie jokes, "Good luck eatin' that food!"

The episode ends with the typical closing prayer and voiceover, followed by a home video titled "Meanwhile in Taiwan" that shows Rebecca struggling to use chopsticks. Rebecca and John Reed cut a cake and kiss, leaving the viewer with a sweet moment that nonetheless focuses on her awkwardness in both cultures, rather than her facility in navigating them. Bhoomi K. Thakore claims that "these *Americanized* representations tend to play up the fact that these characters know little about their ethnic culture and are assimilated and thus acceptable."[74] The series has it both ways, portraying Rebecca as "forever foreigner" based on her inability to pronounce English words *and* as an assimilated and thus acceptable American who is engaged to a white man, never appears with Asian friends, and seems alienated from her home culture. Park Nelson notes that "it is only by understanding racial visibility and invisibility as two sides of a single oppressive ideology that it becomes possible to see that neither is necessarily a good choice."[75] Like other Asian adoptees, Rebecca inhabits a liminal space in which neither Taiwan nor Louisiana feels like home.

The final season's "Razing the Snakes" makes fun of Rebecca's incompetence as manager of the boutique Duck & Dressing, a Duck Commander spin-off business. In the initial scene, Rebecca sits in Willie's office as he chastises her for removing their top-selling T-shirt from the inventory. She explains that she hoped to entice customers to buy other products, but the camera cuts to an interview with Willie that establishes his opinion as authoritative. His voiceover begins while Rebecca is still onscreen, usurping her voice: "You can probably guess by looking at me, I'm not really into clothes, so when Rebecca came to me asking for advice about her clothing store, I knew that what I lacked in fashion sense, I'd make up for with business sense." The rest of the segment cross-cuts between Willie's interview and the scene with Rebecca in his office, until Jase and Si come for a machete to hunt down the snake that killed Miss Kay's pet squirrel. Si's statement joins the two male rescue plots: "Go ahead and take care of Becca's problem at the store. We'll be forming a posse and taking care of this snake," placing her alongside the reptile as a problem to be solved.

74. Thakore, *South Asians*, 45 (italics original).

75. Park Nelson, *Invisible Asians*, 124.

Willie later visits Duck & Dressing to teach Rebecca and Sadie how to run a business, comparing selling clothes to traditionally male pastimes like fishing and playing baseball. Sadie suggests putting a makeover of the Duck Commander men on Instagram, and the plot shifts to a cross-promotional photo shoot. In interviews, the wives talk about how great their husbands look and Si demonstrates his modeling poses. Nobody interviews Rebecca. The problem of her poor sales figures is "resolved" by the Robertson men— fresh from their snake-killing posse—posing before the diegetic and *Duck Dynasty* cameras. Willie's closing voiceover links their sacrifice in both plots: "In times like these, you have to forget about your needs and think about the big picture." The series never provides updates on Rebecca's wedding or business, proving that this cable show has not moved on from Darrell Y. Hamamoto's indictment of network television: "Rarely are the lives of Asian American characters examined on their own merit, and the problems they face in daily life are not considered to be of intrinsic interest."[76] The series finale continues to mock her English when she misspells "Hey" as "Hay" on the T-shirts for Si's retirement party.

Besides Rebecca, there are no extended interactions with Asians. Si's politically incorrect comments about his tour in Vietnam begin in the series premiere, "Family Funny Business," when he discusses his hatred of beavers: "They're like the Vietcong. They only move at night and they live in holes in the ground." Phil says the last part of the line along with him, suggesting that this is a habitual way of talking. In "Frog in One," Korie gets a pedicure and says that she would feel sorry for anybody who had to touch Phil's feet, and a shot of the Asian manicurist provides a brief glimpse of her point of view. In "Governor's Travels," Louisiana governor Bobby Jindal presents the Governor's Award for Entrepreneurial Excellence to Duck Commander. This portrayal of an Oxford-educated Indian American is one of those happy moments when reality manages to slip into reality television, but most of the episode dwells on the family's antics as they prepare for his visit. Jindal appears in the seventeenth minute of the twenty-two minute episode, when Willie discovers him playing basketball with the workers, playfully identified as "BOBBY: Willie's Governor." He is so articulate and likeable that I wish he could have spent more than five minutes onscreen.

Like its references to Hispanic and African American cultures, *Duck Dynasty*'s references to Asian cultures involve consuming products, quoting from movies, or dressing in costumes. In "Samurai Si," Willie receives a sword from a Japanese friend and jokes: "My appreciation for the Asian culture is vast, from the time-honored traditions of the Samurai down to

76. Hamamoto, *Monitored Peril*, 206.

the all-you-can-eat buffet at the Peking Palace." When Willie takes Bella to karate class in "Return of the Beavers," he uses incongruous words like *Namaste* and *¿Cómo está?* while Si blows up a beaver dam with homemade napalm: "There's always room for napalm, boys." Si begins "The Ducket List" by imitating moves from *The 36th Chamber of Shaolin* and takes over for the chef at a hibachi restaurant, again viewing culture through the lens of consumption. In "Renaissance Men," Alan Robertson's costume from the Japanese Edo period inspires Willie's joke: "Edon't matter what time or period it is, you look like an idiot." These superficial engagements with Asian popular culture outnumber the scenes focusing on Rebecca.

"A BETTER OPPORTUNITY FOR A CHILD": THE LATEST ROBERTSON ADOPTEES

The season ten premiere "Willie & Korie's Anniversorry" announces their adoption of white teen Rowdy, whose story unfortunately gets earlier and more attention than the transracial adoptions in the past. Viewers waited two seasons for Will's backstory and five seasons to meet Rebecca, but Rowdy shows up right away. He and Korie sit in the kitchen looking at old family photos, recalling "I'm Dreaming of a Redneck Christmas," and Korie explains: "Rowdy is our new son. We met him last year in April. I was actually speaking at an adoption fundraiser and found out that there was this little boy that needed a home. We met him and fell in love with him immediately and invited him into our family." Willie adds, "And here he is," and a longer shot reveals Rowdy sitting on the interview couch, a position of privilege not yet granted to Will or Rebecca. This discrepancy occurs because season ten is the first to include extensive interviews with the Robertson children, but the timing gives the impression that Rowdy becomes part of the family more easily than older adoptees who remained in the background for years. Rowdy tells his own story in a way that they never did: "I was a little bit nervous about meeting my new family because where I came from, I had no siblings. I was just the only child in my family. Since I was an only child and only had one parent, I never got to go out of state, and so this was also my first time to be out of state. It was awesome." Korie pats his knee and says, "You're gonna be in our family forever." While this interview improves on previous depictions of adopted children as sources of irritation, there is a regrettable contrast between the onscreen treatment of this white child and his biracial and Asian siblings.

The final season episode "Rowdy's Big Day" celebrates his legal adoption. Korie explains, "Even though we adopted Will when he was five weeks old, this was the first time we have actually had this experience to go before the judge." The episode includes interviews with Rowdy, courthouse scenes, and a huge party in which the siblings and cousins read him letters on "What It Means to Be a Robertson." Rebecca's and Will's heartfelt letters to Rowdy may be the high point of the series' adoption advocacy. Will incorporates the Hawaiian language, showing more respect toward Hawaiian culture than the "home of the burrito" jokes in season three, albeit by paraphrasing a Disney film: "There's a word that a lot of people know, and I'm sure you know it too, and it's called *ohana*, and it means 'family,' and family means no one is forgotten or left behind." Rebecca reads: "I don't think I've told you this, but my first dad died when I was your age, so sometimes sad things happen, but we don't really understand why, but just know that you can count on every single one of us." It is moving to see the family reach out to another child, and Willie's final voiceover makes an explicit appeal: "The decision to add a child to your family ain't an easy one, no matter if it's your first or your fifth, but when it comes to adoption, it's a blessing to be able to provide not only a home but a better opportunity for a child." Of course, the reference to a "fifth" child includes (1) John Luke, (2) Sadie, (3) Will, (4) Bella, and (5) Rowdy but excludes Rebecca, reinforcing her ambiguous status in the family. The adoption advocacy rhetoric continues to be color-blind, which may explain its absence in the next episode.

"Disappearing Acts" focuses on the first birthday of Jep and Jessica's newly adopted black son Gus, but never explains how he joined the family. The baby had started to appear in season ten as a strangely mysterious figure with no backstory. The A&E broadcast audience would recognize him from the spin-off series *Jep & Jessica: Growing the Dynasty*, which ran parallel to *Duck Dynasty*'s last three seasons and which we will examine in the conclusion. For anyone watching the original series on DVD or online, his presence seems as inexplicable as that of Will five years earlier, even in this episode that centers on him. In one shot of Jessica holding him, the caption "JESSICA: Jep's Wife" partially covers his face, and he does not have his own caption. "LIL' WILL" and "REBECCA: Honorary Robertson" were bad enough, but the darkest-skinned child simply has no identity. The plot concentrates on Jep learning magic tricks for the party, where we see Gus smiling, clapping, and eating birthday cake. Jep prays, "Lord, we want to thank you so much for little Gus and what he means to us," and Willie jokes: "One day Gus may be responsible for changing Jep's diapers." He seems to be an adopted son, but his status in the family remains ambiguous. While "Disappearing Acts" refers to the magic, it also serves as a symbolic label for Gus's role as bodily present and discursively absent.

Overall, the series portrays the Robertson children of color in ways that marginalize them in comparison to the white children, but the fault lies as much with the A&E producers as with the family members. An anecdote in Missy Robertson's *Blessed, Blessed . . . Blessed* reveals their conflict about the tone of the show. Missy wanted to spread awareness about children born with cleft palate by making an episode about her daughter Mia's bone graft surgery, but the producers balked: "'*Duck Dynasty* is a comedy show,' they explained to us. 'This situation with Mia's surgery isn't funny.'"[77] Southern racial tensions are not funny, and the *GQ* fiasco revealed the high costs of choosing the wrong language or striking the wrong tone when discussing the subject, so the producers may have hesitated to feature Will and Rebecca as main characters. Ironically, they created even more grounds for offense by depicting them in stereotypical ways that garnered cheap laughs but prevented the series from affirming "the authenticity of complicated identities."[78] The producers might have treated their multicultural cast with greater sensitivity and handled the nuances of transracial adoption with greater integrity if they respected their audience and took the family's advice to address complex issues along with the comedy.

77. Missy Robertson, *Blessed, Blessed . . . Blessed*, 170–71.
78. Park Nelson, *Invisible Asians*, 125.

CONCLUSION

This book has offered one answer to Clifford G. Christians's question: "Where are the evangelical attempts to broaden the moral landscape of a modern highly technological age?"[1] We have seen these attempts in Walden Media's reinvention of Susan Pevensie, Jan Karon's exposure of Southern racism in *Home to Holly Springs*, and the Kendrick Brothers' focus on a black family in *War Room*. Christians concluded: "So far the evangelical community has exalted the mass media for outreach, but has had little positive impact on their contribution to the overall flow of cultural history."[2] Although *Duck Dynasty* hardly fulfills Christians's hopes for redemptive television, the Robertsons defended biblical values in the *GQ* scandal, wrote honest nonfiction books about hard topics, and advocated for the adoption of "hard-to-place" biracial and older children. Their popularity reflects viewers' desire to see conservative Christians who are likeable and compassionate. As R. Laurence Moore claims in *Selling God*, "Success is not proof of worldliness, nor flexibility proof of corruption."[3] The most recent texts from the artists examined in this volume reveal further attention to race, class, and gender: Francine Rivers's *The Masterpiece* (2018), Karon's *To Be Where You Are* (2017), Jerry B. Jenkins's *Dead Sea Rising* (2018), the Kendrick Brothers' *Overcomer* (2019), and *Jep & Jessica: Growing the Dynasty* (2016–2017). As the politics of social location continue to preoccupy Americans in the second decade of the twenty-first century, Christian artists are placing them more often in the center of their narratives.

1. Christians, "Redemptive Media," 347.
2. Christians, "Redemptive Media," 354.
3. R. Laurence Moore, *Selling God*, 55.

EMPOWERING ROMANCE IN *THE MASTERPIECE* AND *TO BE WHERE YOU ARE*

The cover of *The Masterpiece* still identifies Rivers as "Internationally Best-selling Author of *Redeeming Love*," and the book includes a full-page advertisement for her most famous novel, but her gender roles have greatly improved. *Redeeming Love* focused on a Christian man kidnapping and imprisoning a fallen woman, and its fairy tale references masked his violent domination. *The Masterpiece* focuses on a Christian woman setting the terms of her romance with a fallen man, updating Charlotte Brontë's transformation of fairy tale imagery in the Victorian feminist classic *Jane Eyre*. This latest bestseller presents an egalitarian relationship between Grace Moore and her handsome employer Roman Velasco, while it explores the scars of foster youth and the identity crisis of its biracial hero.

Like Angel from *Redeeming Love*, Grace suffers from childhood trauma and the worst kind of sexual experience, in this case a failed marriage to an abusive husband and a one-night stand that resulted in her baby son Samuel. Yet her many connections to Jane Eyre are more compelling. Like Jane, Grace is an orphan raised by an aunt who dislikes her. Out of desperation, she goes to work for a dark, mysterious, brooding man; lives on his extensive property; falls in love with him; and flees his offer of sex without marriage, leaving no way for him to find her. She reconciles with her aunt, rejects a pious suitor who offers marriage without sexual attraction, and waits until her hero has been chastened by God before she marries him. Not only the plot outline but many details evoke Brontë's novel. The child Jane cowers in the room where her uncle died, looks into a mirror, and sees "the strange little figure there gazing at me, with a white face and arms specking the gloom, and glittering eyes of fear."[4] The child Grace cowers in the closet where she hears her father shoot himself, and much later she looks into a mirror and sees that "she looked pale, shadows under her eyes and wild-eyed."[5] Just as Jane reunites with her relatives at Moor House and achieves financial independence as a schoolteacher, Grace Moore moves closer to family and sets up a tutoring business.

Roman plays the role of Edward Fairfax Rochester, one of the original Gothic heroes. Rochester sits alone in an ancestral estate haunted by ghostly laughter and broods like "some wronged and fettered wild beast or bird."[6] Roman wanders his empty mansion feeling "like a ghost haunting the

4. Brontë, *Jane Eyre*, 26.
5. Rivers, *Masterpiece*, 467.
6. Brontë, *Jane Eyre*, 420.

place"[7] and harbors a secret identity as "the Bird" who paints graffiti at night to release his pent-up rage. Rochester may have fathered Jane's pupil Adèle during a passing affair; Roman may have fathered Grace's son Samuel during a one-night stand. Rochester's pride crumbles when his mansion burns and leaves him a cripple, and he cries out to Jane three times; Roman has a vision of "the fiery heat of hell"[8] that leaves him with a limp, and God sends him the sign of three people mentioning Grace's name. Both heroes marry their heroines and have a child in the final pages.

Jane's relentless pursuit of egalitarian romance in a harshly patriarchal world has endeared her to generations of feminists. Sandra M. Gilbert notes that "though in one sense Jane and Rochester begin their relationship as master and servant, prince and Cinderella, Mr. B. and Pamela, in another way they begin as spiritual equals."[9] Jane rescues him after a riding accident and from a fire in his bedroom, refuses to be treated as his plaything, and inherits her own fortune before she returns to a subdued man who now "draws his powers from within himself rather than from inequity, disguise, deception."[10] In chapter 2, I argued that *Redeeming Love* retold the Cinderella story in the least empowering way, with Angel as the prisoner and Michael Hosea as the scheming stepmother and the prince who won't back down. *The Masterpiece* echoes *Jane Eyre* in matching its Cinderella with a prince who also needs to rise from the ashes. When Roman leaves a gallery where he is selling meaningless modern art, "he was out the door like Cinderella at midnight."[11] Rivers explores the ways in which both men and women recover from traumatic histories.

While *Redeeming Love*'s cover features a faceless heroine that foreshadows Angel's lack of agency and selfhood, *The Masterpiece*'s cover features the work of a real graffiti artist that foreshadows Rivers's sympathy for urban foster youth.

7. Rivers, *Masterpiece*, 86.

8. Rivers, *Masterpiece*, 302.

9. Gilbert, "Plain Jane's Progress," 485.

10. Gilbert, "Plain Jane's Progress," 499.

11. Rivers, *Masterpiece*, 181.

Cameron Moberg's graffiti art on the cover of *The Masterpiece* signals the novel's compassionate portrait of the urban underclass. Book copyright © 2018 by Francine Rivers. All rights reserved. Used by permission of Tyndale House Publishers, a Division of Tyndale House Ministries. All rights reserved. Cover photograph and mural artwork © by Cameron Moberg. All rights reserved. Designed by Jennifer L. Phelps.

She devotes ninety-three pages to flashbacks that place many of the "romantic" situations from *Redeeming Love* into a context of dysfunction and violence in which both Roman and Grace play the role of the orphan Angel. Roman is the son of a prostitute, narrowly escapes being sold after her death, and finds himself on a remote farm that he cannot leave; Grace grows up without love, marries a dominating and manipulative husband for the wrong reasons, and flees his physical and sexual abuse. Yet both characters take control of their adult lives, make peace with their roots, and reject the consumer trappings of the American dream. Whereas *War Room* never shows the Jordans leaving their trophy house, and *Duck Dynasty* never questions the Robertsons' extravagant spending, Roman finds happiness by selling his mansion, marrying a girl from Fresno, and painting murals in the inner city.

Roman also needs to make peace with his unknown racial heritage. His biracial features add to his mysterious allure: Grace likes his "café au lait skin,"[12] and the first flashback introduces both his attractiveness to girls and "his mixed-race parentage."[13] Jealous of Grace's friendship with his Latino employee, Roman notes that he has been mistaken for Hispanic: "Then again, he'd been mistaken for a lot of things, especially when he traveled and went through security. His mother had been white. It was anyone's guess what the sperm donor was."[14] His female colleague muses: "Whatever mix he is, I don't think he has a drop of Italian blood. Indian, perhaps; Arab, possibly. Black. Not that it matters."[15] Yet Roman's guilt over the death of his friend White Boy symbolizes his ambivalence about his white identity, and his uncertainty about his father torments him. The novel's structure resists definitive answers, with chapters about the present time alternating with nonlinear flashbacks. We learn that Grace's son has "café au lait skin,"[16] but it never becomes clear whether Roman is his father or the racial makeup of either character. Rivers resists the temptation to close off the open-endedness of biracial identity by fixing it into categories that make the world easier to understand at the expense of acknowledging its complexity.[17]

The latest Mitford novel, *To Be Where You Are*, likewise includes former foster youth struggling to overcome childhood trauma. The plot alternates between Father Tim and Cynthia Kavanagh in Mitford and their adopted son and daughter-in-law Dooley and Lace Kavanagh at Meadowgate Farm. Newlyweds Dooley and Lace continue to grieve their traumatic separations from their impoverished birth families as they strive for upward mobility,

---

12. Rivers, *Masterpiece*, 17.

13. Rivers, *Masterpiece*, 25.

14. Rivers, *Masterpiece*, 112.

15. Rivers, *Masterpiece*, 140.

16. Rivers, *Masterpiece*, 165.

17. In contrast to Rivers's fairly nuanced portrait of biracial identity, Grace's struggle to free her baby from the clutches of a Hispanic adoptive family masks white privilege by reversing the situation that most often happens in real life: "Ninety percent of transracial adoptions involve White parents" (Darron T. Smith et al., *White Parents, Black Children*, 23), and women of color more often relinquish their babies. However, this subplot is more complex than it seems, since Grace initially promised the baby to the Garcias and changed her mind after he was born, and Mr. Garcia supports her decision while Mrs. Garcia has an unhealthy dependence on the child. *The Masterpiece* includes a number of sympathetic Hispanic characters, such as Grace's friend Nicole Torres, muralist Hector Espinoza, Roman's teenage roommate José, and Grace's neighbors Juan and Angela Martinez.

while their own foster son, Jack Tyler, struggles to fit into his "forever family." Like Rivers, Karon alternates between points of view, although in this case not limited to the hero and heroine. We see the world through the perspectives of Father Tim and Cynthia; Dooley and Lace; Coot Hendrick, janitor at the bookstore; Avis Packard, owner of the grocery store; Lew Boyd, owner of the Exxon station; farmworkers Harley and Willie; foster son Jack Tyler; housekeeper Lily Flower; Dooley's birth mother and brothers; and many more, for a total of thirty-seven unique points of view. The novel presents inspiring Christian heroines, although it follows the rest of the series in its middle-class bias and tendency to filter stories of Southern racism through a nostalgic lens.

Chapter 3 did not highlight Karon's romance plots or women characters, but *To Be Where You Are* exemplifies her skill in depicting good marriages between intellectual equals. Whereas *The Masterpiece* departed from *Jane Eyre* by making the hero the talented artist rather than the heroine, both Cynthia and Lace work as successful painters with major commissions. Cynthia donates fifteen new paintings to an auction for the Children's Hospital, and Lace paints a mural for a Hollywood actress. Both husbands struggle with their wives' careers but know that it would be selfish to demand their attention. Father Tim muses: "For years he'd been jealous of her creative passions, but in recent years had learned to support and encourage her,"[18] and Dooley expresses a similar sentiment about his wife: "Her art opened her up in a way he couldn't possibly understand."[19] Karon devoted entire novels to these women's weddings, but later books follow them through months and years of marriage. Father Tim says the title phrase to Cynthia: "I like being around the house with you. . . . I like to be where you are,"[20] and Jack Tyler says it to Lace after he wakes up from a nightmare: "I don't want to go in my room again, ever. I want to be where you are."[21] While most romance novels focus on the beginning of a relationship, the series shows capable women balancing career and family over the long term.

Despite the working-class points of view in this novel, Karon reveals her middle-class bias by exaggerating Dooley and Lace's financial struggles and obscuring their class privilege. The newlyweds feel strapped for cash after a $10,000 plumbing disaster, even though Dooley's two-million-dollar inheritance from Miss Sadie Baxter paid for college, veterinary school, the clinic, and the one-hundred-acre farm. They could easily pay the plumbing

18. Karon, *To Be Where You Are*, 6.
19. Karon, *To Be Where You Are*, 24.
20. Karon, *To Be Where You Are*, 148.
21. Karon, *To Be Where You Are*, 160.

bill by asking their parents or using their savings, but Lace's huge payment for the mural allows them to settle their debts, maintain their independence, and place the remainder in Jack Tyler's college fund. Lace does not have to work outside the home, and their staff includes farm hands Willie and Harley, veterinary staff Blake and Amanda, and housekeepers Lily and Violet Flower. The old car in their shed is a BMW. Lace orders battery-operated piggy banks when she decides to save her coins and gives Lily a grocery list including "cashew milk and granola and blueberries."[22] Karon never acknowledges the wage gap that separates Lace's financial security from that of the "Flower girls," whose comical names and personalities conceal any struggles that they may have, just as Tim's claim that his housekeeper is part of the family sentimentalizes their relationship.

The latest adoption plot also privileges a middle-class perspective by insisting that Jack Tyler give up his dialect and his birth name. The battle against lower-class speech has been ongoing in the series: Father Tim corrected Dooley and Sammy, Olivia hired a tutor to correct Lace, Lace corrected Harley, and the Barlowe kids corrected each other. Now Jack Tyler must change his speech patterns to have a prosperous future. Lace writes in her journal: "*It's hard to teach him good grammar with Willie and Harley as models.*"[23] Dialect is fine for her farm hands, but not for her son. Since Jack Tyler has an intense attachment to his full name, the obvious choice after his adoption would be Jack Tyler Kavanagh, but his new parents portray that option as unwieldy and even disloyal, subtly pressuring him to drop his former last name as they once did. However, the novel also questions Father Tim's involvement with the Barlowes, Dooley's birth family: he wonders if he had "insinuated himself too deeply,"[24] Pooh says his removal from the Creek "was like being kidnapped,"[25] and Pauline feels conflicted about Tim's "so-called rescue of several of her children."[26] These moments remind readers that it is a serious thing to intervene in someone else's family.

Father Tim's biracial brother, Henry Winchester, plays a marginal role—four letters from Henry narrate his romance with a woman named Lucille, but it is difficult to follow since more than one hundred pages separate each letter. The focus returns to the domestic servant, Louella Baxter Marshall, when six-year-old Grace Murphy decides to write down her story. Grace clearly represents Karon as she worries that her description of a small

22. Karon, *To Be Where You Are*, 116.

23. Karon, *To Be Where You Are*, 251.

24. Karon, *To Be Where You Are*, 103.

25. Karon, *To Be Where You Are*, 138.

26. Karon, *To Be Where You Are*, 222.

town "doesn't end up *important*,"[27] longs to write something more signifi-cant, and even wears bifocals. Louella's narrative includes intriguing new information about her father: he preached at a church for colored servants; he drove to Atlanta and never came back; and his white employers may have committed suicide. Although "Louella realized there were things she could not tell this child—things too dark and heavy for a child to carry,"[28] and perhaps for a Mitford reader to carry, she describes how the other servants left with their employers when the summer ended: "I was th' only dark skin on this mountain. Some people here was bad to call me by a ugly name. Start with a *n*. You know it, honey?"[29] Grace knows the word, but she real-izes that she must edit for her story to appear in the *Mitford Muse*, just as Karon softened her discussions of Southern racism when she returned to the Mitford series.

Grace's published narrative "Miss Louella: A True Story" contains an extended description of white boys harassing Sadie and Louella on Mit-ford's Main Street in the 1920s, calling Louella "a very, very bad name," and stealing their doll and wagon.[30] A kind white man helps the girls retrieve their possessions, and the story ends with one of the boys returning to apologize almost fifty years later. Everybody loves this heartwarming "white savior" narrative in which Louella makes fried chicken for her childhood tormentor. Louella later tells Father Tim another detail about her parents being treated like slaves: "He loved my mama an' wanted to marry her, but Mr. Baxter run him off, said he better not show his black self in this town ag'in."[31] Yet this scene also ends happily when Louella produces a sepia photograph of her and Sadie "standing in front of their playhouse, happy and proud."[32] Nostalgia continues to overwhelm the miserable details that Louella provides, as Karon subtly draws attention to the challenge of writing honestly about the South.[33]

27. Karon, *To Be Where You Are*, 283 (italics original).

28. Karon, *To Be Where You Are*, 326.

29. Karon, *To Be Where You Are*, 328.

30. Karon, *To Be Where You Are*, 413–14.

31. Karon, *To Be Where You Are*, 428.

32. Karon, *To Be Where You Are*, 428.

33. Karon finally introduces a Hispanic family in *To Be Where You Are*. When Tim is volunteering at the grocery store, he meets first-generation immigrant farmers Pedro and María Sanchez. They don't seriously challenge Mitford's whiteness: they live outside of town, speak broken English, and express nothing but gratitude toward the grocery store owner for his role in their success (266). Their story is a heartwarming expression of the American dream.

Both Rivers and Karon have developed as artists, experimenting with more complex structures while exploring the abuse of women and the traumatic effects of poverty and racism. The first chapter of the Christian edition of *Redeeming Love* is limited to Angel's point of view except one dip into the servant Cleo's perspective, and the first chapter of *At Home in Mitford* is limited to Tim's point of view except one section in which the narrator describes the town. Twenty years later, the first chapter of *The Masterpiece* alternates between Roman and Grace, and the first chapter of *To Be Where You Are* gives the perspectives of nine people with various social locations, including a police officer, janitor, and baker. In the following section, we will explore similar effects in the alternating structure of *Dead Sea Rising*.

RACE, CLASS, AND GENDER IN *DEAD SEA RISING*, *OVERCOMER*, AND *JEP & JESSICA*

Jenkins has certainly not been idle since the *Left Behind* franchise ended and has now written more than 195 books. *Dead Sea Rising*, the first novel in the *Dead Sea Chronicles* series, alternates between three plots. In contemporary Manhattan, archaeologist Nicole Berman learns that her enemies tried to prevent her proposed Saudi Arabian dig by attacking her mother. In Shinar, Mesopotamia, in 2000 BC, Terah's wife gives birth to Abram, the father of the Jewish people. In 1970s Vietnam, Nicole's father Ben has an interracial romance that he never reveals to his wife and daughter. Yet the novel covers only the beginning of a story intended to spread over a multibook series. Though it received 4.1 out of 5 stars on Amazon.com, critical reviewers noted that "the story moves about as far as a snail on cold concrete," "I paid too much for something more like a prequel to a book," and "it spent 312 pages introducing characters."[34] The strong heroines are intriguing, but the lack of character development makes it hard to evaluate the wealthy Bermans' white privilege or their treatment of the multicultural police officers investigating their case.

In a refreshing contrast to *Left Behind*, the novel features intelligent women of faith and critiques the abuse of patriarchal power in ancient and modern times. Nicole left the Harvard faculty to pursue her dream of becoming "the first woman under forty to lead a dig."[35] Although she feels entitled to special treatment due to her wealth, she is an independent heroine who searches for her mother's attacker and easily reads the Arabic threats

34. "*Dead Sea Rising: A Novel* Customer Reviews."
35. Jenkins, *Dead Sea Rising*, 12.

that come in the mail. Her mother Ginny is another "tough woman"[36] who convinced Ben to believe in Jesus, worked for the Berman Foundation until her retirement, and treats her servants with compassion. While Genesis 10–11 focuses on Abram's male ancestors, Jenkins creates his mother Belessunu, a fictional precursor of biblical heroines like Deborah and Esther who worships the God of Noah, denounces her pagan husband's evil schemes, and utters prophecies that anticipate Habakkuk by many centuries: "*Woe to him who plunders many nations, who covets evil gain that he may set his nest on high.*"[37] She insists on raising Abram in her own faith: "I will countenance no opposition on this, Terah! The Lord has spoken, and so have I."[38] Meanwhile in Vietnam, Bian Nguyen attends Saigon National Pedagogical University rather than marry her GI boyfriend, and the alternating structure links Terah's violent misogyny to Ben's violation of egalitarian marriage by keeping secrets from his wife about the war.

These brave heroines are far more appealing than *Left Behind*'s damsels in distress, but Jenkins's attitude toward upper-class white privilege is less clear. The Bermans are major donors to the hospital where Ginny has surgery, and Nicole accepts her luxury room without question. She demands that the police work nights and weekends on her case, although she has little patience for their questions and procedures. When Officer Julia Martinez insists on following protocol, Nicole prays: "I don't know that she's intentionally persecuting me, Lord."[39] When patrolman Duane Decker protests that he's on overtime and needs to leave, she tells him that "you or whoever replaces you is going to have to keep up."[40] When African American hospital worker Kayla Jefferson makes coffee and calls Nicole an inspiration, Nicole treats her rudely but "had a niggling feeling she owed Kayla an apology,"[41] the word "niggling" a tactless choice that flirts with the forbidden word *nigger*. When working-class Catholic Detective George Wojciechowski comes to work on Saturday, Nicole "was glad he did."[42] When Detective Pranav Chakrabarti and Kayla ask to join her dig team, she responds pragmatically: "Having a native Indian and an African American woman on her volunteer

---

36. Jenkins, *Dead Sea Rising*, 152.
37. Jenkins, *Dead Sea Rising*, 42 (italics original).
38. Jenkins, *Dead Sea Rising*, 246.
39. Jenkins, *Dead Sea Rising*, 62.
40. Jenkins, *Dead Sea Rising*, 68.
41. Jenkins, *Dead Sea Rising*, 125.
42. Jenkins, *Dead Sea Rising*, 235.

team would check off a lot of boxes."[43] She never seriously questions her snobbery, nor does the narrator provide a critical perspective.

With the Black Lives Matter movement drawing attention to police discrimination against people of color, it seems disingenuous to base a novel on the "unjust" treatment of a rich white woman. Ben's ethnic Judaism does not entitle the family to around-the-clock service from the NYPD or justify any action that they take against their enemies. Ginny's attacker turns out to be Bulgarian housekeeper Teodora Petrova, working for a mysterious Persian who wants to stop Nicole's dig, and the family seems to care little about her suicide. In the Vietnam flashbacks, Ben shows no remorse for killing the Vietcong since he is protecting his girlfriend. Rather than blaming the Bermans for hiring housekeepers they don't need, using Southeast Asia as the backdrop for their teen rebellion, or pressing for a certain dig to achieve wealth and fame, Jenkins portrays them as victims of Arabic-speaking forces beyond their control. Yet the narrative structure juxtaposes our supposedly humanitarian era with the cutthroat ancient world: the housekeeper Teodora's suicide after she attacks Ginny echoes the servant Ikuppi's suicide after Terah makes him an accessory to murder. Ideally, the series will continue to highlight the ways in which twenty-first-century America falls into the same traps as wealthy civilizations through the ages.

As I was writing the first draft of this conclusion, *Overcomer* was two months away from theatrical release, yet the trailer revealed Stephen and Alex Kendricks' ongoing interest in race and gender and raised questions about whether they could avoid the "white savior" stereotype. The plot that emerges in the trailer is simple: "The town's oldest manufacturing plant is closing its doors,"[44] and the Christian school loses so many students that white basketball coach John Harrison (Alex Kendrick) has to coach cross-country, which he claims is "not even a real sport."[45] The only student who tries out is African American Hannah Scott (Aryn Wright-Thompson). John's black mentors, Principal Olivia Brooks (Priscilla Shirer) and friend Thomas Hill (Cameron Arnett), teach him that every runner matters, and the trailer ends with Hannah streaking toward the finish line against all odds. While *War Room* centered on an African American family, *Overcomer* seems to reverse the trend with a white man helping a black teen. Yet things are rarely that simple at the Sherwood Baptist Church. The *Overcomer* trailer, novelization, and theatrical version resist the "white savior" plot as black

---

43. Jenkins, *Dead Sea Rising*, 272.
44. "Overcomer Trailer," 0:24–0:28.
45. "Overcomer Trailer," 0:40–0:42.

mentors help both John and Hannah overcome their physical and spiritual limitations.

Any film about a white coach and black athlete in the American South raises the specter of *The Blind Side* (2009), a controversial Best Picture nominee in which adoptive mother Leigh Anne Tuohy (Sandra Bullock) coaches her son Michael Oher (Quinton Aaron) to football fame. *Overcomer* could easily fall into the comfortable plotline of the confident white authority figure who rescues a black teen from a dysfunctional birth community that is portrayed as a dead end. Yet the premise also echoes *McFarland, USA* (2015), another sports film inspired by true events, in which football coach Jim White (Kevin Costner) finds himself at a Hispanic high school populated by farm laborers and starts a track team that he leads to a state championship. Living north of McFarland in California's Central Valley has allowed me to hear from the real athletes about how the film collapses events and downplays their Christian faith but fairly accurately captures their poverty and White's long career in McFarland. The film emphasizes White's initial culture shock and his family's assimilation into a richly developed and largely positive Hispanic community. In my favorite scene, he goes with his runners to experience one day working in the fields, gaining a new respect for his team and forever changing the power dynamics between them.

Overcomer also undermines the "white savior" trope with shots of Hannah running fast and strong while her sweating, middle-aged coach jogs along chanting "don't die, don't die."[46] The Christian message disrupts the logic that Matthew W. Hughey describes in *The White Savior Film*, which "separates people into those who are redeemers (whites) and those who are redeemed or in need of redemption (nonwhites). Such imposing patronage enables an interpretation of nonwhite characters and culture as essentially broken, marginalized, and pathological."[47] In this film, both John and Hannah need redemption in the same spiritual sense. The black community exemplifies profound faith, with Thomas rebuking the coach, "For someone who knows the Lord, you're acting like somebody who doesn't," and Olivia telling Hannah, "Your life is worth so much more than this."[48] Hughey's further description of the "white savior" genre uses an evocative metaphor for a Christian film about running: "Whether helping people of color who cannot or will not help themselves, teaching nonwhites right from wrong, or framing the white savior as the only character able to recognize these moral distinctions, these films show whites going the extra mile across the

46. "Overcomer Trailer."
47. Hughey, *White Savior Film*, 2.
48. "Overcomer Trailer."

color line."[49] John may "go the extra mile," but Thomas and Olivia teach *him* right from wrong. Although the trailer includes slightly more shots of the coach than of the black characters, there are twenty-three shots of Hannah practicing, stretching, talking to Olivia, sitting by herself, raising her hands in worship, and running toward the finish line.

Christy Hall of Fame member Chris Fabry wrote the impressive novelization, which was published before the theatrical release and extends the plot far beyond the predictable sports story in the trailer. The third person limited point of view alternates between Hannah, her grandmother Barbara, and John, with more chapters devoted to the African American family than to the coach. The prologue begins with Barbara's flashback to the day that her daughter Janet died from a drug overdose and Janet's boyfriend T-bone dropped off baby Hannah and drove away. At forty-five, "She carried life like a cross. Her back was tired and her knees ached and her ankles were swollen from a full day's work. She was in the prime of her life, but she felt like every part of her had been wrung out like a dishrag, and her hopes and dreams had splattered on the tile, nobody but her to mop the mess."[50] The next chapter jumps to the present day and John coaching a championship basketball game: "He was forty-five but felt twenty-five, and a game like this brought out all the competitive juices."[51] The detail that both characters are forty-five heightens their contrasting experiences, and Fabry continues to juxtapose Barbara's working-class problems and the coach's middle-class problems. Barbara works two jobs and worries about paying bills; John coaches two sports and worries about his retirement. Barbara agonizes about her granddaughter's stealing and whether she'll end up in prison; John frets about his son's attitude and whether he'll end up in college. Fabry never ties Barbara's struggles to Southern racism, but her determination to save Hannah from Janet's fate emphasizes the strong pull of risky behaviors in an environment of poverty and discrimination.

Fabry explores the relationships among the black characters—seemingly unconnected at first but deeply entwined in complex ways—with the same nuance that he devotes to John's recognition that his class privilege has prevented him from developing true faith. Thomas seems like the stereotypical "black best friend" whose life revolves around supporting the white hero until we learn that he is Hannah's father T-bone, now reconciled with God and on his deathbed. We also learn that Olivia paid Hannah's private school tuition because she was Janet's friend and vowed to help

49. Hughey, *White Savior Film*, 8.

50. Fabry, *Overcomer*, 2–3.

51. Fabry, *Overcomer*, 12.

her daughter. Thomas is the wise mentor who knows Jesus, whereas John teaches about the Great Depression and wonders helplessly: "What would FDR do?"[52] Fabry narrates the championship race from the perspectives of Hannah, John, and Barbara, and the story continues for five chapters as the coach realizes, "*I wasn't placed here to help her. She was placed here to help me.*"[53] In the epilogue, an omniscient narrator describes Hannah going to college and sharing her newfound faith.

The feature film could not include all of the novel's nuances, but its emotional power was clear when I finally watched it on Division Street in Portland, Oregon, squeezed into the back row behind a racially integrated church that booked the theater. Without the sidekicks that provided comic relief in earlier Sherwood films, this drama had both men and women weeping. Barbara's role is much smaller than in the novel, but the over-the-shoulder shot when she confronts Thomas in his hospital room allows us to see him from her perspective, and actress Denise Armstrong captures her justifiable rage and painful journey to forgiveness. Other shots reveal Hannah's point of view: blurred images during an asthma attack, close-ups of medical equipment when she is overwhelmed by meeting her father, and the finish line of the championship race. The film ends with the song "Overcomer" by Mandisa, a black gospel singer who has shared her struggle with body image. Between Wright-Thompson's acting and Mandisa's lyrics, the film celebrates young black women in a way that is new for the Kendricks and rare in popular culture of any kind. Whereas the trailer devoted its first shot to the school and its last shot to the coach, and the novel's prologue and epilogue focused on the Scott family, the film begins and ends with aerial shots of the city, reminding viewers that we are all in this together.

The *Duck Dynasty* spin-off *Jep & Jessica: Growing the Dynasty* promised to focus on the white Robertson couple adopting a black newborn, so I looked forward to a show with transracial adoption at the center rather than the periphery. Unfortunately, the series ignores racial issues to an amazing extent.[54] Phil Robertson's prayer at the Baby Blessing in "The Homecoming" is the only oblique reference to Gus's skin color: "There is just one race, Father, in your eyes. It's called the human race." Since newborns do not make for fascinating television—one can only make so many episodes

52. Fabry, *Overcomer*, 72.

53. Fabry, *Overcomer*, 370 (italics original).

54. Since the A&E producers resisted serious themes on *Duck Dynasty*, it's possible that Jep and Jessica pushed for meaningful racial discussions on their show and were overruled. However, whereas *Duck Dynasty* balances humorous antics with heartfelt family prayers, *Jep & Jessica* contains little religious language and does not present any compelling alternative to the emphasis on everyday life in a wealthy family.

about diaper rash—the series quickly shifts its focus to the white extended family, friends, and older children: Lily, Merritt, Priscilla, and River. *Jep & Jessica* does promote foster care and adoption, but its demeaning attitudes toward women, excessive consumerism, and colorblind rhetoric undercut the message that "there is just one race" in the kingdom of heaven.

In contrast to *Duck Dynasty*'s traditional gender roles, *Jep & Jessica* shows Jep avoiding both work and family responsibilities while expressing contempt for Jessica and her mother Kathy as they raise the five kids. We rarely see him at Duck Commander, and when he starts a food truck business in season two, he neglects to bring supplies to the farmer's market, advertise their opening day, and read the contract for their first party. Yet Jessica reveals in "The Homecoming" that Jep has only changed about one diaper per child, reinforcing the notion that childcare is women's work. In later episodes, Jep fails to take the kids to the dentist, plays on his phone during Priscilla's soccer game, and fakes an injury to avoid roller skating with Merritt. He calls Kathy an "old hag"[55] and tells Jessica that "your breath smells like sewage."[56] Although incompetent husbands are staples of sitcom humor, Jep seems surprisingly cruel for a franchise known for family values.

Duck Dynasty chronicles the family's move from poverty to fabulous wealth, and *Jep & Jessica* devotes more time to buying and selling consumer goods than adopting and raising Gus. Indeed, they frame the adoption as the acquisition of a highly desirable product that arrives from a distant warehouse to meet their needs, even though they make no allusion to paying for the adoption or profiting from it with this series. In *Somebody's Children*, Laura Briggs describes how white infertile couples emerged as a market segment, so that "adoption in the 1970s and 1980s became increasingly like a consumer market for parents and less like a solution for children in need."[57] In "The Call," as they wait anxiously during the five-day period in which the birth mother can legally change her mind, Jessica tells Willie and Korie that "we'll know hopefully soon if we can get him." In "The Homecoming," Jep becomes impatient with their long wait at the hospital, and his rhetoric sounds like a complaint about a delayed package: "Usually if somebody says, 'Hey, we got you something. Come pick it up,' okay, we'll go pick it up and leave." Later in that episode, a trip to the drug store for formula turns into a free-for-all in which the family purchases baskets of unnecessary items, foreshadowing the central role of shopping on the series.

---

55. "Enemy of the Skate."
56. "Grandma's Ploy."
57. Briggs, *Somebody's Children*, 112.

Every family event seems to call for an expensive purchase. Jep rents a party bus for his wedding anniversary and a red carpet for Lily's birthday, hires a cleaning service, makes the girls get "a lifetime supply of bras"[58] so that he never has to return to the bra section, and responds to a grease fire by purchasing smoke alarms, fire extinguishers, and solar panels. Jessica takes the girls for mani-pedis to console Lily after a break-up, buys a $1,500 miniature pig, rents a camper for $500 per day, and spends a $200 gift card on new clothes for Gus. In a kind of product placement reminiscent of early television, businesses like Dillard's appear many times. Cell phones are everywhere, and episodes end with home videos rather than family prayers, emphasizing technological mediation rather than divine intervention.

Several episodes represent Jep's shopping as interchangeable with parenting. In "The Punishment," he is so thrilled with his new blender that he says: "This blender is like my baby." When Merritt reminds him that "we have a real baby," he responds: "We have two real babies: baby Gus and baby XR5000." When Jep and Jessica prepare for Gus's legal adoption at the courthouse in "Home Is Where the Chart Is," they spend time shopping for a suit rather than reflecting deeply on their first year as adoptive parents. In "Kick 'em the Bird," the kids want to go bird watching, so Jep heads to T. P. Outdoors to buy binoculars with built-in Wi-Fi, camera, and GPS, and the episode ends with him filming Gus toddling across the lawn and then panning over to his new binoculars. In "Toys R Gus," Jep camps overnight at Game Mechanix with his friends Godwin and Martin to buy a new Nintendo console. As if the episode were a commercial, he often repeats that it comes with thirty games. Meanwhile, Gus can't sleep because his stuffed bunny is in Jep's truck, and Jessica is furious that Jep has chosen video games over their son. They share a tender parenting moment when Jep brings home the bunny and Gus falls asleep, but the episode ends with the emotional climax of the men acquiring the console. The title "Toys R Gus" collapses the two plots, as if a father buying toys for himself has something to do with his son.

The series also contains numerous layers of selling: family members sell products in the diegetic world, the series itself makes money, and the plots about Calvary Jewelry and Jep's Southern Roots advertise the couple's post-series businesses. In the last episode, "Buy, Buy, This American Pie," Priscilla sells candy for a fundraiser while Jep and Jessica launch the food truck business. Jep makes a chalkboard sign that says "In God We Crust," a rare and light-hearted religious reference on a series with less Christian content than *Duck Dynasty*. Giddy with their success, the couple says: "Who knows what the future holds? Franchise!" After the series was cancelled,

58. "Shock and Bra."

they moved their food truck to Texas,[59] and their house went on the market for $1.4 million,[60] demonstrating how their home and business become even more valuable after being featured on television.

My biggest disappointment was the colorblind rhetoric that avoided any meaningful discussion of transracial adoption. Hughey states, "This approach allows whites to maintain their dominant position in the racial hierarchy without directly speaking of race."[61] According to *White Parents, Black Children*, "colorblindness dictates that race should not be mentioned, seen, talked about, or taken seriously when (over)heard; the race rule is this: *see no race, speak no race, hear no race.*"[62] When white adoptive parents teach black children to nurture and educate those who perpetuate racism, "transracial adoption becomes a space by, for, and about White people."[63] Like the parents in this study, Jep and Jessica love their son, but the initial episodes about getting the call and picking him up at the hospital never mention his race. They name him Jules Augustus after two Southern white men: adoptive father Jules Jeptha and Augustus McCrae from *Lonesome Dove*, the cowboy who kills Indians, steals from Mexicans, sleeps with whores, and takes the law into his own hands. Rather than naming him after Joshua Deets, the admirable black man played by Danny Glover, they fold him into a pattern of whiteness as if his skin color is irrelevant.

Jessica's comment that "God placed him in our lives just out of nowhere"[64] erases birth parents from the picture. An interview with the black social worker about the conditions that lead mothers to give up their children would provide insight into Gus's community of origin. Instead, the Robertsons usurp the birth mother's role with pregnancy metaphors: Korie remembers feeling like she was having contractions when they picked up Will, and Jep laments his "post-pregnancy baby fat."[65] The series introduces Godwin's white adopted daughter Johanna to reassure viewers that adoptive parents are the real parents. In "The Ninja Warriors," she says: "I've had people ask me before, well, what about your biological mom and your biological dad? Well, like, this is my mom and dad." In "Home Is Where the Chart Is," Johanna says that she has met her biological family, but they are not the ones who raised her. Rather than planning for Gus to learn about his

59. jepssouthernroots.com.

60. Bracken, "Selling Lakeside Louisiana Home," para. 2.

61. Hughey, *White Savior Film*, 117.

62. Darron T. Smith et al., *White Parents, Black Children*, 40 (italics original).

63. Darron T. Smith et al., *White Parents, Black Children*, 87.

64. "The Circumbration."

65. "The Ninja Warriors."

black heritage, the family makes throwaway references to popular culture like Willie holding up the baby and saying "Simba!"[66] and Jep referring to him as "young Denzel."[67] His transracially adopted cousins remain on the periphery: Will appears in baby photos, and Rebecca appears in the background, although a five-minute interview with them would make a huge difference in educating prospective adoptive parents. The first season received only 3.8 stars on Amazon.com, and some reviewers wished it was more family friendly. One reviewer noted, "Hopefully little Gus will have positive African American role models in his life as he grows up so that he feels secure with who and what he is."[68] Hopefully he will not be too traumatized by having his circumcision featured on national television.

Throughout this book, each author and franchise has revealed surprising twists and defied simplistic analysis. The latest novels of Rivers, Karon, and Jenkins are more nuanced than the works that made them famous in the 1990s, *Overcomer* may be the Kendricks' most heart-wrenching film, and *Jep & Jessica* ironically gave me greater appreciation for *Duck Dynasty*. Christian popular culture has evolved to the point of self-reflexivity exemplified by Millennial comedian John Crist, who mocks the Generation X culture that he grew up with as a pastor's son in Georgia. The video "Christian Breakup Lines" includes zingers like "Hey, do you know Kirk Cameron? Cause you about to be left behind" and "Are you a short-term mission trip? Cause you're doing more harm than good." The latter is typical of Crist's critique of evangelical assumptions about race and class, referring to a growing recognition that short-term missions create burdens for developing countries as they broaden the horizons of self-centered Americans. He follows that joke by waving his hands and saying, "Take that one out. That one's probably too far," acknowledging the sensitive nature of the subject but leaving it in the video.[69] As Millennial and Generation Z artists develop Christian popular culture that reflects their mainstream media savvy and investment in social justice, we must track their ongoing attempts to provide better portrayals of race, class, and gender than we saw thirty years ago. Even the legacy of *Left Behind* can be left behind.

66. "The Homecoming."

67. "LARPe Diem."

68. "*Jep & Jessica: Growing the Dynasty* Season 1 Customer Reviews."

69. Recent sexual harassment allegations against Crist prove that artists' progressive work on race and class does not prevent the abuse of women (Bailey, "John Crist").

BIBLIOGRAPHY

At Home in Mitford. DVD. Directed by Gary Harvey. Studio City, CA: Hallmark Channel, 2017.

"*At Home in Mitford* Customer Reviews." Amazon. https://www.amazon.com/Mitford-Andie-MacDowell-Cameron-Mathison/product-reviews/B07DLTD1BW/ref=cm_cr_dp_d_show_all_btm?ie=UTF8&reviewerType=all_reviews.

"*At Home in Mitford* User Reviews." Internet Movie Database. https://www.imdb.com/title/tt7140696/reviews?ref_=tt_urv.

Bailey, Sarah Pulliam. "John Crist, a Popular Christian Comedian, Cancels Tour After Sexual Harassment Allegations." *Washington Post*, November 6, 2019. https://www.washingtonpost.com/religion/2019/11/07/john-crist-popular-christian-comedian-cancels-tour-after-sexual-harassment-allegations/.

Balmer, Randall. *Mine Eyes Have Seen the Glory: A Journey into the Evangelical Subculture in America*. New York: Oxford University Press, 1989.

Banjo, Omotayo O., and Kesha Morant Williams, eds. *Contemporary Christian Culture: Messages, Missions, and Dilemmas*. Lanham, MD: Lexington, 2018.

Barker, Andrew. "Film Review: 'Left Behind.'" *Variety*, October 2, 2014. https://variety.com/2014/film/reviews/film-review-left-behind-1201319012/.

Barkman, Adam. "'All Is Righteousness and There Is No Equality': C. S. Lewis on Gender and Justice." *Christian Scholar's Review* 36.4 (2007) 415–36.

Barrett-Fox, Rebecca. "Hope, Faith and Toughness: An Analysis of the Christian Hero." In *Empowerment versus Oppression: Twenty First Century Views of Popular Romance Novels*, edited by Sally Goade, 93–102. Newcastle-upon-Tyne, UK: Cambridge Scholars, 2007.

Barrueto, Jorge J. *The Hispanic Image in Hollywood: A Postcolonial Approach*. New York: Peter Lang, 2014.

Beltrán, Mary, and Camilla Fojas, eds. *Mixed Race Hollywood*. New York: New York University Press, 2008.

Berg, Charles Ramírez. *Latino Images in Film: Stereotypes, Subversion, & Resistance*. Austin: University of Texas Press, 2002.

Bergen, Wesley J. "The New Apocalyptic: Modern American Apocalyptic Fiction and Its Ancient and Modern Cousins." *Journal of Religion and Popular Culture* 20 (Fall 2008) https://doi.org/10.3138/jrpc.20.1.003.

Blankenhorn, David. *Fatherless America: Confronting Our Most Urgent Social Problem*. New York: Basic, 1995.

The Blind Side. DVD. Directed by John Lee Hancock. Los Angeles: Alcon Entertainment, 2009.

Blodgett, Jan. *Protestant Evangelical Literary Culture and Contemporary Society*. Westport, CT: Greenwood, 1997.

Bogle, Donald. *Prime Time Blues: African Americans on Network Television*. New York: Farrar, Straus and Giroux, 2001.

———. *Toms, Coons, Mulattoes, Mammies, and Bucks: An Interpretive History of Blacks in American Films*. 4th ed. New York: Continuum, 2001.

Bolz-Weber, Nadia. *Salvation on the Small Screen? 24 Hours of Christian Television*. New York: Seabury, 2008.

Bracken, Becky. "'Duck Dynasty' Star Jep Robertson Selling Lakeside Louisiana Home for $1.4M." *Realtor.com*. December 20, 2017. https://www.realtor.com/news/celebrity-real-estate/jep-robertson-selling-louisiana-home/.

Briggs, Laura. *Somebody's Children: The Politics of Transracial and Transnational Adoption*. Durham, NC: Duke University Press, 2012.

Brontë, Charlotte. *Jane Eyre*. Edited by Beth Newman. Boston: Bedford, 1996.

Brown, Devin. *Inside Narnia: A Guide to Exploring "The Lion, the Witch and the Wardrobe."* Grand Rapids: Baker, 2005.

Bryant, Joseph A., Jr. *Twentieth-Century Southern Literature*. Lexington: University Press of Kentucky, 1997.

Carey, Jacqueline. "Heathen Eye for the Christian Guy." In *Revisiting Narnia: Fantasy, Myth and Religion in C. S. Lewis' Chronicles*, edited by Shanna Caughey, 159–64. Dallas: BenBella, 2005.

Catsoulis, Jeannette. "He Thought This Flight Was Fully Booked." *New York Times*, October 2, 2014. https://www.nytimes.com/2014/10/03/movies/left-behind-stars-nicolas-cage-as-a-pilot.html?_r=0.

Chapman, Jennie. *Plotting Apocalypse: Reading, Agency, and Identity in the Left Behind Series*. Jackson: University Press of Mississippi, 2013.

———. "Selling Faith without Selling Out: Reading the *Left Behind* Novels in the Context of Popular Culture." In *The End All Around Us: Apocalyptic Texts and Popular Culture*, edited by John Walliss and Kenneth G. C. Newport, 148–72. London: Equinox, 2009.

Chidester, David. *Authentic Fakes: Religion and American Popular Culture*. Berkeley: University of California Press, 2005.

Choy, Catherine Ceniza. *Global Families: A History of Asian International Adoption in America*. New York: New York University Press, 2013.

Christians, Clifford G. "Redemptive Media as the Evangelical's Cultural Task." In *American Evangelicals and the Mass Media: Perspectives on the Relationship between American Evangelicals and the Mass Media*, edited by Quentin J. Schultze, 331–56. Grand Rapids: Academie, 1990.

Clapp, Rodney. *Border Crossings: Christian Trespasses on Popular Culture and Public Affairs*. Grand Rapids: Brazos, 2000.

Collins, Suzanne. *The Hunger Games*. New York: Scholastic, 2008.

Courageous. DVD. Directed by Alex Kendrick. Albany, GA: Sherwood Pictures, 2011.

Crist, John. "Christian Breakup Lines." YouTube. February 18, 2018. https://www.youtube.com/watch?v=bb83TYEsIxk.

Davis, Hugh H. "'Sing, My Tongue, the Glorious Battle': Aslan's Sacrifice in Adaptations of *The Lion, the Witch and the Wardrobe*." In *Past Watchful Dragons:*

Fantasy and Faith in the World of C. S. Lewis, edited by Amy H. Sturgis, 67–78. Altadena, CA: Mythopoeic, 2007.

Davis, Walter T., Jr., et al. *Watching What We Watch: Prime-Time Television through the Lens of Faith.* Louisville: Geneva, 2001.

"*Dead Sea Rising: A Novel* Customer Reviews." Amazon. https://www.amazon.com/product-reviews/1617950092/ref=acr_dpproductdetail_text?ie=UTF8&showViewpoints=1.

DeLong, Janice, and Rachel Schwedt. *Contemporary Christian Authors: Lives and Works.* Lanham, MD: Scarecrow, 2000.

DeMar, Gary. *End Times Fiction: A Biblical Consideration of the "Left Behind" Theology.* Nashville: Thomas Nelson, 2001.

Detweiler, Craig, and Barry Taylor. *A Matrix of Meanings: Finding God in Pop Culture.* Grand Rapids: Baker Academic, 2003.

Duck Dynasty. DVD. Performed by Phil Robertson et al. New York: A+E Networks, 2012–17.

Edwards, Bruce L. *Not a Tame Lion: Unveil Narnia through the Eyes of Lucy, Peter, and Other Characters Created by C. S. Lewis.* Wheaton, IL: Tyndale House, 2005.

Ehrenreich, Barbara. *The Hearts of Men: American Dreams and the Flight from Commitment.* New York: Anchor, 1983.

Fabry, Chris. *Overcomer.* Carol Stream, IL: Tyndale House, 2019.

Facing the Giants. DVD. Directed by Alex Kendrick. Albany, GA: Sherwood Pictures, 2006.

Fireproof. DVD. Directed by Alex Kendrick. Albany, GA: Sherwood Pictures, 2008.

Fletcher, Lisa. *Historical Romance Fiction: Heterosexuality and Performativity.* Aldershot, UK: Ashgate, 2008.

Flywheel. DVD. Directed by Alex Kendrick. Albany, GA: Sherwood Pictures, 2003.

Forbes, Bruce David, and Jeanne Halgren Kilde, eds. *Rapture, Revelation, and the End Times: Exploring the Left Behind Series.* New York: Palgrave Macmillan, 2004.

Forbes, Bruce David, and Jeffrey H. Mahan, eds. *Religion and Popular Culture in America.* Rev. ed. Berkeley: University of California Press, 2005.

Ford, Paul F. *Companion to Narnia: A Complete Guide to the Magical World of C. S. Lewis's "The Chronicles of Narnia."* 5th ed. New York: HarperOne, 2005.

Foster, Gwendolyn Audrey. "Consuming the Apocalypse, Marketing Bunker Materiality." *Quarterly Review of Film and Video* 33.4 (2016) 285–302.

The 40onthefloor. "Workin' Man Zombie." YouTube. September 30, 2010. https://www.youtube.com/watch?v=gFCaIspV7n4.

Fowkes, Katherine A. *The Fantasy Film.* Chichester, UK: Wiley-Blackwell, 2010.

Frank, Gillian. "'Ideals of Stability, Order and Fidelity': The Love Dare Phenomenon, Convergence Culture, and the Marriage Movement." *Journal of Religion and Popular Culture* 23.2 (2011) 118–38. doi:10.3138/jrpc.23.2.118.

Fredrick, Candice, and Sam McBride. *Women among the Inklings: Gender, C. S. Lewis, J. R. R. Tolkien, and Charles Williams.* Westport, CT: Greenwood, 2001.

Freedman, Jonathan. "Antisemitism without Jews: *Left Behind* in the American Heartland." In *Antisemitism and Philosemitism in the Twentieth and Twenty-first Centuries: Representing Jews, Jewishness, and Modern Culture*, edited by Phyllis Lassner and Lara Trubowitz, 154–74. Newark: University of Delaware Press, 2008.

Fry, Karin. "No Longer a Friend of Narnia: Gender in Narnia." In *"The Chronicles of Narnia" and Philosophy: The Lion, the Witch, and the Worldview*, edited by Gregory Bassham and Jerry L. Walls, 155–66. Chicago: Open Court, 2005.

Frykholm, Amy Johnson. "The Gender Dynamics of the *Left Behind* Series." In *Religion and Popular Culture in America*, edited by Bruce David Forbes and Jeffrey H. Mahan, 270–87. Berkeley: University of California Press, 2005.

———. *Rapture Culture: "Left Behind" in Evangelical America*. New York: Oxford University Press, 2004.

———. "Rapture Fiction and the Predicament of Christian Male Leadership." In *Left Behind and the Evangelical Imagination*, edited by Crawford Gribben and Mark S. Sweetnam, 15–30. Sheffield, UK: Sheffield Phoenix, 2011.

Fuchs, Cynthia J. "The Buddy Politic." In *Screening the Male: Exploring Masculinities in Hollywood Cinema*, edited by Steven Cohan and Ina Rae Hark, 194–210. London: Routledge, 1993.

Gandolfo, Anita. *Faith and Fiction: Christian Literature in America Today*. Westport, CT: Praeger, 2007.

Gaunt, Kyra D. *The Games Black Girls Play: Learning the Ropes from Double-Dutch to Hip-Hop*. New York: New York University Press, 2006.

Geist, Christopher D. "Popular Literature." In *Literature*, edited by M. Thomas Inge, 117–24. Vol. 9 of *The New Encyclopedia of Southern Culture*, edited by Charles Reagan Wilson. 24 vols. Chapel Hill: University of North Carolina Press, 2008.

Giardina, Natasha. "Elusive Prey: Searching for Traces of Narnia in the Jungles of the Psyche." In *Revisiting Narnia: Fantasy, Myth and Religion in C. S. Lewis' Chronicles*, edited by Shanna Caughey, 33–43. Dallas: BenBella, 2005.

Gilbert, Sandra M. "Plain Jane's Progress." In *Jane Eyre*, by Charlotte Brontë, edited by Beth Newman, 475–501. Boston: Bedford, 1996.

Glover, Donald E. *C. S. Lewis: The Art of Enchantment*. Athens: Ohio University Press, 1981.

Goldstein, Gary. "'Left Behind' Is a Disaster in All the Wrong Ways." *Los Angeles Times*, October 2, 2014. https://www.latimes.com/entertainment/movies/la-et-mn-left-behind-movie-review-20141003-story.html.

Grammer, John M. "Plantation Fiction." In *A Companion to the Literature and Culture of the American South*, edited by Richard Gray and Owen Robinson, 58–75. Malden, MA: Blackwell, 2004.

Gray, Richard. *Southern Aberrations: Writers of the American South and the Problems of Regionalism*. Baton Rouge: Louisiana State University Press, 2000.

Greeley, Andrew M. *God in Popular Culture*. Chicago: Thomas More, 1988.

Greydanus, Steven D. "Calling for Heroic Commitment." *Christianity Today* (October 2011) 56–57.

Gribben, Crawford. "Piety and Polemic in Evangelical Prophecy Fiction, 1995–2000." In *The Church and Literature*, edited by Peter Clarke and Charlotte Methuen, 478–503. Woodbridge, UK: Boydell, 2012.

———. *Rapture Fiction and the Evangelical Crisis*. Darlington, UK: Evangelical, 2006.

———. *Writing the Rapture: Prophecy Fiction in Evangelical America*. Oxford: Oxford University Press, 2009.

Grimm, Jacob, and Wilhelm Grimm. *Grimm's Fairy Tales*. Mineola, NY: Dover, 2007.

Guest, Mathew. "Keeping the End in Mind: *Left Behind*, the Apocalypse and the Evangelical Imagination." *Literature & Theology* 26.4 (2012) 474–88.

Gutjahr, Paul C. "No Longer Left Behind: Amazon.com, Reader-Response, and the Changing Fortunes of the Christian Novel in America." *Book History* 5 (2002) 209–36.

Haddad, Emily A. "Bound to Love: Captivity in Harlequin Sheikh Novels." In *Empowerment versus Oppression: Twenty First Century Views of Popular Romance Novels*, edited by Sally Goade, 42–64. Newcastle-upon-Tyne: Cambridge Scholars, 2007.

Hamamoto, Darrell Y. *Monitored Peril: Asian Americans and the Politics of TV Representation*. Minneapolis: University of Minnesota Press, 1994.

Harders, Robin. "Borderlands of Desire: Captivity, Romance, and the Revolutionary Power of Love." In *New Approaches to Popular Romance Fiction: Critical Essays*, edited by Sarah S. G. Frantz and Eric Murphy Selinger, 133–52. Jefferson, NC: McFarland, 2012.

Hendershot, Heather. *Shaking the World for Jesus: Media and Conservative Evangelical Culture*. Chicago: University of Chicago Press, 2004.

Hilder, Monika B. *The Feminine Ethos in C. S. Lewis's "Chronicles of Narnia."* New York: Peter Lang, 2012.

Holbrook, David. *The Skeleton in the Wardrobe: C. S. Lewis's Fantasies: A Phenomenological Study*. Lewisburg, PA: Bucknell University Press, 1991.

Holden, Stephen. "A Biblically Inspired Tale about Dying and Surviving." *New York Times*, February 2, 2001. https://www.nytimes.com/2001/02/02/movies/film-review-a-biblically-inspired-tale-about-dying-and-surviving.html.

Holladay, Holly Willson. "Reckoning with the 'Redneck': *Duck Dynasty* and the Boundaries of Morally Appropriate Whiteness." *Southern Communication Journal* 83.4 (2018) 256–66.

Hooper, Walter. *Past Watchful Dragons: The Narnian Chronicles of C. S. Lewis*. New York: Collier, 1979.

Hoops, Joshua F. "The Constitution of a 'Moral Issue' through Mediated Representations in Christian Newspapers: Intersections of Faith, Politics, and Whiteness." In *Contemporary Christian Culture: Messages, Missions, and Dilemmas*, edited by Omotayo O. Banjo and Kesha Morant Williams, 27–43. Lanham, MD: Lexington, 2018.

Horsfield, Peter. *From Jesus to the Internet: A History of Christianity and Media*. Chichester, UK: Wiley Blackwell, 2015.

———. *Religious Television: The American Experience*. New York: Longman, 1984.

Howe, Desson. "'Left Behind': Heaven Help Us." *Washington Post*, February 2, 2001. https://www.washingtonpost.com/archive/lifestyle/2001/02/02/left-behind-heaven-help-us/9fa87d90-fdaf-4018-9983-d8adcdbe87bf/.

Hughey, Matthew W. *The White Savior Film: Content, Critics, and Consumption*. Philadelphia: Temple University Press, 2014.

Jacobs, Alan. *The Narnian: The Life and Imagination of C. S. Lewis*. San Francisco: HarperSanFrancisco, 2005.

Jenkins, Jerry B. *Dead Sea Rising*. Franklin, TN: Worthy, 2018.

Jep & Jessica: Growing the Dynasty. Amazon Prime Video. Performed by Jep Robertson and Jessica Robertson. New York: A+E Networks, 2016–17.

"*Jep & Jessica: Growing the Dynasty* Season 1 Customer Reviews." Amazon. https://www.amazon.com/Jep-Jessica-Growing-Dynasty-Season/product-reviews/

B01BBMMYAE/ref=cm_cr_dp_d_show_all_btm?ie=UTF8&reviewerType=all_
    review.

Johnston, Robert K. *Reel Spirituality: Theology and Film in Dialogue*. Grand Rapids:
    Baker Academic, 2000.

Jones, Anne Goodwyn, and Susan V. Donaldson. "Haunted Bodies: Rethinking the
    South through Gender." In *Haunted Bodies: Gender and Southern Texts*, edited by
    Anne Goodwyn Jones and Susan V. Donaldson, 1–19. Charlottesville: University
    Press of Virginia, 1997.

Jones, Darryl. "The Liberal Antichrist—*Left Behind* in America." In *Expecting the End:
    Millennialism in Social and Historical Context*, edited by Kenneth G. C. Newport
    and Crawford Gribben, 97–112. Waco, TX: Baylor University Press, 2006.

Jones, Gerard. *Honey, I'm Home! Sitcoms: Selling the American Dream*. New York: St.
    Martin's, 1992.

Jones, Karla Faust. "Girls in Narnia: Hindered or Human?" *Mythlore* 49 (1987) 15–19.

Jones, Marnie. "'Spiritual Warfare' and Intolerance in Popular Culture: The *Left
    Behind* Franchise, the Commodification of Belief, and the Consequences for
    Imagination." *Studies in Popular Culture* 32.1 (2009) 1–19.

Joseph, Ralina L. "Imagining Obama: Reading Overtly and Inferentially Racist Images
    of Our 44th President, 2007–2008." *Communication Studies* 62.4 (2011) 389–405.

Kaler, Anne K. "Conventions of Captivity in Romance Novels." In *Romantic
    Conventions*, edited by Anne K. Kaler and Rosemary E. Johnson-Kurek, 86–99.
    Bowling Green, OH: Bowling Green State University Popular Press, 1999.

Karkainen, Paul A. *Narnia Explored*. Old Tappan, NJ: Revell, 1979.

Karon, Jan. *At Home in Mitford*. New York: Penguin, 1994.

———. *Bathed in Prayer*. New York: Putnam's Sons, 2018.

———. *Come Rain or Come Shine*. New York: Putnam's Sons, 2015.

———. *A Common Life: The Wedding Story*. New York: Penguin, 2001.

———. *Home to Holly Springs*. New York: Viking, 2007.

———. *In the Company of Others*. New York: Putnam's Sons, 2010.

———. *In This Mountain*. New York: Penguin, 2002.

———. *Jan Karon's Mitford Cookbook & Kitchen Reader*. Edited by Martha McIntosh.
    New York: Viking, 2004.

———. *Light from Heaven*. New York: Penguin, 2005.

———. *A Light in the Window*. New York: Penguin, 1995.

———. *The Mitford Bedside Companion*. Edited by Brenda Furman. New York:
    Viking, 2006.

———. *A New Song*. New York: Penguin, 1999.

———. *Out to Canaan*. New York: Penguin, 1997.

———. *Shepherds Abiding*. New York: Penguin, 2003.

———. *Somewhere Safe with Somebody Good*. New York: Berkley, 2014.

———. *These High, Green Hills*. New York: Penguin, 1996.

———. *To Be Where You Are*. New York: Putnam's Sons, 2017.

Kissell, Rick. "'Duck Dynasty' Premiere Shatters Cable Records with 11.8
    Million Viewers." *Variety*, August 15, 2013. https://variety.com/2013/tv/
    news/duck-dynasty-premiere-shatters-cable-records-with-11-8-million-
    viewers-1200578066/.

Krentz, Jayne Ann. "Introduction." In *Dangerous Men and Adventurous Women: Romance Writers on the Appeal of the Romance*, edited by Jayne Ann Krentz, 1–8. Philadelphia: University of Pennsylvania Press, 1992.

Kreyling, Michael. *Inventing Southern Literature*. Jackson: University Press of Mississippi, 1998.

LaHaye, Tim. *How to Be Happy Though Married*. Wheaton, IL: Tyndale House, 1968.

LaHaye, Tim, and Jerry B. Jenkins. *Armageddon: The Cosmic Battle of the Ages*. Wheaton, IL: Tyndale House, 2003.

———. *Desecration: Antichrist Takes the Throne*. Wheaton, IL: Tyndale House, 2001.

———. *Glorious Appearing: The End of Days*. Wheaton, IL: Tyndale House, 2004.

———. *Left Behind: A Novel of the Earth's Last Days*. Wheaton, IL: Tyndale House, 1995.

———. *Soul Harvest: The World Takes Sides*. Wheaton, IL: Tyndale House, 1998.

———. *Tribulation Force: The Continuing Drama of Those Left Behind*. Wheaton, IL: Tyndale House, 1996.

Lampert-Weissig, Lisa. "*Left Behind*, the Holocaust, and that Old Time Antisemitism." *Journal of Popular Culture* 45.3 (2012) 497–515.

Lee, Earl. *Kiss My Left Behind*. Chula Vista, CA: Aventine, 2003.

Lee, Linda J. "Guilty Pleasures: Reading Romance Novels as Reworked Fairy Tales." *Marvels & Tales* 22.1 (2008) 52–66.

Left Behind. DVD. Directed by Vic Armstrong. Oceanside, CA: Stoney Lake Entertainment, 2014.

Left Behind: The Movie. DVD. Directed by Vic Sarin. St. Catharines, ON: Cloud Ten Pictures, 2000.

"Left Behind: The Movie Trivia." Internet Movie Database. https://www.imdb.com/title/tt0190524/trivia?ref_=tt_trv_trv.

Left Behind II: Tribulation Force. DVD. Directed by Bill Corcoran. St. Catharines, ON: Cloud Ten Pictures, 2002.

Left Behind III: World at War. DVD. Directed by Craig R. Baxley. St. Catharines, ON: Cloud Ten Pictures, 2005.

Lemire, Christy. Review of *Left Behind*. RogerEbert.com. October 3, 2014. https://www.rogerebert.com/reviews/left-behind-2014.

Lewis, C. S. *The Chronicles of Narnia*. New York: HarperCollins, 2004.

———. *The Collected Letters of C. S. Lewis*. Edited by Walter Hooper. 3 vols. San Francisco: HarperSanFrancisco, 2004–7.

———. "Membership." In *The Weight of Glory and Other Addresses*, edited by C. S. Lewis, 30–42. New York: Macmillan, 1949.

Lindvall, Terry. *Sanctuary Cinema: Origins of the Christian Film Industry*. New York: New York University Press, 2007.

Lindvall, Terry, and Andrew Quicke. *Celluloid Sermons: The Emergence of the Christian Film Industry, 1930–1986*. New York: New York University Press, 2011.

The Lion, the Witch and the Wardrobe. DVD. Directed by Andrew Adamson. Los Angeles: Walden Media, 2005.

Locke, Brian. *Racial Stigma on the Hollywood Screen from World War II to the Present: The Orientalist Buddy Film*. New York: Palgrave Macmillan, 2009.

Lundberg, Christian. "The Pleasure of Sadism: A Reading of the *Left Behind* Series." In *Media and the Apocalypse*, edited by Kylo-Patrick R. Hart and Annette M. Holba, 97–128. New York: Peter Lang, 2009.

Lupton, Deborah, and Lesley Barclay. *Constructing Fatherhood: Discourses and Experiences*. London: SAGE, 1997.

Lynch, Gordon. *Understanding Theology and Popular Culture*. Malden, MA: Blackwell, 2005.

Măcineanu, Laura. "Consciously Rejecting the Magic: The Cases of Susan Pevensie and Petunia Dursley." *Gender Studies* 17.1 (2018) 73–83.

Maddux, Kristy. *The Faithful Citizen: Popular Christian Media and Gendered Civic Identities*. Waco, TX: Baylor University Press, 2010.

Magary, Drew. "What the Duck?" *GQ*, December 18, 2013. https://www.gq.com/story/duck-dynasty-phil-robertson.

Manlove, Colin. *The Chronicles of Narnia: The Patterning of a Fantastic World*. New York: Twayne, 1993.

Marshall, Catherine. *Christy*. New York: McGraw-Hill, 1967.

Mathewson, Dan. "End Times Entertainment: The *Left Behind* Series, Evangelicals, and Death Pornography." *Journal of Contemporary Religion* 24.3 (2009) 319–37.

Mazur, Eric Michael, and Kate McCarthy, eds. *God in the Details: American Religion in Popular Culture*. New York: Routledge, 2001.

McAlister, Melani. "Prophecy, Politics, and the Popular: The *Left Behind* Series and Christian Fundamentalism's New World Order." *South Atlantic Quarterly* 102.4 (2003) 773–98.

McCafferty, Kate. "Palimpsest of Desire: The Re-Emergence of the American Captivity Narrative as Pulp Romance." *Journal of Popular Culture* 27.4 (1994) 43–56.

McDannell, Colleen. *Material Christianity: Religion and Popular Culture in America*. New Haven: Yale University Press, 1995.

McDonagh, Maitland. Review of *The Lion, the Witch and the Wardrobe*. *TV Guide*, 2005. https://www.tvguide.com/movies/the-chronicles-of-narnia-the-lion-the-witch-and-the-wardrobe/review/197903/.

McElya, Micki. *Clinging to Mammy: The Faithful Slave in Twentieth-Century America*. Cambridge, MA: Harvard University Press, 2007.

McFarland, USA. DVD. Directed by Niki Caro. Burbank, CA: Walt Disney Pictures, 2015.

Mcleod, Maurice. "Why the Black Best Friend Has Had Its Day." *Guardian*, June 2, 2015. https://www.theguardian.com/global/commentisfree/2015/jun/02/why-black-best-friend-had-its-day-david-oyelowo.

McSporran, Cathy. "Daughters of Lilith: Witches and Wicked Women in *The Chronicles of Narnia*." In *Revisiting Narnia: Fantasy, Myth and Religion in C. S. Lewis' Chronicles*, edited by Shanna Caughey, 191–204. Dallas: BenBella, 2005.

Means Coleman, Robin R., and Charlton D. McIlwain. "The Hidden Truths in Black Sitcoms." In *The Sitcom Reader: America Viewed and Skewed*, edited by Mary M. Dalton and Laura R. Linder, 125–37. Albany: State University of New York Press, 2005.

Metzger, Bruce M., and Roland E. Murphy, eds. *The New Oxford Annotated Bible*. New York: Oxford University Press, 1991.

Miller, Laura. *The Magician's Book: A Skeptic's Adventures in Narnia*. New York: Little, Brown, 2008.

Minnick, Lisa Cohen. *Dialect and Dichotomy: Literary Representations of African American Speech*. Tuscaloosa: University of Alabama Press, 2004.

Mleynek, Sherryll. "The Rhetoric of the 'Jewish Problem' in the *Left Behind* Novels."
  Literature & Theology 19.4 (2005) 367–83.

Modleski, Tania. *Loving with a Vengeance: Mass-Produced Fantasies for Women.* 2nd
  ed. New York: Routledge, 2008.

Monteith, Sharon. *Advancing Sisterhood? Interracial Friendships in Contemporary
  Southern Fiction.* Athens: University of Georgia Press, 2000.

———. "Recent and Contemporary Women Writers in the South." In *A Companion
  to the Literature and Culture of the American South,* edited by Richard Gray and
  Owen Robinson, 536–51. Malden, MA: Blackwell, 2004.

Moore, Rick Clifton. "'Take My Film and Let It Be': Critics and Consecration in Faith-
  Based Cinema." *Journal of Religion and Popular Culture* 30.3 (2018) 143–64.

Moore, R. Laurence. *Selling God: American Religion in the Marketplace of Culture.* New
  York: Oxford University Press, 1994.

Morgan, David. *Protestants & Pictures: Religion, Visual Culture, and the Age of
  American Mass Production.* New York: Oxford University Press, 1999.

Moring, Mark. "A Black & White Production." *Christianity Today* (October 2011)
  55–59.

———. "The Narnia Policeman." *Christianity Today,* December 3, 2010. https://www.
  christianitytoday.com/ct/2010/december/narniapoliceman-dec10.html.

Mort, John. *Christian Fiction: A Guide to the Genre.* Englewood, CO: Libraries
  Unlimited, 2002.

Mussell, Kay. *Fantasy and Reconciliation: Contemporary Formulas of Women's
  Romance Fiction.* Westport, CT: Greenwood, 1984.

Myers, Doris T. *C. S. Lewis in Context.* Kent, OH: Kent State University Press, 1994.

Myers, Kenneth A. *All God's Children and Blue Suede Shoes: Christians & Popular
  Culture.* Westchester, IL: Crossway, 1989.

Nakamura, Lisa. "*Mixedfolks.com*: 'Ethnic Ambiguity,' Celebrity Outing, and the
  Internet." In *Mixed Race Hollywood,* edited by Mary Beltrán and Camilla Fojas,
  64–83. New York: New York University Press, 2008.

Neal, Lynn S. *Romancing God: Evangelical Women and Inspirational Fiction.* Chapel
  Hill: University of North Carolina Press, 2006.

Nelson, John Wiley. *Your God Is Alive and Well and Appearing in Popular Culture.*
  Philadelphia: Westminster, 1976.

Netflix Media Center. "Netflix to Develop Series and Films Based on C. S. Lewis'
  Beloved THE CHRONICLES OF NARNIA." October 3, 2018. https://media.
  netflix.com/en/press-releases/netflix-to-develop-series-and-films-based-on-c-s-
  lewis-beloved-the-chronicles-of-narnia.

Newman, Judith. "And Some Call for a Voice." *New York Times,* January 19, 1992.
  https://www.nytimes.com/1992/01/19/movies/and-some-call-for-a-voice.html.

Nicholson, Amy. "*Left Behind* Is Sinfully Boring." *LA Weekly,* September 30, 2014.
  https://www.laweekly.com/film/left-behind-is-sinfully-boring-5122840.

Nickel, Eleanor Hersey. "'But This Is the *South*': Ambivalent Regionalism in Jan
  Karon's Mitford Novels." *Studies in Popular Culture* 32.2 (2010) 17–33.

———. "'Jesus, Take the Wheel': Evangelical Christianity on *American Idol.*" *Intégrité*
  12.2 (2013) 17–34.

Oke, Janette. *Love Comes Softly.* Minneapolis: Bethany House, 2003.

Olson, Carl E. *Will Catholics Be "Left Behind"? A Catholic Critique of the Rapture and
  Today's Prophecy Preachers.* San Francisco: Ignatius, 2003.

Olson, Ted. "Literature." In *High Mountains Rising: Appalachia in Time and Place*, edited by Richard A. Straw and H. Tyler Blethen, 165–78. Urbana: University of Illinois Press, 2004.

Ono, Kent A., and Vincent N. Pham. *Asian Americans and the Media*. Cambridge, UK: Polity, 2009.

O'Sullivan, Michael. "'Left Behind' Movie Review: Reboot Costs More, Adds Nicolas Cage to Amateurish Mix." *Washington Post*, October 2, 2014. https://www.washingtonpost.com/goingoutguide/movies/left-behind-movie-review-reboot-costs-more-adds-nicolas-cage-to-amateurish-mix/2014/10/01/e7e1ea7a-459b-11e4-9a15-137aa0153527_story.html.

O'Sullivan, Shannon E. M. "Playing 'Redneck': White Masculinity and Working-Class Performance on *Duck Dynasty*." *Journal of Popular Culture* 49.2 (2016) 367–84.

Overcomer. DVD. Directed by Alex Kendrick. Culver City, CA: Affirm Films, 2019.

"Overcomer Trailer—Now Playing." https://www.overcomermovie.com/videos-photos.

Overstreet, Jeffrey. Review of *The Lion, the Witch and the Wardrobe*. *Christianity Today*, December 9, 2005. https://www.christianitytoday.com/ct/2005/decemberweb-only/lionwitchwardrobe.html.

Park Nelson, Kim. *Invisible Asians: Korean American Adoptees, Asian American Experiences, and Racial Exceptionalism*. New Brunswick, NJ: Rutgers University Press, 2016.

Pautz, Johann. "The End-Times Narratives of the American Far-Right." In *End of Days: Essays on the Apocalypse from Antiquity to Modernity*, edited by Karolyn Kinane and Michael A. Ryan, 265–86. Jefferson, NC: McFarland, 2009.

Peberdy, Donna. *Masculinity and Film Performance: Male Angst in Contemporary American Cinema*. New York: Palgrave Macmillan, 2011.

Peretti, Frank E. *This Present Darkness*. Westchester, IL: Crossway, 1986.

———. *The Wounded Spirit*. Nashville: Word, 2000.

Perry, Carolyn, and Mary Louise Weaks. *The History of Southern Women's Literature*. Baton Rouge: Louisiana State University Press, 2002.

Phillips, Michael. "Review: 'Left Behind.'" *Chicago Tribune*, October 2, 2014. https://www.chicagotribune.com/entertainment/movies/ct-left-behind-20141002-column.html.

Powers, Christopher. "Movie Millenarianism: *Left Behind*, Script/ure and the Sleeping Dragon." In *Hollywood in the Holy Land: Essays on Film Depictions of the Crusades and Christian-Muslim Clashes*, edited by Nickolas Haydock and E. L. Risden, 269–89. Jefferson, NC: McFarland, 2009.

Prince Caspian. DVD. Directed by Andrew Adamson. Los Angeles: Walden Media, 2008.

Radosh, Daniel. *Rapture Ready! Adventures in the Parallel Universe of Christian Pop Culture*. New York: Scribner, 2008.

Radway, Janice A. *Reading the Romance: Women, Patriarchy, and Popular Literature*. Chapel Hill: University of North Carolina Press, 1991.

Regis, Pamela. *A Natural History of the Romance Novel*. Philadelphia: University of Pennsylvania Press, 2003.

Riswold, Caryn D. "Four Fictions and Their Theological Truths." *Dialog* 42.2 (2003) 136–45.

Rivers, Francine. *The Masterpiece*. Carol Stream, IL: Tyndale House, 2018.

———. *Redeeming Love*. New York: Bantam, 1991.

———. *Redeeming Love*. Colorado Springs: Multnomah, 1997.

Robertson, Jase. *Good Call: Reflections on Faith, Family, and Fowl*. With Mark Schlabach. New York: Howard, 2014.

Robertson, John Luke. *Young & Beardless: The Search for God, Purpose, and a Meaningful Life*. With Travis Thrasher. Nashville: Thomas Nelson, 2016.

Robertson, Kay. *Miss Kay's Duck Commander Kitchen: Faith, Family, and Food— Bringing Our Home to Your Table*. With Chrys Howard. New York: Howard, 2013.

Robertson, Kay, et al. *The Women of Duck Commander: Surprising Insights from the Women Behind the Beards about What Makes This Family Work*. With Beth Clark. New York: Howard, 2014.

Robertson, Korie. *Strong and Kind: And Other Important Character Traits Your Child Needs to Succeed*. With Chrys Howard. Nashville: Thomas Nelson, 2015.

Robertson, Missy. *Blessed, Blessed . . . Blessed: The Untold Story of Our Family's Fight to Love Hard, Stay Strong, and Keep the Faith When Life Can't Be Fixed*. With Beth Clark. Carol Stream, IL: Tyndale Momentum, 2015.

Robertson, Phil. *Happy, Happy, Happy: My Life and Legacy as the Duck Commander*. With Mark Schlabach. New York: Howard, 2013.

———. *UnPHILtered: The Way I See It*. With Mark Schlabach. New York: Howard, 2014.

Robertson, Sadie. *Live Original: How the Duck Commander Teen Keeps It Real and Stays True to Her Values*. With Beth Clark. New York: Howard, 2014.

Robertson, Si. *Si-cology 101: Tales & Wisdom from Duck Dynasty's Favorite Uncle*. With Mark Schlabach. New York: Howard, 2013.

Robertson, Willie, and Korie Robertson. *The Duck Commander Family: How Faith, Family, and Ducks Created a Dynasty*. New York: Howard, 2012.

Rodríguez, Clara E. "Keeping It Reel? Films of the 1980s and 1990s." In *Latin Looks: Images of Latinas and Latinos in the U. S. Media*, edited by Clara E. Rodríguez, 180–84. Boulder, CO: Westview, 1997.

Rodriguez, Susana. "Boy-Girls and Girl-Beasts: The Gender Paradox in C. S. Lewis's *The Chronicles of Narnia*." In *C. S. Lewis: "The Chronicles of Narnia,"* edited by Michelle Ann Abate and Lance Weldy, 186–98. Houndmills, UK: Palgrave Macmillan, 2012.

Romanowski, William D. *Eyes Wide Open: Looking for God in Popular Culture*. Grand Rapids: Brazos, 2001.

———. *Pop Culture Wars: Religion & the Role of Entertainment in American Life*. Downers Grove, IL: InterVarsity, 1996.

Romine, Scott. *The Real South: Southern Narrative in the Age of Cultural Reproduction*. Baton Rouge: Louisiana State University Press, 2008.

Rowling, J. K. *Harry Potter and the Sorcerer's Stone*. New York: Scholastic, 1997.

Russell, James. "Evangelical Audiences and 'Hollywood' Film: Promoting *Fireproof* (2008)." *Journal of American Studies* 44.2 (2010) 391–407.

Ryken, Leland, and Marjorie Lamp Mead. *A Reader's Guide through the Wardrobe: Exploring C. S. Lewis's Classic Story*. Downers Grove, IL: InterVarsity, 2005.

Santana, Richard W., and Gregory Erickson. *Religion and Popular Culture: Rescripting the Sacred*. Jefferson, NC: McFarland, 2008.

Sawhney, Sabina. "The Joke and the Hoax: (Not) Speaking as the Other." In *Who Can Speak? Authority and Critical Identity*, edited by Judith Roof and Robyn Wiegman, 208–20. Urbana: University of Illinois Press, 1995.

Schakel, Peter J. *The Way into Narnia: A Reader's Guide*. Grand Rapids: Eerdmans, 2005.

Scheck, Frank. "'Left Behind': Film Review." *Hollywood Reporter*, October 2, 2014. https://www.hollywoodreporter.com/review/left-behind-film-review-737580.

Schultze, Quentin J., ed. *American Evangelicals and the Mass Media: Perspectives on the Relationship between American Evangelicals and the Mass Media*. Grand Rapids: Academie, 1990.

———. *Christianity and the Mass Media in America: Toward a Democratic Accommodation*. East Lansing: Michigan State University Press, 2003.

———. *Redeeming Television: How TV Changes Christians—How Christians Can Change TV*. Downers Grove, IL: InterVarsity, 1992.

Schultze, Quentin J., and Robert H. Woods Jr., eds. *Understanding Evangelical Media: The Changing Face of Christian Communication*. Downers Grove, IL: IVP Academic, 2008.

Scott, A. O. "Out of the Wardrobe, Into a War Zone." *New York Times*, May 16, 2008. https://www.nytimes.com/2008/05/16/movies/16narn.html.

———. "Two Wars of Good and Evil." *New York Times*, December 9, 2005. https://www.nytimes.com/2005/12/09/movies/two-wars-of-good-and-evil.html.

Sedgwick, Eve Kosofsky. *Between Men: English Literature and Male Homosocial Desire*. New York: Columbia University Press, 1985.

The Shack. DVD. Directed by Stuart Hazeldine. Santa Monica, CA: Summit Entertainment, 2017.

Shuck, Glenn W. *Marks of the Beast: The Left Behind Novels and the Struggle for Evangelical Identity*. New York: New York University Press, 2005.

Simpson, Mark. *Male Impersonators: Men Performing Masculinity*. New York: Routledge, 1994.

Smith, Darron T., et al. *White Parents, Black Children: Experiencing Transracial Adoption*. Lanham, MD: Rowman & Littlefield, 2011.

Smith, Jennifer Crusie. "This Is Not Your Mother's Cinderella: The Romance Novel as Feminist Fairy Tale." In *Romantic Conventions*, edited by Anne K. Kaler and Rosemary E. Johnson-Kurek, 51–61. Bowling Green, OH: Bowling Green State University Popular Press, 1999.

Smith, Mark Eddy. *Aslan's Call: Finding Our Way to Narnia*. Downers Grove, IL: InterVarsity, 2005.

Stanford University. "About Stanford." https://www.stanford.edu/about/.

Staub, Dick. *The Culturally Savvy Christian: A Manifesto for Deepening Faith and Enriching Popular Culture in an Age of Christianity-Lite*. San Francisco: Jossey-Bass, 2007.

Stiller, Evelyn. "Gaming Armageddon: Leaving Behind Race, Class and Gender." In *End of Days: Essays on the Apocalypse from Antiquity to Modernity*, edited by Karolyn Kinane and Michael A. Ryan, 309–27. Jefferson, NC: McFarland, 2009.

Stoner, Megan. "The Lion, the Witch, and the War Scenes: How *Narnia* Went from Allegory to Action Flick." In *Fantasy Fiction into Film: Essays*, edited by Leslie Stratyner and James R. Keller, 73–79. Jefferson, NC: McFarland, 2007.

Strombeck, Andrew. "Invest in Jesus: Neoliberalism and the *Left Behind* Novels." *Cultural Critique* 64 (2006) 161–95.

Swenson, Joanne M. "From Dogma to Aesthetica: Evangelical Eschatology Gets a Makeover." *CrossCurrents* 53.4 (2004) 566–78.

Swirski, Peter. "'To Sacrifice One's Intellect Is More Demonic than Divine': American Literature and Politics in *Left Behind: A Novel of the Earth's Last Days*." *European Journal of American Studies* 9.2 (2014). doi:10.4000/ejas.10342.

Tankard, Paul. "The Lion, the Witch and the Multiplex." In *Fantasy Fiction into Film: Essays*, edited by Leslie Stratyner and James R. Keller, 80–92. Jefferson, NC: McFarland, 2007.

Tate, Linda. *A Southern Weave of Women: Fiction of the Contemporary South*. Athens: University of Georgia Press, 1994.

Taunton, Larry Alex. "The Genuine Conflict Being Ignored in the *Duck Dynasty* Debate." *Atlantic*, December 22, 2013. https://www.theatlantic.com/national/archive/2013/12/the-genuine-conflict-being-ignored-in-the-i-duck-dynasty-i-debate/282587/.

Taylor, Ella. "*Prince Caspian* Loses Some Magic." *Village Voice*, May 13, 2008. https://www.villagevoice.com/2008/05/13/prince-caspian-loses-some-magic/.

Teo, Hsu-Ming. "'Bertrice teaches you about history, and you don't even mind!': History and Revisionist Historiography in Bertrice Small's *The Kadin*." In *New Approaches to Popular Romance Fiction: Critical Essays*, edited by Sarah S. G. Frantz and Eric Murphy Selinger, 21–32. Jefferson, NC: McFarland, 2012.

Thakore, Bhoomi K. *South Asians on the U. S. Screen: Just Like Everyone Else?* Lanham, MD: Lexington, 2016.

Thurston, Carol. *The Romance Revolution: Erotic Novels for Women and the Quest for a New Sexual Identity*. Urbana: University of Illinois Press, 1987.

Tischler, Nancy M. *Encyclopedia of Contemporary Christian Fiction: From C. S. Lewis to "Left Behind."* Santa Barbara, CA: Greenwood, 2009.

Tolkien, J. R. R. *The Lord of the Rings*. London: HarperCollins, 2004.

Tricomi, Albert H. *Missionary Positions: Evangelicalism and Empire in American Fiction*. Gainesville: University Press of Florida, 2011.

Tuan, Mia. *Forever Foreigners or Honorary Whites? The Asian Ethnic Experience Today*. New Brunswick, NJ: Rutgers University Press, 1998.

Turnau, Ted. *Popologetics: Popular Culture in Christian Perspective*. Phillipsburg, NJ: P&R, 2012.

Turner, Patricia A. *Ceramic Uncles & Celluloid Mummies: Black Images and Their Influence on Culture*. New York: Anchor, 1994.

Turner, Sarah E. "BBFFs: Interracial Friendships in a Post-Racial World." In *The Colorblind Screen: Television in Post-Racial America*, edited by Sarah Nilsen and Sarah E. Turner, 237–57. New York: New York University Press, 2014.

United States Census Bureau. "QuickFacts: Albany City, Georgia; United States." https://www.census.gov/quickfacts/fact/table/albanycitygeorgia,US/PST045219.

———. "QuickFacts: West Monroe City, Louisiana; United States." https://www.census.gov/quickfacts/fact/table/westmonroecitylouisiana,US/PST045219.

Van Leeuwen, Mary Stewart. *A Sword between the Sexes? C. S. Lewis and the Gender Debates*. Grand Rapids: Brazos, 2010.

Veldman-Genz, Carole. "The More the Merrier? Transformations of the Love Triangle Across the Romance." In *New Approaches to Popular Romance Fiction: Critical*

Essays, edited by Sarah S. G. Frantz and Eric Murphy Selinger, 108–20. Jefferson, NC: McFarland, 2012.

Vera, Hernán, and Andrew M. Gordon. *Screen Saviors: Hollywood Fictions of Whiteness*. Lanham, MD: Rowman & Littlefield, 2003.

The Voyage of the Dawn Treader. DVD. Directed by Michael Apted. Los Angeles: Walden Media, 2010.

Walliss, John. "Evangelical End-Time Films: From 1941 to the Present." In *Left Behind and the Evangelical Imagination*, edited by Crawford Gribben and Mark S. Sweetnam, 84–98. Sheffield, UK: Sheffield Phoenix, 2011.

War Room. DVD. Directed by Alex Kendrick. Albany, GA: FaithStep Films, 2015.

"War Room." Internet Movie Database. https://www.imdb.com/title/ tt3832914/?ref_=fn_al_tt_1.

Weaver-Zercher, Valerie. *Thrill of the Chaste: The Allure of Amish Romance Novels*. Baltimore: Johns Hopkins University Press, 2013.

Weldy, Lance. "The Treason of Peter and Susan Pevensie: Incongruous Intertextuality in Adamson's *The Lion, the Witch and the Wardrobe* (2005)." In *Crossing Textual Boundaries in International Children's Literature*, edited by Lance Weldy, 177–91. Newcastle-upon-Tyne: Cambridge Scholars, 2011.

Wiegman, Robyn. *American Anatomies: Theorizing Race and Gender*. Durham, NC: Duke University Press, 1995.

Winchell, Mark Royden. *Reinventing the South: Versions of a Literary Region*. Columbia: University of Missouri Press, 2006.

Winston, Diane, ed. *Small Screen, Big Picture: Television and Lived Religion*. Waco, TX: Baylor University Press, 2009.

Woods, Robert H., Jr., ed. *Evangelical Christians and Popular Culture: Pop Goes the Gospel*. 3 vols. Santa Barbara, CA: Praeger, 2013.

Wright, Greg, and Jenn Wright. "C. S. Lewis and the Media: Cinematic and Stage Treatments of C. S. Lewis's Life and Works." In *Scholar, Teacher, and Public Intellectual*, edited by Bruce L. Edwards, 257–81. Vol. 4 of *C. S. Lewis: Life, Works, and Legacy*. 4 vols. Westport, CT: Praeger, 2007.

Yaeger, Patricia. *Dirt and Desire: Reconstructing Southern Women's Writing, 1930–1990*. Chicago: University of Chicago Press, 2000.

Yahr, Emily. "A&E Retracts Its Suspension of 'Duck Dynasty' Star Phil Robertson." *Washington Post*, December 27, 2013. https://www.washingtonpost.com/ lifestyle/style/aande-retracts-its-suspension-of-duck-dynasty-star-phil- robertson/2013/12/27/116181b4–6f44–11e3-a523-fe73f0ff6b8d_story.html.

Yan, Holly, and Dana Ford. "'Duck Dynasty' Family Stands by Suspended Patriarch." *CNN*, December 20, 2013. https://www.cnn.com/2013/12/19/showbiz/duck- dynasty-suspension/index.html.

Young, William P. *The Shack*. Los Angeles: Windblown Media, 2007.

INDEX

stereotypes *(continued)*
  and multiculturalism, 105–6
  positive, 142, 148
  racial, 14–17, 62, 91–98, 133–40,
    142–43, 146–51, 160, 166,
    170–71, 176–77
  and Southern authors, 102
Stiller, Evelyn, 106
Stoner, Megan, 39
Strombeck, Andrew, 105
Strong and Kind (Robertson), 164–65
structures of narrative, 188, 192, 194
Susan Pevensie (character), 20–46
  at Aslan's death, 23–24
  and battle, 27, 35–39
  critics of, 31–33
  and feminine role of, 43–46
  in *The Horse and His Boy,* 26–27
  in *The Lion, the Witch, and the
    Wardrobe,* 21–26
  Marian significance of, 23–26, 29
  and maternal role of, 21–23, 27–29,
    38
  in *Prince Caspian,* 27–29
  and publishing order, 26n26
  and removal from narrative, 29–31
  and romance in *Prince Caspian,*
    40–44
  visual rhetoric of, 33–35
Swenson, Joanne M., 104
Swirski, Peter, 104–5
systemic injustice, 6, 11

"'Take My Film and Let It Be'"
  (Moore), 156–57
Tankard, Paul, 39
Tate, Allen, 78
Tate, Linda, 79
Taunton, Larry Alex, 160n9
Taylor, Barry, 2
Taylor, Ella, 40
Teo, Hsu-Ming, 54
Thakore, Bhoomi K., 179
"The Joke and the Hoax" (Sawhney),
  150
theological themes in Hollywood
  film, 3

These High, Green Hills (Karon), 82,
  82–83, 86–87, 89–90
"This Is Not Your Mother's Cinder-
  ella" (Smith), 58
This Present Darkness (Peretti), 11–14
Thompson, Donald, 4
Thomson, Cassi, *128*
Thrill of the Chaste (Weaver-Zercher),
  4
Thurston, Carol, 52
Tischler, Nancy M., 5n5, 99
To Be Where You Are (Karon), 89,
  101, 188–92
*Toms, Coons, Mulattoes, Mammies,
  and Bucks* (Bogle), 133, 170–71
tom stereotype, 135
transnational adoption, 175–81
transracial adoption, 164–67, 170,
  181–83, 188n17, 197–201
Tribulation Force (LaHaye and Jen-
  kins), 120
Tricomi, Albert H., 104
Tuan, Mia, 177–78
Turnau, Ted, 3, 5, 8, 164
Turner, Patricia A., 91
Turner, Sarah E., 143–44

Understanding Evangelical Media
  (Schultze and Woods), 4
*Understanding Theology and Popular
  Culture* (Lynch), 2
UnPHILtered (Robertson), 161–62,
  168

Vanderbilt University, 78
Van Leeuwen, Mary Stewart, 46–47
Variety (magazine), 129
Veldman-Genz, Carole, 65–66
Vera, Hernán, 15, 132, 136, 142, 152,
  160
violence, 64, 95–96
visual rhetoric in Narnia series, 33–35
The Voyage of the Dawn Treader
  (film), 20–21, 35, 44–46
The Voyage of the Dawn Treader
  (Lewis), 29–30

Walden Media, 20–21, 45–46

www.ingramcontent.com/pod-product-compliance
Lightning Source LLC
Chambersburg PA
CBHW030106030726
47498CB00007B/2275